New York Times and USA Today Bestselling Author

LORA LEIGH

LEGACIES
Shadowed Legacy

ELLORA'S CAVE®
ROMANTICA® PUBLISHING

What the critics are saying...

୪໑

"This is one powerful story full of lush imagery and dialogue that snaps and crackles. And the love scenes, well, they defy my humble descriptions." ~ *A Romance Review*

"Ms. Leigh is truly one with this story as the reader will feel when they read *Shadowed Legacy*... Run to get this wonderfully expanded and revised series and find yourself drawn into a world where magic, passion and love transcend the centuries. The *Legacy* series is truly one of the best paranormal series to date. Ms. Leigh is a gifted and superb author that should be on anyone's reading list if you like complex characters, an engrossing story and a tale woven from the legends." ~ *Love Romances*

An Ellora's Cave Romantica Publication

www.ellorascave.com

Shadowed Legacy
ISBN 9781419954603
ALL RIGHTS RESERVED.
Shadowed Legacy Copyright © 2005 Lora Leigh
Edited by Sue-Ellen Gower.
Cover art by Syneca.

This book printed in the U.S.A. by Jasmine–Jade Enterprises, LLC.

Electronic book Publication October 2005
Trade paperback Publication July 2006

This book is a work of fiction and any resemblance to persons, living or dead, or places, events or locales is purely coincidental. The characters are productions of the author's imagination and used fictitiously.

SHADOWED LEGACY

છ૭

Dedication

ଈ

To Patricia Rasey, who taught me point of view
when no one else could.
Momma Sue, who always listened and enjoyed the books.
And Lyn Morgan, who so loved my warriors.
You helped this series to live when I was certain I would
never get it "right". Thank you all for all the time and
effort you gave me. And thank you for being friends.

Trademarks Acknowledgement

ଈ

The author acknowledges the trademarked status and trademark owners of the following wordmarks mentioned in this work of fiction:

Land Rover: Land Rover

Lear Jet: Learjet Inc.

Maserati: Officine Alfieri Maserati S.P.A.

Foreword

ℰ

There is a legend near forgotten by time, and hazy to even the oldest memory. A legend that has never been told by those who wield the pen, but lives in the hearts and souls of those who wield the sword. The legend of the Shadow and the Earth Mistress.

Legends abound, mystic in proportion and told of only in whispered words. Legends of a warrior blessed by the gods, given life immortal and gifts of strength and power never fully known. And the tale of a daughter of the earth, whose gentleness and warmth healed a warrior's heart, only to see it ravaged, torn asunder by a bargain met and made for the fragile promise of victory in another day.

The Guardians had gifted unto a man, whose honor and heart were bold, strength and power untold. A warrior blessed with sight, scarred by battle, and enduring life unending. His only thought, his only dream, that of vanquishing the evil that is Jo Nar. An evil not of this earth, not of this land, that would enslave the souls of men, and bring destruction to all that Mother Earth has protected and preserved.

Mother Earth chose her own as well. A daughter of wisdom and of beauty. Whose gifts of power would aid him in battle, aid him in healing. To this daughter she gave the gift of the earth itself. A power untold, whose secrets whisper in an aura of mystic force.

The Earth Crystal, created and fashioned for her protection and his strength. The heart of the earth, given to the heart of the warrior. Power in full measure, longing and passion enriched with devotion. The Shadow's heart was captured, held true, and blessed in the eyes of man and immortal alike.

The bargain had been made. Fate and Destiny whispered the rules, for the time was not at hand. Such blessings were for later, such richness of love repayment for the service completed, not for the battles not yet fought. For men of love, passion and heart know only fear of the loss, the blood to be shed, and the battles to come.

Payment must be made.

Betrayal and blood, death and loss. Memories were then as dust in the wind, a soul held in limbo, a heart held bound by the shadows of a grief unknown.

Screams haunt dreams, whispered passion haunts the mind. A warrior bound to one whose face was true, whose heart was as black as the pits of the farthest hell. A woman coming to rebirth, soul restored, passion known. A heart seeking, whispering, gathering in strength for the day of awakening.

And the Heart of the Earth, returned to its keeper, a power unimagined. A woman whose face and heart is true, who must vanquish the bonds of magic, of memories severed, of a heart scarred by greed, betrayal, and loss.

The Shadow Warrior and the Mistress of the Earth Crystal will be reunited. Power untold shall flow, secrets shall be revealed, and betrayals met with honor and truth. Beware, Jo Nar, for the time is at hand. Beware, dark forces, for truth shall walk the land.

Open your eyes, Mistress of power, of truth and love. Dominion in passion, power in truth, a warrior born in rage, in grief and pain. Submission in touch, heated life, devoted heart. A woman gifted, the time is at hand. Awake, Mistress of the Earth, secrets revealed. Crystal dreams, blood and death. Awaken, dear heart, the payment is met.

Prologue
France

&

She came to him, whether he wished it or not. And though he had always known only hatred, only abiding fury when faced with her in the past, now he knew only gentleness. He needed to kiss the pale pink perfection of her soft lips, needed to touch the full curves of her breasts. He wanted to see his cock enveloped by her hungry lips, wanted to bury his lips in the soft heat of her cunt. He hungered for her, as he never had anything in his life before this.

Her nipples, hard little points of tempting fruit, beckoned his lips, his stroking tongue. As she knelt before him, he could do no more than lean forward and envelop a tip with his hungry mouth. He was greedy for her, his desires ravenous. She was warm, heating the cold wedge of hatred that surrounded his heart and made him long for her. Made him long for her kiss, her touch.

His engorged cock was a raging beast between his thighs, throbbing, demanding the tight heated clasp of her cunt. She would be silken fire and slick liquid relief. She would be the end of centuries of self-imposed celibacy.

His hands gripped her small waist, feeling the delicacy of her body and he knew, knew beyond a shadow of a doubt, that she was much stronger than she appeared. And still his lips sipped at her nipples. He could not get enough. His teeth tugged gently as she cried out, trembling before him, her nails delicate pinpoints of fire against his scalp as she held him to her.

He drew back, staring at her, seeing the differences in the curve of her face, the warmth of her eyes. The resemblance to Antea was strong, yet he knew this was not Antea he held in his arms.

"Who are you?" he whispered as he moved to press her back to the bed.

Lithe and graceful, she lay before him, her emerald eyes dark and heavy-lidded as she watched him move between her thighs, watched him with sensual pleasure as his fingers feathered over the dewy curls then slid through the moist slit. She gasped, her hips arching as her hands clenched at the sheets beneath her.

"I would see you bare here," he told her, his voice roughened by the thought of even those delicate curls removed, leaving her tender flesh vulnerable to his every touch. "You will remove this for me."

She smiled. A mysterious, female smile that warned him she would not be easily tamed. His cock jerked as he envisioned the many sensual ways he could convince her.

"Make me," she whispered, a challenge that had his eyes narrowing in purpose.

"I will find you soon," he growled. "I know this well for the dream it is, but I will find you. Do not remove the fleece, and you will not feel my lips caressing you there, or my tongue stroking the liquid from your body."

She jerked against him, her eyes widening, a whimper issuing from her lips. The movement caused the tip of his finger to press against her. It tucked between her swollen cunt lips, kissed the honey-soaked entrance to her vagina.

"Promise me you will do this thing for me," he urged her as he caressed the tight entrance, every muscle in his body tense as he fought for control. "I would feel you silken and soft against me as I do this."

He slid inside her slowly, feeling her vagina clench as his finger invaded her. Her muscles stretched around the intrusion as he pressed inside the slick portal. His hand held her thighs apart as he watched the mating of his body with hers. The sight of her most tender flesh parting for his finger was nearly more than he could bear and still hold fast to his control.

"Promise me," he whispered again as he retreated, his breathing quickening at the sight of her glistening juices as they clung to his hard finger.

"I promise," she cried out when he would have slid from her snug cunt. "Anything. I promise. Please, don't stop. Please."

He pulled her up, into his arms, knowing that having her lay before him in such a way was tempting his control past bearing. God, how he wanted her. If he took her now, he feared he would savage her. *Just a moment,* he thought. *Just until he could find the control he needed to ease her into their joining, rather than throwing her into it.*

But he couldn't stop his hands from smoothing over her back, or from pressing her closer to his chest as he fought for breath.

"Tell me who you are. Where to find you," he growled impatiently. "I cannot take you, and not even know your name."

She tensed in his arms, as though in fear.

"Remember me," she whispered, desperation and fear reflecting in her voice. "Remember me, Devlin. Save me."

He held tighter to her now, terrified that something, somehow, would reach out and snatch her from him. His lips touched her neck, his tongue whispered over the delicate shell of her ear. Her hand, so soft and silken, rather than calloused as he remembered Antea's being, smoothed over his shoulders to his waist. He sucked in a hard breath as it then traveled to the hard plane of his stomach.

"Touch me," he growled, needing it as he had never needed anything in his life.

The touch of her hand on his cock had him nearly spilling his seed onto the bed. Her grip was warm, tentative, almost shy. Her fingers explored the thick shaft, tracing the bulge of the veins, the flared head that throbbed beneath her touch. *Sweet mercy.* He fought the eruption he could feel boiling in his scrotum. She set him on fire. He needed more of her, always more of her.

Before he could question himself, or his voracious need, his lips covered hers, his hands pulling her tighter against his body as he bore her to the bed beneath him. Her hand gripped his hip then, her moan echoing in the air around them as he made his way between her thighs.

Then the dream shifted.

Devlin watched as Chantel came awake groggily as she was dragged roughly from sleep, stumbling in clumsy disorientation as the guards hauled her out of the room and down the long corridor toward the dungeon's entrance.

He could feel her. Sense her thoughts, her emotions, the terrible driving fear that had his gut clenching in agony, in a need to hold to her, to save her from what he could feel she knew awaited her. Disorientation filled his mind as it filled hers. Fear. Knowledge. And his soul screamed at what he knew awaited her.

The drugged fog that had held her in peaceful slumber was slowly dissipating beneath the fear and the laughing jeers of the soldiers. What was it they had said when they jerked her from her bed? What dark evil could they have meant about Oberon and Jonar sharing their pleasure?

Too quickly it seemed, Chantel stood before the dark lord, feeling bereft, naked without the crystal, which had been stripped from her. She could feel the missing part of her, the link to her sisters, to her father, that she had grown used to in such a short time.

A link she knew was about to be severed forever. The moment she had glimpsed the expression in Jonar's eyes, she had known that her death was at hand. And Devlin felt it. He knew it. In this dream, he resided along with her in the horror beginning to unfold. He didn't just see the nightmare she awoke to, but he was feeling it himself.

The destiny Mother Earth had predicted so many years ago was now at hand. There was no longer reason to fear the day coming, nor to worry about the deceptions practiced. There was now only the time for acceptance.

God help her, but she prayed the pain would be brief. The horror she knew would follow her even unto death, but it was now the pain before death that she feared. That, and the terrible emptiness she knew she would leave behind.

Chantel could no longer feel the power of the crystal, or the strength that had once been inside her. She felt weakened, frightened, though she was determined that this monster would never see that fear.

"So, you are the daughter of Konar." He watched her with eyes a brilliant blue, and lacking in any warmth or mercy.

Chantel could feel her heart thunder now in fear as he watched her. She fought to breathe, to remind herself that it was for the greater good. One day, the Shadow would be victorious because of the sacrifice she now made. But may Mother Earth and God have mercy on her, for she feared had she the choice now, she would turn away from what was to come.

Beside him, Oberon sat on a low-built, crude stone altar. The leer on his face was nearly more than she could bear.

Chantel's skin crawled as she watched his hand move slowly between his own thighs, watching her as he massaged the erection that had grown beneath his pants. The sight of it sent icy chills of horror racing over her skin.

Chantel prayed her heart would burst from the fear before the stench of his evil could touch her.

"I am Chantel. Daughter of Galen," she repeated, standing tall, proud, as she knew her father would expect her to, despite the trembling in her body. Proclaiming herself now would do no good, she knew. She had ensured her own death when she accepted Antea into the castle.

Chantel hoped she did not beg when the end came. She felt these creatures would relish her pleas. She had a feeling that when the time came, she would be more than willing to. But begging would do her no good.

"Then show me the necklace which proclaims you as the daughter of the sorcerer," he suggested quietly. "The talisman he gifted to his daughters."

"It has been stolen from me," she whispered, meeting his eyes and glimpsing a strange fury within them as she blinked back her tears. "The other woman that you held stole that which was mine. The first in a circle of four gifted to the daughters of Galen, chosen by Mother Earth to wield her power."

"Cease!" His voice echoed with anger as her calmly spoken words began to fill him with doubt. "Only a child of Konar's could speak with such strength as she faced me. Only the daughter of my bastard brother would know the words to say. The child of Galen is *released, as I swore she would be. Now you, Antea, shall die, just as I swore to Konar you would."*

"Konar's daughter is not I," she whispered, fighting the breathless fear that threatened to take her voice. "But even she is innocent in this vendetta you wage against the Guardians."

"As was my daughter innocent." He spoke harshly, his voice filled with an anger she knew must have grown over the years. "You cannot dissuade me, Antea. I swore to Konar the fate you will now receive."

"What are you going to do?" She could not resist the fear in her voice, or the force in which she struggled against the men who held her. "Oh God, please no…"

Their touch burned her, the evil of their lusts, the pleasure they gained from her pain-filled cries pushing them to greater depravities as they forced her to the stone altar in the center of the room. Hard, brutal hands held her, jeering voices laughed at her pleas.

Had she known this would be her end, she knew she would have never faced this destiny. Shame filled her as they took their pleasure of her. Horror clawing through her soul at the knowledge that there would be no way to hide the degradation or the horrible proof of how easily she was defeated.

No part of her body was sacred, none left untouched. The sounds of their pleasure, grunts of male exertion and lust filled her mind with a haze of agony as she cringed from them, screaming out in pain, hearing their laughter echoing around her again and again.

When they finished, Oberon jerked her roughly to her feet, sneering, his lips twisted mercilessly as he watched her, sneering at her nudity, her shame. In his hand, Jonar held a small wand. She had heard of this weapon. One that would wound and maim from within and yet never touch the skin. Aiming it at her stomach, he pressed the side and a ray of light lit the area at her navel.

Her body heaved as she felt the flesh tear inside her abdomen. Screams were but a harsh cry as the breath left her body in a pain so resounding it nearly broke her mind as she fell limply to the floor.

The agonizing pain lasted only briefly. But she knew that whatever this damage had done would soon take her life. As the heat in her subsided, she looked up at him, knowing that in her life she had never known hatred as fierce as what she now knew.

"Jonar?" She could barely put sound to her voice as he leaned near, mild curiosity on his face.

"Yes, my dear," he inquired, satisfaction filling his eyes as he regarded her dying body.

"I am Chantel. Daughter to Galen. Sister to Arriane. She will know, Jonar, that you have taken that which she loves. She will know, and she will hate you forever."

She watched as Jonar's eyes widened in sudden shock, his face paling. He opened his mouth to speak, but was halted by the door to the altar room swinging open.

"The Shadow Warriors, sire!" the guard screamed out desperately. "They have breached the fortress and now come this way. God's blood, but the Shadow is cutting through each man who gets in his way."

His eyes came back to hers.

"Chantel," he whispered, grief, resignation and regret filling his eyes.

"You will burn in hell for this day," she swore. "And the Shadow will be the one to light the fire."

"Come now, Jonar, we will deal with this later," Oberon yelled from the door. "Come now, while we can still escape."

Jonar shook his head, then turned and rushed out the door, leaving Chantel alone in her grief and her pain. She closed her eyes, knowing Devlin would soon be there. Knowing there was nothing she could do to ease the horror of what he would find.

Devlin felt the horror of her thoughts, just as he felt the horror of the rape. He could feel his soul screaming in pain, his very spirit burning in flames of agony. What she had suffered no woman should face, no matter the future outcome. He was in her mind, a part of her soul, and knew then the sacrifice she had made for so many.

He felt the tears that fell down her cheeks himself, the sobs that racked her, her cries as the pain seeped slowly throughout her body.

It hurts, oh God, Devlin, it hurts so badly, *she cried silently.*

Then suddenly, she was no longer alone. Chantel opened her eyes as her sisters ran through the door, each dressed in men's clothes, their crystals beacons at their breasts. They had come for her, hoping to save her.

Chantel heard Ariel's terrified cries as they found her on the floor. Heard her tearful pleas that Mother Earth surely would not have allowed this.

Then she felt herself being lifted, heard the anguished cries of her sisters as they wrapped a blanket carefully about her and held her in their arms.

As their cries echoed in the room, she felt the warmth of their crystals as they were laid about her neck. The pain began slowly to ease, but Chantel knew that nothing could stem the tide of death that was slowly cresting over her.

"I will kill them myself, Chantel," Ariel the warrior woman swore, knowing it was by Antea's betrayal that such had happened. "They shall not escape unharmed."

Chantel lifted her hand to the tear-streaked face of her sister, and touched her gently. She would have spoken, would have tried to ease the tears had she not heard the tormented cry of the warrior as he burst upon the scene.

And then he was there. Through her eyes, he watched himself, saw his own horror, the bleak fury and knowledge that all he had fought for was being taken from him. He knew his own pain, and hers as well.

Chantel saw his ravaged, terror-shocked face as her sisters eased back. The fire of fury in his black eyes, the disbelief that left him shaking as he eased her in his arms.

"Chantel." He touched her face, her neck, then looked in horror at the spot she knew marked her stomach. Then tears ran slowly from his eyes as his gaze came back to hers. "I tried. I tried to reach you. Oh God, baby, I tried."

From her navel, her lifeblood slowly oozed from her body. She had felt the warmth when it began. Jonar's weapon was amazingly efficient. The wound so vicious that even magic could not heal it.

"Do something!" Devlin raged, his eyes lifting to the sorcerer who fell to his knees beside her.

Chantel turned her eyes to her father, as her grip tightened on her warrior's hand.

"Remember your vow," she whispered raggedly, feeling the sluggishness which seemed to make it hard to speak. "You must do as you swore now."

"She will pay," Galen promised her softly, his eyes wet with his own tears. "They shall all pay for this, Chantel."

"No." She shook her head slowly, feeling the drowsiness drifting over her. "Use her, she has the power to do so. She can help. Remember, Father, she is a sister as well."

"Chantel." Devlin's voice whispered over her senses as though from a distance. "Hang on. Do not leave me. Please God, Chantel, do not leave me."

His tears, the ragged agony reflected in his voice was a wound deeper and more painful than the one Jonar had given her.

"I love you, my warrior." She smiled up at him as she felt the life slowly begin to drain away from her body. "I shall always be close."

She heard his screams of denial as darkness closed gently over her, and for an instant, hatred flared in her for the sister whose betrayal had caused it. Just as the same hatred flared with Devlin. Consuming. Overriding. A black, murderous rage that penetrated centuries of magic and began to pierce the fog of forgetfulness.

"Chantel…" He came out of the bed, fury and rage pulsing, pounding through his body even as the knowledge that it was not reality slid through his soul, as his cell phone rang in demand.

His chest heaved for breath, his hand reaching for his gun before he could shift from nightmare to reality. He shook in the grip of an agony he couldn't define, memories that drifted away as though they had never been, but left a remnant of loss to sear his soul. His hand reached up to touch his face, his fingers coming back, damp with his own tears. He could feel the moisture in his eyes, the cries in his heart as he trembled, shaking from the vividness of the dream.

He knew the face as Antea, the conniving, vindictive bitch he had once been wed to. The emotion though... He shook his head, drawing in ragged breaths as he remembered a love, an adoration for the woman whose lifeless body he held in his arms. That woman had owned his soul. Antea had owned naught but his contempt.

The dream drifted within his head now, hazy, details suddenly impossible to grasp as he fought to remember her name, her death. Antea had not died in his arms, and had she done so, he would have felt no grief. But this woman, treasured above all others, had taken his soul.

Shaking his head he jerked the phone off the bed stand, checked the display number then flipped it open.

"Devlin here, how can I help you, Ducaine?"

"Shadow...I need your help..."

Chapter One
Middle East Desert
Present Day

ဆာ

It had been too easy. Chantel had known it all along. Taking out the Blackthorne agent and retrieving the crystal should have been more difficult. From the moment she had stepped into the back entrance of the Embassy, she had known where he was awaiting her. Just as she had known with each step she took that she was coming closer to the power that was hers alone.

She trembled now, in the grip of that power, yet more helpless than she had ever been in her life. Because she had been betrayed. She had taken the crystal from the agent only to be captured as she awaited extraction. How had they known she would be there?

She had gained the power, but would she now lose her life in the attempt to possess it? That question tormented her as she felt the building warmth that enveloped her. The crystal was safely cushioned between her breasts now, hanging on the chain her mother had given her so long ago.

You'll know its use when it is time, her mother had assured her as she lay dying. *Your destiny and all you know will one day change, Chantel. Wait for it, watch for it, for its gifts are more than you can imagine.*

At the time, those words had terrified her, bringing to mind the nightmares that only her mother had been able to comfort her through. But now she understood. As she had stood before the enemy agent, that knowledge had swirled around her like a rapidly growing mist.

The agent's fear when she had confronted him, and his warning, now echoed through her mind. *Jonar will stop at nothing to destroy you.* And now Jonar was on his way. She could feel it. Knew it with every harsh breath she took. He was coming, and she was hanging there like a sacrificial lamb for the slaughter because her father had refused the help she needed.

Betrayal. And not just by the one who had revealed her presence, but also by the one who could have saved her from capture.

Fathers are supposed to protect their daughters. Especially when the father was in a position to call out every military force in the United States if he needed to. But there had been no help from him. She had waited at the pickup area, had prayed as she had never prayed before, but rescue hadn't arrived. Rather, the enemy had found her.

"I have the crystal, Father, but they know I have it. I need pick-up." Her desperate call via the satellite cell phone had fallen on deaf ears.

"You went out on your own, Chantel," he had stated coldly. *"There will be no pick-up. The mission was unsanctioned."*

She remembered the shock, the horrifying fear that had ripped through her chest at his words. He wasn't going to send pick-up? She was a government agent, his fucking daughter. And he wasn't going to send someone to extract her?

"Dammit, you left the file for me, what do you mean it was unsanctioned?" she had screamed back at him. *"For God's sake, all I need is pick-up."*

The connection had been severed with no response.

And she had waited. And waited. And he had sent no one. She had just enough time to call her brother, to leave a desperate message on his machine. To tell him she loved him, if she didn't make it out alive. And that their father, the man sworn to protect them, had betrayed her.

Now, nearly twenty-four hours later, Chantel found herself imprisoned, hanging from a damned meat hook by the ropes at her wrists, and still help had not come.

She had tried to concentrate on the crystal, praying it would help her.

The information she had found in the file that had been waiting on her desk the day she left for Montrovia, had contained a legend of mystical warriors, or alien Guardians and the power of the crystal. While reading it, she had known, *known* to her very soul that it wasn't merely a legend. That this was her destiny.

Her back, thighs and buttocks smarted with a fire that only the lash of a cane rod could bring. Her breasts throbbed in pain from the lashes along the upper mounds. Thankfully the pain wasn't disabling. She sneered. The bastard guard administering the lashes had left, nearly foaming at the mouth. Each time he drew back to deliver a full blow, some force thickened around her, slowed it, lessening the impact.

"Who are you?" the guard had screamed at her. *"Antea. Jonar says you are Antea. Are you Antea? Release the crystal and we will let you go. Whore that you were, it is a little enough exchange."*

She had screamed her name until she was hoarse. She was Chantel. Only Chantel.

"Only Antea can wear the crystal," the guard had charged. *"You are Antea. Release the crystal. Give it to me, and you will live."*

She would die first. She would never release what was hers alone, what had always been hers. Never Antea's. And who the hell was Antea anyway? She remembered Antea, she wasn't certain from where, or how. Someone she had tried to protect, Chantel thought, her mind dazed with fear and pain. Someone who had betrayed her. Who had betrayed the crystal.

She was not Antea.

Chantel trembled in fear. Jonar would be there soon and no force on earth could halt the pain he would bring her.

Terror lay thick in her throat, tightened her chest. She didn't have much longer. She trembled, shuddered as much from fear as she did the cold that wrapped around her. She refused to die here in this dirty little hole. Not like this. Trussed up like a damned chicken and helpless to save herself.

The crystal was a hard, heated throb at her breast. Imploring, commanding, demanding that she get free. Her wrists were already bloody from her struggle to escape, the raw marks around them setting fire to her nerve endings as she struggled once again.

The crystal heated further as she struggled, as though to give her strength.

Devlin. Where are you? She cried out his name silently.

She had known him only in her dreams, but each second the crystal throbbed at her breasts, she knew he was real. The heat surrounding her surged as she cried out to him. A breath of sound whispered at her ear, an airy caress drifted over her stinging back.

The dreams that had haunted her for a lifetime swept through her mind. The dark brooding warrior, his black eyes filled with life, love and passion, his hands stroking her, holding her. And his voice. His voice was magic on the wind, whispering through her mind as it had her dreams.

He had to be out there. She had felt him…sensed him, as though he were a shadow walking at her side, for years. The moment she had placed the crystal around her neck she had heard his voice at her ear, a sigh in the breeze. And she had known he existed. Knew he was out there. Somewhere.

"Time to go." She swung around as the guard swaggered back into the room.

His greasy black hair fell over his forehead, nearly hiding his beady brown eyes. The scar across the left side of his face gave him a menacing appearance that was more than deserved. The bastard liked to hurt people. She suspected he preferred hurting women.

"Go where?" Her voice was raw from the obscenities she had screamed at the bastard earlier.

"Jonar's on his way. He wants you ready for him," he sneered. "Time to get ready, little girl. He and Oberon have several pleasures in store for you."

Oh, she was ready. Her body stilled as she gathered her strength, knowing that when he released her the pain in her wrists and legs would be tremendous. She couldn't wait any longer for rescue. She had to get the hell out of there before Jonar arrived. She sent a silent, desperate plea to the crystal for strength, and a strong one to the heavens for mercy. But she was aware that every particle of her being was searching, reaching out, screaming one man's name.

Devlin.

The guard reached up, the long-bladed knife in his hand, and cut the ropes. Agony swelled in her arms, her legs, and her collapse wasn't totally feigned. She went to the floor, crying out before taking a deep fortified breath. When he bent to her, she moved.

A heated burst of energy vibrated through her body as she twisted around, giving her strength, and easing the pain as she made her play for escape. She felt the knife slice across her thigh as she came up with her elbow, slamming it into his groin. She twisted, gasping for breath, her hand going for his wrist, and the knife she would need to defend herself.

Agony sounded in his cry when her nails bit into the flesh of his wrist, her fingers burned, heated, as hot as the crystal itself. The knife came free in her hand, but he seemed to have found the strength to move as well. He jumped for her, a snarl of rage on his lips as she stiffened her elbows, the knife poised in front of her.

She didn't know who was more surprised—him as he felt the knife sink into his chest, or her as she felt the blade slide in. Her stomach heaved at the sensation of firm flesh giving way to sharpened steel, the sucking sound of its welcome and the dying gasp of the man receiving it.

She moved, rolling to the side as he fell, a strangled moan on his lips. She didn't wait around to relieve her heaving stomach, as much as she wanted to. She grabbed the clothes they had stripped from her. Her jeans and the long manly shirt. Her bra and panties were just gone. Her sneakers were quickly laced, her socks missing from the pile. She grabbed the automatic rifle sitting just inside the door and slipped quietly from the cell.

She was only distantly aware of the strange, emerald aura that began to pulse around her from the crystal as she made her way down the corridor to the back exit where she had been brought in. Pain that she knew should be disabling her was only a hard ache. The blood at her thigh was minimal, the bruises on her body aching but not slowing her down.

She could hear voices in the other rooms, male laughter and raucous jeers as the guards laughed amongst themselves, but no one sounded an alarm. They seemed more than cheerful, secure that they had done as ordered, that Jonar would be pleased.

She slid carefully through the opening of the exit door, nervous, watching the shadows as she moved into the darkness of night. She was alone. Alone as she never had been in her life. Even James, her beloved brother, had been unable to help her. Her heart clenched, her soul screaming out silently. Why hadn't her father even tried to save her?

Devlin. Where are you? The silent cry echoed through her head. He had been her last hope. When she realized no one else would come, she had thought surely he would.

They were nothing more than dreams, she told herself fiercely then. Dreams couldn't save her.

She was alone.

Devlin. Where are you? The words echoed in his head again, driving him insane with his inability to answer her. As the jet landed on the hidden airfield, pulling into the camouflaged metal building that would hide it during the extraction, the voice pleaded with him. His body tightened, both in preparation of the coming mission and in sexual anticipation. She had tormented his dreams for nearly a year now. She had brought sexual desire when before there had been none, and soon, he would have her.

For centuries he had searched for the Earth Mistress, the woman prophesied to wear the crystal of power once again. He had believed throughout the years it would be the simpering bitch he had known as Antea. But this couldn't be Antea. The voice calling out to him filled his soul, striking a fire inside that allowed him to glimpse into the mist of memories that had been hidden in his mind for so long.

She didn't know who she was, but she was not the vile being he had so despised and many had called his wife so long ago.

He knew her name. Chantel. And he knew the man who had been hiding her for so many years. Retribution would be sought for that alone.

Her present identity was a puzzle. Chantel. He knew that name, though he couldn't place her face in the past. All he had were the dreams. Dreams of a time long ago of a woman filled with magic and mystery and a smile that lit his heart.

"I have her pinpointed." Joshua pulled out a rough map of the nearby village. "Two days ago a guard was killed and a prisoner escaped. Rumored to be female, though the guards denied it. Jonar is in residence now, coordinating a search as the villagers hunker down, hiding in terror while his beasts roam the streets. We'll find no allies here, but neither should we find enemies other than those of Jonar's main force."

Joshua pointed out the area of her last known whereabouts. A small, nearly forgotten village, far from where she had been taken outside the Montrovian Embassy.

Devlin rose to his feet. He slung the sheathed sword over his back then picked up the long leather coat he usually wore over it.

"Is our contact in place?" he asked, referring to the double agent who often traveled with Jonar.

"She's there," Joshua sneered. "She's providing what cover she can for the girl, but says she'll be found soon if we don't hurry."

"Jeep is ready," Shane, the huge Viking warrior, reported behind Joshua. "Extra ammo and mounted machine-gun is in place."

"I have the occupants here under control." Derek's brogue attested to the fact that he did indeed control the minds of the few who staffed this little known landing strip. "We're ready to head out."

Devlin could feel the echo of the earth crystal, a warm, bright energy that called to him as it hadn't when Antea had worn it. The woman who had once claimed the title of his wife. Violence surged inside him at the thought. She was no wife of his. He remembered the vows, remembered eyes so impossibly green, a face that filled his vision, yet the woman he remembered awakening beside was not the woman he remembered wedding. She looked the same. And yet she didn't. She had sounded the same, and yet she hadn't. She had worn the crystal. A crystal said to belong to one woman and one woman only. He had been told that woman was Antea. His soul believed otherwise.

Devlin. I'm frightened. Her words drifted along his consciousness. His powers, more subtle, yet stronger than all those of the other three combined, reached out for her. He touched her. For a brief instant, he touched her. Her pain, her fear, hunger and need, they all filled him. She was fighting for her life, and she was alone.

Soon... He found himself fighting to send her what comfort he could, knowing the chances of her sensing his thoughts as he had hers, were nearly nonexistent.

"Joshua, when we return, I want Michael at the castle." There would be no more trips to the Agency. No more favors granted with no questions asked. Any man who would so betray his daughter deserved nothing less than death. "A man does not betray his daughter for no reason. I would know why."

Devlin glanced at Joshua as he nodded his head in agreement. The jeep accelerated into the night. No lights, since there were none of them that needed the aid of the piercing headlights on the front of the jeep. As Shadow Warriors, they were part of the night, and could see as well as any creature that lived within it.

He stared out at the endless landscape of sand, reining in his impatience as he fought to assure the voice reaching out to him that he was coming for her. He leaned his head against the seat, stared up at the night and wondered at the remembered screams of pain, her blood on his hands, and a grief that made him ache for his own death.

Twisting, churning inside him, emotions raged and pulsed. Forgotten feelings, dreams only once hinted at, they all seemed to be focused within his mind now. The cold centuries stretching behind him were over, yet what was coming he wasn't certain.

Chapter Two

ഇ

The next night, Devlin stared across the dark street at the woman, seeing the brilliance of dark emerald-green eyes, the thick silk of moonlit white-blonde hair, the pure perfection of classical elegance in the delicate features of her face. The crystal that lay at her breast was worn with grace, with a familiarity that proclaimed her the owner of it. Yet, she was nothing like the woman she resembled. Antea would have been a pale imitation of this woman.

She was dressed in jeans, torn and ragged, smeared with blood. The large man's shirt of dark gray cotton hung on her slight frame. A black baseball cap was pulled over her hair, tendrils of the white silk laying along her neck. She was sweat-dampened, her delicate features streaked with dust, her eyes large and brilliant with fear and pain.

At the moment, plastered against the shadowed wall of the cement house, she watched the deserted street suspiciously, her body poised for flight. As graceful and yet as wary as a doe during hunting season. She knew she was being watched. His lips tilted in a mocking smile as her gaze met his, yet he knew she could not see him. His powers kept him invisible, a part of the shadows, yet he could see her as clear as daylight.

She trembled, from the cold, and from fear. The desert was not a friendly place, neither during the night, nor the day. And this forgotten village was the least of hospitable places.

"She knows we're here." He spoke softly into the communications unit attached to his head. "She hasn't seen me, but she's aware."

His eyes narrowed as he watched her. He could see the fear shimmering along her body. Fear and courage.

Devlin listened intently as Derek, Shane and Joshua verified their positions around her. They had been searching for her for hours that evening, knowing her general location, but unable to get an exact bearing on her until the past hour. He shied away from looking too deeply into how he had managed to do it. As though by instinct, his gifts had homed in on her and the low vibration of mystical power her crystal held.

Shadows he had been unaware of within his own mind were shifting and coalescing. As though knowledge that had been previously hidden from him was now fighting to be revealed.

She held the powerful automatic rifle loosely in her hands, braced against her chest as she breathed roughly. She had been traveling at night only, hiding through the day, fighting to escape the area she had become trapped within. He could feel her frustration, her sense of helplessness.

Chantel.

The name whispered through his mind. He had been unaware of the crystal's resurrection until her brother James had called. It was then that Devlin had learned of a friend's deception and a father's betrayal. He had been shown once again that no bond was secure, and that saving a life meant nothing in the grand scheme of power and games that existed in his world.

Chantel.

Was she Antea reborn?

He stared at her, seeing the resemblance, yet sensing the difference. A difference reinforced by the hardness of his engorged cock, the steadily rising lust that flowed through his body.

He had never desired Antea. Her very scent had often made him ill, staring into her face caused black rage to engulf him. Staring at this woman caused him to hunger, as he could never remember hungering before. A greedy need to touch, to taste, to consume the passion he knew would fill her small body.

He smiled in anticipation of the coming sensual battle. As though she glimpsed the movement, she stiffened. Her finger lay ready on the trigger of her rifle, and he watched as she took a deep breath, her head falling back against the cold stone wall. And it was then he saw her tears. A slow shimmering trail along her cheeks before she wiped them dry with the sleeve of her shirt.

She bit her lower lip, and began to move.

"Clear her way. We want her out of town before we show ourselves to her. Let's do this discreetly," Devlin warned the others.

He followed her, his movements flowing from shadow to shadow, a part of the night, blending into the dark. She glanced behind her often. Stopping, hiding, aware that she was being followed, confused by the fact that no one had approached her, that no shots had shattered the stillness of the night. No cries of alarm had warned the soldiers who paced the town of her movements.

She was aware that she herself had passed no soldiers. She was confused, fighting to figure out why. Unaware that there were those ahead of her directing the movements of anyone who would stand in her way. She wouldn't come with him easily. Distrust would be a part of her. After all, her father had betrayed her. Who else could she trust if not him? Yet, she would come with him. She would eventually trust him and, he assured himself, she would scream in abandon beneath his body, begging for his touch as she had in his dreams. She was his, and soon she would realize it.

* * * * *

32

She was being followed. Chantel stopped once again, holding herself deep within the shadows of a silent home, listening intently. She could hear the wind, the echo of voices several streets over as one guard called to another. At her breast, the crystal she had stolen the past week hummed with a joyful vibration. A warmth, a resonating power that filled her, invigorated her, terrified her.

She had known the moment she had received the file on the mysterious necklace, that it was hers. A part of her dreams. A part of her destiny. But was that destiny the passion and need with the haunting lover who invaded her dreams? Or was it her death in a cold stone room as he bent over her, screaming out her name?

Chantel. She fought the whisper that seemed to echo through the night. She wiped at her cheeks once again, furious with herself for the tears that escaped. She had to find her way out before she was seen, before she gave in to the helplessness filling her. There was no time to stop and cry.

She shuddered in fear at the thought of Jonar capturing her again, the memory of that stone room and her own blood playing out in her mind. The night she had spent in that cold little room awaiting Jonar's arrival, praying for rescue, had been a nightmare. Escaping from it had been a miracle.

She rubbed her thigh, trying to ignore the pain from the knife wound the guard had managed to deliver. A guard who would never torture another woman. The bastard was resting in hell now, his own knife buried in his chest.

His blood still coating her hands.

A racking chill attacked her at the memory of it. She fingered the trigger of the rifle and moved again. The sun would be up soon, and she would have to hide during the daylight hours. She had little hope of surviving this mission. Her only prayer was that the desert stole her life, rather than the hell she knew Jonar had in store for her.

Devlin.

He couldn't be merely a dream. She fought the clenching pain that flared in her chest at the thought. He had to be real. He had to be out there somewhere, waiting on her…

She eased from the wall and began to make her way slowly along the edge of the deserted street. She was careful to stay in the shadows, to be quiet, to blend into the night. She was extremely careful to heed the pulse of the crystal. A wrong turn and its heat would intensify. The right turn and a gentle, comforting warmth would fill her. She was heading out of town, staying on the back streets, and moving closer to the inhospitable emptiness of the desert beyond.

She would have preferred to steal a vehicle, but in the silence of the night, and with martial law in effect, she knew she would never escape with it. Her best bet was the canteen of water strapped to her hip and a prayer that she could reach another town soon, one she could find help in. Sure as hell there was no help to be found here.

Chantel glanced behind her once again. Her skin prickled with awareness, though the crystal hadn't warned her of danger. She was being watched, followed with calculated interest. Something or someone had been trailing her all night, but had yet to show itself. And no matter how hard she tried, she couldn't seem to catch sight of them.

She was almost clear. If she moved from the protection of the house, then she was entering the desert. A vast sea of sand and body-chilling night temperatures. Blistering heat during the day. She took a deep breath as the warmth intensified at her breast. Time to move.

She was insane to obey a piece of rock.

Keeping as low as she could, she moved from the shelter of the house and entered the desert. The waist-high dunes cast enough shadow in the dimness of the cloudy night to allow her to slip unseen from the town. She was careful to keep the rough highway in sight, knowing it had to lead somewhere, rather than allowing herself to become lost in the desert around her.

Only death could await her here, but it beat what she knew Jonar had in store for her.

When the few lights that still glimmered within the town behind her could no longer be seen, she collapsed at the base of one of the dunes. A quick drink, not much. She would need the water to sustain her tomorrow through the blinding heat she knew was coming.

Exhaustion nearly overcame her at the thought as the pain in her leg seemed to intensify. What she wouldn't give for a warm bath, a soft bed. Devlin's warmth holding her close.

She shook her head, a bitter sound of laughter left her chest.

"Yeah. And the tooth fairy is real too," she muttered mockingly as she bent her head, her fingers probing at the wound on her thigh. Thankfully the bleeding was minimal considering her exertion. She took a deep breath and closed her eyes for just a second.

"Bad place to rest, darling." Her eyes flew open.

She didn't scream. There was no breath to scream as a sudden shadow tore the rifle unceremoniously from her hands and tossed it away. There was only reaction. She kicked up, catching him off balance as her foot met his lower abdomen. He grunted and went backwards.

She was on her feet, running. The rifle was lost. Her only chance was flight. Within seconds a heavy manacle wrapped around her waist, pulling her to a stop as her legs tangled instinctively with those behind her. Another male grunt sounded as they went down, then a chuckle as she tried to ram her elbow into the hard stomach behind her.

Before she could react, before she could do more than scream in throttled rage he twisted her to her back pinning her beneath him. Her arms were stretched above her head while long, thickly muscled thighs enclosed her in a grip that sent agony racing through her wound.

Chantel clenched her teeth to hold back a wail of pain, determined that she wouldn't let the bastard know he had hurt her.

Within seconds he shifted again though, his legs clamped at her knees.

"Damn, she's a wildcat this time," another voice spoke from behind him. "I don't remember Antea fighting when held beneath a man's body."

She struggled furiously as that hated name echoed in her mind.

"Bastards!" she yelled furiously. "I'm not Antea. Do you morons have sand for brains? Who the bloody hell is Antea?"

How many times had she screamed that denial at her tormentors as they held her? How many denials did it take before a moron could see sense?

"Easy, baby." Dark, amused, the man who held her down sounded more gentle than tormenting. "We're here to help you, Chantel. Not to hurt you."

She stilled her struggles. Yeah, she thought, like she believed that one. She licked her dry lips nervously, waiting. Two could play at this game.

"Then get off me," she suggested hoarsely. "You're hurting me."

Then her eyes widened as the clouds above her shifted. The moon shone down on them all and she was given a glimpse of the man holding himself carefully above her.

Midnight black eyes burned with purpose. Long, shaggy black hair fell over his aristocratic features. The hilt of a sword could be seen behind his left shoulder, the belt of the scabbard crossing his hard, muscular chest.

The breath stilled in her throat as the familiar features were shown in sudden stark relief.

It couldn't be him. Her imagination was playing tricks on her. There could be no other answer. She had believed. From the moment she put the crystal on she had felt the connection, and though she had believed he would come for her, a part of her hadn't. Not really. Not to her soul. Until now.

"Welcome back, Chantel," he greeted her, his voice formal with only a hint of deepening lust. "It's a pleasure to have you beneath me once again."

There was a flash of confusion in his eyes then, in his expression, as though the words confused him as much as they did her.

His thighs loosened at her knees as shock filled her system and the need to escape, to run, to find someplace, anyplace to hide just long enough to make sense of the events suddenly sweeping through her life.

Her knees rose forcefully, intending to connect between his thighs with a force that should have pushed his balls into his throat. Instead he shifted at the last minute, his hard thigh taking the brunt of the blow as she scrambled to her feet, half crawling as she fought to escape the vision that should not have been there.

Instead, she found herself pushed into the sand, the heavy weight holding her down effortlessly as hard hips pressed into her buttocks. A scream of outrage escaped her lips as she felt his cock, a hard, engorged length of heat pressing against the crevice of her buttocks through her jeans and his pants.

Even more mortifying was her sudden response. Her hips jerked, her teeth grinding together as she only barely managed to contain the sudden need to rub her buttocks against the hardened length. To kneel before him in submission, her hips raised like a bitch in heat, eager to mate.

She didn't think so!

"We can do this the easy way, or the hard way," he informed her, his voice steel-hard despite the black velvet pitch, indicating that either way, it would be his way. "You can stop fighting and listen to reason, or I can carry you kicking and screaming through the desert. But be warned, it's been a hell of a long time since I've had a woman, and every time you wiggle that tight ass against my dick that way, it just makes me want to fuck it more. Now settle the hell down."

She stilled, breathing hard, gasping as his lips caressed the shell of her ear as he spoke. She closed her eyes, fighting the weakness invading her body, the incredible hunger flaring inside her.

"Now, all shit aside, you're in a hell of a mess, baby," he continued. "And I'm your only way out. Do you want to continue fighting me, or are you ready to listen to reason?"

Dreams existed after all…

Devlin.

Chapter Three

☙

Chantel wasn't exactly ready to listen to reason, but she stopped fighting. As she did, the warmth of the crystal eased at her breast, and its psychic summons seemed to still. It was at peace. Unfortunately, she was only more confused.

"Derek, get the jeep," he ordered from above her, still holding her securely to the ground. "Let's get the hell out of here before the sun comes up."

A shuffle of movement from her right had her turning her head. She watched as a dark figure loped out of sight.

"Shane, contact the jet. Have it running and ready to go. Inform them of our ETA. Joshua, keep those damned soldiers in the city as long as you can. All limits are lifted for the time being. Her safety is top priority."

Nothing he was saying made any sense. She heard a vehicle start up nearby, and though no lights cut through the darkness she was aware that it hadn't been far away.

"Now," he breathed out roughly. "Are you ready to get the hell out of here, or do you want to try for another shot at de-manning me first?"

"I'll refrain for now," she promised sarcastically. "Now get the bloody hell off my back, you sadistic son of a bitch." His cock still pressed against her. The almost imperceptible movements of his hips were making her insane.

He moved away from her. A flowing, graceful movement accomplished so quickly that at first she was unaware he was gone. When she realized it, she struggled to her feet, fighting not to limp as her thigh burned in agony.

She faced him then, barely able to make out his features with the cover of clouds that had moved in once again.

"James called us in." He spoke of her brother with easy familiarity. "He found the files and the notes used to draw you in after your call to him. Now, are you ready to trust us?"

She felt her throat tighten with tears, her over-exhausted body threatening to collapse beneath a wave of emotion.

"James?" she whispered. "Not Father?"

"I haven't spoken to your father," he assured her carefully. "Did he know you were here?"

She shook her head, disbelief rolling through her, a part of her howling out in misery.

"Know?" she whispered the betrayal. "I contacted him days ago. Days ago..." She shook her head, the last hope she had held in her heart that there was softness in his heart for her, dying. She raised her eyes to his as she fought to keep her body straight, to keep from collapsing to the sand in pain.

She couldn't see his expression as clearly now, but she felt the rage washing over her as he started to speak. Before the words formed, the jeep moved in beside them.

"Let's go."

Moving swiftly, he jerked the scabbard off his back and tossed it to the back floorboard. He gripped her arm, pulling her with him as he jumped into the front seat and lifted her into his lap.

"Excuse me?" she squeaked, one hand bracing on his shoulder, the other against the raised windshield in front of her.

"There's no room for you in the back." His voice was clipped as he held her still against him while the other two jumped in.

Within seconds, the jeep sped across the slight distance to the highway. Once it met with smooth pavement, it accelerated quickly, eating the distance with a surge of power.

Chantel didn't know whether to scream in rage or laugh in hysterical relief. So the desert wasn't going to kill her after all. But the life-sized version of the legend holding her appeared no less merciless than the desert had.

And he was Devlin. She knew he was. He had to be.

"James called you," she whispered then, fighting to control the lump in her throat, the fears that she was wrong. "You didn't hear me?" She had screamed for him for days. Surely to God she hadn't she been crying out for a dream and nothing more.

He tensed. She could feel every muscle in the hard body pressed against her tightening dangerously as swirling power erupted around them, pressing in on her. And it wasn't the power of the crystal

"Rest. We're an hour from the jet at least." His hand moved to her head, pushing it against his shoulder, though no answer was forthcoming.

"It couldn't be a dream," she whispered, knowing pain and exhaustion had worn her down, dazing her, as the lack of sleep left her nearly incoherent, but surely not insane.

"I came for you," he told her then, his head lowering until his lips were but a breath from hers, his words for her ears only. "Didn't I tell you that I would come for you? Didn't I warn you that you wouldn't escape me for long? Tell me, Chantel, did you clear your woman's growth from that pretty little cunt, or do I get to?"

Her breath caught in her throat. She blinked up at him, barely aware of the fact that she was fighting for breath, that panic was slowly building inside her chest. She could feel his anger, his lust. It built around her, inside her, swirling through the mix of emotions and dim dreamlike memories that filled her.

"I thought I was dreaming." Her breath hitched as hope flared inside her. "That you weren't real."

"Oh baby, I'm more than real. But are you?" he growled an instant before his lips lowered to hers. As though he could no longer fight the need, or perhaps he knew the building hysteria was slowly filling her. Whichever, the dominant, possessive thrust of his tongue and the carnal hunger of his lips replaced it.

Chantel could only moan in pleasure, in relief as her hands gripped the arm that held her to his chest. Pleasure swamped her senses now, desire firing in her body until her cunt clenched with moist, desperate need as she felt his hand clenched at her hip.

She whimpered, forgetting that they weren't alone, forgetting that he was still little more than a stranger, a dangerous unknown entity who could kill her in the next breath. Adrenaline still coursed through her veins, fury filling her body at her father's betrayal, and he was offering her an escape. A heady, pleasure-filled experience that engaged all her senses.

His hand moved from her waist, smoothing up her arm. His fingers cupped her cheek as his lips moved slowly, sensually on hers. His tongue licked at her lips, twining with hers as though learning the taste and texture of her kiss. The caress touched not just her lips, but her soul.

In this, he was familiar. In this, the passion of those vivid dreams returned full force, reminding her of the heady ecstasy to be found in his arms. Her breasts became swollen, her nipples throbbing beneath the material of the shirt. Her cunt, silky and bare, her intimate hair waxed away in an uncomfortable procedure that left her wondering at her sanity, ached for his touch.

Breathing roughly, he pulled back from her, gazing down at her with heated desire.

"Soon," he whispered.

She shook her head, fighting the attraction, fighting demands that pounded through her system as his head lowered, his lips taking hers once again before she could deny the passion between them.

His lips slanted over hers. Devlin couldn't stop himself, couldn't deny the demand that he touch her, that he assure himself she was truly there and that he wasn't mistaking the hot, desperate lust rising inside him. It had been too long since he had felt such lust. Too long since he had touched, had needed. Had he ever needed like this? He knew he had. He could feel the knowledge that he had. Yet those memories were hidden, dark and distant.

He should be revolted. He had despised Antea, though he had never been certain why. Her men had not bothered him. Who touched her, who shared her bed, never concerned him. But this woman... He growled as her lips opened beneath him, accepting the hard stroke of his tongue, the demand in his kiss. He would kill the man who attempted to touch this woman.

Beneath his lips, silk and satin moved enticingly. Her tongue twined with his as a soft whimper of female longing sighed from her throat. Her arms twined around his neck, her breasts pressing into his chest as she fought for air beneath the hard demand of his caress.

She was fire and light. Heated need arced through his body, making his cock throb in a hard beat of passionate demand. He wanted to rip the jeans from her body. He wanted to push his cock hard and deep inside her and hear her cry out his name as she begged him for more. Lust was a wild, untamed beast inside him, fighting for supremacy over the logic that had always guided him.

His hands gripped her waist as he pulled her closer, his thighs bunching as he pressed his cock against the rounded curves of her ass. Those sweet curves were a temptation all their own. But first, first he needed to slide inside the tight, velvet grip of her pussy. She would be slick and hot around him, fist-tight. He knew this as he had never known anything. And he wanted her.

She was never still. She gave him no time to consider the lust that suddenly flared between them, no time to rein in his control or his desires. Her hands smoothed over his shoulders, gripped them, tested the muscles there as she tried to get closer, to draw deeper into his body.

"Chantel." He groaned her name, knowing that now was not the time, not the place for such overriding physical demands.

He pulled back from her lips, as greedy as his own, and fought for self-control.

She stared up at him, her eyes overly brilliant, the pupils enlarged, exhaustion, pain and lust shifting in her pale face. And confusion. Still not certain if she was awake or dreaming once again. The minute he had the time to show her the difference between dream and reality, he vowed she would no longer question how real he truly was.

"Rest." Hands threaded through her hair, experiencing the soft, silken feel of the thick mass. Like silver moonlight as he pressed her against his shoulder.

The fall of silk brushed her shoulders with the loss of her cap. The cap had shielded her expression, hid the glory of her hair and the unique line of her delicate face.

She rested against him now, her breathing still fast, shivering in the cold night air of the desert. He reached back to the floorboard of the jeep and pulled free one of the large jackets they carried to hide the swords they wore at their backs. He wrapped her in its warmth, held her to his chest and began to pray. He prayed that the shifting shadows hid her true identity, for he knew if she was indeed Antea, then his life would be a greater hell than it had been for the past thousand years.

Chantel hadn't expected to sleep. She hadn't expected the chill that had invaded her bones to be replaced with warmth. The fear and adrenaline-laced nerves to be replaced by peace.

The jacket smelled like Devlin, sandalwood and spice, and heated male. She snuggled into its warmth, burrowing closer to his chest, and slept.

She awoke as the first pale rays of dawn were beginning to streak across the sky. The jeep had come to a quick stop, the hard jerk bringing her groggily from sleep. She stared around at the rough airstrip, the single metal building that had been strung with camouflage netting. Inside was a small, sleek Lear Jet, its motor purring in the stillness of the early morning.

"Let's get the hell out of here," Devlin ordered them as he moved from the jeep, carrying her in arms as sturdy and strong as the limbs of an oak as he strode quickly into the building. "Jonar will have his planes in the air before the sun is up completely. We need a head start."

They rushed into the plane, two of the men heading for the cockpit as Devlin helped Chantel strap quickly into her seat, ignoring her dazed attempts to awaken fully. She wanted to sleep. To burrow back into his arms where it was safe and warm.

Within seconds, they were speeding down the runway, lifting clear and heading into the clouds.

"Joshua?" Devlin glanced behind them at the other hard-eyed warrior.

"Clear for now." His voice resonated with a power that she couldn't understand. It was a deep resonating sound that pricked at the shifting mists in her mind. Like memories barely formed.

She glanced back at him, her gaze meeting the brilliance of his amber eyes. They were like liquid gems, glowing, swirling with power. He was familiar. Not as familiar as Devlin was, not as familiar as the dreams that had filled her of the man who had been her lover, if only in her dreams, but she had a sense of knowledge. A confused feeling that there was much more to him than there was to the others.

Mystic. The word whispered through her mind. She frowned, fighting to sweep aside the confusion to the truth.

Antagonism suddenly rose inside her, confusing her with the sense that this man had done something, at sometime, against someone she loved. As she watched him, she saw a fragile young woman, her eyes wide with pain and betrayal, her soul screaming out in agony.

Chantel, do not! The young woman's frightened cry echoed around them as a curse passed Chantel's lips. Flames rose then to surround the dark-haired woman, enveloping her in heated power. Joshua's rage, Devlin's fears, and like the phoenix born in flames, the woman emerged. Dry-eyed, her heart protected, but only for a time. Only for a short, distant time, until his emotional betrayal ended in her downfall. He had refused to love her, refused to allow his heart to open. He had denied her his strength.

Her fists clenched as he arched a heavy black brow, smug knowledge curling about his lips.

"Joshau," she whispered. "The betrayer."

She didn't know why she was so certain that the mispronunciation of his name was correct. But she knew by the silent snarl on his lips that it was.

His face tightened as anger darkened his eyes.

"Antea, the bitch," he growled back.

She smiled weakly. She made certain the curve of her lips had little to do with amusement, and much to do with her disdain.

"Only in your worst nightmares," she said with deceptive gentleness. "Jonar's man spent nearly twenty hours trying to convince me that I am someone I'm not. Do you think such a perfect sneer from you can do what he couldn't?"

She was convinced reality had receded the moment she placed the crystal around her neck. The world she existed in now had nothing to do with the cold, often stark life she had lived before. This world was filled with magic, with power, with beings she knew weren't completely human, and yet were much too human for even their own peace of mind.

"Enough, Joshua," Devlin ordered as he unclipped his seat belt and rose to his feet, his voice hard, commanding. "Keep us hidden while I attend to her wounds. Don't play games with Jonar either, we can't afford a mistake right now."

Joshua glanced at Devlin. His eyes narrowed, his long fall of thick black hair framing his savage features. He nodded abruptly, then leaned his head back against the seat, closing his oddly colored eyes.

Chantel watched him curiously, wondering at the thickening of the air around them, a power, not unlike that she had felt in the stone, surrounding them. It wasn't natural, but neither was it evil. She knew the feel of evil.

"Come on." Devlin stood before her then, extending his hand out to her. "Let's go check those wounds and get them cleaned out before they set up infection."

She stared at the large, tanned hand. It was calloused, but she knew it felt sensual rather than rough against her skin. Broad, long-fingered and filled with strength. She watched as she laid her hand in it, seeing how fragile her fingers looked against him.

Helping her to her feet, Devlin led her across the interior to a small converted bedroom that had been built in the rear of the plane.

"Would you like to explain this Antea person to me?" she asked wearily as she collapsed on the cloud-soft comfort of the mattress. She would give anything to curl beneath the covers and just sleep.

"Undress." He released her to move to the overhead compartments beside the bed, obviously ignoring her.

Sensation speared through her belly at the order. She could feel tingles of response racing over her, through her, piercing her erogenous zones.

"I don't think so." She sniffed peevishly. "You can get your jollies somewhere else, bad ass. Answer my question."

A medical case bounced on the bed beside her.

"You can take the damned clothes off willingly, or I can strip you. It's your choice," he ordered in a voice that brooked no resistance. "Now do as I said, undress. Make it now."

She crossed her arms over her breasts and stared up at him as she lifted her brow in defiance.

"Chantel?" His voice was patient, his black eyes were cold and filled with purpose. "Have you ever seen gangrene? I've been in Jonar's hellholes, and sanitation is not his main priority. Do you really want to risk such an infection?"

"I asked a question," she reminded him, refusing to back down. "Who is Antea and why does everyone want to believe it's me?"

He inhaled deeply. "She was the former mistress of the crystal you wear. It's said only she can control its gifts." He watched her intently, those black eyes probing into her, filling her with heat.

"Actually, it said only the true mistress could control its powers," she snapped in return. "Don't play games with me. I read the legend too."

The look he gave her was cold, hard. "Then you know as much about it as the rest of us do." He inclined his head mockingly. "Now undress, Chantel, before that wound becomes infected. We'll discuss the rest later."

She stared into his eyes, chips of black ice on the surface, a cauldron of shadows and heat beneath. And he had no intention of telling her anything more. It was in his voice, in his eyes. She would do as he said, or he would do it for her.

Gathering her courage, she stood up and shed her jeans as quickly as she could before sitting back down, though she kept her shirt on. She knew her back was bruised, abraded, but hoped it wouldn't require anything more than a hot bath to ease it.

He knelt in front of her, his fingers going to the gash on the outside of her thigh.

His overly long black hair was shaggy and in his earlobe he wore a small gold hoop. It was incredibly sexy on him. He opened the med kit, cleaned his hands with an alcohol hand cloth, then bent to inspect the gash on her thigh. Long, nerve-racking minutes later it was cleaned and bandaged. The scratches along her thighs were treated. The welts on the sides of her lower legs were examined closely.

"Bastards," he muttered as his fingers smoothed over a nasty bruise.

Chantel flinched, remembering the cane rod that had inflicted the damage.

"Take off the shirt now, and lay on your stomach," he ordered when he had done all he could from the position she was in.

"I'm just bruised…"

She didn't dare. Her breasts were swollen, the nipples hard, tight peaks of aroused hunger, throbbing, begging for his touch. Her pussy was damp, her clit swollen. She couldn't risk it, couldn't chance the loss of control. Not now, not when the sense of familiarity was so deep, the arousal climbing higher.

She was too tired she knew. Adrenaline still spiked her blood, sensitizing her nerve endings as the power whipping around them caressed her already violently aroused flesh.

"There's blood caked on the back of the shirt, Chantel. Remove it." His voice brooked no refusal.

Her lips tightened as she stared at him.

"No."

"Chantel, I am not above ripping that shirt off your back and holding you down while I attend your injuries. I'm not asking you to do anything here. I'm telling you."

The dominant tone of his voice should not have caused excitement to spike through her body, but it did. She was shaking, trembling with the power of the lust clawing at her system, demanding relief.

What the hell was wrong with her? She had never, at any time, felt such overpowering desire, not in her dreams and never in the midst of such danger.

"And that should make a difference?" she snapped, more frightened of the dampness she knew would show on her bare flesh than she was of what he would think of her nakedness. It was depraved. The whole time his fingers had moved over her wounds her cunt had pulsed in an agony of arousal.

She wanted them inside her. She almost whimpered at the thought. She wanted his fingers parting her pussy, slamming inside her vagina, fucking her into what she knew would be a mind-shattering climax.

"If you would prefer, I will turn around while you take the damned shirt off and lay down. But you will take it off." She could see the same lust glittering in his eyes. "Your way or my way. It doesn't matter to me."

"Does everyone obey you instantly?" she cried out, furious with her needs as well as his. "I'm not one of your warriors to take your orders." She would not lose all control with him. She would not humiliate herself by begging him to fuck her as she knew she wanted to do. Instead, she fortified herself with her anger, her rage.

"My warriors understand the value of treating their wounds. Even Joshua is not as intractable as you are being," he pointed out impatiently.

"Joshua is a jerk." Flashing memories of arrogance, smug smiles and tormented amber eyes flashed through her mind.

"But a smart one," he growled. "Now take the damned shirt off, Chantel."

"No."

He sat back on his heels, staring at her through narrowed eyes.

"You're acting like a child," he snorted.

Before she could move, he gripped the shirt, ripping buttons from their holes and pushing it back over her shoulders as he flipped her over on the bed.

The comforter rasped her nipples, causing her to whimper at the pleasure as she felt his eyes caressing. She shouldn't feel that. A look shouldn't be physical. But his was. And the heat that stroked her flesh nearly had her lifting her hips in demand.

"Good God in heaven." His voice was rough, filled with fury as he held her hips and arms to the bed. "Who was the bastard who dared do this to you?"

Breathing heavily, Chantel strained against him, fighting his hold. Her back didn't hurt nearly as bad as her leg had and the pain of the wounds was nothing compared to the ripping need in her pussy. Surely the sight of her back couldn't be that severe?

"Lay still." His voice was a sharp whip of fury that had her stilling immediately.

His hand smoothed over her back, pressing here and there as she gasped out at the feel of his hands against her. There was pain, the bruising was bad she knew, but the pain was so overshadowed with pleasure that she nearly mewled like a cat in heat.

"If you get up, I'll paddle your ass," he bit out as he moved off her. "Dammit, Chantel, do you have any idea how bad infection is? Have you lost your senses?"

She stayed still, silent, her legs carefully closed, thankful that the shirt still covered her bare buttocks. Jonar's damned guards had managed to lose her panties and her bra, leaving her with nothing to shield her nakedness now.

His hands smoothed over her back, the burning sting of the alcohol pads almost making her forget the fire between her legs. If he would just stop with the soothing whispers, the soft touches, then maybe her pussy would stop that infernal throb.

Chantel thought he was nearly done. Thought for sure the torment would ease until he jerked the shirt from her hips, holding her down as she instinctively fought for the protection of the cloth.

"Who did this?" For all the softness of his voice the latent threat seemed to throb around her.

"Does it matter?" she cried out, knowing the curves of her buttocks had to be colored from one side to the other. The bastard guard had taken exceptional delight in striking her there.

"It matters." Fury roughened his voice, the promise of retribution heavy in the tone. "Answer me."

"He didn't exactly introduce himself," she snarled back as she fought pain and ecstasy. "I don't know who he was. He had a scar across his face, and really bad body hygiene. What can I say? We weren't exactly in a formal setting."

She shuddered, the vivid memory of the guard's death, at her own hand, causing her stomach to clench sickeningly.

"The skin isn't broken, but sitting down won't be comfortable for a while," he growled, his hand smoothing over the trembling flesh of her ass

The muscles clenched involuntarily as she felt a flare of heat invade her anus, shocking her. She wanted to lift to him, to feel him part her there, his finger moving to the snug little entrance... No. Oh God, where the hell was her control?

"It's not exactly fun now," she strangled as his finger ran down the top of the crease between the round curves. "What are you doing?"

As though he could read her mind, his finger tucked into the narrow crevice, moving slowly, steadily to the highly sensitized opening just below.

"Wondering," he said roughly then. "Wondering if you obeyed the orders I gave you within that dream. Did you remove it, Chantel, or must I?" He sounded as though he would enjoy it too. Her clit swelled further, the enraptured flesh throbbing in longing.

A shudder worked through her body.

"You shared those dreams with me," he whispered. "I know you did, I saw the knowledge in your eyes, your recognition of me. Did you do as I bid you, baby?"

She stiffened, her heart racing now, her drenched cunt throbbing with a heartbeat all its own. His hands were incredibly gentle on her bruised butt, smoothing over the abused skin, heating her body with the most incredible sensations of pleasure. She almost whimpered at the warmth, the tenderness in his touch. Had anyone ever touched her so gently?

"How did we dream together?" Chantel fought for breath as he moved for only a second, his hands lifting from her rear. When he returned, a whimper of pleasure couldn't be contained as she felt him smooth a soothing, cool cream into her flesh.

Hot barbs of need prickled at her cunt, making her thighs tighten, her breasts ache.

"It doesn't matter how," he whispered, leaning down to caress the curve of her buttock with his lips before tracing the narrow cleft as she shuddered beneath him.

Chantel jerked at the heated touch, a whimper escaping her lips as the silky slide of her juices eased past the lips of her pussy. His tongue was moving against her, licking into the crevice, coming closer, so very close to the depraved ache filling her. She wanted his tongue. Wanting it driving in her pussy, licking the entrance to her ass. She wanted a touch she knew to be as perverted, as unnatural as the power suddenly filling the small room, pressing in on her, fueling her lust.

"Your thighs now," he whispered, his voice rough. "The salve will soothe the bruises. Part your thighs for me, Chantel, let me see your bare little pussy."

Chapter Four

๕๑

Chantel trembled, but she was helpless to deny him as his hands parted her bruised thighs, his voice a harsh growl as he cursed the guard who had taken the cane rod to her. His fingers were a healing caress as they trailed from the top of the inside of her thigh, to her knee, and back again. The backs of his fingers whispered over the swollen lips of her cunt, making them ache, *need*. She had never known such intensity of emotion in her life.

Then his touch was gone, but only briefly. Within seconds, she was moaning from a pleasure that burned through her nervous system like an inferno of sensation. His hands were hard, but not rough. They whispered over her skin, yet the touch was firm enough to smooth the satin coolness of the salve into her skin while she quivered with sudden, sharp pangs of clenching desire that shot from her thighs to her aching vagina.

"Chantel, turn over for me," he whispered then as his fingers glanced over the wetness of that soaked silk. "I can't take you, not as tender as you are. I swear I will but touch you."

She fought for breath. She couldn't believe she was allowing him to turn her over, to gaze down at her with those fiery black eyes as he knelt above her. Then they narrowed, the muscle in his jaw pulsing with fury as he glimpsed what she had forgotten about.

Several long welts and bruises marred her flat stomach, her full breasts. They weren't the most painful, nor the most serious, but the dark blue marring of her skin wasn't a pleasant sight.

She glanced down at her hard-tipped breasts, her face flushing at the hardened state of her nipples rather than the bruises above and below them.

"I will find him," he growled. "The one who did this to you. And I will kill him slowly."

Her gaze flickered away from him as she swallowed hard.

"He's already dead," she whispered.

He watched her closely, a question in his eyes, his expression filled with regret, with ragged hunger.

"By your hand?" he asked her, his voice soft.

Chantel felt her lips tremble as she remembered the instant the knife had sunk into the undefended chest.

"I had to get free." She fought to explain herself, explain the taking of a life that filled her with regret, despite the circumstances. "He wouldn't let me go. We struggled for the knife…"

"He is better off dead by your hand than by mine," he bit out. "He would have known great pain, Chantel, had I been the one to exact vengeance for your injuries."

Her eyes widened at the violence in his soft voice. The room pulsed with it, with a power she feared could reach beyond the plane and would have struck her assailant in his tracks, if he still lived. The crystal lay silent at her breast though, neither warm nor cool, complacent in his presence even while his fury raged. Then he bent to her, as she watched, her eyes widening in shock as his tongue extended and stroked over the marks of pain.

Her body jerked, her womb spasming with such pleasure that it felt as though it would jerk through her abdomen. Her clitoris swelled, throbbed, aching with a physical pain that she knew only his touch would ease.

Involuntarily she arched closer to his moist caress, a moan ripping from her lips as the near orgasmic delight shook her body. He watched her carefully, his eyes filling with lust as his face drew into lines of sexually charged emotion while his tongue stroked her nipples, the curve of her breast, before returning once again to the hard tip.

"Feel good?" he whispered softly before his lips parted over her aching nipple, enclosing it in a heat that whipped through every cell in her body.

Her hands clenched in the comforter of the bed, her head grinding into the mattress as she fought to breathe. Oh God, had she ever known anything that felt as good as his touch, outside her dreams? Then his tongue curled over the stiff peak of her breast. Her hands released the comforter, speared into his hair, hanging on for dear life as his mouth covered the tip of her breast, then drew on it firmly. His tongue flayed her nipple, stroking, curling around it as she twisted against him.

She was moaning his name. She couldn't stop the soft entreaties from whispering past her lips as he groaned against her, the sound vibrating against her sensitive flesh. One hand held his weight above her, the other stroked the skin of her waist, her abdomen, edging close but never touching the swollen mound of her cunt.

Then his lips rose, ignoring her protesting cry, only to move to the neglected nipple of her other breast. He stroked, licked, then covered the peak, drawing on her as his fingers traced erratic designs on her lower abdomen. She arched to his hand. Dear God, she didn't want to beg, but she was close, so damned close.

His hand paused at the top of her cunt, his fingers barely touching where the flesh curved, where her clit ached with such need she wanted to scream.

"Did he strike you here?" he asked her, his voice rough. "Are you bruised?"

"No," she gasped, arching her hips closer. "No, not there."

His fingers moved then as he drew back. He knelt between her splayed thighs and stared down at her, his breathing hard, rough. Savage intensity marked his expression, drawing the flesh tight over his high cheekbones as he stared at the dew-rich, silken folds of her cunt.

"I won't take you," he swore. "Not now. Not yet."

But that didn't stop him from lowering his head slowly, his mouth moving to the syrup-slick flesh that awaited him. An agonized moan of pleasure tore from her lips as she felt his tongue, wet velvet and fiery heat, stroke down the slit, gathering the cream that had amassed there as he hummed in pleasure at her taste.

Her legs fell further apart, her eyes closing as rapture flared, nearing, so close. Just a little more.

She lifted to him, her knees bending, her pussy pulsing.

"Devlin, you have a call out here." Joshua's voice was an unwelcome intrusion into the lust-thick atmosphere of the room.

He jerked against her, a harsh indrawn breath following another long, slow lick of his tongue along the parting lips of her cunt before he raised his head.

"Take care of it," Devlin half-growled, half-yelled, frustration echoing in his voice.

"Sorry, man. This one's not my call. You better get out here." Joshua's voice, knowing and mocking, set her face to flaming in embarrassment.

Devlin glanced up at her, his arousal clear in the glitter of his eyes, the flush of his cheekbones and the heavy sensuality in his lips. He cursed in a low, nearly violent voice before bounding off the bed.

Walking to a small recessed closet, he jerked out a midnight-blue silk shirt, then tossed her a pair of men's drawstring sweat pants.

"These will be more comfortable, and risk less chance of infection," he bit out as he helped her sit up. "Dress. We shouldn't be far from Hunter Castle now."

He helped her into the clothes, making certain the silk shirt was buttoned correctly, then rolled up the legs of the pants above her ankles. When he was certain she was ready, he jerked the door open.

Chantel was dazed, fighting to understand the sudden desertion when ecstasy had been so close within her grasp.

Joshua stood there, his arrogant face holding the slightest smirk. "Trust me, you don't want to miss this call," he told him softly, though Chantel caught the words.

"Stay close by in case she has difficulty," Devlin snarled. "Her jailer caned her, Joshua. At least attempt to spare her your bitterness for the time being."

Chantel found the strength to roll her eyes. Devlin was more furious over it than she had been. It was actually less than she had expected from Jonar's henchman. Despite the pain, she had found the guard's fury amusing. He would pull back for a blow that should have cut her to the bone, but just before it connected, some force would deflect the strength of it.

The crystal, she knew. She had grown accustomed to the burst of heat at her breast as she heard the whine of the stick. Then the guard's growling, animalistic rage when the blow didn't connect as he intended. Joshua's face paled slightly at the knowledge though, and his expression lost its casual mockery as Devlin brushed past him.

"No blood, no tears," she told him mockingly as she watched him now, standing silently in the doorway. "Don't worry, Joshua, I don't expect you to pretend to like me. I wouldn't want you to have to carry such a burden."

As she said the words, a spearing thought burst through her mind. He carried the guilt of such a thing already. He had deceived a lover, wiped away a spell of strength, and caused her downfall. Once again, she saw the phoenix's flames that enveloped the black-haired beauty.

"There was no need for the bastard to cane you." He seemed uncomfortable with whatever emotions the thought of it caused within him.

"There's no need for many of Jonar's and his demons' cruelties." She smiled tightly, misty images, memories, flitting through her mind as she watched him. "Torture is torture, whether inflicted physically or mentally. Wouldn't you think?"

His expression hardened as anger sparked in his oddly colored eyes.

"Devlin doesn't remember you." The smug smile was back in place as he leaned against the frame of the doorway watching her, his eyes glowing with amusement and a hint of anger.

Chantel sighed deeply, sitting down on the edge of the bed as she fought to bring her rioting system back under control.

"That's okay," she said simply, a bitter smile twisting her lips. "I don't really remember him either."

But she did. In her heart, in her dreams, she remembered him. Sighing wearily, she looked down at the glowing emerald within the crystal and wondered at the secrets of the past. She tucked it beneath her shirt once again, knowing that for now there would be no answers. Confusion raged within her mind as she stared back at the warrior. Glimpses of knowledge that she couldn't place flitted within her mind. The other three men with Devlin — Joshau, Derek, Shanar. As though she had once known them, and yet couldn't place them. The small bit of memory earlier when she had faced Joshau, or Joshua she reminded herself, had been one of the most telling.

But Devlin she had dreamed of. For years, she had dreamed of him. And now he was here. And with him came more questions than answers.

"Will you tell me who Antea is?" She stared back at him curiously then, tilting her head as she watched the anger that flowed through his eyes.

"Antea was a whore," he growled. "Devlin will not see you as who you were before. He does not remember. He will know you only as the whore he thinks you to be."

The cruel words slipped easily past his lips. She wondered if they passed his soul as easily.

She licked her lips before raking her teeth over the bottom curve hesitantly, staring up at him in dawning knowledge.

"You know," she whispered, coming to her feet as she faced him. "You know the truth, the past."

His smile was as sharp as a knife, a cutting blade of mockery.

"I know Antea's deceit was no greater than your own, Chantel, if you are indeed Chantel. And I tell you now, the magic of Hunter Castle will allow no one within its cursed halls to hear the truth of the past. It will be interesting to see how you fight the demons you gave birth to so long ago."

Chantel trembled beneath his cold regard. His eyes were like chips of amber ice, but beneath, the flame of fury burned. His accusation grew in her mind, swirling through her brain like echos of memories lost. And she hated it. She could feel that knowledge, just out of reach. So close and yet so very far away.

"What did I do?" She could feel his hatred now, brushing against her, fueled with his rage and pain.

He tilted his head, his long hair flowing over his shoulder like a cape of the darkest midnight.

"You destroyed the man he was," he rasped, his voice throbbing with violence. "You and that crazed sorcerer destroyed the warrior who laughed and knew how to love. Just as your sisters destroyed the rest of us. I curse the day we made the journey to that bewitched castle, and if I could go back, I would kill you all myself to save those I call brothers the pain you wrought."

Chantel shuddered. She shook her head, silently protesting his words, protesting that she could be a part of what he accused. Yet deep inside, she feared in some small way, he was right.

"What did I do?" she repeated fiercely. "You can't make statements like that and not explain what you're talking about." She needed to know, needed to understand the battle to come. And there would be a battle, she knew.

He smirked. A cruel twist of his mouth that sliced through her soul.

"I swore when you returned I would repay you for drawing me into your web of deceit," he growled. "I know what is coming. I know the past and your secrets, Mistress. And I'll be damned if I will tell them one moment sooner than I must." He laughed bitterly then. "And it will do you no good to go to the others. Galen made certain of that. They have forgotten, Mistress. Every memory they ever had of you is gone."

The blow struck just as he intended. But with the pain bloomed a certainty that struck back in response.

Her eyes narrowed on him. Rage beat within him like the frightened wings of a captive eagle. Yet, the rage was for himself, not for Devlin or the others.

"Selfishness," she whispered. "Were you always more concerned with your own pain than others', Joshua? You seek vengeance for yourself, not for them."

She watched as his swarthy expression paled just slightly. Then a flush of anger mantled his cheekbones as he pushed his hands into the wide pockets of his pants as though fighting to keep them in control.

"I learned the necessity of it once, long ago, in a battle that began with your deceptions," he sneered. "I will not stand in the way of, nor will I aid you in what you face, Mistress. You face it alone."

"I face it with Devlin," she reminded him.

He tilted his head in acknowledgement. "You do at that."

"According to the legend of the crystal, my victory or defeat will tie into yours as well. Yours and the others who stand with Devlin. There are four crystals, four Mistresses. None of us stand alone."

His head raised, his nostrils flaring as he breathed in deeply. His jaw clenched with anger as she drove the information into a particularly sensitive spot, it seemed.

"In ways, Mistress, we all stand alone," he bit out. "Remember this conversation well. Should you use me in the way you used me in the past, I will carve your heart from your chest myself. Remember that." His hand came from the pocket of his pants, his finger pointing at her imperatively. "Remember, for your very life and that of Devlin's may well depend upon it."

He turned from her, stalking from the doorway, leaving only the emanations of his anger behind him, and Chantel's own fears. Her eyes narrowed as the crystal soothed her. The ever-present mists of knowledge shifted for but a second, allowing her to see Joshua, snarling, enraged as he faced a fragile young woman who watched him with pain and with love.

She muttered a growl of frustration as she pulled herself up on the bed. Her body still hummed from Devlin's caresses, need rocketing through her system like a plague. She stared up at the ceiling, feeling the soft vibration of the plane's engines, the hum of power they discharged. At her breast, the crystal vibrated with its own warmth, its own power. She was comforted, inside and out, despite the confusion and the arousal. Her eyes closed, and before she knew it, the exhaustion of the past twenty-four hours swept over her.

Pulling the comforter to her shoulders, she sighed, allowing her body, if not her mind, to finally rest.

Chapter Five

ℰ

Hours later, Chantel found herself ushered unceremoniously into a large, fortress-like castle and up a flight of stairs to a large, opulent bedroom.

"I'll be back later," Devlin informed her, his voice cold, hard, as he turned and left her standing in the middle of the room.

After the door closed behind him, she heard the lock engage, and sighed wearily. Locked in. Now didn't that just cap it all off.

She took a deep breath, stilling the anger and the fear rising inside her. She had no idea where she was, or who these men were. Not really. She knew Devlin from her dreams, knew that the crystal responded to his power, and that she ached for him. She knew she could be going insane.

Stilling her nerves, she gazed around the room rather than focusing on her present predicament. A fire burned in the fireplace on the far right. In the center of the wall across from her was the largest canopied bed she had ever seen in her life. Thick velvet curtains were tied back at the huge posts, and a cushiony velvet-blue comforter covered the bed. A bedside table and chair sat beside it on one side, and a door that she hoped led to the bathroom on the other. At the other end of the room were several long, narrow windows. Beneath them a walnut chest that gleamed from the low lamp that sat atop it.

Plush, thick, pale cream carpeting lined the floor, and ancient tapestries hung from the stone walls.

"At least it's not the dungeon," she sighed wearily, exhausted now that the adrenaline that had once poured through her body was slowly easing.

A hot bath—and she was praying a meal would come soon, she was starved—and then she would sleep like a baby in that big bed. She eyed it longingly. If she dared lay down there for a second, she would be out like a light.

She pushed her fingers through her hair tiredly, grimacing at the limp state of the silken strands. A bath first. If there was a bathroom behind that door. She toed her sneakers from her feet, then began unclipping her gun holster. They had let her keep the gun. Not that it could hurt one of them, she grimaced. But she would keep it with her just in case. A bullet might not stop one of them if it was needed, but it could very well slow them down.

It was unreal. Grasping reality and holding onto it was becoming harder to do as minutes passed and she was given the time to consider what had happened in such a short time.

She swallowed tightly as she turned the doorknob to the nearest door, thankful that it was a bathroom. It was a large, decadent bathroom, complete with garden tub and a separate shower. Gleaming porcelain, marble floors, narrow, tinted windows and thick rugs in a rich sapphire blue hinted at the wealth of the owner.

She adjusted the water in the sunken tub and poured a liberal amount of bath foam from the selection along a small shelf above it. The scent of gardenias, light and fragrant, began to fill the steamy atmosphere as the tub filled.

Undressing quickly, she dropped her borrowed clothing to the floor. She checked the gash on her leg. It was raw, angry looking, but not too bad, which surprised her. The wound should have been much worse. With a sigh, she stepped into the sinfully hot liquid silk that awaited her. A groan, a breathless whimper of mingled pain and bliss, escaped her lips.

Chantel washed her hair quickly, then leaned back against the tub, resting her head on the curved lip. Sore, tight muscles relaxed as the heated water soothed her chafed and bruised skin. The smell of blood and fear eased beneath the flowery fragrance of the bubbles, lulling her into a gentle, drowsy state. Too much had happened to her too soon. Too much was out of her control. She needed to drift, to relax and allow the strain of the past day to ease through her, out of her, before she could think clearly.

"You should not sleep in the water." The dark voice had Chantel jerking upright in alarm. She reached for her gun, her eyes widening, her head turning to meet the light scowl that filled Devlin's face.

He was hunched by the tub. His powerful legs bent, holding his weight easily as his eyes flickered to the thick foam that covered her breasts. Biting back a curse, she sank back into the water, unwilling to display herself to his heated gaze. And her traitorous body wasn't helping any. Her nipples had peaked for him instantly, her breasts swelling as his gaze raked her bared curves.

"I hope you brought dinner." She frowned up at him, wondering how he had managed to sneak in without her seeing him.

Chantel lifted her hand from the gun, easing back into the concealing suds.

"Dinner will be up soon," he promised her, his gaze finally rising to meet hers. "I felt we should talk first."

Chantel felt her mouth go dry. His voice wasn't conducive to pleasant conversation. He sounded furious.

"Oh, ready to answer questions now?" she asked him as she arched a brow in a move that she knew drove her father crazy.

He frowned. His midnight-black brows came to a fierce vee between his eyes, a contrast to the soft fall of silky black hair that fell over his forehead. His sun-darkened face was lined with weariness, his black eyes so cold they chilled her. She took a deep breath, determined she wouldn't flinch beneath the look.

"I thought perhaps you would be ready for that small chore." He watched her expectantly.

Chantel almost smiled. He acted like he expected her to suddenly begin spouting venom rather than truths.

"What would I know that could help you?" she asked him. "That I haven't already told you?"

"Your father believes you know more than you are telling, Chantel," he said softly, watching curiously. "I just got off the phone with him, and he's highly suspicious of you at this moment."

Chantel rolled her eyes. Her father always thought she knew more than she was telling. It was a fact of her life. Knowing it didn't alleviate the hurt, but neither did she dwell on it any longer.

"My father often sees deceit where there is none. He's a spy, Devlin. It's natural." But was it?

Her breath caught in her throat as his arm moved, extending toward her. His finger touched her collarbone, traced it until it came to the heavy silver chain. There, he inserted his finger beneath the heavy links, lifting the crystal until it cleared the water.

Light fractured against the stone for a second, spilling a rainbow of hues over her skin as she glanced down at it.

"If you aren't Antea, why then does the crystal she wore accept you?" Insinuation lay heavily in his voice.

Chantel bit back the pain that flared inside her at the question. She turned her gaze back to him, staring up at him, meeting those cold eyes head-on.

"I need to finish my bath," she finally whispered. "I'm too tired, and too hungry right now to play games with you. I don't know who wore it before, but it was meant for me. The crystal is mine, but I am not Antea."

She remembered him in her dreams. Remembered his touch, his kiss, even the sound of his laughter and his tears. The warning Joshua had given her about the magic of this castle played through her mind. She could feel it, that magic, woven into the very air that filled the castle. And she knew whatever had happened in the past, whenever it had been, the memories were as dim within his mind as they were within hers.

"What are you playing, if it isn't a game?" he asked her, refusing to move. "How much do you remember, Chantel? Exactly what have your dreams brought you?" His finger ran along her collarbone again.

Chantel breathed in roughly. It was more than obvious that once again her father had spread his malice and suspicions. The dreams that had begun in late childhood were so filled with blood and agonizing pain, that she wanted never to relive them.

The sensuality of the caress sent a spear of longing through her body that lodged almost painfully in the center of her womb. She struggled for breath, fighting against the riotous desires that enflamed her body.

"Glimpses of hell," she finally whispered painfully, fighting to forget the horror of those dreams with the same strength she fought not to pant at his touch. "Now, if you will kindly leave, I can complete my bath, and hopefully get some food."

She couldn't hide her accelerated breathing. She watched as his gaze went to her breasts, his lashes lowering as he watched their heavy movements. She forced back a whimper as she watched the dark color that ran beneath his cheeks, and felt the heavy tension that suddenly descended between them. His touch was more heated than the water, the calloused finger that rubbed gently below her neck throwing her senses into a maelstrom of sensations.

His gaze rose slowly to meet hers, heated now where it had been cold before, a flame of lust flickering in the midnight depths as he watched her. Lust and confusion. He frowned down at her as though he couldn't quite believe his desire for her.

Back and forth his finger moved, stroking a sensual fire in her that caused her breasts to ache, the muscles of her cunt to clench with the need to be filled. Her clit was a pulsing ache, begging for his touch. She had to bite her lip to keep from begging him to ease the fiery longing that flamed through her body.

"Your skin is so soft," he whispered into the heavy silence of the room. "It makes me want to touch you forever."

Her eyes were held captive by his as she fought for breath. She wanted nothing more than to have him touch her forever. Every part of her, every inch of flesh, screamed out in longing. Her vagina heated, searing her with need as it pulsed and throbbed in reaction. She wanted his touch. Forever. His possession. Forever.

When she didn't speak, he sighed softly, his finger retreating, leaving a path of fire and need in its wake. He rose to his feet, watching her carefully as he did so, his eyes brooding, intense.

"I've laid a gown and robe on the counter," he told her, his voice pitched low, rough with desire. "I'll be awaiting you in the bedroom. Your dinner should be up soon."

He turned and left the room as silently as he had come in. Chantel shook her head, fighting for breath as she watched him leave. He never made a sound, even when he closed the door behind him. Like a phantom, she thought, or a ghost from the past.

Devlin watched as Chantel walked slowly from the bathroom, her lithe body covered by the light green, floor length linen gown and robe. She was covered properly, barely any skin showing to entice him, yet still his heart rate increased as she entered the room. Not to mention what his dick did. That traitor was thick and hard and begging for freedom, for a change.

His conversation with her father had done nothing but raise more questions than he had to begin with. Michael hadn't been the least concerned about his daughter's welfare. Even more disturbing was the cold, biting remark that they would have been better off had Jonar still held her.

"Your dinner will be here soon," he told her as she turned those dark green eyes on him.

Her gaze was vulnerable, yet filled with strength. She was wary of him, but determined. She wasn't shrinking before him, nor calculating her chances of lying to him. He wanted to shake the mental fog from his head, the shadows that hid some secret knowledge that he couldn't quite bring forward. She was a vision of silken beauty, unlike anything he had known before. Soft, sweetly scented and drawing him like a bee to honey.

"Thank you," she whispered, standing before him, her eyes bright, watching him with fragile hope, with wary fear.

He could not reconcile it within himself. She was identical to the traitorous Antea in nearly every way. But had Antea's eyes been such a deep, emerald green? He knew her skin had not been so soft, her body so perfectly formed. Antea's eyes had lacked the brilliance of uncut stones, but had been dulled by her greed and lusts instead.

"I did not bring you here to starve you," he finally snorted. "I'm sorry it's taken so long, there was much I had to do before I could get back to you, and Kanna needed time to prepare the food."

He watched as she ran her fingers through her damp hair, feathering the soft strands around her face, making his hand itch to touch it. Antea's skin had been coarse. Her hair, though thick, had been rougher than the silk that adorned Chantel's head. Her skin had been pale, not the color of the finest cream and the most delicate blush of a pale rose.

Michael had done all he could to convince Devlin that she was Antea. A belief Devlin rejected as fiercely as his body had once rejected the bitch who had dared call herself his wife.

As he started to speak, a knock at the door halted the words he would have said. Words he was certain would bring the light of battle back to her brilliant gaze. He found earlier that he liked the furious sparkle that would light her eyes and flush her cheeks. She was a spitfire, and it made him wonder if she would be as hot in other ways.

"Enter." He turned to watch Kanna and Joshua enter the room. Joshua bore a heavy tray filled with the serving dishes that held Chantel's dinner. Kanna moved behind him, curiosity lighting her soft brown eyes.

Kanna appeared no older than Chantel herself, yet the other woman had raised him and the others and looked after their estate the few times they were taken for healing by the Guardians, and she ran the castle in a manner that gave Devlin the freedom to battle against Jonar at will.

Chantel stood silently on the other side of him, watching the other woman with a wary expression. Kanna was dressed in jeans and a light cotton sweater, her long, nut-brown hair pulled back into a low ponytail at the back of her neck. She held herself with confidence, but a bit of nervousness.

"Kanna, may I present to you, Chantel. Michael Ducaine's daughter, and the Mistress of the Earth Crystal. Chantel, this is Kanna, she is the Castle Retainer," Devlin introduced them, watching Chantel intently for any animosity she might show.

"Hello, it's a pleasure to meet you." Chantel clasped her hands before her in a gesture of nervousness as her gaze flickered to Devlin, then to the food Joshua was setting on the small table across the room, then back to Kanna.

"It's a pleasure to meet you as well." Kanna cast Devlin a questioning look. He could only shrug in response.

"I am aware I should be acting some way that I'm not," Chantel finally said without a hint of apology, though her voice was amused. An amusement that made Devlin narrow his eyes at her in warning. "But I'm honestly too tired and too hungry to try to figure out how I should act. I'm sure Devlin will be able to convince me of it soon though."

Kanna cast him a surprised look. Devlin could only sigh and shake his head. He had no idea how to deal with this woman, and she wasn't helping in the least.

"The meal is a light one, since it's so late," Kanna said softly. "We can talk tomorrow."

"Thank you." Chantel's smile was one of gracious acceptance. Her lips were fuller, Devlin suddenly thought. They weren't thin, or pinched, as Antea's had often been.

Joshua and Kanna left the room quickly, leaving Devlin to watch as Chantel went over to the table and sat down. She uncovered the first plate, a soft hum of appreciation leaving her lips as she found the large roast beef sandwich that lay inside. Sweet tea filled the glass that sat beside her plate, and she sipped from it quickly before looking back at him. She checked beneath the other dome to be certain a sandwich filled it as well before turning to him.

"Father will tell you that I only have manners when I need them. After the hell I've already been through, I figure I'm entitled to eat rather than stand on ceremony," she informed him casually as she lifted the sandwich to her lips.

Devlin strode to the table and sat down before his own meal. He wanted to keep her within his room for now. Keep her in sight until he knew better what she was up to, and who she was.

They ate in silence. Chantel glanced around the room often, but said nothing to him. He knew she had noticed the bed turned down, his gun and knife in their holster and sheath lying on the side table. She didn't say anything though.

The sandwiches were finished quickly, leaving them sitting in silence as she leaned back in her chair and watched him quietly. He finished his wine, watching her, seeing not just her fear and nervousness, but also her complete exhaustion.

"You should prepare for bed now." He rose to his feet, moving to her and helping her from her chair.

She moved with the careful, controlled movements of one who was finally realizing exactly how sore her body was. Thankfully, none of the abuse had been severe. The wound at her thigh was healing, but the bruising was still uncomfortable, he knew. With rest, he was certain she would be healed within a day or two.

He reached out, his fingers touching her cheek, amazed at the warmth he felt there. Her lips trembled as his thumb smoothed over them, her breathing increasing to a rapid tempo of desire. He would have bent to kiss her then, to taste the sweetness of those lips.

With a startled jerk she moved away from him, shaking her head.

"Tell me first that you know I am not Antea," she whispered desperately, causing his chest to tighten with the need he saw in her expression.

Devlin pushed his fingers restlessly through his hair. What was he supposed to say to her? Right now, the only thing he was truly certain of was his overriding lust for her. All other things he could not be certain of in any way.

"Now is not the time for this, Chantel," he sighed. "We are both exhausted, and you are running on nerves alone. You need to rest."

She shook her head, the white silk of her hair brushing along her neck as she denied him. She was pale, yet she still fought him. His lips quirked at the core of steel he could sense beneath her soft, graceful exterior.

"I need answers." She shook her head, her somber expression pricking at his conscience. "Who do you think I am?"

Devlin could only shake his head. "I don't know. But I know for a fact I never got hard for Antea. For you, my dick is so hard I'm about to come in my pants."

Chantel lost her breath. Her eyes flickered to the erection that strained his jeans, then back to his confident expression. Her mouth dried, then watered. Her cunt did worse than water—she expected it to start dripping down her thighs any minute now.

She jerked as he reached out again, carefully smoothing a strand of hair from her face, tucking it behind her ear. The overwhelming gentleness of the act, the deliberate restraint coupled with the intense lust in his eyes had the anticipation, the adrenaline surging through her body.

"Tell me you do not feel it." His voice was a grating, harsh tone. "Tell me, Chantel, that your body does not hunger for mine in the same way. Tell me, and I will leave you alone in this bed, in this room, rather than sharing it with you as I intend to."

Her eyes widened. "Sharing it?" she gasped. Now why hadn't she expected that one?

She shook her head, backing away from him as he continued to stalk her with predatory intent. It shouldn't turn her on, shouldn't make the heat flare hotter inside her that he would stalk her in such a manner. She should be furious. Instead, she was horny. Anticipating the chase, as well as the capture. Sick puppy that she was.

"Sharing it," he repeated. "This is my room, Chantel, and my bed. And there you will sleep, next to me, where you belong."

Her back came up against the wall, preventing her from retreating further as his body stopped within a breath of her. Fire licked over her flesh, heating her, raising the temperature of the room until the air was stifling, hunger and need tearing through her mind. She could feel it. Awareness, blistering and consuming, working through her, making her ache until she wondered if anything could satisfy the incredible burning hunger raging through her.

"Who says I belong here?" she panted, well aware that she was melting against him, her body refusing to struggle despite the demands her mind made of it. "And I did not agree to sleep with you, Devlin."

He smiled, a slow, sensual curve of his lips as his lashes lowered in a sexy move that had her heart racing in excitement.

"I like having you helpless before me," he told her, his voice dark, erotic. "And soon, I intend to have you helpless beneath me."

Her body flooded with weakness.

"I haven't agreed to any of this," she cried out desperately, keeping her palms flat against the hard muscles of his chest, though it did nothing to budge him.

"Nor have you rejected the idea." His hands spanned her waist, holding her still as his head lowered, his lips grazing her cheek. "Perhaps you do not intend to reject it?"

"Stop," she bit out, pushing harder against him as she struggled against his hold, against the sensation of his touch. Her skin was too tight, too aware of him, too susceptible to him.

He moved back as her knee cocked, a thread of laughter glittering in his eyes.

"You do not have to agree to sleep with me. You will do so anyway. There is no room for discussion," he said in a hard voice as she moved quickly.

Chantel turned back to him, anger and desire warring equally inside her body.

"You can't force me, Devlin." He placed her hands flat against the wall as she faced him, fear and need both tangible forces within her body. "I won't allow you to."

"I will not force you to accept my body." The cultured baritone was sexier, huskier. "But I will force you to sleep where I can keep an eye on you. I do not trust you, Chantel. Not you, nor that crystal, not yet. Until I can, I will make certain you can cause no mischief."

Her eyes widened as anger overshadowed need and built like an inferno within her body.

"Are you insane?" she demanded furiously. "What do you expect me to do? I don't even know where the hell I am."

"I expect very little, but I am prepared for many things," he warned her ruthlessly. "And I will not stand here and argue with you. You can sleep in the bed, or on the floor, it matters not. But the floor gets pretty damned cold, *wife*."

Chantel's eyes widened in alarm, but it was nothing compared to the shock that sped across his face. He looked like a man that had been slapped silly with surprising violence. He shook his head then, anger glittering cold and hard within his eyes.

"Go to fucking bed," he bit out, stalking to the door as the tension in the air thickened to a smothering level. "And for God's sake, be asleep when I return."

The door slammed behind him, then the lock clicked into place with a sound of finality. Chantel stood staring at it, unable to respond for the simple fact that she could not make sense of a single emotion running through her body. She was insane, she thought, because the strongest feeling running through her was that of joy. He had called her wife.

Devlin stood atop the battlements of the castle and gazed out at the darkened valley below, hours later. The wind whipped at his clothes, tore through his hair, but did nothing to clear the fog from his brain. Why had he called her wife? And why did the title seem to fit her when it had never fit Antea? The word had stuck in his throat and had sent agony flaring though him if another had dared to call Antea by that title. Wife. He had sworn he had no wife.

He propped his hands against the half-wall that protected those who walked along the area from carelessly falling. His eyes closed and he could have sworn he heard her gentle laughter. It wrapped around him, soothed him in ways he could not name.

He had called her wife, and he could feel the tie that bound them in that manner. He remembered, in a hazy distant part of his memories, a marriage, a binding, and happiness that made no sense. All he had now was that infernal mist that hid the secrets within his brain and emotions he could make no sense of.

He remembered, ages ago, after first coming to the castle. His memories of this place had no beginning, though he knew he had not always been here. He remembered the journey to the castle, the battles and blood before his arrival here. After that, he could not bring his life into focus until the memory of awakening, perhaps after drinking too much, with Antea beside him.

Fury had filled him. A black rage unlike anything he had ever known had washed through his body, and from that moment he had hated her. Hated her so desperately that he would have killed her himself on many occasions. All that stayed his hand was that he could not bring to mind a single reason why he would hate her so desperately.

And now there was Chantel. Her name came easily to his lips, soothed a part of his soul that had lain in wrenching agony for centuries. He longed to touch her, needed to touch her, to hold her, to immerse himself in the heat that he knew was a part of her. Vibrant, living silk. He closed his eyes, remembering the feel of her. Her kiss, her skin, the heat that was a natural part of her.

"You fight the mists of time too desperately. You should relax and allow it to come as it will."

He whirled around to confront the tall, stocky form of the sorcerer, Galen. The man was not as tall as Devlin, but muscular, and well-built. He was an able warrior alone, and his gift of magic made him a formidable opponent.

"Aren't you dead yet?" Devlin growled in irritation. The sorcerer invariably brought confusion and anger whenever he came to Devlin.

Laughter drifted on the breeze as Galen joined him at his sentry point. He stood and stared out into the night, his expression reflective. The sadness that seemed so much a part of the sorcerer in the centuries past was noticeably absent now. He seemed concerned, but his smile was lighter, his eyes lacking the shadows of the past.

"Do not harm this woman," he finally said, the warning thick within his tone.

"I have never harmed a woman," Devlin bit out, more than offended. "Why would I begin with this one?"

He crossed his arms over his chest, staring back at the other man furiously. Who was Chantel that she could have such an effect on both of them?

"Because she has the looks of one you hate. Because you cannot accept yet, that there is more to her than what you see," Galen suggested.

He knew there was more to her than what he saw, and this was his problem. Knowing, and yet not knowing, what she was to him.

Devlin sighed wearily. "I may not know who the hell she is, old man, but I know who she isn't. That woman is not Antea. But I would know exactly who she is now, and I have a feeling you know."

"She is Chantel. You would hear no more than that, no matter what I say, warrior," Galen sighed sadly. "Sometimes, my magic is greater than even I anticipate."

Devlin frowned. He would have questioned the sorcerer further but the need for it seemed to slip through his fingers.

He frowned, knowing there was more that he should ask, aware suddenly of the many times this had happened over the centuries.

"I called her wife," he said instead. "Suddenly she stood there, refusing to share my bed. And I called her wife. I cannot imagine why I would do so. I remember no wedding, no vows, none except that that my soul seems to whisper whenever she is near."

Perhaps he was as bewitched as Michael accused him of being.

Galen nodded slowly. "Magic whispers and shields my warrior. Continue to listen with your heart, rather than your ears, and its secrets will be yours."

Devlin grunted at the sorcerer's riddle.

"Jonar will stop at nothing to take her now that she has escaped him once." Devlin knew this, and was terrified he could not adequately protect her. "If he took her once, he could do so again."

"The crystal protected her," Galen said, his voice thick with satisfaction. "She is the true mistress, Devlin. It would protect only the one it was destined for. It aided her, and gave her strength until you could find her. You must now give it time to teach her."

"Antea was given the gem," Devlin growled, his fists clenching in fury at the memory of her. "She was mistress as well."

Galen said nothing to this. He only shook his head sadly. "There is only one mistress, Devlin. No matter who may wear the crystal, only one shall control it. As well as your heart."

"Am I crazy, old man?" he finally asked wearily. "Would I not remember had I loved this woman? Would I not know?"

Galen turned and looked at him shrewdly, his eyes glittering with power and with knowledge.

"Tell me, warrior, do you not already know?"

* * * * *

"Daughter, awaken," the voice whispered through her mind, soft and maternal, a sound of such purity and gentleness that Chantel's heart surged with fondness.

Her eyes fluttered open, but drowsiness held such sway on her mind, that she wondered if she still yet slept. Then she knew she must be, for the wavering figure by her bed was nearly transparent. Transparent, but so gentle and filled with compassion that it brought a lump to her throat.

The figure was ghostly, a pale white that didn't lend much to the overall features of the spirit who watched her. This wasn't her mother, at least not the one who gave birth to her. But Chantel knew in her heart that this figure was as maternal as any birth mother could hope to be.

Wonder and awe filled her. She blinked up at the beauty of the form, seeing the compassion, the gentle pure love that surrounded her, and felt her soul begin to ease.

"I remember you," she whispered, sensing a familiarity, a bond as deep and old as time.

"You have returned. My joy knows no bounds. But now you must ease in your fears. You must accept the crystal and the power. You can no longer sleep in ignorance, but must instead awaken to truth."

"I am not Antea," she told the vision firmly just in case this vision was under the same misapprehension as everyone else seemed to be.

"You are not Antea," the Mother agreed with a gentle smile. *"You are Chantel, and the power and the promise that was Chantel returns to you now."*

The vision shifted, her arm waving. Chantel gasped breathlessly as the mists in her mind shifted and power flooded her body. Blazing heat and awakening secrets surged through her, rioting through her mind with the force of a tidal wave.

She was the Mistress of the Earth.

She breathed in hard and deep as that knowledge sank into her very pores. The power was hers, as was the warrior. The memories were still shrouded, awaiting something, she wasn't certain what. But she knew. Knew in her heart, in her soul that she was truly the wife Devlin had named her.

"Give yourself to the power, Chantel. To the earth. It awaits you with open arms and a heart of gladness. Sleep now, child, and awaken knowing your promise, and the strength that fills you."

Her eyes closed once again. As her head settled into the pillows of Devlin's bed and sleep folded around her, she could have sworn she heard the door open, and Devlin's whispered prayer for strength.

Chapter Six

ഇ

Devlin watched Chantel sleep the next morning. She was lying in his bed, her head resting on his pillow, so he figured he had the right. Besides, it was either watch her or touch her and he wasn't certain if his self-control was strong enough, should she demand that he stop. And that feeling alone convinced him that this couldn't be Antea. The very thought of her sharing so much as the room he slept in had sickened him. Yet Chantel... He could allow her to sleep no place else.

From the first moment that he had looked into those brilliant, expressive eyes, he had seen something he hadn't even known was missing in his life. No, he took that back. He had known it was missing, had felt its absence for more centuries than he wanted to count, with no idea what it was until he saw her. Felt her, touched her.

Now, he lay next to her aching to touch her, kiss her. He wanted nothing more than to experience once again the passion that had flared between them in that damned plane.

He could have devoured her then. Had Joshua not interrupted them, he doubted he could have stopped. Chantel had fired his blood, his lust, in a way that had been damned hard to resist.

Had she not been wounded, abused, he would have been unable to stop himself. Desperation flared through his body and his cock, unlike anything he had known in his life. She filled him. Filled his senses and his thoughts, and made him question his very sanity.

Chantel was finally where she was meant to be.

He would never allow Chantel to sleep in any bed but his own. She was here, and she would stay here until he sorted through the conflicting feelings raging through him.

His hand lifted, his fingers softly touching her cheek as her eyes slowly fluttered opened. She sighed deeply, a small frown crossing her face as she blinked up at him sleepily.

"You're here," she whispered, her gentle voice drowsy. "I thought I had dreamed you again."

She had dreamed of him, just as he had dreamed of her.

Through the veil of her lashes, he glimpsed the incredible brilliance of her emerald eyes. So dark and filled with secrets, knowledge. He felt that if he could only stare into them long enough, he would find the answers he was seeking.

"No dream," Devlin told her huskily, turning his head to place a kiss in her palm, which had reached up to touch his cheek. "I'm really here."

The silken feel of her hand against his lips was exquisite. Devlin had never felt such soft skin, nor tasted anything so delicate. She was spring after a hard winter, a promise of heat and passion unlike anything he had ever known.

"'Bout time," she sighed in pleasure as he pulled her closer to his body.

Devlin nearly groaned aloud as Chantel's tongue slowly ran over her sleep-dry lips. He wanted that moist little tongue against his own. Stroking him, laving him with moist silk. His cock jerked in response. Damn, to feel her tongue there, licking the sensitive flesh, sucking him past all boundaries of control. He barely restrained his growl of need.

He would find out soon, he promised himself. He would taste her until he could sate himself with her, then allow her to taste him in a similar manner. Perhaps then, he could figure out why he desired her so deeply.

"Such restraint," Chantel whispered up at him seductively, her eyes dark, her lips beckoning. A temptress with the eyes of an innocent. A contradiction that was shredding his self-control. As though she belonged in another place, another time. "I would not have expected such patience after such abstinence."

"You're playing with fire," Devlin whispered as her hand moved from his face down his neck, then to his naked chest. "I may not be able to stop this time."

"Did I ask you to stop last time?" she asked him, breathing quickly as his hand moved to her waist.

Devlin's fingers bunched in the material of the gown as he considered ripping it from her body.

Patience, he cautioned himself. Chantel was here, warm and beckoning, no need to rush or to frighten her with the strength of his passion. For once, this was no dream. There was no need to hurry, no need to fear the strength of his hunger.

"You can't say I didn't warn you," he groaned, his voice dark and rough.

Slowly, Devlin warned himself once more. He feared he would be unable to heed that voice for long.

His head lowered, his heart thundered. When his lips took hers, it was like sinking into a maelstrom of sensation so powerful, so heated, it shook his very being.

Slowly, he drew her closer against him, feeling the warm weight of her breasts through the fine linen nightgown she wore. He didn't understand the incredible need that filled him, the lust when before there had been a barren wasteland of impotency.

"So warm and sweet," Devlin whispered against Chantel's lips as he slowly sipped at the sweetness she offered.

His tongue licked her lips gently, probing softly at the corners until they opened for him and he was allowed entrance.

It was so much better than anything he had ever known. Better than anything he could have hoped for in the nightmare his life had become. Chantel was all the heat and delicate passion he had dreamed of for so damned long.

"Such beauty." His voice was soft as he rose above her. "Never have I seen such beauty."

Chantel's eyes were dazed with passion and need. Her face delicately flushed, her breasts rising and falling swiftly as he watched her. He could ask for nothing more perfect than the arousal of this moment. An arousal he hadn't known in a thousand years.

Chantel felt fire scorching through her as Devlin watched her. Her body was heating, her skin sensitizing. If he didn't kiss her soon, she knew she would die of the desire for it. In her sleep-dazed reality, little existed but Devlin, and the continuation of the dream that had filled her senses before waking.

Her breasts were swollen, the nipples aching with fiery longing as her cunt clenched in desperate need. She was empty, throbbing, she needed him inside her, needed his lust rough and hot, hard and deep. She wanted him to take her with the same wild hunger that reflected in the endless black of his eyes.

When his lips touched hers, so warm and soft, she melted. Her lips opened, her hand clutching his back to pull him closer. Her eyes closed against the extreme pressure of the caress as she arched against him.

Devlin whispered her name against her lips, his voice hoarse with hunger as his hands clenched at her waist. His tongue slid seductively over her lips, probing against them until they opened further for his possession. There was no need to rush, as there had been on the plane. No need to try to gorge on the heat and seductive pleasure rising between them. But Chantel needed to gorge. She whimpered as she fought for the rougher touch, the dominant possession that she knew was so much a part of him.

She wasn't certain how she knew, but she knew the outcome of the incredible passion flaring between them. She knew the explosive heat, which would build, only to explode in a pleasure unlike any she had ever known in her life. She knew his touch would bring it. She knew his kiss would ease it.

As the buttons on her gown were slowly released, the edges pushed apart, her breathing escalated, the hardened mounds rising toward him demandingly. There was no embarrassment, no fear. There was only wonder as Devlin's head raised, his black eyes lowering until he could gaze upon the flesh he had revealed.

Chantel felt her breasts swell and harden further as her pussy became wet, hot, so hot she felt she would burst into flames if he didn't touch it soon. Her breathing escalated until she was fighting for every lungful of air. She had never known that a man could look so sexy and hot outside her dreams, that the expression on his face could make her womb clench with such force.

"You're beautiful," Devlin whispered, his hand lifting, his fingers touching one breast gently.

Chantel lifted to his touch, her eyes drifting closed, a startled cry trapped in her throat. Electricity tingled from his fingertips to her breasts, shocking her with the pleasure of his caress.

With a rough groan, Devlin bent to her once again, stealing her lips in a carnal, demanding kiss as his hand cupped the slope of her breast gently.

"This hunger for you will drive me insane." His voice was rough as his lips moved to the tender skin of her neck.

Chantel twisted against him, her head falling back to allow greater access to the sensitive skin he was caressing.

Her hands gripped his shoulders. Her body moved against him demandingly as he took his time tasting her. His tongue tangled with hers, his lips demanding her response, her hunger. It surged from her with a force that left her gasping as she felt his knee wedge between her thighs, his upper leg pressing against the damp folds of her pussy. She rocked against him, aching, needing as she had never needed before.

Chantel cried out in wonder when those hungry, diabolical lips reached her breasts. The pleasure exceeded every expectation and dream she had ever had. His tongue stroked over the hard, elongated point with rasping demand. The heat of his mouth seared her, enflamed her. He sucked the tender point into the moist depths of his mouth and drew on her with a firm, deep motion that had her jerking in response. She was shuddering, violent tremors quaking through her as a high, keening cry escaped her throat.

She twisted beneath him, pleading for more, her muted cries demanding as her hands gripped his hair, her back arching from the bed. She had to have more of his touch before she went insane from the need.

With a deep groan, Devlin's hands went to her gown, jerking it quickly to her thighs. She arched toward him, well aware of her nudity and the shocking dampness between her legs. Her pussy ached. It was on fire, desperate for his touch.

"Please," she cried out as his hand trailed along her thigh. "Please, Devlin."

His gaze rose to hers, heavy-lidded, hungry.

"Do you have any idea what I want to do to you?" He stared down at her, fierce, conquering. "Any idea of the many ways I will take you?"

Her breath caught as his fingers slid over the swollen, slick lips of her cunt.

"Not yet," she gasped. "But I trust you're getting ready to show me."

A sensual smile curled around his lips, making the blood thunder through her veins in anticipation. His finger ran over the plump curves until it came to the swollen bud of her clit.

He circled it teasingly before running down the humid slit once again to test the readiness of her vagina.

She felt the heat of his finger burrowing between her flesh, sliding easily through the syrupy juices until he was circling the opening to her vagina slowly.

"I could easily make you scream in need, Chantel. Is this what you wish?" he asked her seductively as his palm cupped the curves of her cunt.

"Do I have to scream to prove I need?" she panted roughly, pressing against his palm, needing a deeper, hotter touch.

She groaned at the slight pressure on her clit. Not enough. She needed more. She could feel the sensations building in the sensitive bud, the pulsing ache that threatened to drive her insane.

"Easy," he whispered, his hand moving slowly, too slowly, against the heat he cupped in his hand.

Chantel stared up at him in dazed pleasure. His expression was savage, carnal, his eyes glittering with wicked heat, his face flushed with his lusts. His hair fell over his forehead in disarray and his lips were a bit fuller, more sensual than before. Just looking at him made her melt.

Her thighs clenched on his hand. Fire swept through her womb as his palm massaged her soaked pussy, driving her to distraction with his teasing. She arched closer, pressing her aching clit tighter against the palm of his hand.

"So hot and wet," he whispered sensually as she stared up at him. "Greedy baby."

She would have snapped out a sharp retort for his comment if he hadn't chosen that moment to press harder against her desperate flesh, grinding his hand into her burning clit.

Chantel nearly came off the bed. Her hands caught in his hair, dragging his lips to hers, as her action seemed to break the fragile thread of his control. His lips devoured her as his finger pressed into the ultrasensitive entrance to her pussy. He sank in to the first knuckle, then retreated and returned until the small, teasing thrusts were making her insane with desire.

Devlin's body, harder, larger, levered over her as his lips and tongue plundered hers, setting off such riotous sensations that they left her gasping, crying out for more. His fingers were never still between her thighs. As one finger pressed heatedly into her liquid hot vagina, his lips moved hungrily past her cheek, her neck, his lips latching on her breast and drawing the nipple into the greedy depths of his mouth.

His tongue was a flaming lash of pure pleasure at her breast, his fingers torturous in their explorations of her cunt. Chantel cried out as her body arched against him, her head thrashing on the pillow as sensations built and rushed through her body like an avalanche of impending ecstasy.

"Oh God, yes," she panted breathlessly. His lips moved to her other breast, his tongue stroking, lips suckling. "Oh God, Devlin, I don't know if I can stand it."

"You will bear it." His head rose from the full mound of flesh he had been caressing. His gaze locked on hers as his fingers moved between her thighs once again. "At least for a while longer."

Her eyes widened and a gasp escaped her as his fingers traveled lower, circling the tight entrance to her anus, massaging it with lazy, tormenting strokes as he alternately pressed against it.

"Devlin," his name stuttered from her lips as her fingers tightened in his hair.

She stared up at him, uncertain, but not frightened.

"I'll take you there, eventually," he whispered, his voice rough, heated. "When I know you're ready, when I know you can take me. I'll push inside this tight little hole."

The tip of his finger entered her, stretched her with hot intent.

Her hips arched again, her muscles clamping on the invader as she watched his head lower. Carnal determination marked his features, his black eyes nearly glowing with the lust rising inside him. She had never seen such a look on a man's face. A hunger that transcended anything she had ever known.

His finger slid into her tight hole to the first knuckle as his tongue slid slowly through her creamy slit. The small bite of pain and the hard lash of pleasure were nearly more than she could stand.

"Devlin, please." Her hands tightened in his hair as he glanced back up at her.

"I'm a very hungry man, Chantel," he whispered. "And this is a feast I am not willing to deny myself."

He lapped at her again. From the entrance to her clenching vagina, up to the fiery demand of her swollen clit. As he licked, the finger burrowing into her ass slid a little deeper.

Chantel could barely breathe. The feel of his finger massaging muscles never before touched was nearly enough to send her into a climax alone. She had never imagined such delicious sensation. Part pleasure, part pain. Pure wicked delight.

"More," she whispered, her head tossing on the pillows as his tongue circled her clit in a slow, mind-destroying stroke. "Please. More."

"You like this?" His finger retreated, gathered more of the slick juices seeping from her pussy then pressed back into the hot channel of her anus with a firm thrust.

Chantel shuddered, a cry breaking from her lips. She shouldn't feel such pleasure at the mild bite of pain. Shouldn't be racked by such intense desire to feel the hard, thick length of his cock pressing into her there.

"Soon," he whispered against her pulsing clit, as though he knew her shameful desire. "Until then, I will give you this."

She was dying. Chantel swore it must be death as his mouth became ravenous on her pussy. The licking, sucking sounds of his mouth on the drenched flesh had her womb clenching in a desire so strong she was nearly dazed with it. She fought for breath, fought for her sanity as he licked her, then cried out pleadingly as he fucked her with smooth, determined strokes of his tongue.

"Please," she begged raggedly, lifting to the plunging caresses as her pussy wept in furious demand. "Devlin, please take me. I can't stand it," she cried out, her body assailed by an inferno of sensations.

He moved back, taking a last, slow lick of her syrupy juices as his finger pulled free of the tight clamp of her ass. Her hands slid to his shoulders, her nails biting into his flesh as he rose above her. Her desperate moans and heated cries a match to his rougher, darker growls of male need as he positioned himself between her spread thighs.

Chantel's gaze lowered, her eyes widening as his hand moved to grip the thick length of his turgid cock. The mushroom-shaped head was thick and pulsing, a pearly bead of creamy pre-cum beading along the tip.

Then her head tipped back as she cried out in desperation. He ran the head of his erection through her wet, sensitive slit before lodging it at the gripping, weeping opening of her cunt.

Chantel shifted against him, anticipation rising as she whimpered at his needlessly slow movements. She would have begged for more. Would have pleaded for him to hurry and take her now. The words were on the tip of her tongue when a hard, fierce pounding sounded at the bedroom door.

Her eyes widened in horror as Devlin bit out a vicious oath.

"Later," he bit out the sharp command as his cock jerked against her, making her eyes close in need.

"Devlin, it's an emergency," Joshua called out, his voice filled with concern, and demand. "You're needed now."

Devlin fought to deny he had heard the sound for one dazed minute. Then it returned, louder, stronger than the first time.

"In a minute," Devlin yelled impatiently, then took a deep calming breath. His cock throbbed at the entrance to Chantel's vagina as her dewy heat kissed it beseechingly.

Chantel shook her head in denial as he stared down at her. It was too soon to stop, the sensations too deep and powerful to stifle, he knew. But he also knew no one would disturb him unless it was imperative.

"Stay right where you are," he whispered harshly, his body protesting the delay forcibly. "I'll be right back."

Devlin didn't want her to move an inch. He had every intention of finishing what they had started. Chantel nodded, watching him as he rose from the bed, careful to replace the drapes so the sight of her nude body would still be hidden.

Out of sight definitely did not mean out of mind, Devlin thought impatiently as he jerked a pair of jeans on, struggling to zip them over his stiff cock as he strode quickly to the door.

"What?" he jerked the door open, frowning at Joshua's somber expression.

"Sorry to interrupt." There was an edge of censure in his tone. "We have a problem."

"What sort of problem?"

Devlin was suspicious. He knew Joshua. Knew his dislike of Antea before, and knew he was not above causing problems himself, if he thought the situation warranted it.

"There are some children missing from the village. A brother and sister."

A fist punch to his gut warned him that it was nothing so simple as two children wandering off. Jonar had struck, just as

Devlin had feared. But not at the castle or at Devlin, at the village he protected instead.

"How long have they been missing?" He quickly turned possibilities over in his mind.

"Since morning that they know of," Joshua answered softly. "The children were last seen at bedtime. When the parents went to awaken them this morning, they were gone."

"Are the others ready to go?" he demanded as he moved to his closet, grabbing out a shirt and boots.

He moved quickly to dress, despite the regret that lay heavy in his loins. Damn Jonar and his evil, and his insane belief that he could conquer all that was good in this world. His evil was such that no one was safe. Not women nor children, innocence nor beauty.

"We're awaiting you in the great hall," Joshua informed him.

"Give me five minutes." He closed the door in Joshua's face as he saw the curtains on the bed moving.

As the door closed, Chantel came from the bed and began a frantic search around the room. Her expression was intent, her hair mussed, a flush of desire still radiating in her face. But her eyes were brilliant, glowing with secrets and warmth as she glanced at him from across the room.

"What are you doing?" Devlin quickly pulled on his shirt, then his socks as he watched her.

"What the hell did you do with my clothes?" Chantel rounded on him as he finished the laces on his boots and rose from the chair. "You aren't leaving without me."

Devlin turned from the door in surprise. He watched as she faced him in determination, dressed only in her gown, and holding a pair of leather sneakers in her hand.

"Why are you looking at me like that?" she bit out angrily. "Yell for someone and find my clothes."

Impatience flared inside him. He didn't have time for this, neither did he want her outside the castle grounds, where she would be completely unprotected from Jonar's fury. It was imperative that he keep her sheltered within the magic that Galen kept wrapped around his former home.

"I don't have time for this, Chantel." He turned the doorknob and opened the door. "I'll be back later. Go back to bed or something until I return."

He didn't have time to explain, nor to ease her worry. They had to find the children quickly, if there was anything left to find.

"Don't you leave without me, Devlin." He paused at the depth of emotion he heard in her voice, and the crystalline clarity that glowed in her eyes.

At her breast, the crystal glowed with a faint, emerald aura. Protecting her. His teeth clenched in fury. Jonar had kidnapped those children or had them kidnapped to draw her away from the protection the castle afforded her. Devlin would be damned if he would give the bastard a chance to strike at her.

"I don't have a choice." He shook his head at her. "There's nothing you can do there. You don't know the area or the people. Stay here, I'll be able to work better if I know you're out of the way."

Chantel watched the door close behind him, shock holding her stiff and immobile. She had never been so summarily dismissed. It was as though her help, her insight wouldn't matter. As though she didn't matter.

She stared at the closed panel in disbelief, in anger. Damn him! He was like fire and ice, blowing hot then cold until she was never certain where she stood with him or what he believed. And it was breaking her heart...

She wasn't needed. She took a deep, hard breath and turned to look at the curtain-shrouded bed. Had she even been needed there? Or was it just an urge, an itch he needed to have scratched? The slick flesh between her thighs reminded her that she had her own itch, one she would be damned if she wanted him to scratch now.

Had she really convinced herself that he had needed her in some way? Had she allowed her dreams of him, and the connection the crystal seemed to forge, to deceive her to that extent? She must have, because surely he neither wanted, nor needed her with him now.

Devlin didn't want her in his way. This wasn't her home, it wasn't her people, and therefore, she had no business sticking her nose outside the castle walls. And yet, everything inside her denied that this could be the truth.

Slowly, Chantel moved back to the bed, pushing the curtains aside to sit on the mattress, staring down wearily at the sneakers in her hand. She would have helped find the children. Surely every available person was needed. Whether they knew the land or not. Yet, he had dismissed her offer of help as though it had meant nothing.

She shook her head. She placed the sneakers on the bed and jerked the borrowed robe on angrily. She couldn't remember a time in her life when she had felt so humiliated, so cast aside. At least he hadn't locked the door this time. She left the bedroom, following the path they had taken the night before, back to the great hall.

Chantel arrived in the large room just as everyone else had left. The huge doors swinging shut echoed eerily through the stone room. Chantel stood in the center of the hardwood floor and looked around. There were no lights left on, no fire burning in the hearth.

The silence echoed around her, weighing against her until she felt her chest tightening with the pain of it. There was no one left in the castle. Chantel knew she was the only one, and that feeling ripped into her with the force of a slashing knife.

She didn't want to be alone, didn't want to face the hours ahead of her in this dark hulking piece of stone. She wanted to help find the children, wanted to heed the urgency of the crystal. Something was wrong, she knew it, and yet there was nothing she could do.

She stared around the shadowed room, her gaze pausing at the blackened fireplace. The empty, yawning mouth set within the stone wall seemed to mock her loneliness. Several feet away from it, two large, thickly cushioned maroon velvet chairs looked inviting, yet still lonely.

"I would have gone with you, Devlin," her words echoed softly around the room. "I could have helped."

Chantel lifted the crystal from her gown, staring at the faint green aura surrounding it. She could have aided them. She wasn't certain how yet, but she knew she could have.

She sighed deeply, her lips compressing as she looked around the room once again. The silence pressed in on her. The sense of desertion filling her was unsettling.

"I should have gone home." She turned and headed for a doorway at the other end of the room as she muttered the words aloud. "At least I knew where to find my damned clothes there."

It was a long, tedious search for the clothes that had been taken from her the night before. During the search, she found four sections which branched off the main castle. And a huge inner courtyard set in the middle.

The kitchen, laundry room, pantry and freezer storage room were set in the back of the main part of the castle, accessible from the courtyard or the short hall, which led from the great hall.

In the laundry room, she found her jeans, but the bloodstained T-shirt she had worn was nowhere to be found. She borrowed a dark blue shirt that obviously belonged to one of the men.

If they objected to her wearing it, Chantel would remind them to be certain she could find her own clothes next time.

She carried the clothes back to Devlin's bedroom, showered and dressed and then wandered moodily back to the great hall. The damned place was too quiet, too eerily familiar to suit her. As she looked around, she glimpsed the small table lamps set around the room. She walked to the couch, reaching across the arm to find the switch.

As she made contact with the switch the room began to spin dizzily around her. Bracing herself on the arm of the couch, she lowered her head, closing her eyes as she fought to keep from passing out.

It was then that the pain hit. Great blinding waves of it striking mercilessly into her skull as she cried out in agony. Her hands clutched her head as a great wave of light pierced her skull. She fell to her knees, her hands reaching out blindly to grasp the cushions of the couch.

Agony resonated through her brain as she fought against the pain. She cried out Devlin's name. A plea, searching for something, someone to hold onto as she tried to fight the clawing, pounding forces beating themselves into her skull.

"Stop fighting it, Chantel." She thought she knew the voice, but couldn't open her eyes to identify the body, which suddenly knelt at her side.

A pair of hands lifted her gently to the couch, and she felt rather than saw the figure kneeling beside her.

"Stop fighting it," he ordered her again, his hands now touching her head, palms cupping it. "Relax. Let the power in, you can't keep it out."

"Make it stop." Her hands reached out to him, searching desperately for something to hold onto as her hands clenched the thick, soft material of whatever he wore upon his arms.

"It won't stop, Chantel. But it will stop hurting. Don't fight it, let it into you, see what it's bringing you."

"It hurts."

"It hurts because you're fighting it." The voice became harsh, demanding. "Relax, girl. Take deep breaths. Relax your forehead. Slowly, let it in."

Let it in? It would kill her. She clenched her fingers, clawing now at the hands wrapped around her head.

"Do you want the answers, Chantel?" The hands tightened on her head. "Do you want to control the crystal? I thought you were a fighter as you were before, not weak-willed like the imposter who stole your birthright."

Chantel fought past the pain, tears now wetting her face as the agony radiated throughout her entire body. She was a fighter — she wouldn't allow this to defeat her.

"I am fighting," she cried out.

"You're fighting the wrong thing. You're fighting the power, the answers. You're fighting yourself. Relax. Take the energy and the pain will recede."

Chantel gritted her teeth, groaning harshly as she fought to do as she was ordered. She was not weak, like she knew Antea had been. She was the Mistress of the Crystal, and she would damned well prove it.

She took a deep breath and let it out slowly. She forced her muscles to relax, a feat she considered of immense proportions considering the pain gripping her.

The hands at her head became caressing, the voice soothing as it whispered instructions to her. *Breathe. Relax. Open your mind to the power.*

Chantel breathed slowly, deeply. One by one, she forced the muscles in her head to relax.

The light surrounded her, pulsing against her. She could feel the warmth all around her, inside her as she allowed it to enter her body. She became lighter, freer, drifting on a cloud so light and pure it transcended anything she had ever known before.

"Now, listen to me closely, Chantel," the voice whispered from a distance. "I'm going to release you now. When I do, you will open your eyes. Then the crystal will show you what it's seeking to."

She didn't want the voice to release her. She whimpered softly, fighting to open her eyes.

"Not yet," he cautioned her. "When you no longer feel my presence, then it will be time."

She shook her head.

"This is your journey, Chantel. You must take it alone. The crystal is with you. It is all you need. It will guide you, dear. It will keep you safe."

Suddenly, the presence was gone. The warmth inside her became stronger, her senses opening until she felt the protection that had been promised to her.

Then, she opened her eyes.

She blinked, turning around and gazing at her surroundings.

A cave. It was dark, and she could feel the cold on the outer edges of the green aura around her.

She listened closely, hearing the children crying farther back into the cave. Chantel walked slowly toward that sound, noticing as she did so, how the darkness around her was lit by the aura. She went slowly, cautiously.

What sort of dream was this? She could smell the damp, stale air of the cave, hear the whimpers of the children just ahead. She rounded a bend in the stone-enclosed tunnel, and there they were. The children had been placed side by side. The thick blanket, which had been wrapped around them, had fallen away. They rested against the wall of the cave, still crying, bound together by ropes.

"Daniel," the little girl whimpered. "I'm so cold."

"I know, Cammy. So am I." The little boy's voice trembled with his fear as well as the cold.

Chantel gasped, causing the children's eyes to open, then widen in amazement.

She moved to them quickly, but it only took her seconds to realize that she couldn't release the knots holding them. Her hands passed through them as if they were as insubstantial as air.

"It's a ghost," the little girl cried out, shrinking away from her, tears running faster down her dirt-smudged cheeks.

The children began to cry harder, the sound ripping through Chantel's heart quicker than a knife.

"Well, I guess I look like a ghost." She looked down at the green aura surrounding her body, then back to the children. "But I'm not dead. Just sort of here."

The little boy watched her suspiciously, still crying, but apparently more willing to listen than his sister.

"You must be very cold." She wished she could wrap the blanket back around them. She couldn't, but perhaps she could help them do it themselves. "If you pay attention to me, and do exactly as I tell you, perhaps we can get the blanket back where it belongs."

"He said it would keep us warm." The little boy tried to stem his tears enough to talk to her. "It did, but we tried to get loose, and it fell off."

"Well, let's see if we can get your sister to stop crying." She looked at the little girl now. "It will take teamwork from both of you, and concentration to get the blanket back where it belongs."

The little girl shivered, and fought to stop crying. Chantel watched her, smiling encouragingly as the child's breath hitched, and the tears slowly lessened.

"Come now, don't be frightened of me," she pleaded with the girl. "I promise, I just want to get you warm until your family can find you."

"They won't," the little girl wailed. "We've been waiting...and waiting."

"Yes, they will." Chantel hoped that promise was fulfilled. "Now come on, let's get that blanket back around you, so you can stay warm until they get here."

"Do you hear that?" she asked the children, listening closely.

"No." Daniel shook his head, listening as well.

She heard the sound again, distant and faintly fragile.

"Hang on a second," she told them, suddenly aware of where it was coming from. "I'm going to the front of the cave, I think I hear someone."

"Be careful," the little boy fretted. "Those men are waiting on someone. I heard them talking, how they can catch who they want by waiting outside."

"They won't see me," she promised. "I just want to be certain of something. Okay?"

Daniel nodded, watching worriedly as she rose to her feet and began to move to the front of the cave.

When Chantel had rounded the bend once again, she sat down, leaning against the wall, and sighed heavily. She couldn't leave the children, but she had to let Devlin know where they were.

She could hear Devlin's voice screaming at her, an edge of desperation coloring his voice. He was definitely the impatient type. She hoped he showed a bit more patience during sex. She would have smiled at the thought if she weren't so certain that at that moment, Devlin was feeling no humor at all.

Chantel closed her eyes, concentrating on the voice. For long moments, she tried to return, but each time she opened her eyes, she was still in the cave, and Devlin was becoming furious.

"Dammit, stop screaming at me," she muttered, trying to find the answer to her return.

There was a sudden silence. He was no longer screaming within her head. She could feel instead total confusion.

"Devlin?" she whispered his name tentatively, wondering if she had indeed lost her mind. "Are you there?"

* * * * *

Devlin stood back in shock as her voice suddenly whispered from inside the soft green aura surrounding her. They had been trying to break through the aura for nearly half an hour, but none of them had been able to approach her.

"Chantel, what the hell is going on here?" He knew his voice was rough, ragged. He had run out of patience within the first few minutes of finding her and being unable to awaken her.

"This is so strange." There was the slightest hint of fear in her voice, he noticed. "Talking to a voice in my head isn't normal for me."

"What are you talking about, Chantel?" He could only shake his head as he watched her.

"I'm in a cave with the children, Devlin. It's very cold. They're bound, and scared and hungry. They say there are men waiting outside…"

"Chantel, this is crazy," he broke in, staring down at her furiously. "You're right here on my damned couch." He watched her sigh regretfully.

"You have to listen to me, Devlin," she pleaded with him. "The children are here, in this cave. They were kidnapped to lure someone here. The men who took them are waiting outside now. You have to believe me. What about the old guy? The one who was there when this happened? He'll tell you."

"Old guy?" Devlin turned and looked at the others in question.

Kanna and the other warriors shook their heads in confusion. As Devlin had thought, there was no old man who worked within the castle, only Galen could have come to her. He bit off a curse, wondering what in the hell the sorcerer was up to.

"Chantel, there was no one here but you."

"He was there." There was no expression on her face. Her lips moved, but other than that, she looked like a corpse lying on his couch. Her face was deathly pale, her eyes shadowed. She was terrifying him.

Devlin closed his eyes, shaking his head. When he reopened them, he turned to the men behind him.

"Joshua." The Mystic was the most sensitive of the group, but would he know the difference between reality, and what Chantel had created in her own mind?

"Her body's here, but her spirit isn't." He looked as confused as Devlin felt. "If you subscribe to the theory, you could say she's experiencing some form of astral viewing." He spoke of the psychic ability to allow the soul to wander while still living.

"What about the children?" he asked him. "Did you sense anything earlier, any traces of Jonar?"

"None." Joshua shook his head. "I couldn't sense the children, but I didn't sense Jonar, either."

"Do you think I'm lying, Devlin?" Devlin could hear the hurt in Chantel's voice.

Devlin grimaced, raking his fingers impatiently through his hair. They had spent the better part of the day combing the mountain for the children. It was nearing dark now with no sign of them.

Devlin was tired, worried and at his wit's end with the search, or any clue as to the children's disappearance. On his return home, he had wanted to do nothing but relax before the search resumed the next morning.

When he had walked into the castle to find Chantel laid out on the couch like a damned corpse, with that eerie green glow around her, he had lost all ability to think or move for precious seconds as he stared down at her.

Devlin felt, in one brief minute, he had stepped into a nightmare he couldn't understand. In it, he had heard his own screams of grief, and saw her lying bloodied and dead within his arms.

"Tell me where you are. What's going on?"

Devlin listened intently as she relayed the information about the cave and the children. When she offered to go outside and see if she could find the men watching the cave, or give a better description of the area, he shook his head.

"Stay where you are," he told her. "If the children can see you, so can those men. Go back to the kids, maybe they know where they are."

Devlin waited impatiently before he heard her voice again.

"Daniel." He was shocked at the sudden, soft, maternal quality in her voice. "I need you to help me for a moment. I need you to tell me where we are."

How unusual, he thought. Antea had hated children.

There was a long silence, during which Devlin could feel his own nerves wearing thin.

"Near the old mines?" he heard her question. "Do you know anything else about where we are?"

"The old mines are on the north side of the mountain, Devlin." Derek spoke softly from behind him. "Hard to get to in daylight, let alone night since the mountain slides last year."

If the cave was being watched, the best time to get in there and back out would be under the cover of the night.

"Ask the children how close to the mines, Chantel. Ask them if they've ever been there before."

He waited impatiently as she talked to them.

"So, you've never been in this area before?" Her voice was light, easy. She was being patient with them, unwilling to let them know that there were others who could hear her. "How do you know where we are then?"

Once again, Devlin waited.

"The men mentioned the mines? What else did they say?"

The waiting was killing him, Devlin realized, as he felt the fine sheen of perspiration along his forehead.

It took nearly thirty minutes to get the information they needed from the children. Thankfully, little Daniel had been smart enough to pay attention to what his kidnappers had talked about as they dragged him and his sister up the mountain.

"Okay, I've pinpointed the location." Devlin heard Shane's triumphant exclamation, soft though it was. "It will be damned hard to get into without being spotted, but we can do it."

"Chantel, we have your location pinpointed. You can come back now."

"I'm going to stay right here." He was surprised at the determination in her voice.

"Chantel, you don't look well. I want you to come back,"

Silence. There wasn't a breath of sound for the space of a minute.

"We'll just sit tight." He knew she was talking to the children. "I promise my friends will be here soon, then we can all go home." She placed emphasis on the "all". There was no mistaking whom she meant the message for.

"Damn stubborn woman," he muttered, then turned to Joshua and barked out orders for the preparations to head into the mountains.

It took less than twenty minutes before they were once again headed out the door. This time, they knew where to go, and what they were looking for.

Devlin and Shane would head for the cave to collect the children, while Joshua and Derek took care of whoever or whatever was watching for them.

They had their orders to bring the men to the castle, preferably alive. Both men were capable of killing the kidnappers if the need arose, but both were also aware of the advantages of questioning them first.

"I want that cave entrance secured before Shane and I enter it," Devlin ordered Joshua. "Whatever it takes. We have no idea what could happen to her if something happens to those kids while she's still there like that. She has to stay safe."

"She should have come back while she had the chance," Joshua muttered.

"But she didn't." Devlin turned on him, keeping tight rein on the anger building inside him. "So you make damned certain she has the chance to come back after we rescue those kids."

Devlin stared Joshua down for long seconds before he received the slight acknowledgement Joshua gave with the nod of his head.

Devlin wanted Chantel back. He wanted answers to the questions raging through his mind. Was she Antea? And if she was, how had this incredible change occurred? He had to know, just as he had to know why he heard her screams echoing through his head.

Chapter Seven

ഔ

The four men split up at the base of the north side of the mountain. Devlin and Shane headed for the caves that sat above the old mines, while Joshua and Derek moved ahead of them to intercept and contain whoever might be waiting for them.

The danger, Devlin knew, was in the fact that none of them had felt Jonar or the presence of any of his men earlier in the day. There was no doubt who was behind the kidnapping—only Jonar would dare strike against Devlin or his village.

In the past, it had always been easy to know when Jonar was in the vicinity. Any time he or his men were in a position to strike against them, their unique psychic abilities would warn the warriors of their presence. They hadn't felt it this time. Which meant Jonar had sent men he knew would not have a chance in a fight against the warriors. It also meant there would be another trap waiting somewhere close to the children.

Keeping silent, Devlin motioned to Shanar to cover their advance into the mountain. He had no doubt that Joshua and Derek would take care of the men watching the cave's entrance, but Jonar had been known to leave more than one surprise waiting for them.

They moved through the shadows of darkness, with nothing but the full moon to light their way. Too much light to suit Devlin, and he hoped not enough for whoever awaited them.

The moon was high, shining brightly above them when Devlin received the signal from Joshua that he had the men watching the cave contained.

With a sigh of relief, Devlin moved quickly to the entrance, watching carefully for any sign of hidden dangers.

As he stepped beneath the stone overhang, he paused, his eyes locking on the thin, nearly invisible wire that lay across the entrance. The least amount of pressure would set off an explosion, which would bury the unaware as well as the children he could hear singing, farther into the cave.

He and Shane stepped carefully over the wire. Devlin wouldn't risk the children's lives in the attempt to disarm it immediately.

Devlin's eyes narrowed as the partially hidden red light in the stones overhead alerted them of the second trap. Signaling to Shanar to stop, he surveyed the area thoroughly. There, along the opposite wall, infrared sensors had been placed, attached to a trigger, which would set off yet another deadly explosion.

"Fuck!" His curse was but a breath of sound.

It would be impossible to get around this one. They would have to disarm it before they could get to the children. Disarming it would not be easy.

Devlin moved aside carefully as Shane came in closer to survey the trap.

"Good one," Shane grunted with a tight grimace.

Carefully, the big warrior opened the tool bag at his side, extracting the required tools to disarm it. He motioned for Devlin to move away from the area. Devlin shook his head quickly. He wasn't about to go anywhere. If that trigger was released, then the children would die. By the looks of it, he would possibly have a few seconds to round the bend and give them a small measure of cover should it go off.

He knew how ineffectual he would be against falling rock, but he also knew he would never be able to live with any other choice if that device was set off.

Those children were part of the village he had taken custody of over six hundred years ago. When Galen had disappeared, leaving the castle and its lands in Devlin's hands, he had exacted that promise from him. Care for those who were his. The village had been his. It was now Devlin's.

Shanar shook his head, and then moved carefully to the highly sensitive area where the trigger had been positioned. They listened to the conversation of the children and Chantel as Shanar worked intently to save them all.

"Do you think Poppa will find us, Chantel?" Devlin heard the little boy's voice ask her hesitantly.

"Oh, someone will find us soon, I'm sure. I'd lay my bets on Lord Devlin. He seems like the capable sort."

"Poppa says Lord Devlin doesn't care about the villagers. Maybe he won't care that we're lost." The frightened voice of the sister had Devlin closing his eyes in regret. "He's never around, and every time someone wants to bring in new stuff, he says no."

"What sort of new stuff, Cammy?" Devlin was surprised that he could imagine concern and worry shadowing Chantel's face as she spoke.

"Jobs." The little boy piped up. "Uncle Jaime wanted to build a fine factory in the valley for everyone to work at, but Lord Devlin said no. He owns all the land, you see."

"Perhaps Lord Devlin had his reasons for refusing. It's very beautiful here. Maybe he didn't want something that would mess that up."

"Uncle Jaime says he doesn't want things to get better for the village. He says Lord Devlin just wants us all to leave, so he can do whatever he wants and no one knows."

"Sounds strange, huh?" Chantel commented. "What sorts of strange things does he expect Lord Devlin to get into?"

"Dunno," the little boy answered. "But Mister Drake, who owns the bar, thinks they're vampires. He says that he knows they should be way older than they look."

Damn villagers were thinking too much, Devlin thought. He would have to have a talk with the barkeep, it would seem. Now was not a good time to disappear for decades, so he would have no choice except to intimidate instead.

"Oh, I don't know about that, Daniel." Devlin wanted to shake his head at the image of the gentle smile he could see on her face. "Some people don't look old for a very long time."

"So, you don't think they're vampires?" Daniel asked. "'Cause I really am tired of all that garlic Momma keeps putting around the windows. It smells bad."

Garlic? Devlin closed his eyes tightly for a brief moment. Perhaps letting civilization come to the village wouldn't be such a bad idea. It sounded as though they were trapped in the middle ages.

"Aunt Calista worked at the castle. She says they're not vampires, 'cause she couldn't find their caskets. But she told Momma about the other funny stuff she found," the little girl piped up. "The one with the weird eyes is a killer. He had a real gold knife with dried blood on it."

Devlin's eyes narrowed. That dagger had come up missing about the time Calista had come to work for them. He had forbidden Joshua to use his psychic abilities against the castle help to find it. Perhaps in that, he had made a mistake.

"Perhaps he had used it to hunt with, and forgot to clean it," Chantel's voice suggested softly. "I really don't think any of the men of the castle are killers, Cammy. I stayed there all night last night and not once did anyone come after me with a knife."

The two children giggled, and he wondered what she had done that they found so amusing.

"Gotcha." The soft expulsion of sound from Shane signaled the trigger had been deactivated.

Devlin breathed a sigh of relief, and then turned to look behind him. The first thing he saw was Joshua's furious face. He had heard the conversation as well.

"I'll take care of it," he warned Joshua before the other man could get a chance to head out for vengeance. "I'll get the dagger back."

Devlin imagined he could hear the grinding of Joshua's teeth.

"Calista is mine," his voice was a guttural growl.

"No." The single word was like lighting a match to Joshua's growing temper.

"Well, it's about time you guys got here." Chantel bathed them all in a soft glow of warmth as she entered the outer part of the cave.

Devlin forgot all about the little thief Calista as he stared at the vision radiating the emerald glow of the Earth Crystal.

Devlin was speechless, mindless. Had he ever seen a more beautiful sight, he wondered? He knew he hadn't. Chantel stood before him, glowing like a candle within that damned green light, her lips still holding a smile of amusement.

Desire, hard and hot, kicked him in the stomach and caused his cock to harden, his blood to thunder through his veins. Damn her, how was she doing this to him?

"Go back to the castle now," his voice was harsh and conveyed none of the emotions rioting through him.

He watched as the amusement slowly died on her face and the somber, saddened eyes rose to his once again.

She nodded slowly, then moved away from him.

"How long before the children will be home?" she asked Shane as she passed him. Devlin could hear the soft vein of hurt in her words.

"Within an hour." Shane's softened voice infuriated Devlin. He had hated Antea more than any of them, believing her to be the cause of his own wife's death because of her refusal to use the crystal's power. And here he was softening toward the woman who could very well be her incarnation. "We'll be back at the castle not long after."

She nodded. "I'll likely be asleep. I'm very tired."

* * * * *

The door bounced against the tapestry-covered stone wall as light blazed in the room, jerking Chantel awake and to her feet in a defensive stance as her eyes cleared and focused on a furious Devlin.

He was pissed. Well, he wasn't the only one.

His eyes almost glowed from within the tight, hard contours of his savage features. His lips were thinned, his eyes narrowed in a way that caused the muscles of her abdomen to clench in nervous anticipation.

"This is *not* my bedroom," he growled, with dark emphasis on the "not".

Chantel felt her heart race in excitement, in mingled anticipation and anger.

"No kidding," she threw back as though in surprise, watching his eyes narrow further. "That should tell you something, big boy."

Surprise lit his gaze for a long, tense moment.

"Would you like to know what this tells me?" He advanced on her, a slow, stalking movement that had her lifting her head proudly, refusing to back down. "This tells me that you wish to live dangerously, Chantel. That it is your intent to fire my temper and my lusts to a point that controlling them becomes difficult. Why would you wish to do this?"

She sniffed with censorious sarcasm. "Really, Devlin. To be perfectly honest, I didn't give a damn one way or the other. I'm not a pet for you to pat on the head and send to its bed when you no longer have the time to play. I won't be pushed aside so conveniently."

He frowned, stopping several feet from her and watching her as male irritation flashed across his face.

"That was not what I intended," he snarled.

"I don't care what you intended, that is what you did. Now go away and leave me alone. I'm too tired to deal with you and your dumb male perspective." She crossed her arms over her chest, watching him as he regarded her with narrowed eyes.

His brow arched as arrogance washed over his face.

"My dumb male perspective may keep your naïve little ass alive one of these days," he bit out. "Do you think Jonar is playing games, Chantel? That he does not intend to kill you? Painfully."

Pain, searing and agonizing, ripping through her body, destroying her from the inside out. She remembered well the event that had played itself out in her dreams.

"I'm very well aware of what he could do," she bit out painfully, the memory of her nightmares washing over her. "I'm not a fool and I won't be treated like one, nor am I a child for you to protect or order about. I have fared quite well through my life without you standing guard over me like a big bad shadow of death. I sure as hell don't need it now."

"And I won't allow you to risk your life needlessly," he growled, covering the distance between them.

Before she could do more than gasp in surprise, he had swung her into his arms and was striding quickly from the room.

"What are you doing?" She pushed at his chest, surprised and furious by the display of strength that kept her from escaping him.

His arms were like steel bands around her as he strode through the darkened castle. No matter how she pressed or pushed, they wouldn't be budged until he entered his bedroom and tossed her on the bed she had slept in the night before.

"You will sleep here, where you belong." His voice was calm now, his expression filled with satisfaction.

Anger consumed her. That he could believe she was so easy to control was like a fuse lit to her suddenly explosive temper. She moved to jump from the bed, but he countered her, stepping in front of her, staring down at her with such male confidence that she wanted to smack it from his face.

"I will not allow you to order me around this way." Her voice vibrated with her fury. "I will not sleep with a man who doesn't even have enough consideration to listen to me when it's important."

Devlin pushed his fingers through his hair as he gazed down at her with an expression of confusion.

He grimaced apologetically. "You are right, Chantel, and I will pay more attention in the future. But I will not allow you to punish us both by sleeping away from me."

"Don't patronize me, Devlin," she snarled, feeling an overwhelming desire to kick him. "It's been an exhausting day, and I'm not up to dealing with your damned arrogance."

"My arrogance wasn't what I intended to give you," he told her with flashing irritation. "And if you are so weary, then you can sleep here just fine. Beside me, where you belong."

"You can't order me to sleep with you," she reminded him fiercely. "You don't own me."

But he did, to an extent. Chantel could feel the knowledge pulsing through her body, her suddenly soaked cunt. He owned her heart, and he filled her soul.

"Argue all you wish." The snarl that lifted his lips assured her he was brooking no refusal. And unfortunately, he was bigger than she was. "I will not allow you to sleep anywhere but beside me, where I know you'll be safe. For God's sake, do you have any idea what you did to me when I saw you shielded within that glow, unable to reach you, to touch you?"

His hand reached out to touch her then, his fingers cupping her cheek, his thumb grazing over lips that had suddenly gone dry as he stared back at her with eyes filled with agony.

"I was all right," she whispered, suddenly confused, taken aback by the bemusement that entered his expression.

"For a moment, Chantel, I was in another place, another time that I still do not remember. I saw your blood, and I heard my own screams." He shook his head with a tight, jerky movement. "For a moment, the memory was fresh and terrifyingly real. Then it was gone, as quickly as it had come."

Chantel stared into his face, seeing the questions in his eyes, hearing the remembered pain that tore at him. Mists and shadows twisted in her mind, obscuring memories, knowledge. What must she do, she wondered, to break past those veils of time?

Her hand raised then to his chest as his thumb caressed her lips, sending sparks of heated desire showering through her body. Her breasts ached to feel his touch, her nipples becoming swollen, engorged in demand. Between her thighs her pussy throbbed in rhythm to the blood pounding through her veins. The muscles there rippled as heated juices spilled along the plump lips.

"That is my nightmare, my memory," she whispered as she felt his heart pounding beneath his shirt. "Your screams as I lay dying in your arms. And I don't know if it's past or future that I'm seeing."

"Which is why I cannot allow you to risk yourself." A thread of anger returned to his voice as his fingers moved along her cheek to thread within her hair. "Don't you see? If he took you, Chantel, he would have no remorse in your death."

"I didn't have the crystal then," she argued as his fingers tightened the barest bit within the strands of hair he had gripped between them. "He can't touch me as long as I wear the crystal."

His eyes narrowed as he glanced at her chest, then back to her eyes.

"Would you have removed that crystal to save the lives of those children?"

Her eyes widened as his words penetrated her dazed senses.

"Do you see, Chantel, why I cannot allow you to leave the protection of the castle grounds? Not yet, not until we know what we face. You would sacrifice yourself for the life of a child. I cannot allow that." His voice was tormented, his expression arrogant and domineering.

"I can't hide forever, Devlin," she told him softly as she moved from the bed. "And neither can you. One day, you'll have to see that."

He caught her arm as she went to move past him.

"You will sleep with me." There was no give in his voice.

"Do you really think you can command me as easily as you command others around you?" she asked him softly, staring him steadily in the eye.

His brows snapped into a deep, dark frown. The black in his eyes seemed to glow as his irritation flashed through his expression.

"I never command unless it is needed," he growled. "I would ask nothing from one of my men that I would not do myself."

"And what of me?" she pointed out. "You're asking me to surrender my pride and everything I believe in and cower before you."

"Chantel, that is untrue." He shook his head, his hand reaching out until his fingers could smooth over her cheek. "I do not ask that of you."

"Don't you, Devlin?" She moved away from his touch then. "You left this morning without even questioning my insistence to go with you, or why I felt it was needed."

He tucked his hands into his jeans pockets, watching her with a look of such male outrage that she nearly smiled.

"I wanted only to protect you," he growled. "There was no ulterior motive."

Chantel shook her head, seeing so much more than what his words conveyed. His expression was rife with confusion, hesitation, and his own sense of honor. Having it questioned bothered him on a level he wasn't comfortable with.

"I don't want to be protected," she told him firmly. "I'm not a weak little woman who needs to hide behind a big brave warrior for protection. I've protected myself against Jonar and his men before, and will likely do so again. You can't protect me, Devlin."

He sighed roughly. "You are a danger unto yourself," he bit out. "This isn't a game, Chantel."

"Do you think I don't know that already?" she asked him furiously. "My entire life is riding on this. My life, as well as the sisters who come after me. I'm not a fool as you so clearly think I am."

"I don't believe that," he argued as he crossed his arms over his chest. This was not the fragile woman of his dreams. Or had the woman in his dreams ever been fragile? Soft-spoken, he had learned over the centuries, did not mean a lack of strength. It would not mean a lack of desire.

"Don't you?" She pushed her hands through her hair as she felt overcome with exhaustion, with a sadness that pierced her heart. "A part of you still believes I'm Antea. Still believes I'm not worthy of your trust, or your consideration. I won't tolerate that, Devlin. I don't care who you think I am, you will still treat me with the respect I deserve, at least as Mistress of this crystal."

His eyes narrowed as her challenge thickened the tension in the air between them.

"Do I call you by her name?" he growled out. "My dick wouldn't harden like steel, Chantel, if I believed you were that bitch."

Chantel felt her womb clench at his explicit words. What was it about this man that any hint of the sexual awareness between them could weaken her?

"She was your wife—"

"She was no wife of mine," he bit out viciously, his hand suddenly slicing through the air. "I may not have my memories, I may be confused as hell, but I know she was no wife to me."

"You were married to her," she reminded him. "You told me so yourself. That makes her—"

"Call her wife again and I will become violent." His scorching reply halted her words.

Chantel felt like rolling her eyes. Were all men this incredibly stubborn?

"Fine," she sighed roughly. "But that doesn't change the point of this argument. Stop trying to protect me. I don't want it. Nor will I allow it."

She watched him steadily, her mouth drying, her heart accelerating at the expression that slowly came over his face.

"I will not lose you," he snarled, jerking her into his arms, binding her to him with the simple use of his strength as his head lowered, his lips drawing back from his teeth in a feral snarl. "Do you understand me, Chantel?" His voice vibrated with fury, pain. "I will not cease to protect you. I will not cease to stand guard over you, and by God, I will not allow you to be taken from me again."

His lips covered hers, his tongue plunging past her lips as lust, fury, and desperate need swirled in the air around them. She couldn't fight him. Couldn't fight the agonized groan that echoed against her lips, that gentled his furious kiss into one of dominant need, aggressive surrender.

His hands roamed over her shoulders, pulling at her robe until he had it off her shoulders, her arms, the material falling away from them as he backed her into the bed.

Chantel was powerless in the grip of his needs and of her own. Her hands rose to his shoulders, then to his hair as she fought for the hunger in his kiss that had always turned ravenous. His tongue stroked over hers, tangling with it, stoking the fires of her passions higher, hotter.

She heard the rend of material, felt her gown fall away from her and the cool air of the room washing over her heated body. Devlin's groan was one of greed, of desperate hunger. His hands roamed over her naked back with forceful determination, with heated promise.

"I cannot control my hunger for you," he growled as he tore his lips from hers, his hands pulling hers from his hair as he shifted back from her. "God help us both Chantel, if I don't fuck you, I'm going to lose what is left of my mind."

He was a man riding the edge of his control, and from the look he gave her, it would take very little to push him over.

Chapter Eight

ഇ

Chantel's eyes widened as he tore his shirt from his back. His boots were a bit of a struggle, but within seconds they were littering the floor and his jeans were quickly following suit. She caught only a quick glimpse of his erection, thick and long, as he lifted her into his arms and pulled her onto the bed with him.

"Devlin," she gasped as he pulled her over him, his hand locking in her hair as he pulled his lips back from hers.

"Tell me no, now, if this is your intent," he bit out, staring into her eyes with a gaze that raged with lust. "Seconds from now will be too late."

His body was hard beneath hers, warm and tense with his passion. She smoothed her hands over his hairless chest, feeling the ripple of his instinctive response as it passed through his muscles.

His dark male nipples beaded as her fingers passed over them. She smiled, staring up at him as she leaned forward, allowing her tongue to prod one experimentally. He reacted as though she had taken a whip to him.

Devlin jerked, and with a powerful move reversed their positions. Before Chantel could do more than gasp, she was beneath him, her body arching as she cried out at the heated lash of his tongue on her suddenly straining nipple.

"Do it now. Don't make me wait." Pulsing sensations of exquisite pleasure tore through her body, convulsing her womb, clenching her cunt as it released more of its silky liquid between her thighs.

"Not yet," he growled. "But soon. Dear God, it will have to be soon." A second later his mouth covered the hard peak he was tormenting with each swipe of his tongue.

Chantel arched to him, gasping, dazed with bone-melting sensations that tore through her. His mouth drew on her, suckled her firm and deep as his tongue lashed at the beaded tip. He didn't allow the other breast to feel neglected either. His fingers plumped the full mound, his thumb and forefinger caressing the nipple, rolling against it with a pressure that had her crying out in heated longing.

Sharp, addictive and fueled with a bond she didn't understand but accepted nonetheless, Chantel reveled in the pleasure his touch brought. Her hands smoothed over his shoulders, his biceps, feeling the bulge of muscle, the tensely held control he fought to hang on to.

Chantel moaned, moving against him as his mouth moved to her other breast, feeling the sharp inhalation of his breath as the slick, desire-damp flesh of her pussy rubbed against his straining cock.

Her own breathing became more labored as the added sensation spiked through her. She rubbed against the engorged length again, feeling it pulse, throb against her swollen clit. Below, her vagina wept in emptiness, in sharp hunger for the steel-hard erection that lay just out of reach.

Devlin's head rose from her breast, his eyes swirling black flames, his expression savage in his lust. She licked her lips, tempting him, her pleasure flaring higher as she saw the reaction in his narrowed eyes, the further flushing of his hard cheekbones.

"Temptress," he growled as her hands ran over his chest, then left his body so they could cup her own breasts, lifting them to him as her fingers grazed over the engorged nipples.

He swallowed with a tight movement as his hips moved, grinding his cock against her flared clitoris with a stroke of heat that had her moaning his name.

"Yes, do that," he whispered. "Caress your pretty breasts for me."

His head lowered again, his lips moving to her ribs, traveling with pinpoints of sensual fire across her stomach, her abdomen, then going lower. Chantel's breath suspended as he blew a heated wash of breath over her straining clit. Her hands moved from her breasts to touch him, only to have him catch them in his grip.

"No," he whispered. "Touch yourself. Caress your nipples as you please while I pleasure you. There can be no sight more tempting, Chantel, then a woman willing to show her lover what pleases her."

He released her hands, watching carefully as they moved back to her breasts. A sensual smile of arousal shaped his swollen lips. His hands moved to her thighs as he slid further between them, parting her as he watched her with that dark, sensual stare.

"I crave the taste of you," he whispered, causing her to whimper with the physical pleasure his words brought.

She cried out when he touched her, her fingers tightening on her nipples as her head ground into the pillows with the explosive shards of feeling that tore through her.

His tongue curled around her clit, a hot, torturous lash of exquisite fire that had her vagina pulsing in agonized need. His tongue was a greedy instrument of pleasure, a tormenting stroke of near rapture that had her begging each time it curled around her clit, licked it, stroked it with a slow gentleness that had her quivering for more.

Her fingers twisted her nipples as each stroke of his tongue drove her higher. The added flare of heat, of exquisite need only driving her higher, yet refusing her the final explosion she knew she needed.

When he pulled back from her again, she screamed out at him in need, almost rising from the bed to jerk his head back between her thighs. His hand pressed her back, his expression dark, dominant, as he watched her with a sudden, sexual demand.

"Have you ever taken yourself over?" he asked her softly as his fingers slid through the honey-slick slit of her cunt.

Chantel shivered in reaction to the heat of his touch. His finger circled her clit, massaging the swollen little bud with his thumb as she gasped and twisted against the fiery longing that shuddered through her.

"Answer me," he growled. "Do you pleasure yourself, Chantel? When the dreams torment you of pleasures only distantly remembered upon waking, do your fingers steal into the dampness of your pussy as you complete your journey?"

"Yes," she gasped, tormented past reason as he stroked her with the softest touch. "Please, Devlin. Don't make me wait like this."

"Do you use your fingers, or other devices as well?" His fingers slid below, to her weeping vagina. He circled the small opening, watching her with hooded eyes.

"Why?" she cried out, her body jerking at the sensual promise of his fingers slipping inside her.

"I would watch you," he groaned, reaching up to pull one hand from her breasts.

Chantel trembled as he pulled it between her thighs, settling her fingers against her throbbing clit.

"Show me," he demanded heatedly as a fingertip slipped inside her pulsing entrance. "Show me, Chantel. Let me see you find your heights, then we will see if I can make you go higher."

She was helpless, caught in a web of such intense lust she knew she had no hope of breaking free. Her fingers moved on her own slick flesh, running over the plump lips, through the fiery slit until they circled the pulsing, pleading nubbin of her clit.

His eyes tracked each movement, his fingers moving in slow, sensual strokes against the opening of her vagina, testing its grip, the wash of liquid that coated his fingers, and the need that surged through her body.

Chantel kept one hand on her breast, her thumb and forefinger tormenting her nipple with each heated, sensual caress. Her fingers tracked over her pussy, slid between the swollen, plump lips, and rasped her clit. She circled the hard bud, massaging it with firm, lingering strokes as she felt two of his broad fingers burrow into the opening of her pussy, stretching the tender entrance, sending an agony of pleasure exploding through her body.

She cried out his name as she arched to him, her fingers tightening on her nipple as her hips began to jerk against the invasion, attempting to drive him deeper as she fought for the orgasm building in her womb.

Her fingers moved faster, harder against her clit as it throbbed, pulsed in time to the spasms that ripped through her cunt. Whimpers of need echoed in the room, the sound of a male groan of despairing lust joined the chorus of passion sounding around them.

"How beautiful you are," he groaned as her thighs tightened around his hand, the lash of sensation intensifying through her body. "Your pussy glistening with your juice, your face flushed in need. Let me see you come for me, Chantel. Come for me, as you have never come before."

The words pushed her over the edge, as his fingers slid deeper inside her, thrusting gently, peaking the rapture building in her cunt. Chantel screamed as her hips arched, her fingers stroking the explosive release from her clitoris as her fingers tightened on her nipple to the point of pain.

She was dying. A thousand stars were exploding inside her, and she was only vaguely aware of Devlin coming over her. The thick, hard intrusion of his cock inside her vagina took her breath as her orgasm clawed through her womb and rippled over her. The hard thrust inside her, the stretching, searing pleasure so intense, so deep, it defied anything she could have imagined. Her body convulsed as another climax quickly followed the last.

The twinge of pain as he tore through her virginity only intensified the explosive ecstasy ripping through her. And he gave little concession to it. His control had shattered. His hard male cry echoed at her ear as his thighs pushed hers farther apart and his hips began a hard, driving rhythm that had his cock pounding inside her with strokes so deep she felt they reached her soul.

The thick erection separated her muscles, filling her until she was certain there was no room for more. Her cunt clenched around him in greedy hunger, her juices flowing around him, easing his way as he powered into her over and over again.

The sound of honey-slick flesh slapping together, of moist, hungry pussy devouring the hard length of his dominating cock was the most erotic, most intensely sexual sound she could have imagined. Her legs wrapped around his waist, locking him in place as her arms wrapped around his shoulders. She could do nothing but hold on and fight for her sanity against a pleasure so intense, so overriding that she could do little but fight for her breath as licking flames of yet another release began to build inside her.

She twisted beneath him, crying out as she felt the warning ripples flutter in her womb. Her cunt convulsed, tightening further, gripping him, milking him, making each thrust harder, deeper. Her vagina, tortured in its greed, spasmed against his cock.

Devlin cried out then, his thrusts increasing as his erection seemed to thicken, throb inside her. Each breath that passed her lips was a cry now as she felt the next, harder explosion begin inside her. As it began to pour over her, his shout of completion sounded in her ear and he drove deep, savagely hard inside her pussy as his cock began to jerk, pulse, and the searing explosion of his seed began to spurt inside her.

Chantel knew death then. The power of her release imploded her body, tightened her cunt, milked more of his jetting sperm as she felt her own juices explode from her body.

Breathing was forgotten as she was racked by one shudder after another, convulsing her, ripping through every muscle as she shook in its grip. She was reborn in the explosive climax. Like the phoenix, like birth, and the air around them. Visions flashed through her mind. One moment there, the next second gone. But she saw passion and love, and a bond that would never be denied.

As the last shudder ripped through her, Chantel collapsed against the bed, finally aware of the soothing murmurs Devlin whispered at her ear, the soft, consoling tone of his voice as he eased her back. Her chest heaved for breath, much as his did. Sweat soaked their bodies, and the smell of passion wove around her senses.

Devlin moved beside her then, pulling her into arms that felt sheltering and protective. For the first time in her life, she realized how much she needed that. To be held and to feel protected, even though she needed to make her decisions for herself. The contradiction confused her, but she was relaxed enough, exhausted enough now that she refused to let it worry her.

"Sleep with me," he whispered into her hair, his voice dark, filled with a need that now went beyond the physical. "Do not leave our bed again, Chantel."

He meant it as an order, she knew, but she heard the thread, faint though it was, of a plea. A plea she could not deny.

"No. I won't leave our bed again," she agreed, her eyes closing as he pulled the blankets around them.

He enfolded her with his warmth, his strength. Chantel drifted asleep, content, secure, for the first time in her life. As exhaustion claimed her, she wondered at the warmth at her breast, the power of the crystal that seemed to wrap around not just her, but Devlin as well.

Chapter Nine

ഇ

"Eventually, I'm going to need my own clothes," Chantel muttered the next morning as she slipped from the bedroom.

Devlin had left earlier, but not before he had taken her again, and then again. The night had been a series of orgasms designed to drive her insane. When he left, she had been slipping into sleep once again, certain she would never find the strength to move. But something prodded at her, urged her to get up, to dress. Something, she wasn't certain what, that she couldn't ignore.

She was dressed now in another pair of overly large men's sweats, and one of Devlin's silk shirts. The silk was comforting against her abused flesh, the sweats loose and non-chafing on her buttocks and her tender thighs, but a pair of her own soft cotton day pants would have felt much better, she thought. They sure as hell wouldn't have sagged as bad.

She had no bra. No panties. Dammit, she was even wearing Devlin's socks. They were so large that the heel came well past her ankle. She wanted to growl in frustration. To top it off, he thought she was going to stay in that damned bedroom until he decided to let her out. She didn't think so. It hadn't taken any more than twenty minutes to pick the lock and gain the freedom she was looking for.

As she did, a sense of familiarity swept over her as she walked down the hall and descended the staircase to the great hall. Like filmy memories, not yet clear, ghostly in substance, she remembered walking this way before. But she hadn't been sneaking through the castle like a thief. She had walked through it with purpose, with confidence. She had been a part of it.

She shook her head as she paused at the landing, peeking around the stone wall to see if the great hall was empty. A smile crossed her face as she realized it was. She entered the large room, moving slowly toward the fireplace and the two wide, maroon velvet chairs that faced it.

She frowned, swallowing tightly as some unnamed emotion seemed to attack her. Regret? She had sat there, awaiting deceit, treachery. Her hand smoothed over the back of the nearest chair, her eyes closing as she fought to see past the misty veil in her mind. The memories were there, she knew they were. Waiting for her to find the key to unlock them. But what was the key?

"How in the hell did you find the strength to drag yourself out of bed?" Devlin's patient, though in no way pleased voice had her spinning around in surprise.

Dear God, it should be a sin for any man to look so damned sexy. He was dressed in jeans and boots, a blue silk shirt tucked into the low-riding waistband, a wide black belt circling his lean hips. The bulge beneath those jeans was more than worth a second look, but not while he was watching so closely.

"I was tired of lying there alone." She frowned at him fiercely. "Besides, I wanted to see more of the castle than just that damned bedroom."

He crossed his arms over his chest, narrowing his eyes on her as she faced him with her hands braced on her hips. Damn him, the Lord of the Castle routine was really starting to get on her nerves.

"You needed to rest, and I have things to do," he told her carefully as he came toward her.

His arms unfolded from his chest, coming down to his sides as his long, muscular legs began to clear the distance between them. Chantel gripped the back of the chair, seeing the sensual warning in his expression, in the controlled movements of his body. If she had ever seen a more sensually ready male in her life, then she couldn't remember it. And he wasn't just horny. He was pulsing with heat. The power of his lust throbbed in the air around them. It wrapped around her, increasing her awareness of her own femininity, her own weakness in the face of his strength.

He should have been sated from the night before. Hell, she should have been, but the answering ache of her own arousal clenched the muscles of her vagina and had her juices coating her cunt lips.

He stopped, inches from her, staring down at her with a heavy-lidded gaze that sent spears of sensation exploding in her pussy. She felt her vagina heating, moistening. Her body had no pride when around him, no sense of self-preservation. All it had was need.

She crossed her arms over her swelling breasts, hoping to hide the erect state of her nipples as she stared up at him. She still wasn't comfortable with the new development of their relationship. Wasn't comfortable with the needs he inspired in her.

"I feel like a prisoner," she griped self-consciously. "Stay here, stay there. I have a mind of my own, you know?"

"Had I wanted a prisoner, I would have locked you in the dungeon." His long-lashed eyelids lowered further as he stared down at her lips. "Though, the idea has some merit."

Chantel breathed in deeply. Her patience was wearing thin. Very thin.

"Excuse me for having a mind, oh revered ancient one," she grunted mockingly. "I'll try to do better in the future."

"Hmm. You do that." He nodded abruptly. "Now that you're free, exactly what did you consider doing? You would have done better to rest as I wanted you to."

She rolled her eyes, suppressing the need to stomp his leather-shod feet.

"Don't treat me like a child, either. I deserve better than that. You aren't the only one involved in this mess, Devlin.

This is my life too." She couldn't still the impatient demands inside her, the unnamed memories and desires that filled her.

"As it obviously was once before," he pointed out coolly as his gaze flickered to where the crystal rested beneath the shirt she wore. "And that being the case, we must be certain whose life you're reliving. The one we all remember, or the one you claim to be."

Her eyes widened. "Been talking to Joshua again, have you?" she snorted. "You know I'm not Antea. You can feel it, the same as I can. Don't start playing games with me now."

His stance shifted. Rather than facing her, he stepped behind her, his head lowering until his cheek touched the side of her head, his words whispering over the shell of her ear.

"I have never played games, Chantel," he assured her softly. "Every event in my long life has been deadly serious. Don't make the mistake of believing I would begin now."

Chantel shivered as she tried to step away from him. He stopped her, his hand gripping her hip lightly, his fingers flexing in warning. He would stop her if she attempted to move further.

His hard chest cushioned her head as his fingers moved from her hip to her abdomen, pressing her back against him. She could feel his cock, engorged and hot, through their clothes. The ready tenseness of his body seemed magnified as he surrounded her.

A sense of vertigo filled her. Hazy images of other times attacked her mind. Times when his sensual promise had filled her with a heady sense of female power. A knowledge that her touch, her kiss, could turn his cool rage to heated desire. She trembled at that knowledge, terrified of stoking that heat and burning herself within the flames.

Her hands gripped his wrists as one hand lay on her abdomen, the other at her hip. His fingers flexed against her, as though his need to allow his fingers to touch her further was being held in check by the thinnest threads of control.

"What is this," she breathed harshly, "if it isn't a game? I don't like being manipulated, Devlin."

He grunted, rubbing his cheek against her hair. "And you are no stranger to manipulation?" he asked her curiously. Or was it mockingly?

"I don't manipulate," she gasped when his lips touched her ear, his tongue stroking the outer shell with a whispered caress. "It seems to me that you're the one playing games here."

His fingers flexed against her once before he turned her quickly in his arms. He stared down at her intently, his eyes brightening as the force of his desire wrapped around her. Her hands gripped his shoulders, her hips tilting at the feel of his erection pressing into her abdomen as his head lowered to her.

"The great hall is a little public for this, don't you think?" Amusement and fond warmth echoed in the familiar voice behind her.

Chantel whirled around. She stared at the older man, frowning, knowing she had never met him, but knowing that, like the castle, and the man who held her, he was familiar, perhaps even more familiar than the others.

Devlin sighed.

"Chantel, meet the sorcerer, Galen, the former owner, sometimes inhabitant and all around mischief-maker of Hunter Castle."

Galen snorted, his blue eyes twinkling in amusement. "He makes me sound like a rambunctious toddler, doesn't he?"

He stepped forward, his husky, muscular body moving gracefully as he came to her. Rather than shaking her hand, or greeting her jovially as she would have expected, his arms wrapped around her in a hug she would have thought would be reserved for only someone most beloved.

"It's good to see you back, Chantel," he whispered for her ears alone. "Damned good, child, to see you back."

The crystal at her breast flared with warmth, comforting, joyous warmth. Chantel fought for breath as the wispy memories overwhelmed her. Laughter, tears.

I do not like this bargain you have begot, Chantel. The distant memory pierced her heart as she heard his pain.

All will be well... Her own voice was shadowed with pain, with loss.

She shuddered in reaction as she pushed away from him, staring up at his face, then turning to Devlin. Galen watched her with fondness and warmth. Devlin watched her with cool, curious detachment. She shook her head as she backed away from them both, fighting to put a distance between her and the hazy memories rising to the surface.

Remember me, Devlin, let your heart never forget. Her own desperate, pain-ridden voice echoed around her.

"Chantel?" He stepped forward now, his black gaze concerned as he watched her.

Chantel shook her head. She fought the blinding heat that wanted to suffuse her body, the fear that wanted to take possession of her sanity.

"Let her alone, warrior," Galen ordered, his voice strong, determined. "You cannot save her from this. It is her decision alone."

"What decision?" she bit out, frightened, angry. "Where do I have a decision in this at all?"

"The same as you made centuries before, you must make now," Galen told her gently. "The decision to live, child, is often much harder than the decision to die."

Pain speared through her head, washing through her body as the crystal hummed at her breast. Imperative. Demanding. She felt herself stumble beneath the force of it as she whimpered in distress. Her hand went to her head, her gaze to Devlin.

A mist formed over her sight as she saw more, and yet less than she needed.

"I am no whore, Sir Devlin," she told him, standing firmly before him.

The scene flashed yet again.

"Have you betrayed me?" he asked her, his eyes dark, suspicious.

She gasped as his hands manacled her arms, jerking her to him as she swayed on her feet.

"Sorcerer, what magic do you practice now?" Devlin bit out, his voice furious, his body tight with his anger. "Let her be."

Chantel stared back at Galen, seeing the sadness in his eyes, and more. There was always more. Always so much more surrounding her that she should sift through. She shook her head then, unable to deal with the shifting memories, the all-consuming sense that she had indeed deceived all those around her.

She shook her head, fighting the need to question him, to know the truth. For once in her life she was terrified of facing the destiny that she had always known was to come. For the first time, she was terrified that she could indeed be Antea.

She jerked away from Devlin, staring at them both for long, pain-filled moments. Whispered accusations, a scream of rage and women's tears drifted around her. She had deceived. And she had died. She could feel her face paling, her stomach roiling with dread as she shook her head in denial.

"I'm not Antea," she whispered. "I can't be Antea."

Before they could stop her, she ran. Up the stairs, back to the room he had locked her in earlier, back to the silence. She prayed for the peace she needed to sort through the disjointed memories, and the sense that she would never be the same again.

"Let her alone," Galen hissed when Devlin would have sprinted after her. "Give the memories time to return, without your lusts clouding her vision."

"My lusts?" Devlin turned back to him furiously. "What of your games, old man? What are you doing to her mind?"

"I do nothing but give her the chance to remember," Galen argued back. "I expect her to be no one. I suspect nothing of her, and expect only great things of her accomplishments. What, my fine warrior, do you expect from her? Deceit? Lies? Each time you look at her, it is with suspicion and lust in your eyes."

"How else am I supposed to look at her?" Devlin turned on the older man, furious at the lecture he was receiving. "Do you know, old man, exactly who she is?"

Galen smiled. "Of course I know. She is Chantel, just as she says she is."

Devlin felt his jaw bunch in frustration. This was getting him nowhere.

"I don't want her to be alone while she's so upset," he bit out. "Now get out of my way so I can go check on her."

"And why would you care?" Galen questioned softly. "Antea was nothing to you then, she would be nothing to you now. Only a great and abiding love would have followed you all these centuries, Devlin."

Devlin snorted. "That or an old man's insane magic," he growled, stepping around him as he made his way to the staircase.

"Devlin." He paused on the first step, looking back at the sorcerer, seeing the old man's worry and concern. "Chantel is dear to me. More so than you could know. Tread carefully."

Devlin frowned at the words that sounded too much like a fatherly warning. He shook his head, fighting the feeling, the possibility of such a thing. Galen had three daughters. *A crystal, the first of four, bound by blood, bound by love...*

Antea had not been Galen's daughter. Devlin knew this. Knew for a fact that the sorcerer had hated her, despised her as he had despised no one else on this earth. He would not have given the crystal to a woman whose heart held the treachery Antea's did.

The thought wanted to slip from his grasp, to slide into the murky depths of those shadowed dreams that tormented his sleeping hours. He felt the pressure along his face as his jaw bunched, fighting against the need to let it escape as it had so many times before.

"I practice no magic on you, Sir Knight," she told him softly as she moved to the small table and poured him a healthy measure of wine. Turning back to him, she sipped slowly from the goblet herself before extending it to him. "I am here to practice the gentle art of cleansing your body, and perhaps your heart, if you would allow it. I've shared your dreams, warrior, surely now you will be willing to share the reality of it with me."

Devlin stopped as he approached his bedroom door. Same bedroom, same woman, yet he knew it was a different time. He shook his head, his fists clenching as he remembered his wonderment, his surprise that a woman so graceful and filled with warmth would be so accepting of him, a man of blood and battle.

Where had the memory come from? There were no others to accompany it, as though it was there, twisting about in his memories on its own.

Then he saw her, on her knees, just a shadowed image, yet the implications of it had his cock spike-hard. Staring up at him, drawing his straining erection into the heat of her mouth. Then, just as quickly as the image flashed through his mind, it was gone.

Furious at the loss, confused by the twisting shadows in his own mind, he jerked the door open and stalked into the bedroom, only to pull up short as he slammed the door behind him.

The afternoon sun speared through the window, bathing her in golden rays as she tossed the sweatpants across the floor furiously. She turned to him, naked, flushed, her breasts swollen, her nipples peaked, aroused. A distant portion of his mind urged him to go slowly, a contradictory image of her, too innocent for the lusts raging through him, and merging with that image was the woman who faced him now, sensual, hungry, well able to sustain the desires he hadn't realized had grown over the centuries. Whatever she may have been, he knew in that instant, he hadn't fully known her, not until now. Not until this time.

Her green eyes widened, then widened more when his hands went to the waistband of his pants.

"You're mine," he growled, moving to her as he loosened his belt, then the buttons of his jeans. "Whoever the hell you are, whoever the hell you were, you're mine now."

The collision of memories, lust and need. An echo of some emotion he couldn't grasp, yet he knew went far deeper than any he had known before. She stood before him, hurt, angry, a woman riding the edge of her own sanity, and he couldn't bear to see her hang there. Couldn't take the risk that she would topple over. That once again, whether he remembered or not, he would lose her.

"So much is begging to be free," she whispered as he pulled her into his arms. "So much that I can't make sense of."

His hands ran over her smooth back, down to the tempting curve of her buttocks. Those sweet curves flexed beneath his hands, her back arching, a whispering moan sighing from her lips.

"I need you again," he groaned as his lips caressed hers. "Now."

Her hands pulled at his shirt, buttons slipping, or tearing, free of the material as she fought to get to his flesh. Her fingers were warm and silky-soft on the muscles of his chest. He shrugged the shirt from his arms, his lips covering hers, his tongue stroking into her mouth as he reveled in the strength of her desire. He could taste it, feel it in her questing fingers and straining body as she lifted to him.

She tore her mouth from his then, her lips moving to his chest, teeth and tongue rasping over the hard male planes as he held her head to him. Had he ever known anything so hot, so sensuous?

The night before, he had controlled her passions. Deliberately, ruthlessly, he had touched her in ways that left her gasping, giving her little time to consider ways of destroying his self-control. But the temptress who had awakened to him was having no more of that. Each time he tried to pull her to him, she slid away, her mouth finding another sensitive inch of his flesh to torment. Where her touch was concerned, each inch of his flesh was sensitive.

"I want to touch you," she whispered as her tongue stroked over the hard male nipple that tightened at her touch. "I want to know you as you know me, Devlin."

Her lips stroked lower, her hand reaching between the loosened front of his jeans to grip the straining length of his cock as she pushed at the material. His breathing became labored, his muscles tightening as her head lowered. His hands clenched in her hair, but he did nothing to halt her stroking caress. His cock was pounding, throbbing, anticipation tightening it further as her mouth moved with excruciating slowness toward it.

She pushed his jeans past his hips, but once they cleared the area she was most interested in, she forgot about them. Devlin couldn't have cared less. His cock was spike-hard, throbbing, the thick head pleading for attention.

"Tease," he groaned as her lips roamed his abdomen, her teeth scraping his flesh sensually as his hips jerked involuntarily. By the time she finally wrapped her mouth around the near to bursting head, he would lose all control and spill his seed before experiencing the joy of her mouth.

His muscles tightened at the thought as he damned near quivered in excitement. He was like a youth with his first woman, unable to get enough, unable to last long enough.

Her soft laughter was like a breath of heat over the straining crown of his erection. His hand tightened in her hair, hearing her gasp of pleasure, feeling the wash of her tongue over the tip of his engorged erection.

"Like that?" he growled, his hands tightening once again in the silken strands he held prisoner.

Her moan was like a flame on the head of his cock as her lips parted, her tongue washing over it. He grimaced, fighting for control. He could feel perspiration dotting his skin, anticipation straining his muscles. When her mouth covered the engorged head of his cock, he nearly spilled his seed with a shameless act of loss of control.

Her tongue was a moist flame, her mouth searing heat around his long-neglected flesh as she went to her knees before him. She wrapped one hand about the shaft, her other caressing the heavy weight of his scrotum. Her mouth moved on him sensually, suckling the head of his cock with deep, lazy draws that had sensation spiking through his body. Her tongue was never still. It licked over the pulsing head, stroked beneath the flaring tip, caressed him with such hungry movements that a moan ripped from his throat.

His hands tightened in her hair, his teeth clenching as she groaned around his cock. He filled her mouth until each vibration was yet another pleasure to stroke across it.

"God, Chantel, you're killing me." He couldn't hold back his groan as her tongue swirled over the bulbous head then her mouth sucked at it deeply, firmly.

His thighs trembled as he fought to hold back his explosion. He looked down at her. Her gaze was raised, her hungry mouth filled with his flesh, stroking down, then back, leaving several inches of the shaft glistening and wet. Then her tongue swirled, her mouth sucked, and he had to close his eyes to maintain his control.

Sensations intensified. Her felt every delicate flexing of her mouth — the suction that caused his scrotum to tighten, her teasing fingers that stroked over his shaft and the drawn sac below and caused his thighs to tremble with his need to thrust hard and deep inside her.

"Oh yeah," he whispered, unable to still the words that fell from his lips. "So hot, baby. So good and hot." His fingers flexed in her hair, tugging at it, and she moaned around the violently sensitive head again.

Her tongue found the underside of the flared tip, probed and licked, and he gritted his teeth as he fought the building pressure that threatened to push him over.

"Sweet, baby," he groaned, the lust building through his body. "Chantel, darlin'…"

The suckling pressure increased. Her mouth slipping heatedly over the head of his cock, then back again. Pleasure streaked from his engorged erection, traveling through his body like forked lightning as his hips flexed, pushing back, fucking her mouth with short, hard thrusts as he fought to steal every moment of the pleasure that he could.

His abdomen tightened, his loins burned. He was close. So close. He could feel the head of his cock flaring, his seed barely contained.

"Enough," he growled, his eyes opening to stare down at her, to see her eyes so hot and dark, her cheeks flushed, her expression hungry.

He tried to pull back. Tried to spare her the humiliating loss of his control. But her mouth followed him, suckling him, destroying him. He buried his cock nearly to her throat as she moaned around the thick flesh, and felt his climax take him. His sperm erupted from the tip of his cock, exploding into the hot depths of her mouth, only to have her moan, and draw another explosive eruption from him.

Devlin heard his own cry, felt the sensations that streaked up his spine, that enveloped his mind in such erotic pleasure that he wondered if he would survive. His cock pulsed, over and over, shooting its liquid desire into the hungry depths of her mouth. And she took him, took each eruption and moaned for more.

Fighting for breath, Devlin eased his cock from her mouth, amazed at the stiffness, the renewed passion that pulsed through his body, despite his violent release. His hands gripped Chantel's arms, drew her up, then pushed her back to the bed.

"Lay back," he growled as he sat in the chair by the bed and reached down to unlace his boots. "Touch yourself. Let me see how wet you are for me, baby. How much you need me."

She smiled. A siren's smile of knowledge. She lay back, her legs spreading, her hands smoothing across her breasts then down her flat stomach to the glistening flesh of her pussy.

That sweet mound was the color of peaches and cream. Flushed creamy lips were slick with the nectar of her passion. And inside the narrow slit, the sweet pink flesh was revealed. Her fingers circled her swollen clit, her moan breathless and needy as she licked her lips in anticipation.

One boot was off, the other nearly untied when her fingers slid farther down, gathering the sweet juices on her fingers before she lifted her hand. He watched, mesmerized, as the tip of her finger disappeared inside her lush mouth.

His brain exploded. The man fell before the beast of lust, and he forgot about the boot, or the jeans tangled around his legs. The short distance to the bed was no problem. He lifted her legs, braced his knees and thrust his cock inside the lava-hot volcano of her gripping pussy. Her muscles, tight as a fist, hot as lightning, flowed around him, tightened, spasmed as he felt her juices aid in his penetration.

"Oh God, Chantel." He came over her then, his hips thrusting inside her, giving her no time to adjust to his thickness, no time to do more than wrap her legs around his lower back and hang on for the ride, which was what he wanted anyway.

He lifted her hand as he thrust inside her, sucking her fingers into his mouth, groaning at the delicate taste, the erotic sweetness of her desire for him. She was arching beneath him now, her other hand gripping his shoulder, her head thrown back, her face flushed with her need to climax. She was the most beautiful sight in the world to him. Her hair splayed out around her, her cunt gripping him, rippling with her pleasure.

Devlin clasped her to him, all reason having been buried beneath the onslaught of his lust. He drove his cock inside her, the feel of her heated channel making him insane with the snug grip. She was strangling him, killing him with pleasure. His cock was a needy, voracious beast intent on fucking her as hard and as fast as Devlin could throw his hips against her.

The sound of wet flesh, the feel of his scrotum slapping the delicate flesh of her ass, was destroying him. His lips released her fingers, his head buried at her neck and he drove harder, deeper inside her. He could feel his orgasm building again, the hot rush of sensation streaking up his spine warning him that the explosion was near.

Then he felt her come apart beneath him. She cried out his name, her voice husky, desire-rich and emotion-laden as she stiffened, her pussy tightening, milking him, drawing on his cock with a force her mouth had lacked as her orgasm rushed over her. Devlin was but seconds behind her.

He thrust again, hard and deep, and could hold back no more. Once more his seed rocketed from his cock, filling her, exploding inside her with a force that had his body jerking, trembling and his cry echoing hoarsely around them.

He collapsed beside her long minutes later. His jeans around his ankles, her body plastered to his side. He couldn't bear to let her go, to be separated from her for even a moment.

"Chantel," he whispered her name, needing an affirmation of her, to know she was indeed with him.

"Hmm, Devlin." Her hand smoothed weakly over his chest. "I can sleep now."

She breathed out deeply and stilled in his arms. Surprised, Devlin looked down at her to see that she was indeed asleep. His legs were numb, his cock still half hard, and his mind in turmoil, and she was sleeping. He sighed deeply. Hell, life was getting better.

Chapter Ten

ഇ

Dawn had barely risen when the explosion rocked the castle. The bed rocked and the stone walls groaned with such a shuddering impact that Chantel was nearly thrown from the bed.

A volatile curse ripped from Devlin as he jumped from the bed, dragging her with him, his arms wrapping around her to steady her as the room jolted once again and the walls heaved.

"Son of a bitch," he cursed again as another quaking explosion shook the room.

"Dress." He threw her the sweat pants from the day before and a large men's shirt as he disappeared into the closet.

Chantel struggled into the clothes as another blast rocked the structure. One after another, the violence of the attack shook the room with enough force that it should have leveled the castle.

"What the hell is going on?" she screamed out at him as he emerged, dressed in formfitting black from head to toe, a sword strapped to his lean hips and death glittering in his eyes.

She struggled into her sneakers then grabbed her pistol from the dresser, checking the clip quickly.

"Here." His voice was hard, his hands rough as he strapped a lethal dagger to her thigh. "Bullets won't work, Chantel. If by chance they breech the castle, a dagger to the heart is all that will kill them."

"What?" The dagger sheath extended from her thigh, nearly to her knee. The weapon itself would have to be almost a foot long.

She stared up at him in confusion, fighting to make sense of what he was telling her.

"To the heart." He grabbed her shoulders, shaking her in emphasis. "If they breech the castle, Chantel, take no chances. Swear it to me. Hide first. Should they find you then use that dagger. With the protection of your crystal, it could save you until I reach you."

He was yelling at her as another hard blast rocked the room. Chantel fought to understand what was going on around her. Devlin's words, the warning heat of the crystal at her breast, her own fears.

"Devlin, we have two dozen immortals dropping into the valley." Joshua burst into the room, wild-eyed, his black hair flowing around him, his amber eyes glowing with menace. "The magic of the castle is holding, but they're headed to the village."

Devlin's head swung around to the warrior, dressed similarly, sword in hand as he faced him. He turned back to Chantel.

"Swear it to me before God," he yelled desperately. "I must go defend those outside the castle. Swear to me you will not leave the castle, that you will take no chances. Swear it to me."

"I swear," she screamed, unable to do anything else.

Menace pulsed in the air around them, the discordant hum of energy gathering, the shuddering, explosive sound of a violent discharge and the protesting shudder of the castle that had them all fighting to keep their footing within the room.

"Chantel, come with me." Kanna rushed through the doorway, dressed in a fashion similar to the warriors. "Go, Devlin. I will care for your lady."

Before Chantel could do more than gasp, he bent his head, his lips pressing roughly, heatedly against hers before he tore himself from her and rushed from the room.

"What the fuck is going on here?" Chantel demanded above the roar of the violent assault being waged upon the castle.

"Jonar," Kanna bit out. "Come with me. We must be prepared for any injuries they sustain."

Chantel rushed after the other woman as she moved quickly through the castle. The huge fortress shook with each blast, but not a single stone dislodged from the walls.

"What the hell is he using?" she yelled as she rushed to keep up with the other woman.

"An energy blast that he has managed to hold on to," Kanna bit out. "We have destroyed most of his unnatural weapons over the centuries, but a few he managed to protect. This is one we have not been able to destroy."

They entered the great hall as a particularly violent blast caused the floors to rock beneath their feet. Stone dust whispered from the ceiling, causing Chantel to eye it nervously.

"Hurry, we have a lot to prepare." Kanna looked back at her quickly before speeding up as she passed the kitchen, turned the corner and entered a darkened stairwell.

"We're going further underground," Chantel bit out as she hurried to follow the other woman. "Is that a good idea?"

"If you so much as stick your head out a window, Jonar will have it cleaved in two," Kanna informed her fiercely. "Never doubt he is not watching for you."

The walls groaned beneath the weight of the blasts above. Dust shimmered through the air, the ceiling groaning beneath the impacts.

"Seems wrong to go down when what's above you is so damned heavy," Chantel said nervously.

"The castle is protected. You are safe. Those who fight beyond it are the ones in danger. Come, there is much that must be done in case of injuries." Kanna's voice was stern, imperative.

The dimly lit stone stairs curved around for what seemed like forever. The small lights along the ceiling dimmed occasionally from the blasts above, but never gave out. Finally, a brighter light glowed from above and Chantel moved faster as Kanna increased her pace.

When they entered the large underground cavern, Chantel could do nothing but stop and stare in shock. It was a technological nightmare, or an alternate reality that she would just as soon escape.

Between her breasts, the warning throb of the crystal had eased to a light, comforting warmth, which did little to ease her fears. The cavern was brightly lit. On one wall a low counter held several computers, their monitors dark, unused. A larger monitor was attached higher on the wall. She gasped as she watched the action moving across the scene. It could have been an action adventure flick worthy of the most imaginative screenwriter. But she recognized well the tall, broad-shouldered form that wielded a sword like a demon intent on destruction.

Devlin wasn't giving his enemy a chance as he entered the fray outside a small village. There were over a dozen of what appeared to be the enemy. There were only four of the warriors.

"My God. It's suicide," she whispered.

The screen went blank. Swinging around she faced Kanna furiously.

"We don't have time for this," the other woman bit out, though there was a thread of compassion in her tone. "If they are wounded, no matter how desperately, the Guardians will ensure that they are brought here. We must be ready. Help me to get the stasis chambers prepared."

The stasis chambers were long, cylindrical units with the appearance of a coffin. The bottom was filled with a thick, supportive gel that rippled when Chantel touched her finger to it.

"Check all the cables and wires leading from the end of it. They must all be securely fitted into the main power control along the base of the unit. Now hurry, it takes a while, and the battle will be over soon."

Chantel did as she was bid. There were dozens. They ran from the top of the unit, a glass-shielded covering with small metal plates where the cables and wires fit. Under the glass shield, a strange-colored wire extended through the plate.

Shaking her head she checked the first unit, going quickly from wire to wire, cable to cable, as she made certain they were all attached securely.

"Each unit is individually assigned to one of us," Kanna explained as they worked. "It can hold us for days, or for centuries. I don't understand the technology, but the Guardians have perfected preserving life in these units. As long as a warrior is reached before their heart is cut from their chest, or their heads severed from their bodies, then they can be repaired, healed. Though sometimes, it takes centuries to do so."

Chantel shook her head as she worked. She didn't want to hear this. Didn't want to know that Devlin could be taken from her as effectively as death, and yet still be alive.

Chantel rose to her feet after checking the last cable on the unit she had been going over, and moved to the next. Silence filled the stone chamber as they worked through the next hour. It was meticulous work, but kept her mind and her hands occupied. She was frantic for news, and kept glancing at the dark screen that could have allowed her to know if Devlin had been injured or not.

She was ready to question Kanna further when a sudden static burst from a receiver on the other side of the room echoed around them. Kanna rushed for it, pressing one of the brightly lit buttons.

"Kanna, get Joshua's unit ready. It's bad." Devlin's voice was imperative, commanding. "Jonar has flown with his wounded and the rest of us have only minor injuries. Joshua has taken the worst of it."

"How bad?" Kanna bit out.

"It's bad, Kanna," he growled. "We're nearly to the castle now. Get his unit ready."

Chantel stood aside as Kanna rushed to one of the farthest units. She hit one of the buttons on the side, and a small keyboard, lights glowing and revealing strange curved symbols, slid from the end of the coffin like a bed. Kanna's fingers flew over the keys. The unit lit up, the dark blue gel in the bed rippling as waves of warmth mystified in the cool chamber.

"He knew the secrets, and the past," Chantel said slowly as she watched Kanna work. "He was the only one who knew."

"Who?" Kanna glanced up at her in surprise.

"Joshua," she said softly. "He was the only one who knew."

Kanna snorted. "He thinks he knows every damned thing."

There was a wealth of fondness in her voice, despite her caustic reply.

"We're coming down, Kanna." Devlin's voice suddenly sounded from the stairwell.

Chantel scurried out of the way, her eyes widening as the men rushed into the room. Devlin was bloody from head to toe. Several scratches covered his face. His black uniform-like clothes were ripped in several places, yet he appeared unharmed.

Derek was holding his arm, where a makeshift bandage was wrapped around it, and the giant known as Shanar carried a weakened Joshua. The wound was to his chest, deep and severe. He had already lost an untold amount of blood, and even more stained Shanar's chest.

He was rushed to the unit and placed in it carefully, but before they could close the lid, he struggled against them.

"I need to talk to her," he growled. "Now."

Devlin's head whipped in Chantel's direction. "See what he wants. He's nearly dead and he's trying to play the fool."

Chantel moved over to the unit, staring down at the bloodied bandage on his chest.

"Do not deceive him again," Joshau snarled. This was not Joshua, the mocking bitter warrior she had come to know. Whoever, whatever Joshau was, it showed now in the glow of his amber eyes, in the commanding tone of his voice and the arrogance of his pallid expression. "Do so, and when I awaken, I will kill you myself, Lady. Do you understand me?" His voice was weakening as the life slowly drained from his body.

"I swear to you, I won't deceive him," she swore painfully, seeing for the first time his dedication, his worry for those he fought with. *Joshau, the prince.* She shook the thought away, staring into his eyes, knowing he would not allow the healing without her reassurance.

Agony filled his expression, darkened the gold of his eyes. She could feel him reaching out to her, feel a million emotions swirling in the air around them.

"Dammit Joshua, we have to seal this unit..." Devlin cursed as blood ran from more than one horrendous injury in the warrior's body.

And still he stared up at her, his lips tightened, moved as though he would speak as power shimmered in the air around them. For the briefest moment an image flashed in her mind. A young woman, long black hair flowing around her, her sapphire blue eyes reflecting a misery that echoed from the soul. The same woman she saw each time she felt this man's power. And regret. For a timeless moment, she felt his regret.

"I will protect her," she promised him then, sensing a need she wondered if even he understood. "Even from you."

He fought to breathe, his amber eyes watching her for a long second before he nodded abruptly.

Chantel stood aside then as the lid was lowered. Kanna keyed in several short commands to the keyboard, and suddenly a thick, red mist began to fill the unit.

Chantel drew in a deep, steadying breath before she turned to the others. Her eyes narrowed on Derek. "How bad is the arm?" She moved to him, reaching for the bandage.

"You cannot ease me, Lady," he whispered, moving back from her regretfully. "I am undeserving of such mercy." He turned and strode quickly from the room.

"That man carries a burden of the soul," Shane said softly, his graveled voice rough, filled with regret.

Chantel watched the larger man as he shook his great shaggy head and turned to Devlin. "I need to shower and sleep. Do you require anything before I retire?"

Devlin shook his head. "Rest, Shanar. Jonar won't stop with this attack. We need to be at our best for the next round. I'll call for you if you're needed."

Shanar nodded, then he too left the room.

Chantel faced Devlin then, gazing at him in confusion.

"Were any of the villagers harmed?" she asked him, afraid to hear the answer should she learn there had been any deaths.

His shook his head tightly. "They did not reach the village. And you? Everything is okay?"

He moved to her, reaching out to touch her before he saw the blood that stained his hands. He drew back, then watched in surprise as she took his hand.

"You need to bathe and rest as well," she told her.

She turned to Kanna, intent on asking about a meal for him when the other woman turned to her. Kanna was exhausted herself.

"Are there any servants to prepare a meal for them?" she asked her.

Kanna shook her head. "I'll bring something up…"

"I'll help you prepare it," Chantel told her decisively before turning to Devlin. "Bathe. I'll have a meal up soon. Get the blood off your body so I can see for myself that you're not hurt."

"You will come with me." His hand gripped her arm, his expression suddenly brooking no argument, no fight. "I need you, not food."

Chantel gasped as he moved steadily for the stairwell, pulling her behind him, his grip gentle, but determined. She could see the sexual intent in his hard body, feel the lustful heat coming off him in waves. Her pussy clenched at the sudden domination in him, the male need, relentless, demanding emotions. He was filled with adrenaline, with lust. She could see it in his black eyes, feel it in the way he pulled her behind him. And she knew if he turned to her, she would see the thick bulge of his erect cock beneath his pants. She shivered with desire, in her own feminine heat. More than willing to follow him into the coming sensual battle.

"Undress." His voice was stark, grating in its intensity as he pushed the door closed behind them and turned to face her.

Chantel felt her mouth go dry. His expression was tight, savage with his lust. His eyes were black coals in his taut features, his cheeks darkening with a brick flush that emphasized the heat in his eyes.

"So romantic." She arched a brow mockingly, though her fingers went to the buttons of the large man's shirt that she wore.

Devlin grunted. "I've been more centuries than I can count without a woman. I'll be damned if I'll do without what I need now."

Centuries. Her heart softened even as it beat out of control with the needs warring inside her.

"Centuries?" she whispered as he finished unlacing his boots and pulled them from his feet.

He ripped the shirt over his head then tossed the leather supply belt after it before he looked at her. When he did, he stopped. Chantel watched need and emotion rage in his eyes.

He shook his head as though confused, as though he were fighting through the same morass of emotions and shattered memories, as she was herself. He stood before her, his bronzed chest bare, rising and falling with his hard, quick breaths.

"Centuries," he growled desperately. "And God's truth, Chantel, if you don't undress quickly, you will have the clothes torn from your body. I can wait no longer."

He unzipped his pants, releasing the straining, engorged length of his cock. Heavy veins stood out in stark relief along the dark shaft. The plum-shaped, purplish head throbbed as a small bead of pearly liquid rose from the tiny slit atop the crown. Chantel's eyes widened, her mouth watered.

"Time's up," he growled.

Before Chantel could do more than gasp he had jerked her to him. His hands were excitingly rough, demandingly hard as he pulled her into his arms. His lips slanting over hers in a kiss that sent a thrill of escalating lust pounding through her body. He was demanding, his tongue thrusting forcefully between her lips as he took the kiss he wanted.

He was voracious in his demand. He ripped the shirt from her back, either forgetting or uncaring of the fact that it was his to begin with. Then his hands were tearing at the waistband of her sweats, his moan filled with hunger and desperate need as the material tore in his impatience to get to her moist, hot cunt.

His tongue drove into her mouth repeatedly, twining with hers as a hard male groan vibrated against her lips. He ate her lips, a hungry male in full arousal and making no apologies for it.

Chantel's system exploded with excitement. Her vagina clenched, the lips of her cunt pulsing, swelling and becoming sensitized with her own escalating desires. Rioting sensations of pleasure, erotic greed, and tormented need tore through her body.

She whimpered as her womb clenched so tight and hard she felt the breath being driven from her chest as she nearly climaxed from the excitement alone. He pushed her sweats roughly past her hips, down her trembling thighs.

"I can't wait." He tore his lips from hers as he pushed her over the side of the bed. "I can't wait, Chantel. God help me, I have to…"

She felt the bulging head of his cock notch at the weeping entrance of her vagina. She screamed out, pleasure and fire burning through her body as he surged inside her, hard and forceful, parting the muscles of her pussy with the heated length of his throbbing cock.

Chantel's back arched involuntarily as pleasure streaked through her body. Her hands clutched at the blankets as he gripped her hips.

"Bend over." Hard hands pushed her back into position.

His fingers gripped her hips again, his thighs bunched and he began a hard, driving motion that whipped every nerve in her body into a frantic dance of tormented lust. He stroked the clenching, nerve-rich tissue with repeated thrusts that burrowed to her very womb, pounding inside her as she tightened the muscles of her pussy to hold him deep inside.

The pleasure was akin to pain. The brutal lance of sensations had her fighting for more, desperate for the hard punch of the orgasm that she knew would rip through her body at any thrust now. She needed. Oh God, she needed him so desperately.

Her hands bunched in the blankets as she fought to hold herself in place. His hands, quick and demanding, lifted her thigh until her knee was braced on the mattress as well, giving each thrust a deeper, more agonizing level of sensation.

Chantel panted for breath as her pussy tightened further around him. She couldn't get enough, yet he filled her until her muscles burned with protest, and with greed.

The sound of hard cock and moist hungry cunt filled the room. The slap of fiercely pounding flesh, the suckling heat of her vagina, and the explosive mix of sensations were much more than a quick desperate mating. The fire lit in her pussy raged through her body, then exploded in a cataclysmic rush of release that left her screaming his name as feminine fear streaked through her brain. Could she ever survive such a rush of pleasure?

There was no choice. Her body rocketed as her orgasm ripped through her at the same moment that she felt his cock swell further, throb then explode in the tight depths of her pussy.

She twisted in his grip, fighting the rush of sensation, but caught in the throes of his own desperate release he had no intention of releasing her. His hands held her tight to him as his semen exploded inside her, pushing her higher, tossing her mercilessly into the maelstrom of ecstasy.

She heard his harsh male shout as though from a distance. Heard the dark, emotion-rich quality of it that her soul gloried in. But the hot bursting rapture that engulfed her left little room for other senses to operate.

She shuddered in his grip. Trembled as her cunt tightened around him with a final, convulsive burst of sensation before she wilted to the bed. She felt his erection slide free, still hard, still achingly hot.

As she lay there fighting for breath, he turned her to her back and tenderly picked her up in his arms and carried her across the room. She didn't even have the strength to protest, to voice her disagreement of his decision to force her back to reality. The dreamy mists of their echoed passions still enfolded her in a web of blissful contentment.

"I could have used a nap." She tried to pout as he lowered her into the chair that sat to the side of the large, recessed tub.

"As could I," he grunted. "But first I need to bathe. And I want you with me."

She gazed up at him, tall and strong, and still intensely aroused. His cock glistened with their combined moisture, the dark, engorged crown throbbing occasionally in need. She licked her lips.

"Such a look will surely get you in more trouble than I believe you are looking for at this moment," he told her, his voice rough with his body's demands.

She couldn't take her eyes off the heavy erection. The thick veins that ran through it throbbed beneath the satiny flesh with a pulsing rhythm of desire. Lethargic from her earlier climax, Chantel had never imagined that she could heat with passion again so soon. But her blood began to thunder through her veins, and heated longing invaded her vagina.

She slid to her knees, aware of the tensing of his body as he watched her, the tight jerk of his engorged erection. His scrotum was bare of any intimate hair, soft as velvet as she cupped it in her palm. The thick stalk of his cock was a work of art to her eyes. Sculpted to perfection, the ridged veins giving it a muscular, roughened feel that she loved when he was clasped deep inside her pussy. But she wanted to taste him now. Wanted to draw the bead of pre-cum that once again drew to the tip, into her mouth. Wanted to taste their combined releases from the hot flesh that throbbed before her eyes.

"Chantel," he whispered her name, his voice echoing with his growing excitement.

"I've never done this except with you." She glanced up at his expression, her heart jumping at the intent anticipation on his expression. "But I want to, Devlin. I want to do it again."

His expression was tight, the bones displayed beneath his flesh in stark relief as lust once again began to fill the air.

"Then do it," he growled. "Before I die from the—" He groaned, a low male sound of hot, exquisite pleasure as she licked her tongue over the pulsing head, tasting herself as well as him. An erotic blend of sweetness and tart flavors. "I will die before you get me in your mouth," he bit out.

She was in no hurry. Not this time. Not with this. She wanted to taste every inch of the hard male flesh that brought her such pleasure. She painted his cock with her tongue, licking him like candied ambrosia. The salty, slightly musky scent made her ravenous for more. The taste was dark like a storm coming across the sea, whipping the land with the promise of its caress.

She licked the pearly drop of fluid from the tip, savored the silky feel of it, the male taste of it, then took him into her mouth as she longed to do. His hips jerked, as though flayed with a whip, driving the bulging head deeper into her mouth, firmer against her suckling lips.

Her tongue washed over the engorged head, probing beneath the flared edge, glorying in the hard moan that tore from his chest. Her hands gripped the straining shaft, uncertain what to do now that her mouth was filled with the wild taste of his passion. She knew only his taste, his hard heat, and she relished it.

"Like this, baby." His voice was strained, hoarse with his arousal as his hands moved to hers, teaching her to stroke the broad stalk, to cup the silken scrotum.

Each new touch had him straining closer to her, his hips thrusting against her, stroking his cock in and out of her mouth with shallow, controlled thrusts.

Devlin watched the enflamed, engorged crown of his cock stretching her pink lips, disappearing into the scalding depths of her mouth, and wanted to howl at the pleasure. Her tongue was hot as it licked and stroked the pulsing knob. Like whipped satin heat it licked over him, destroying his control.

Her hand, so small and graceful, had no hope of encompassing the width of his erection, but with the aid of her warm saliva, slid firmly up and down the stalk as her other hand caressed his scrotum as it drew tight against his body. He could feel his seed heating in the depths of his cock, the pressure building at the base of his spine that warned him his release was imminent. A release he fought to hold off.

He wanted to watch her, the way her fragile eyelids closed over those brilliant eyes, her white-blonde lashes caressing her flushed cheeks. Then they would open, and those bright emerald eyes glanced up at him with such a look of searing need and emotion that he nearly lost the fight to hold back the eruption threatening to explode past his control.

"Chantel," he groaned her name, every muscle in his body tightening as her shy, hungry suckling of his cock had it jerking, his balls twitching as he fought his release. "Decide now, baby. Continue this, and you will find your mouth filled with my seed. Stop now, or I will not be able to control it much longer."

Her flush darkened, her eyes glittering with a sudden, hungry lust as he spoke. Her mouth tightened on him, moving over his cock with ever-quickening strokes as her hand pumped along the shaft, drawing his seed from the very depths of his loins.

His hands tightened in her hair. It was so soft, so silky. He fought to concentrate on it, to concentrate on anything other than the wet velvet rasp of her tongue and satin lips over his straining cock. His thighs tightened convulsively, bunched as the muscles in his stomach clenched. And she watched him. Watched his fight to hold back the explosion, his indecision in giving her what she so clearly wanted.

Against his will, his cock jerked, a pulse of semen spilling from the tip as he gritted his teeth, fighting the boiling detonation only seconds away. At the taste of him, she moaned. A low, erotic sound of appreciation as her tongue investigated the small slit at the tip of his penis as she licked over him.

His vision blurred. His world narrowed down to her suckling lips, her tormenting tongue, her stroking hands, until he cried out hoarsely as his release rocked through his body. His cum shot from the tip of his cock, splattering in the tight grip of her mouth, against her hungry tongue. He tried to pull back, to keep from burying his cock down her throat in his mad drive for completion, but she only followed him.

Spurt after spurt of his semen exploded into her mouth as she groaned hungrily, her mouth tightening on him, her tongue stroking the pulsing head as though greedy for more. And he provided more. Another hard, agonizing pulse of fire tore through his body and exploded in her mouth as his hands tightened on her head and his body shuddered with the violence of his release.

When he could look at her again, it was to see her leaning back from him, staring up at him, her pert little tongue licking sensually over her lips to catch a few stray drops of his creamy seed.

Reaching down, he drew her to her feet, entranced by the drowsy sensuality in her expression.

"Devlin, I climaxed," she whispered wonderingly as his lips touched her forehead. "You weren't even touching me."

The small tremors of that release still shook her body and lent to her voice a soft, sensual cadence.

He looked into her face, wondering, not for the first time, at the welling emotion that filled his soul and tightened his throat. He didn't know who she was, or why he could touch her when he had been unable to touch another woman in centuries. But she was his. This he knew to the soles of his feet, and this time, he vowed, no one would take her from him.

Chapter Eleven

ೕಾ

The next morning, Chantel was dressed in yet another of Devlin's big shirts, this time a soft gray silk, and a pair of Kanna's sweat pants that were just a bit snug on her. Thankfully, the shirt covered the material that stretched over her ass as though she had been poured into it.

Barefoot, nerves riding high inside her, she left their bedroom, intent on finding Devlin. The crystal was throbbing at her chest, the dreams of the night before harrowing and insistent. At brief moments, the veil of mists would shift in her mind, terrifying her with the shadowed images of the past. At least, she hoped it was the past, and not visions of what was to come.

She moved swiftly down the wide stone steps and intended to pass through the great hall and into the kitchen where she hoped to find breakfast. As she entered the large room, she stopped in her tracks. Now she understood the warning pulse of the crystal, the nerves that ate at her composure.

Standing tall and forbidding in the center of the room, several large suitcases around him, stood her father. She glanced around the room, hoping to see Devlin, yet realizing they were alone.

"Hello, Father," she finally greeted him softly.

The look on his face wasn't welcoming, nor was it concerned and caring. Not that she would have thought it would be. She knew her father well enough to know that her life wasn't his main concern.

"I brought your things." He nudged one of the suitcases with his boot before casting a particularly sneering look her way. "I disposed of the sexual aids you had collected. Really, Chantel, I thought better of you."

Her face flushed as she stared back at him, furious now. It wasn't that the articles couldn't be replaced so much as he had made it his business in the first place.

"You showed me your opinion of me already," she bit out. "Why didn't you send help? Why did you let Jonar's men take me, Father?"

Her fists were clenched at her sides as she fought her fury. She had fought to forget those harrowing hours as she hung in that nasty cell. Fought to forget the pain and the horror of what her father had allowed to happen.

"The mission was unsanctioned. I had no authority—"

"You're lying to me," she cried out bitterly. "You could have sent a pick-up in and no questions would have been asked. You could have stopped it. Why didn't you?"

His expression was cold, his eyes flat and hard as he watched her.

"Dear God, you hate me," she whispered, suddenly seeing what she had refused to see throughout her life. "You hate me. Why? Why couldn't you love me? What would it have taken?"

"All it took was honor," he bit out. "I can respect honor, Chantel."

She shook her head, confused, disbelieving.

"When have I ever shown dishonor?" She forced the tears back, forced back the pain and the regret. So much regret. "Were the nightmares a sign of dishonor?" She remembered well his black anger each time she had them. "Or perhaps my lack of interest in the suitors you brought to me was a sign of my dishonor?" She tilted her head, watching as his blue eyes glittered furiously. "Or perhaps it was my refusal to believe I was unworthy of your love? Which was it, I wonder?"

His lips quirked in a gesture of distaste.

"You think Devlin will save you from the mess you're in?" he finally asked her, completely changing the subject in a way that had her floundering to follow him. "Don't bet on it, Chantel. He hates you. Hates everything you are and everything you represent."

Chantel flinched. "That isn't true."

No man could hate a woman that he had shared such passion with, surely? He touched her as though she were a dream, as though he had awakened from nightmares to find pleasure instead. That wasn't hatred.

"Do you think that because you share his bed, that he holds any affection for you?" he asked her with sarcastic disbelief. "Men can disassociate their emotions from their cocks, daughter. Surely you knew that."

It felt as though a brand were being seared into her soul. She swallowed tightly, fighting to hold back her anger and her pain. She had dealt with the bitterness, the cold unconcern and frigid disapproval, all her life. Chantel suddenly realized just how weary she was of trying to love her stern parent, or of trying to make him love her.

"Why do you hate me?" she finally asked him, past trying to make excuses for his bitterness toward her. "What did I ever do to make you hate me, Father?"

"You deceived and you betrayed, and you played the whore when you should have played the devoted wife," he spat out, his fury suddenly manifesting itself as he watched her with such rage that she took a step back from him. "Did you think in the years I've known these men that I didn't learn what you were?"

"Are you crazy?" she cried out. "For God's sake—"

"Do you think I didn't know who you were? That I wasn't aware of what a dishonorable harlot you had been?" He sneered insultingly.

Chantel's eyes widened. "You think I'm Antea?" she cried out in disbelief. "I've paid all these years, endured your hatred because you think I was the reincarnation of another woman? Father, how could you believe…"

"I am not your father." His hand sliced through the air as fury pulsed around him. "That bitch mother of yours dared to take a lover while I was gone. Dared to betray me and all I stood for. You are a bastard, Chantel, and I refuse to claim you any longer. Perhaps. Perhaps I would have, had your honor been strong enough…But I've seen you, twitching your ass at the Agency, teasing the agents, twisting them around your finger and messing with their weak minds. Even your brother, myself, ensuring we lust for you…"

"My God, you're insane!" she screamed out in denial, backing away from him, horrified by the filth pouring from him. "You're lying. I've never done any such thing. I wasn't like that and neither was mother. It's a lie."

She remembered her mother, so quiet, so filled with sadness and broken dreams. Surely it wasn't true, she raged inside. Surely her mother would not have allowed her to suffer this way without telling her the truth.

"I made that bitch swear on your life and on your brother's that she would never breathe a word of the truth," he sneered. "Do you think I wanted the world knowing what a whore I had married? What a whore I then raised?"

"Stop!" she cried out, her hands fisting at her sides as she fought to make sense of the scene playing out between them. "Stop lying to me."

But was he lying? She had always wondered how any man could treat his own flesh and blood so cruelly. Perhaps he could do it because she truly wasn't his daughter.

"I have never lied to you." He drew himself stiffly erect, though she could see his body vibrating with his fury. "I've grown tired of this charade, is what I've done. Grown tired of the vow she forced on me in return. I would have kept you from Devlin. Would have kept his sanity intact by never allowing you access to that cursed crystal if I could have."

"But you sent me there." Confusion and a spearing agony of loss attacked her heart. "You left the file in my office."

He grunted in disgust. "I have no idea how that file got there. It wasn't by my hand."

"The phone call the night before?" she whispered, feeling something inside her shudder with his hatred and the truths finally being revealed. "The message on my machine wasn't about the crystal?"

"The message was in regards to an assignment, Chantel," he bit out. "I needed you in Afghanistan to help your brother. It figures that you went off on your own rather than helping those who needed you. Thankfully, James came out of it okay." There was a wealth of pride, of love in his voice for his only son. A tone he had never used for his daughter.

Her heart beat hard and painfully. Tears tightened her throat, but she refused to allow him to see them shed.

"I'm not Antea." She shook her head, overwhelmed with the bitter pain that washed through her body.

Her father tucked his hands into the pockets of his slacks and regarded her quizzically. "You are the very image of the portrait once hidden in the upper chambers of this castle. I knew that when you were just a teenager. Do you think he hasn't seen it, Chantel, that he doesn't know who and what you are? Do you think even Galen is unaware of it? He destroyed the portrait when I mentioned it. Sliced it to ribbons because no one could bear to have your image within this castle."

The crystal fought to soothe the ragged emotions welling inside her. She could feel the waves of maternal warmth that emanated from it, the comfort it tried to provide. But there was no comfort for this loss. Not yet. She had lost her mother years before, and had spent the rest of this time dreaming that the day would come when her father would realize his mistake in not caring for her. Even her beloved brother James was kept separated from her by the distance of their jobs, except on those rare occasions when no one else was available to help him.

She felt adrift now. Alone. Her enemy was more powerful than anyone could imagine, and he wanted her dead. Who would grieve for her if he managed to kill her? Did even her brother still remember the bond they once shared when she was a child? Would anyone shed tears now?

She wrapped her arms across her chest, fighting the assault of a loneliness she could barely manage to breathe through. Who was she? She didn't know who she was in any way now. Not who she had been centuries before, or even who she was now.

"Devlin knows I'm not Antea." She whispered the hope as she stared back at her father, praying this was another nightmare, and that soon she would awaken.

"Has he said he knows you aren't Antea?" he asked her cruelly. "Or is he merely giving you enough rope to hang yourself with your own deceit?"

"That's enough, Michael." Devlin's voice sliced through the animosity that filled the air between father and daughter.

Chantel turned to him, her heart breaking in her chest as she watched his hard, uncompromising features. His eyes were cold, his gaze boring into her father as he stepped into the room from the opposite hall.

Dressed in jeans and a white shirt, his thick black hair tied back and his black eyes narrowed on them, he looked imposing, savage, as he moved with deceptive laziness into the room.

"Chantel? Are you okay?" As he neared her, she saw something flare in his eyes, a fury he couldn't hide even though he fought to. A fury at her?

Of course it was her, she thought. She looked like Antea, it didn't matter who she was. All that mattered was who she could be.

"I brought her clothing. I assumed you wouldn't want to risk traveling from the castle with her." Michael turned to Devlin, cool, unconcerned about her, more worried about Devlin traveling with her, than her leaving the castle herself.

How was she supposed to contain the pain that drove through her soul like spikes of fiery steel? He had never been a father to her, but she had always had the hope that one day he could be. Now, even that had been taken from her.

"Thank you, though I've already planned a trip to Paris to replace her clothing." He surprised both her and Michael with his announcement.

"Do you think that's wise?" Michael asked him carefully. "Jonar will surely attack."

"And I will take all precautions." Devlin stepped before her, his hand reaching out, his thumb smoothing over her cheek. Only then was Chantel aware of the dampness on her cheeks. Tears. She was shocked that there was any emotion left inside her to shed them.

"I'm sorry." She swiped her hands over her face, attempting to wipe them away. "I didn't mean to."

Tears were forbidden. An expression of weakness, of guilt. This was what the man who had called himself father had taught her at a young age. God, how was she supposed to express her pain?

"It's okay, baby," he whispered.

Chantel stood in shock as his words pierced the swamping pain inside her. She shook her head, moving away from him, fighting for composure. She could see the derision on her father's face, his fury that Devlin had shown her even that small kindness.

"Devlin, a trip to Paris with her should be out of the question," Michael objected once again. "We can't afford to lose you or one of the other warriors."

Devlin ignored him as he caught Chantel's arm, pulling her back against him, staring down at her with a dark frown as she tried to pull away from him.

"Michael, it is Chantel that we cannot afford to lose." His voice was like the sharpest blade, cold and biting. "I believe you have caused her enough damage for this day. I understand there are things we need to discuss before you leave. You know the way to my office, I will be there momentarily."

Chantel stood still in shock, staring up at him, seeing the fury in his eyes as he stared at her father.

"Devlin, don't let her deceive you," Michael sneered. "Have you forgotten who she is?"

"Evidently, this is exactly what I have done," Devlin replied cryptically. "Please do as I ask." The dark forbidding tone of his voice caused Chantel to shiver with the air of danger that suddenly wrapped around them all.

She glanced in Michael's direction, catching the promise of retaliation that glittered in his eyes. He said no more though as he sniffed his displeasure then strode quickly through the arched hallway Chantel had come through, heading for wherever the office was located.

"We will discuss this after I have dealt with this meeting," Devlin told her as Michael disappeared. "Kanna has a meal awaiting you in the kitchen. Go eat, and then I will take you to the gardens when I'm finished."

Chantel drew back from him, shaking her head.

"Tell me you don't believe I'm Antea," she whispered desperately, her hand gripping his arm as she stared up at him. "Tell me you believe in me, Devlin."

His hand reached up once again, his thumb smoothing over her still damp cheek, his expression still, neither belief nor disbelief reflected there.

"I believe you're Chantel."

Her body jerked as agony resonated along every nerve ending. If he believed she wasn't Antea, he would have said so. He had assured her that he didn't play games. The blow to what was left of her emotions nearly staggered her. She shook her head, drawing back from him now as he released her. She fought to breathe, to draw in air when all she wanted to do was curl in a ball and howl in agony.

"You have a meeting to attend." Her voice was hoarse, scraping against her raw throat as it blistered from the tears she held tightly in check.

"Chantel," he sighed and would have continued.

She shook her head, holding up her hand as she turned from him.

"Just go." She wouldn't let her voice tremble, wouldn't allow her agony to overwhelm her. "Just go, Devlin."

She headed for the kitchen, but only because she knew it was the quickest way to escape him. He expected her to eat. Let him expect until hell froze over, but she would allow him his illusions for now. She just wanted to escape. Just for a while. Just long enough to come to grips with the fact that her life, and her heart, had just been destroyed.

Devlin watched Michael as he talked, his eyes narrowed, his mind not so much on what the man was saying, as it was on the look in his eyes, the fury in his expression. He admitted there had always been something about the other man that caused him to pause. But he had always ignored it, not wanting to draw himself deeper into this man's life.

Reincarnation was a bitch. Devlin could count at least three lifetimes for every reincarnated person he knew. He met up with them often. In the village alone, all but three he had known through more than three lifetimes. A warrior he had fought with in the Colonial wars, who had followed him into battle. Another he had fought with against Spain, still another from Korea. A serving lass who worked at the same bar she had worked in over a hundred years before, a child he had carried from a battlefield, dead of his wounds. Often, the looks were nearly identical. Sometimes though, the resemblance was merely passing.

That was the case here, Devlin realized, suddenly seeing what he had avoided for so many years. Why had he avoided it? Why did the animosity from a previous lifetime follow to this one, when he had no knowledge of why there would be such anger toward the man?

Because he had known, even in that first incarnation, Aaron had not been completely sane. He had aligned himself with Antea, lusted for her, bedded her, but just as Devlin knew Chantel had not been Antea, he knew it had not been Antea that Aaron had truly craved.

He watched as Michael paced to the large French doors, his voice furious as he cataloged imagined sins against his stepdaughter. As he did, Devlin saw him for who he had been. The resemblance was passing, but as Devlin opened his senses, allowed the powers his mind held to probe into the soul of the man, he saw the man he had been. And through Michael's hidden memories of that past life, he saw another. For a moment, a brief passing moment, Devlin saw life. The promise of spring in eyes such a clear brilliant emerald green that Antea's weaker-colored eyes could never do justice to. He saw hair of spun white-gold, falling in masses of rich lustrous waves, rather than the limper, thinner strands of Antea's. For a moment, for just a moment he saw her, knew her, loved her... Only to have the vision and the knowledge retreat. But this time, it did not disappear. It lingered in the back of his mind, subtle, teasing, tempting his memories.

He sighed wearily. Michael was ranting about honor and justice, truth and pride, and beneath it all a building lust for the child who thought of him as a father ruled his heart.

He propped his foot on the handle of the lower desk drawer as he leaned back in his chair and watched the other man. Devlin fought to keep his anger stemmed, to watch patiently rather than reacting hastily. Until he knew the dangers they faced then he couldn't kill the other man as he wanted to.

He rubbed his chin with his index finger as Michael paused in his tirade and turned to face him once again.

"So?" the other man questioned him harshly. "What will you do?"

If Devlin remembered correctly, the question was in regards to the trip he had planned for Paris.

"I haven't changed my mind." He shrugged. "And you have given me no reason to do so."

"She has clothing," Michael bit out.

But not clothing befitting her station. That thought caused Devlin to frown. She should be dressed in silks and satins, wearing clothing fashioned by the most talented designers, not off the rack at the nearest discount store as he suspected she was used to.

"Tell me about the rumors of the price Jonar has placed on her head." He refused to argue further over a trip he was determined to make.

"A million," Michael snorted. "Every damned assassin worth the title will be watching for her now. She's a danger to you."

"It seems to me that I am the danger to her," Devlin pointed out calmly. "Were it not for her connection to the crystal, and ultimately to me, Jonar wouldn't worry about her in the least."

"Which is why she is a danger to you," Michael bit out. "Surely to God you aren't going to let her get to you, Devlin? You've told me yourself that reincarnation is steadily accurate to past lives. Once a whore, always a whore."

Devlin's fist clenched as he came forward in his chair now.

"Call her such again, and you'll not live to regret it, my friend," he growled, well aware that the anger pulsing inside him was building in strength. "I have listened to you rant for nearly an hour now, and have heard nothing that persuades me to believe that Chantel has ever acted dishonorably."

"And what do you call the damned sex toys she kept?" Michael's face flushed in furious lust, though Devlin knew the other man had convinced himself otherwise. "Do you believe she has never been with a man, likely more than one?"

"I know she has been with only one." He rose from his chair now, placing his hands on the desk carefully to keep from using them against the other man. "Me, and only me."

Michael's eyes widened. Devlin remembered clearly informing the other man long ago exactly how long it had been since he had known sexual desire. He had often worried that it was an effect caused by the gifts the alien Guardians had given them. Now he wondered himself at the reason.

"But you're impotent." Michael shook his head, paling at the information. "It's not possible."

Devlin shrugged as he straightened to his full height, watching Michael carefully.

"Apparently, I'm not," he said softly. "Whatever Chantel used the toys for is none of my concern. Had she not been a virgin, it would be none of my concern. Just as it is none of yours. She is not your daughter. By your own words, she is nothing to you. So it does not matter."

"You are letting her destroy you for the thrill of lust," Michael snarled. "Jonar will defeat you for sure this time, Devlin. As he nearly did the last time she had her hand in your life."

The mistakes of his life crowded upon him then. He had told Michael too much he now knew. Had trusted him too far in the information he had been given. He should have never held back his powers all these years. He should have used them, tested them, he would have known instantly then who

Michael was and what he was doing to the child he was raising.

"Then it will be my decision to allow it, and none of your concern. Is this not correct?" Devlin asked him softly. "Don't make the mistake of presuming upon our friendship in this manner, Michael. I won't allow it."

On his desk, a brass paperweight began to crumple in on itself, the sound of the crushing metal causing Michael's face to pale. The seemingly effortless power displayed was more of a threat than words could have ever been.

Michael's eyes were caught by the sight of the paperweight. Devlin knew the object was still twisting, a slow gyrating dance of destruction as it literally collapsed upon itself.

"Kanna has prepared your room," Devlin informed him. "I would request that you stay a night or two, until I've investigated the threat against Chantel in more depth. As her acknowledged father, your life too could be in danger."

Michael nodded, his eyes still on the twisted metal that had once resembled a golden ball. When he raised his eyes, Devlin saw the deceit that became quickly shuttered in his gaze. He restrained his urge to crush the bastard's body as he had the bronze ball. Some things were just overkill.

"You will regret this," Michael said slowly. "I would have protected you."

Devlin's lips quirked. "Worry over your own protection, Michael. I have Chantel's and mine well in hand. Now come, I would find her and attempt to undo the damage you have wrought."

"You don't believe she's Antea, do you?" Michael asked him, his voice heavy with sarcasm once again. "Who else could she be?"

Devlin paused. It was a question that was beginning to bother him more with each passing hour.

"I do not know who she is," he finally admitted. "I only know what she is, and what she is not. She is the Mistress of that crystal, the first of four that will eventually defeat Jonar. I know this. And she is no whore to be so reviled by a man who lacked even the honor to uphold a responsibility he accepted himself at her birth. In giving her your name, you accepted her as your child." Fury burned in Devlin's heart as he remembered the pain in Chantel's eyes. "You destroyed your own honor, Michael, in your disregard for her safety. This I know. I will not forget that you left her in that fucking cell to rot beneath Jonar's hand. I will not forget that you nearly destroyed her. And God help you, but I pray I can control my rage long enough to allow you to live until you leave this castle."

He waited for no argument from the other man. Jerking open the door to the study he stalked from the room, fed up with the man's animosity, his stench of unreasoned hatred. For now, there was no choice but to tolerate it. Devlin needed answers. Michael's presence prodded the crystal in an attempt to protect Chantel from the pain her father caused. He had seen it, a dim aura beneath the shirt she wore as she faced Michael in the great hall. They needed the secrets the crystal held, the secrets that Chantel held. And he needed her now, as he had never needed anything he could remember.

* * * * *

Chantel had found her way to the gardens on her own. She had bypassed the kitchen and slipped silently out the door, fighting to hold back her tears, to hide the weakness her father — no, her stepfather — had always associated with guilt.

Guilt? She wandered through the cool shade of the low-branched trees as she made her way deeper into the middle of the garden. Where was the guilt? She remembered the dreaded whippings with his belt when she was younger, the caustic cruelty of his words as she grew up. She remembered the last time he had hit her, a full-faced slap that had so enraged James that he moved both of them from the house. Yet, she didn't remember any guilt. She didn't remember being guilty of any of the crimes he had accused her of in the past, and she sure as hell wasn't guilty now.

She stepped deeper into the lengthening shadows of an overgrown arbor and sat heavily in the padded swing that rested there. The tears fell slower now, but the betrayal still weighed heavily in her heart.

He had been willing to let her die. The sharp pain that seared her chest nearly stole her strength as her breath hitched and she fought yet more tears. He had known Jonar would catch her, had known she would die. Dear God, he had thought she would die. And all because he believed she was the reincarnation of Antea. Would even Antea have deserved that?

I love you, sister. Chantel flinched at the memory, hidden as quickly as it came. She shook her head, fighting the return of the tormenting visions, the whispered memories that were never clear.

She leaned her head against the back of the swing, not even trying to stop the flow of tears now. Rage beat at her like the wings of a wounded bird, fluttering furiously in her chest. The warmth of the crystal enfolded her, seeking to comfort her, but there was no comfort. Her mother was gone, her brother in ever-increasing danger, and now her father wasn't even her father, and she had no fucking idea who she was anymore. She was sleeping with an immortal who hadn't had sex in a thousand years, and only God knew what was coming next.

A mirthless smile crossed her lips. This destiny she had so eagerly awaited all her life was destroying every belief she had ever held.

"Destinies are strange things. Named such for a reason. Just as Fate demands the price, Destiny exacts the payment."

Her eyes flew open. Galen sat stooped in front of her, his blue eyes concerned, filled with sympathy.

Chantel sat up and attempted to wipe the tears from her face. It was a useless exercise, since more fell to replace them.

"I never cry," she whispered, lowering her head to hide the tears as she laced her fingers in her lap.

"Ah, child, tears cleanse the soul. I have cried often myself." His hand reached out, large and broad, calloused from years of labor.

Chantel looked into his eyes, her heart clenching at the warmth, the sympathetic pain in his eyes.

She shrugged heavily. "He was never a father anyway, it's really no loss I guess." She wiped her cheeks, clamping down on her furious emotions to still the trail of tears.

Breathing in deeply, she attempted to smile.

Galen pulled a clean handkerchief from his pocket and, rather than giving it to her, wiped her face himself. Tenderly, as a parent would a child.

"Please." Her hand caught at his. "I don't want to cry more."

His lips twisted into a smile edged with bitterness.

"The bastard shouldn't have been so cruel to you. And he will pay for leaving you in Jonar's hands, Chantel. Mother Earth does not allow her own to be so cruelly victimized."

"You're very nice," she whispered, her voice hoarse as she fought for control. "But Mother Earth, I am certain, has much more important things to do."

He shook his head somberly. "Don't you know, child? That crystal sets you apart for all time. You *are* her child. One of four, most beloved by her. Has she not come to you yet? Has she not shown you her joy in your return?"

Her eyes widened as shock filled her. Her hand went to where the crystal lay beneath the silk. Maternal, warm and comforting, that had been the feeling it had brought her since the moment she had placed it about her neck.

"I thought I dreamed of her," she whispered, thinking of the misty image that had come to her in Devlin's room.

"No, child." He shook his head, his hand taking hers as he patted it gently. "It was no dream. She is there for you, if you but call to her. Reach inside yourself, and you will know the way to her."

"Another riddle," she sighed wearily. "And how am I supposed to reach inside for this knowledge, when all the reaching in the world doesn't tell me the past I shared with Devlin, or how I deceived him?"

Galen braced his elbows on his knees and stared back at her intently.

"Do you believe you deceived Devlin, Chantel?" he asked her curiously.

"Can you deceive in love?" she asked him, frowning as she searched for the answers. "I feel somehow, I may have hidden something from him that he needed to know. Joshua indicates that I lied to him. I know I loved him, though." She heard the desperation in her voice, a pain she didn't understand, but knew she felt. "I loved him more than my own life."

"Then any deception you would have done would have been to save his life, perhaps?" he suggested. "You are worrying about the small things, child. You should be searching for those answers to the bigger picture."

"The secrets of the crystal." It wasn't a question. The answer hit her full force.

"Just so." He nodded. "In discerning the powers you hold, you can then open the memories of the past. The crystal holds it all, Chantel. All it has seen, and all that has been done before it, is forever saved for you to know. You just have to find it."

He rose to his feet, his head cocking to the side as though listening.

"Devlin is coming for you. He's none too pleased with Michael, nor himself at the moment." He looked down at her and smiled gently. "Be at ease, daughter. Soon, all will be well."

Before she could question him further, he was gone. He moved around the arbor, making little sound, and retreated from the gardens. Chantel breathed in deeply, wondering if she would ever stop feeling as though her own insanity was only a step away.

Then Devlin was there. He stared down at her, the midnight-black of his eyes filled with anger, lust and questions. So many questions. She swallowed tightly, staring up at him as her emotions bombarded her. How could she still the pain they were both feeling? How could she make him believe, when there weren't even memories to back her?

"God help us both," he finally whispered as he continued to stare down at her. "Because I don't even care if you were Antea."

Chantel clamped down on her fury with a self-control she was unaware she possessed. Rising to her feet she faced him with her own shattered emotions, her own betrayals.

"Be certain to let me know when it does matter to you, Devlin," she said painfully. "Because I have a feeling your belief may be all that saves any of us."

She walked quickly away from him. Torn between screaming and the tears longing to fall. They were running out of time. She could feel it, sense it with every breeze that blew across the valley, every whispered moan that sounded in the wind. And she was terrified he would never believe in time.

Chapter Twelve

∞

"God help us both, because I no longer care if you were Antea."

Chantel slammed the bedroom door behind her, Devlin's words still echoing through her head. She was breathing heavily, fighting her tears and her anger. Her fists clenched at her sides as she fought down the searing pain. He didn't believe in her, he just didn't care either way. At least her father believed *something,* even if that something was totally preposterous.

She clenched her teeth, fighting for control, then kicked at the suitcase that sat beside the door. Her eyes narrowed. Damn them all. She was sick to her back teeth of the constant suspicion, the questions, the shuttered looks. Devlin should know, even if her father—no, her stepfather, she reminded herself. Even if her stepfather didn't know better, then Devlin should have.

The throttled growl that escaped her throat surprised her as she stared at the suitcases. Her clothes, likely everything Michael could have packed, were there. Her apartment was gone. Her life was gone. What did that leave her?

Her breath hitched at the sudden realization that it left her alone. Bound to a man who suspected she was the reincarnation of a woman he had once despised, his men suspecting at any moment that she would betray them all. And the only person who knew the truth was stuck in some damned alien life unit being healed. The world had gone to hell around her and she couldn't seem to halt the events spiraling out of control.

The crystal pulsed between her breasts, a gentle reminder, a soothing indication that she was not entirely alone, nor had she ever been.

Her eyes narrowed as she gazed around the room. It didn't matter what Devlin thought. Didn't matter what any of them thought. She was the Mistress of the stone, the Mistress of this castle and that of the village beyond. This was her home, and Devlin was her warrior. He would see this in time. Until then, she had other things to see to. The knowledge hit her with a mental force that nearly had her swaying.

She saw the village, knew it was in need. She saw Daniel, his clothing scruffy, the cupboards in his home nearly empty. Shops closing. The inhabitants slowly leaving, and the land becoming saddened from neglect. She blinked, shaking her head. This had nothing to do with Devlin. Nothing to do with Jonar.

This is your heritage, Chantel. All that was yours returned to you. The ethereal voice of the maternal spirit whispered around her.

It was hers. It was her inheritance, her people. She threw one of the suitcases on the bed and opened it quickly. She had hidden within the castle long enough. She understood the dangers involved in leaving the protection of its enchanted walls. Just as she well knew the dangers if she was caught by Jonar again.

She touched the crystal at her neck. It had guided her to safety before, and it would do so again. She needed to get away. Away from the suspicion, away from Michael's hatred, and her own fears. She saw Daniel once again. The little boy flashed before her eyes, as he was at the caves, as he had been centuries before. His engaging grin, his bright eyes. A flash of sadness as he left, never to return. Where had he gone? What had happened to him?

She dragged low-cut jeans from the suitcase, and a light summer blouse that would flirt with the waistband of her jeans when worn. She dressed quickly, pulled on socks and sneakers, donned another cap and slipped from the room.

Moving carefully from the bedroom, she made her way to the large front doors and slipped soundlessly through them. It didn't take long to find the garage that held an assortment of vehicles. All with keys hanging in the ignition. A smile lit her face as she rubbed her hands together in anticipation. She jumped into the shiny red Land Rover, prayed no one noticed her leaving, and started the ignition.

Within minutes she was speeding from the castle yard and heading down the road toward the village. The crystal at her breast was calm, which meant for now, she was safe. The day was clear and warm, the village only a few miles from the castle and Chantel was eager to see it, and to see Daniel and Cammy once again.

The village entranced her as she drove through it. It was small, the brick roads narrow and flanked by brightly colored buildings. The storefronts were lined with an array of various goods — fruits, vegetables, clothes and shoes.

There were several people on the sidewalk, a horse actually passed on the opposite side of the street, followed by a black Maserati. She was charmed by the old-world atmosphere mixed with just a hint of the modern.

Chantel parked the vehicle in front of a bakery at the end of the street, pocketed the keys and then checked the amount of currency she had stuck in her pocket before leaving the castle. She hoped she had enough to purchase some of the gifts she wanted to take to Daniel and Cammy. If she could find them.

At the bakery, she learned where they lived. The short, round little woman who worked the counter informed her of the family's hard times. If she were going to see them, she thought, they could probably use a baguette of bread. Chantel purchased two when she learned the family was quite large.

"Poor *bebes*," the rotund woman had murmured as she talked about the family. "Hard times for all in these days. Very hard times."

The father, Jemaine, had been hurt the year before when a truck he had been working on fell. He still wasn't walking well. Chantel was horrified to learn that. Where was the public assistance he should have been able to draw from?

"Public assistance?" the woman exclaimed, her rapid French hard for Chantel to follow at first. "The only assistance we have is Lord Devlin, when he decides to make an appearance."

Chantel's eyes narrowed. "I see." She paid for the bread and accepted the bag the woman held out to her. "So Lord Devlin doesn't come around very often?"

"He was here last year when Kanna was sick." She smiled a bit mockingly. "They needed bread for the castle."

Chantel left the bakery feeling less than charitable toward Devlin.

She stopped at the vegetable market. There, she was greeted by the tall, thin proprietor with a smile and bow.

"Good morning, *Mademoiselle*. I would guess you are Lord Devlin's lovely guest. We are honored."

"Why, thank you." She smiled a bit hesitantly.

"Is Kanna sick again?" He frowned down at her. "Are you needing produce for the castle?"

"Um, no." She shook her head. "I was wanting to take a few things to Daniel and Cammy. Could you help me with that?"

His face fell. "Of course," he answered, though he was less than enthusiastic. "It has been rough on the family this year. Their Poppa will appreciate your help."

Chantel bought a little more than she thought she needed to, simply because the more she chose, the happier the owner appeared to become.

When she left the shop, she made a quick detour to the Land Rover, stored her purchases and began again. At this rate, she thought, she was going to run out of money soon.

Chantel's next stop was a little farther up the street. She stopped at a candy store and purchased some sweets. Once again, she was reminded of the fact that the last time anyone from the castle had been seen was while Kanna was sick. She wondered if Kanna was the cook as well as hostess.

Chantel browsed through several more shops, though she bought only a few things. She wanted to save enough currency to purchase something from the meat market.

With each stop, Chantel became angrier. It was obvious the village was suffering. The people had few jobs and few possibilities of any coming in.

The local shops were on the verge of closing down, simply because no one could buy from them. From what she learned, Devlin had most of the supplies for the castle brought in, rather than buying them from the village.

Several of the villagers worked at the castle, but only on a needed basis. Once a year, a dozen women were employed to come in and work for a week cleaning each room in the castle.

Chantel left the meat market with several roasts and quite a few things she had to say to Devlin. She had run out of money, but had told the butcher to please begin a tab for the Lord of the Castle. Someone would be in to pay it in a few days.

Excitement had glossed his rosy cheeks and his effervescent thanks had made her feel like a fraud. She was acting like the Lady of the Castle, when she feared she might end up little more than a guest for a while.

Putting these feelings aside, Chantel crossed the street, stopping in a small mercantile. There, she chose several things she wanted for herself. Among them, a lovely pair of leather boots.

Chantel arranged to have them delivered to the castle later, for a small fee. She put those purchases on a tab as well.

As she went from store to store, she realized she was likely running up a hell of a bill in Devlin's name. She shrugged philosophically. If he didn't want to pay it, then she would arrange for the payment herself. She made a brief reminder to stop in at the small bank and arrange for a transfer from her bank in the States. She also made a note to arrange for all supplies to the castle to be brought from the village. It was ridiculous. The quality of goods was exceptional—there was no excuse for Devlin to have his supplies flown in from elsewhere.

That she was taking responsibility for something that was likely not any of her business really didn't matter. The people were the responsibility of the castle and its owner. She would see to it that Devin realized that.

When she left the last store, she glanced at her watch, wincing at the time. She hoped she would have enough time to reach the small farm of Daniel and Cammy's parents before dark.

She gave a brief thought to sending a message to the castle regarding her whereabouts, but changed her mind.

Dinner wasn't for several hours yet, and there was always a chance she would be back before then.

* * * * *

Devlin stood in the entrance to his bedroom, frowning. He looked around at the scattered luggage, the one opened case, and narrowed his eyes in suspicion. Opening his senses, he felt for the lingering psychic vibrations from her, trying to discern her whereabouts. He sensed her anger, her pain and her worry. But he couldn't figure out where she had disappeared to.

He could feel her passion, heated cries of release that had his cock throbbing in instant anticipation. But no Chantel. He had been searching for her for over an hour now, and was slowly realizing that she wasn't in the castle.

He took a deep breath, exhaling with careful control as he fought to rein in his temper. She couldn't have been taken from the castle grounds, so that only left one answer. For some unknown, scatterbrained reason, she had decided to leave on her own.

He stalked back to the great hall to find that the other members of the castle had assembled there as well, each of them having searched a designated area and coming up empty-handed.

"Where the hell did she go, then?" Devlin's enraged voice echoed through the room as the warriors, Michael and Kanna stood before him.

They had searched every area of the castle and still had not found a trace of her.

"I told you it wasn't a good idea to leave her alone," Michael spoke up smugly. "She always did find trouble when you gave her half a chance. Just as you often told me Antea could do."

Devlin glanced over at him. The other man looked more pleased than concerned with exactly how vulnerable Chantel was outside the castle walls. Devlin closed his eyes, pinching the bridge of his nose with his fingers.

"Regardless of what Antea was capable of, we still have the problem that Chantel is missing." He emphasized the names for reasons that even he was not certain of. "Now, I want her found."

"There's a Land Rover missing from the garage, Devlin," Shane spoke up. "One of the workers could have taken it, but it's one of the newer models and they aren't prone to mess with those."

"Where the hell would she have gone?" His gaze went to Michael.

Michael could only shake his head, causing Devlin's frustration to rise.

"I told you she would be a problem," Michael reminded him.

"We've searched every end of the castle, Devlin," Kanna told him. "She's not here. She had to have been the one to take the vehicle."

"Damn." He gritted his teeth as he fought to hold back the more vile curses rising to his lips. "Kanna, get on the phone. Call Montrose in town and see if anyone has seen her there. If she's there, then Montrose will know."

Kanna nodded, but before she could move more than a few feet, the doors to the castle opened and Chantel stepped into the great hall.

Chantel met the accusing stares directed at her with a lift of one delicate eyebrow.

The warriors, Kanna and her father stood looking at her with varying degrees of frowning displeasure.

"Am I late for dinner already?" She shifted the bags she carried and moved farther into the room. "I assumed I was early."

Chantel faced the occupants of the hall with a lifted brow. Kanna, Shanar and Derek appeared more amused than angry. Devlin and Michael were furious though.

"Just where have you been?" Devlin stood looking down at her coldly.

Oh, she really didn't like that dictatorial tone or the look on his handsome, aristocratic face.

"I've been shopping." She lifted her bag as though he hadn't already seen it. "Something that's done very rarely around here, evidently."

Chantel waited on Devlin to pick up the clue. She wondered if it was just a male thing that he ignored her last statement.

"Do you think this is a game, Chantel?" He frowned down at her, crossing his arms over his chest.

Lord of all he surveys, or so he thinks. She would have laughed if the angry glint in his eyes weren't so bright. This was a man looking for a fight. That was okay, because she was damned well in the mood to give it to him.

"Is what a game, Devlin?" Chantel tilted her head as she watched him curiously. "Shopping? No, I don't consider it a game. I take it very seriously, actually."

From the corner of her eye, she caught a glimpse of the other warriors turning away. Was Shane fighting a grin? She didn't imagine he knew how to grin until now. She wondered if any of them knew how to laugh. She had seen very little in the way of laughter in the castle since coming here.

"By the way," she stated as she set her bags on the floor and moved further into the room. "I have some deliveries coming tomorrow afternoon. I'll need to borrow enough money until I can have some transferred to the bank in town."

She imagined she could hear him grinding his teeth, as his jaw bunched and his brows lowered even further.

"The bank in town is too small to carry many funds," he informed her tightly. "I'll take care of any money you transfer."

Chantel tilted her head thoughtfully, considering the evasive look in his eyes.

"I don't think so, Devlin." She smiled graciously as she said it, though she was far from feeling it. "I've already discussed it with the bank manager. I'll have money available by the end of the week."

Complete silence reigned. Evidently, few people had the nerve to turn down any offer he made.

When no other comment was made, she faced them with a bright smile and turned to Kanna.

"Is there anyone who can get the rest of my packages from the Land Rover and bring them up to my room?"

"I'll get them," Shane offered, heading out the door. "Just leave the other stuff sitting there and I'll get those as well."

Chantel watched him leave the room and then turned back to Devlin.

"Was there anything else you wanted? If not, I'll go upstairs and get ready for dinner."

"There are several things I want," he bit out. "I want you to stay within the castle grounds at all times. And no more sneaking off to town to shop."

He made shopping sound like a curse.

Chantel narrowed her eyes, her lips thinning with anger at his imperious tone. There was nothing that grated on her nerves worse than being ordered to do anything.

Chantel understood the safety issues, but she also understood her own power to detect the danger when it was coming closer. She had heeded the warning of the crystal and headed home earlier, just in case Jonar was watching her closer than she suspected. She wasn't a fool, nor was she Devlin's servant to be ordered in such a manner.

"I will go shopping when and where I please," she informed him softly. "And I refuse to argue with you in front of everyone. If you want to fight, then at least have the decency to do so in private."

"Uh, Chantel." She turned to her father's protest with surprise. Strange, she thought, she had expected anger from him rather than the tolerant amusement she heard in his voice. Another game?

"Perhaps a little discretion on your own part wouldn't be amiss," he suggested softly.

187

"I will agree with you in this instance," Devlin bit out, evidently intent on having his say now. That suited Chantel fine. Now was as good a time as any to state her position.

"Discretion would be fine," she agreed. "If I weren't already so angry with you to begin with." She turned back to Devlin in anger. "I just came from a village of over four hundred people who are suffering from no jobs, no income and little food. It appears even the landowner can't lower himself to hire, nor to buy from them and provide jobs. He sends out for whatever he needs."

His expression tightened, his eyes going flat and cold.

"The village is doing fine," he informed her coldly. "They are self-supporting."

Chantel's eyes widened, then narrowed at the unfeeling tone of his voice. It pierced her heart, a physical pain growing into a fury she could have never imagined

"They are poor. They have no health care, no options and no resources to leave. Haven't you noticed how few young people are left in the village? They leave as soon as they can to find jobs. It was your responsibility to care for my people."

Her angry outburst was met by a surprised, suspicious narrowing of Devlin's gaze. "Your people?"

She raked her fingers through her hair, fighting for control.

"The people," she amended, feeling like a coward, yet unable to explain her feeling of belonging there. "They are your responsibility, Devlin."

Clueless, she thought, just absolutely clueless.

"The village is doing fine," Devlin told her again. "I can't afford to have it grow, Chantel. Being who we are, that would generate too much damned interest."

He crossed his arms over his chest, staring down at her implacably. He watched her with cool interest, as though testing her, pushing her. She hated that feeling.

"No excuse." She shook her head. "If you feel that way, why don't you at least buy from the grocer and butcher in town? Why don't you employ more of the villagers on the castle grounds? All I've seen is a gardener who can't possibly keep up with it all. You need at least a dozen maids here, as well as a cook."

Chantel faced him furiously, uncaring that Kanna, Derek and Michael watched them with varying degrees of emotion. What he had allowed was criminal. It would continue no longer. Not as long as she had a say in it. And she did have a say in it. Her hands braced on her hips as she tensed, preparing to fight.

"Kanna does fine," Devlin argued. He looked ready to strangle her.

"Actually, Chantel's right," Kanna broke in, her voice holding a trace of amusement. "We could use more help around here."

"We tried that," Devlin reminded her, his voice sharp. "Remember Calista? The thief?"

"Still no excuse." Chantel shook her head at the pitiful excuses they were coming up with. "I refuse to allow this to continue, Devlin. End of argument. I'm going to get ready for dinner now." She turned, heading for the stairs.

"Chantel." Devlin's voice, quiet and somehow deadly, stopped her in her tracks. "You aren't the Lady of the Castle here, don't try to make unwanted changes."

The flush on his face, the fire in his eyes, would have sent anyone else running. She wondered a bit distantly why she wasn't frightened.

Instead, she moved closer to him, until her face was directly below his own, their lips only inches apart.

"Wrong," she snarled, suddenly more certain of herself than she had been in years. "I am the Lady of this Castle, and we both damn well know it."

She pouted a perfect whisper kiss toward his lips and then turned away.

"By the way," she called out as she reached the door to the hallway, "I have some people coming by for jobs day after tomorrow. Kanna, I'll need your help getting a list together concerning what sort of help we need."

Chantel disappeared as she turned the corner, leaving the great hall in complete silence.

Devlin turned slowly to Michael. Temper simmered dangerously close to the surface. He was aware of his fists clenching and unclenching in fury.

"Not my fault." Michael shook his head, his expression superior. "I warned you she would be nothing but trouble."

"Is that what you call it?" Devlin questioned him sarcastically and then turned to his men.

Derek was still standing at the doorway, his own eyes narrowed thoughtfully.

"Derek," Devlin snapped, bringing the other man's gaze slowly back to his own.

"I don't understand it, either." He shook his head. "Be damned, Antea hated the village."

Exactly. Devlin had been thinking the same thing. Antea had been quite adamant that if he was going to bring in help from the village, instead of Paris, then she insisted they do their work where she didn't have to see them.

Antea had detested the village and anyone or anything from it.

"Well, it would appear Chantel doesn't feel the same," Kanna spoke up softly. "What do you intend to do about that, Devlin?"

Devlin shook his head. What the hell was he supposed to do? Chantel had been right. She was Lady of the Castle and they all knew it. There was something right, natural, about knowing that. Accepting it.

"Maybe we should keep Joshua's rooms off limits," Derek suggested with a grunt. "He'll be pissed when he comes out of stasis."

"If I have to suffer, then damned if he won't as well," Devlin bit out furiously. "He should have been more careful, as I warned him to be."

Derek shrugged. "Joshua won't like it, Devlin. He's still pissed over that dagger Calista stole."

"And I don't blame him," Michael bit out. "You're letting the bitch control you, Devlin."

Devlin went still. He could feel the fury gathering, building inside him and he was determined to control it. But he would be damned if he would let Michael stand there, within Chantel's home, and be so abusive toward her.

Glassware rattled at the bar across the room as he approached Michael. Violence wrapped about them all as his powers nearly surged past his control.

"Show such disrespect to her again, Michael, and you'll regret it. While within this castle, you will treat her with all due respect. Do I make myself clear?"

Michael stared at him for the space of three seconds before his eyes dropped.

"You'll regret this," Michael said hoarsely, angrily. "But if you are so intent on your own destruction, then so be it. A belt applied to her backside might be your only recourse now."

Devlin raked his hands through his hair in frustration. Dammit, his life was going to hell. What the hell was he supposed to do with Chantel? She was making him crazy. And Michael wasn't helping matters.

Devlin wanted to hit something. He wanted to follow her up to that room, throw her on the bed and show her why she was Lady of the Castle. Because she belonged to him.

"If I were you, I'd establish my authority early," Derek spoke up, the Irish lilt in his voice deepening as he fought his laughter. "She showed a little bit too much spunk, if you ask me."

"Perhaps Derek's right." Shanar slapped him on the shoulder as he walked back into the room. "Establish your control now, while you still can."

Devlin stayed silent. His fists were clenched, his muscles felt strained from the force he was exerting to keep from going after Chantel. They weren't helping any.

"Dinner will be ready as usual," Kanna said softly as she passed him, moving from the room. "Perhaps the steak would be best for you to chew on, rather than Chantel. She looked ready to bite back."

Chapter Thirteen

ॐ

She was like a steady, enduring flame. Graceful, moving about the castle as though she had always been a part of it, as though she had been the soul that was missing from it all these centuries. As though she had been the part of his soul, missing all his life. It was a strange feeling. He was furious that she was changing his world so quickly, so abruptly. He was on edge, awaiting yet another attack from Jonar, certain that her headstrong determination would result in disastrous consequences.

And her very stubbornness aroused him as nothing else ever had. It had him so damned aroused, needing her so desperately, he was certain he would explode from the waiting. He watched her through dinner. His eyes narrowed on her, his cock throbbing in a painful reminder of its need to bury inside her. The tension grew thicker as the meal progressed, the silence heavier, and all Devlin could think about was fucking her until she screamed for mercy.

When the dishes were finally cleared away, he rose to his feet and moved to her intently. She watched him, her emerald eyes glittering in anger, in her own arousal. She wore those damned jeans again. They hugged her hips and legs like a second skin, a small line of bare skin showing between the material of the jeans and the silk of her short blouse. Beneath the shirt, he watched her nipples peak behind the covering of silk and the fragile lace of her bra.

"We need to talk." He gripped her arm, steering her through the great hall, the kitchen and into the dark expanse of the gardens outside. Moonlight washed over her, making the white-blonde of her hair seem ethereal, almost unreal. Her emerald eyes were dark, suspicious, as she glanced up at him from beneath lowered lids.

"I won't change my mind about the castle," she bit out as he drew her into the sheltered copse of low trees. The branches interlaced with each other, creating a dense, protective canopy.

"Fuck the castle," he growled, turning her to face him. "Do you have any idea the risk you took today, Chantel? How easily Jonar could have taken you? Or even the Guardians, were that their intent? Have you no care at all for the consequences of your actions?"

He was furious. The memory of the bruises that covered her body the night he had found her, the knowledge that Jonar would inflict more pain than she could believe possible, flirting with his fears. Damn her, she seemed intent on giving her enemies the perfect opportunity to take her.

"I was safe." She crossed her arms beneath her breasts, facing him with such determined stubbornness that he wanted to shake some sense into her. She was too headstrong, too intent on giving Jonar the chance he needed to kill her.

"You are never safe, Chantel," he bit out, his hands moving to grip her arms. "Don't you understand that? Didn't you learn that lesson in that godforsaken desert while his men had you?"

She took a deep breath, her tongue licking over her lips, leaving those full curves glistening in the dim light that filtered through the trees. His cock jerked, remembering the feel of that moist, playful tongue along his most sensitive flesh. Damn her, she was making him crazy.

Her hands braced against his chest, her fingers curling against him as she shivered beneath his hands.

"I have to do what needs to be done." She shook her head, staring up at him imploringly. "This must be done, Devlin. The village is dying."

"Better the village than you." It was all he could do not to shake her. It was all he could do not to tear the clothes from her body and fuck her into a screaming, quivering climax. Or would it be him screaming and quivering? He was starving for the taste of her.

"You aren't being rational about this," she protested heatedly, pushing against his chest. "You can't let so many people suffer. It isn't right."

Devlin shook his head, his fingers itching to caress her skin. He wanted to tear that shirt from her, rip the lace of her bra and immerse himself in the full mounds of her breasts. He couldn't remember ever being so horny in his life. In centuries. He had never wanted anything more than he wanted her at this moment.

As he stared down at her, her eyes widened. "Oh no, you don't." Her hands pressed harder against his chest. "You can't win this argument with sex, Devlin."

"There is no argument," he growled. "You will cancel these employment interviews. That's all there is to it. At least until Jonar is destroyed." That should give him plenty of time to change her mind.

She shook her head slowly, her lips tilting into a mocking grin. "Sorry, babe, it's not going to work. Why don't you tell me why you are so determined to stay locked alone in this castle?"

Because alone was less of a risk.

"It is too dangerous," he growled. "Jonar could convince anyone. Anyone, Chantel, to make an attempt on your life. He could use any of those people against you."

She breathed in deeply. "It's a chance we have to take. I won't hide this way, Devlin. Even for you. And I will not see that village neglected any longer."

He stilled. She said the words so easily, as though her life meant so little.

"And if he takes you from me?" he asked her tightly. "If, by your own hand, you allow your own destruction…"

Something exploded inside him. A sudden searing knowledge that somehow, she had sacrificed herself once before. That she had died to save others. Had left him alone, drifting...

An agonized howl echoed through his mind as the past fought to merge with the present. His heart ripped from his chest, leaving him lost, bleeding with sorrow before the mists rushed into place once again, hiding the truth, dimming the pain. But nothing could steal the suspicion, the certainty that he had loved her, loved her with all his soul and that she had sacrificed herself.

His teeth clenched, his hands trembled as he fought to bring the memory forward, but it was as elusive as all the others. Only that knowledge remained, with nothing to prove the truth of it.

"Not again." His voice was ragged, despairing as he jerked her to him. "Do you understand me, Chantel? Not again."

His lips covered hers. Hard, sure, intent on convincing her, forcing her to realize that he would not allow it again. His tongue pressed between her lips as she gasped out in surprise, tangling with hers, drawing the heat and passion from her as she moaned against his lips.

She arched into his body, her hands pushing at his chest as his smoothed down her back, gripped the sweet curves of her ass and lifted her closer to the painful erection between his thighs.

Hands that once pressed against his chest now moved to his shoulders, then his head. Her hands gripped his hair, her fingers clenching in the strands like a lazy cat flexing its claws against his scalp. The erotic feeling had his body tightening in anticipation.

She pulled herself tighter against him, moaning against his kiss. She was a living flame in his arms, and she was burning him alive.

Chantel's head tipped back as Devlin's lips moved hungrily from hers to the curve of her neck, then to the upper swells of her breasts. She could feel the heated rasp of his tongue as it stroked over her skin. The scrape of his teeth, the velvet touch of his lips. The heated caress echoed through her body, hardening her nipples, making her vagina flame in need.

"I want you here, now." He whispered the words into the valley of her breasts, his moist breath searing her with the lightning stroke of pleasure that suffused her body.

His hands moved to the front of her jeans, his fingers working at the button then pulling the zipper down.

"Stand still." His voice was hoarse as she twisted against him.

Chantel trembled as he knelt before her, her breathing rough as she fought to draw in much needed oxygen as she stared down at him. He drew her jeans down, catching the waistband of her thong as he slid it over her hips.

A moan broke from her chest as she felt his breath on the swollen lips of her cunt. The soft, heated caress had the thick juices easing from the entrance of her vagina, preparing her, heating her for his possession.

"So pretty," he whispered, placing a kiss on her thigh, so close, yet so far away from her aching flesh.

His hands moved along the backs of her thighs, then cupped her buttocks once again. His fingers massaged the flesh as her hands gripped his shoulders, desperate for something to hold onto as her knees weakened beneath his touch.

"Devlin, please," she begged, her thighs clenching as his tongue probed at the small line between her leg and her cunt.

"Do you have any idea the things I want to do to you?" he growled as he laid his cheek on her thigh, his breath wafting over her sensitive cunt. "I want to taste every inch of you, Chantel. Fuck you until you're screaming for mercy." His hands clenched at her ass, spreading the soft cheeks apart slowly. "I want to take you in every way a man can take a woman."

Chantel tensed as his fingers moved along the shallow valley of her buttocks. Her hands clenched on his shoulders as his finger slid against the damp heat of her cunt before it pressed against the small entrance to her anus. She gasped, feeling it part the soft tissue, the tip of his finger entering her heatedly.

"Devlin." She didn't know if it was fear or excitement that had her whispering his name.

"You would scream my name then, Chantel. And not in pain, but in a pleasure you could never imagine." His tongue stroked along the slit of her pussy as she rose to her tiptoes in shock.

His finger slid to its first knuckle inside the hot channel of her anus. Part pain, part intense pleasure, seared the virgin tissue with its forbidden eroticism. Chantel was shocked at the response of her body. Heat whipped through her, clenching her womb, catching her breath on a shocked gasp as his finger caressed, thrust lightly, pushing her deeper into the vortex of sensuality that she never knew existed.

"Devlin…" She couldn't find the strength to stand straight on her own. Her knees trembled. Her body shuddered. Only his arms held her upright.

"I want you there, Chantel," he growled against her cunt, the sound vibrating against her clit. "I want to take you, fuck you in a way you have never imagined. Show you a pleasure that will sear your senses." His tongue stroked her clit.

Chantel was lost. A soft scream escaped her throat as she exploded. Her release spilled to his lips as they moved to the entrance of her vagina. Tasting her, drawing the heated juices against his tongue, humming his approval against the swollen lips of her cunt. Slowly his finger eased from her, his tongue stroking the liquid silk that spilled from her body as she shuddered in his arms.

"Come to me, Chantel." He drew her down, to her knees, turning her, his hands smoothing over her buttocks as he placed her before him.

Her jeans were bunched above her knees now, as he pulled them only partially up. It was obvious he meant to bind her legs together, and she shook beneath his touch at the thought. Uncertainty lent an edge to her arousal, the feminine fear of the unknown made her tremble beneath his light caress.

"Moonlight becomes you." He pushed the blouse farther up her back, his mouth trailing kisses to the cleft of her behind. "Your body is like a silken dream, Chantel. A feast for the senses that I want only to gorge myself on."

She heard the zipper rasp as he loosened his pants.

"So pretty before me. Giving to me. Tempting me."

"If you don't take me I'm going to kill you." Her fingers bit into the grass beneath her.

His chuckle was dark, strained, as he lifted her hips.

"Mine." His cock nudged at her anus, then slid to the spasming cunt awaiting him below. He surged inside her.

Chantel's back arched as a strangled scream tore from her throat. Thick and hard, his cock thrust past the tight muscles of her vagina, searing her with the abrupt entrance and the violent pleasure that tore through her.

His cock throbbed inside her, each hard pulse of blood that raged through the thickened muscle echoed in the depths of her cunt. She gasped for breath as he lodged inside her, his hands clenching on her hips as his growl of pleasure washed over her.

"Never," he bit out. "Never can I remember knowing such pleasure, Chantel. Only in my dreams. Only in my dreams have I known this."

He moved, dragging the thick erection from her gripping pussy.

"Damn. So tight, Chantel. So tight and hot." He surged inside her again, as she thrust back against him. The sound of wet flesh and desperate moans echoing around them.

Chantel fought for breath as she tightened her cunt on his pulsing cock. He stretched her, burning the tender tissue with a pleasure-pain that threatened to drive her insane. Her hips swayed, her buttocks pressing into his loins as the head of his cock caressed the deepest reaches of her vagina.

"I want you to scream." He came over her, one hand braced on the ground beside her, the other moving to the straining bud of her clitoris.

Her breath caught as he began to move. Long, deep powerful strokes as he began to fuck her fiercely. His fingers massaged her clit, sending sensation after sensation streaking to her womb, gathering strength, then surging through her body.

The muscles in her stomach tightened as the hard strokes set her cunt on fire, burning her with pleasure. She jerked beneath him, fighting to breathe, to survive the onslaught of his possession.

"Take all of me," he growled, his lips at her neck, his teeth raking her flesh as he nipped at it erotically. "All of me, Chantel."

Deeper, harder. Her legs tightened, her cunt gripping the powerful cock as it threatened to explode her sanity. Pleasure built inside her until it was a ravening beast howling for release. She cried out his name, and still he drove her higher. She begged, pleaded, and still he held her back even as he kept the deep, hard thrusts powering inside her.

Then his fingers covered her clit, pressed, rotated, and the world exploded around her. Her screams were torn from her throat as she felt his cock pump inside her, harder, deeper, then the hard, hot jets of his seed began to pulse inside her quaking pussy. She screamed his name. She screamed for her own sanity as her climax ripped through her stomach, her chest, her soul, flinging her outside of her own body in a kaleidoscope of color and light.

Thankfully, breathing was an instinctive response. When she could no longer find the strength to cry out his name, scream out her pleasure, still, her body breathed. When the only thing that kept her upright was his arm gripping her hips, still she lived.

His cock was buried tight inside her, still hard, still flexing in pleasure as her upper body collapsed slowly to the grass beneath her. She shivered as the pulsing staff slid from her body. His hands caressing, soothing, as her lower body crumpled to the ground as well.

She could only lie there, exhausted, astounded, as he rolled her to her back and adjusted her clothing. She was lost in a sea of emotion, of sensation.

"Ah, love, best you aid me in fixing your clothing, else your father will find you in a way he may never recover from."

Frowning, she opened her eyes. Her breath nearly stopped in her lungs, the world tilting, as she blinked up at Devlin in amazement. It was Devlin. A much younger, softer Devlin. His hair was longer, though his body was just as hard, just as broad. Sunlight caressed them, rather than moonlight. The intertwining branches of the overhead trees sheltered them.

"I'm frightened." She wanted the darkness back. Wanted to return to what she remembered, rather than a time she had forgotten.

He touched her cheek, his black eyes filling with emotion as he stared down at her.

"I'll protect you always. Without you, my Lady, I am nothing. I am lost, and my life without meaning. I would surely surrender every breath in my body, should aught take you from me."

Her breath caught in her throat.

Promise me, Father. The words echoed through her head. When the time is at hand, swear to me you will...

"No." She closed her eyes, her heart racing out of control, fear striking a blow to her body that caused her to flinch in dread. "No. Not by my hand. I did not will this. I did not." Yet she had. Whatever Devlin had lost within his own memories, whatever she had lost herself, she had willed.

"Chantel." His voice was harder now, husky with satiation, yet hoarse with fear. "Dammit, Chantel, open your eyes this instant."

She blinked up at him. Her throat was tight with unshed tears, her heart aching, bruised. What had she done so long ago? And what now would her punishment be?

He watched her carefully, closely, and she could only shake her head, could only fight the pain that bloomed inside her body.

"I love you," she whispered. "I have always loved you."

Chapter Fourteen

ஐ

She wasn't Antea. Devlin watched as Chantel moved through the great hall, greeting prospective employees, her movements graceful, her smile gracious. The knowledge didn't just hit him. It wasn't a blinding impact or a sudden realization. It was just there. As though he had always known it.

He, Shanar and Derek watched from different points of the room, ready to protect her if need be. She had assured him the crystal would protect her. That should danger come, then she would be aware of it. He prayed to God she was right.

At the moment, his thoughts were less on danger and more on the delicate sway of her hips, the thrust of her breasts beneath the midnight cotton of her shirtdress. He wanted to see her in silk, in satin, in creations designed specifically for her beauty. He was appalled at the worn look of her department store clothing, considering the income he knew her father generated.

Beneath the dress, he knew she wore a matching thong. He had seen it lying out on the bed as she showered. Her lacy bra was the same dark blue that framed the upper curves of her creamy breasts perfectly. His eyelids lowered as his cock throbbed.

Damn the aggravation of Jonar, Michael and whatever damned curse was working against them. No sooner had she whispered her declaration to him the night before than Michael's voice had called out to them through the gardens. Imperative, furious, he had called out Chantel's name, demanding her presence.

Unwilling to allow her to face the fanatical anger of her stepparent, he had sent her through the French doors of his office, with instructions to go on to bed. Exhaustion had lined her face as she had nodded quickly, following his instructions with no hint of an argument, which surprised him. When he finally dragged his own weary body to bed, she was sleeping. When he would have tasted her sweet flesh once again that morning, an imperative knock at their bedroom door had sounded.

He suppressed his growl as frustration ate at him. There had to be three dozen hopeful applicants moving about the hall, casting wary, curious glances his way, or watching Chantel with a gleam of speculation. And he didn't even want to think of the men that crowded around her as she spoke. Tall, mortal men. Men eager to hear the soft cadence of her voice, to look into the beauty of her eyes.

His fists clenched as he fought the monstrous jealousy. He watched her closely, knew her gentle humor and soft smiles were merely a part of her warmth, and not meant to tease or to tempt. But they tempted him. Teased him with the memory of the hot clasp of her tight pussy, her whispered moans of rising pleasure, and pleas for release.

"I can't believe you're allowing this." Michael stepped to his side, watching Chantel with dark anger.

"Don't you have an agency to run?" Devlin asked him curiously. "I'm certain Jonar or other factions of Blackthorne are causing havoc somewhere in the world right now."

The other man tensed. "Are you asking me to leave?"

Devlin narrowed his eyes, never taking his gaze from Chantel as she interviewed the prospective employees. Finally, he nodded thoughtfully.

"Yes, Michael, I believe I am. This situation is stressful enough for Chantel. She does not need the added weight of your hatred." He watched as she cast a wary glance at her father, then at him.

Devlin allowed the corner of his lips to lift. The only way he knew to reassure her. Smiles were not common within the castle, and he knew few times when he had been tempted to do so. But now, he felt compelled to give her that small acknowledgement that all was well.

He saw the surprise that lightened her eyes, the easing of the fear in her gaze. Her stepfather frightened her. Why, he wondered? He was tempted to ease the control on the powers he possessed and to open himself to the knowledge. Michael would have few blocks against the immense strength of Devlin's awareness, and yet he hesitated. He had carefully reined in his powers centuries ago, realizing the information that poured in affected his control, and his ability to maintain a distance between himself and those who walked on the periphery of his life.

"She's careful, because she knows I'm watching her," Michael bit out. "If I leave…"

"Then she will be herself, freer," Devlin finished for him. "I have no doubts regarding her, Michael, but Chantel must be relaxed, else the crystal will never reveal itself to her."

His eyes narrowed as one young man pressed closer to her. He tensed, immediately dropping his guard, sending out a psychic shield between Chantel and the young man as his mind delved into the other's. He flinched, in shame, in anger. Hunger drove the boy, but not the hungers of the flesh. A hunger to survive, to prosper. A mind reaching out, desperate to learn and to grow. To feed the small family he had taken responsibility for.

"You are making a mistake." Michael's voice fairly shook with his anger.

Devlin shook his head, his mind still occupied by the glimpse of the boy. He liked to build things, to create with his hands. Devlin sighed. There were a few repairs that perhaps the castle needed after all. Frustration ate at him. He didn't want to get involved in the lives of these people. That would make them much too vulnerable to Jonar's cruelty.

"It is my mistake to make, Michael. I'll arrange for Shanar to fly you back to the States tomorrow."

"I don't need Shane to fly me anywhere." Michael's voice was filled with fury. "We can't afford to lose you, Devlin. You are all that stands between the world and Jonar."

Devlin turned to the other man slowly, fighting an anger that surged hot and bright inside him.

"No, Michael, Chantel is all that protects the earth now. She is the Mistress of the power the earth gives only once. Only once, Michael. Whoever the hell Antea was, she wasn't the Mistress, and she wasn't Chantel. And I will no longer allow your unjust hatred to affect her. I have had enough. Now prepare to leave her home, and to return to your own."

Michael paled. His eyes widened in surprise, then narrowed in fury.

"You will regret this, Devlin. You'll see. Only my presence controls her."

"Only your presence hampers her ability to find her happiness," Devlin corrected, fighting to keep his tone low, his power in control. "You will do as I say now."

Devlin sent out a silent call to Shane. Within seconds, the large warrior stood at his side, watching Michael coolly.

"I'll expect you to be ready at dawn." The Viking's voice was graveled, strained. Though Devlin noted it, he said nothing.

Michael's nostrils flared as he breathed in roughly. He looked from Shane to Devlin then turned on his heel and stalked from the hall.

"He is more trouble than he appears," Shane remarked softly as they watched him leave the room.

"Not for much longer," Devlin growled. "Make sure he's on that damned plane if you have to carry him aboard yourself. I want him the hell out of this castle."

"He was trouble in his first life, and not much better now," Shane grunted. "At least he doesn't have Antea this time to aid him in his schemes."

Devlin flinched. His body went still, tight, at the sudden flashing memory of Michael in his Aaron incarnation held by chains of magic, broken, despairing. Beside him, Antea sniveled in fear, her eyes wide, pleading.

If you haven't the stomach for it, then I will…" His own words drifted through his mind. *I'll find her, Galen, and I'll kill her.*

Agony seared his soul, stopping the breath in his chest, clenching about his heart as Chantel's screams echoed in his head. His head whipped around as reality and vision collided. She stood in a ray of sunlight that speared through the high windows on each side of the fireplace. Her hair glistened, her sweet smile filled with warmth as she spoke to another woman. A shy little blonde who kept casting him curious glances.

Sarah. The name ripped through his consciousness. Her expression calm and gentle, confusion and understanding in her eyes as she lay in his arms. Arms that held her not as a lover, or even as a brother. The arms of a man who looked into her green eyes, and saw only the emerald gaze of another.

His heart was pounding in fear, rage and anger. Conflicting emotions tore through him as the vision slowly receded. Devlin shook his head, fighting for more, trying desperately to bring back the memory that refused to be called forth. But he held what little had come to him. It was there, a part of him, as rich and as clear as if it had happened just that day.

"Devlin?" Derek stood beside him as well now, watching him in concern.

He looked from one man to another. His eyes narrowed as anger washed through him yet again. "Joshua is Guardian. Enchantment does not touch him."

He fought to breathe through the force of his fury.

Derek shrugged. "We all know this."

"He has memories we have been denied," Devlin growled. "She is not Antea. She is Chantel. She was Chantel, and by God, that cursed sorcerer and that bastard half-breed Guardian have hidden the knowledge of her from us somehow."

He looked to Chantel, seeing the concern on her face as she looked to him. Sadness. A knowledge hidden—not now, but then. His fists clenched. Remnants of deceit pulsed in the air around him, threads of whispered cries, a promise, a searing passion, an agonizing loss. The memories of the emotions, if not the memories themselves, were there. And Chantel was the center of it all.

"We have a cook, an assistant, eight housemaids on rotation, a dozen people for the outside work, carpenters, masons, and plumbers. I've been checking around the castle and there's quite a bit of work to do. I believe we'll be able to employ most of the village for quite a while, getting everything together…"

The door crashed closed. Chantel pivoted, going instinctively into a defensive stance and staying there when she saw Devlin watching her furiously. Surprise sped through her system. He had been perfectly civil, if a bit aloof during the interview process. When he had asked to speak with her in his office, she had expected a bit less than rage.

"Too many?" she asked archly.

He stood across the room, his arms crossed over his broad chest, his feet planted apart as though entering battle. His expression was dark, forbidding.

"Where is Galen?" The question was more confusing than his anger.

"I don't know. He's your sorcerer," she pointed out. "I think it's your job to keep up with him, not mine."

Silence filled the room, a shiver working up her spine as she felt the magic, the pure power that seemed to wrap around them. She stared into his eyes, black pits of first fury, then slowly dawning knowledge. His expression went blank for a second, despair, then confusion racing across his face.

"I loved you," he whispered hoarsely. "I was wed to you. You were my wife. Tell me, Chantel, why that bastard sorcerer stole your memory from me."

Fear washed over her. Her lips dried with it as phantom fingers of electricity seemed to work over her scalp, as her heart began to race out of control. Her skull tingled and for a moment, just the barest moment, the fog inside her mind seemed to shift.

Promise me, Father. The words echoed around her as remorse tore through her soul.

"I'm not sure…" But she suspected.

As she spoke she felt power course around her. The emanations were barely felt, yet thick and strong. Like velvet cuffs, they sought to entrap her mind, to search her secrets. Instantly the crystal flared to life. Warmth shielded her, protected her.

"Stop," she bit out. "Do you think I'm lying to you?"

"I don't know," he growled, advancing on her now. "But I have a very bad feeling, Chantel, that somewhere in the past, you deceived me once. I would know if you would do so again."

"I won't deceive you." She shook her head, fighting her own knowledge that she had indeed held something back during that misty past. "I swear to you, Devlin, I won't."

Promise me, Father. The words whispered around her again.

"Even in an attempt to protect me, you would not deceive me?" he asked her, his voice silky smooth and all the more dangerous for it.

Chantel stopped. Instinctively she wanted to deny his suspicion that she would deceive him for any reason, and yet she couldn't. The words wouldn't come to her lips, wouldn't give voice to the lie she knew they were.

"I would protect you with everything that I am," she finally whispered, knowing beyond a shadow of a doubt that if it did mean her life, she would protect him.

"No!" His voice rose as his hands clamped on her shoulders. He stared down at her, fury seeming to overwhelm him. "You will not, ever, Chantel. Never will you sacrifice yourself for me, do you understand this?"

She licked her lips nervously, her hand rising to touch his cheek as she stared up at him. His expression wavered as tears filled her eyes. "And what of you?" she asked him softly. "Would you swear the same? That you will not sacrifice yourself for me, or because of my death?"

He paled. Slowly the blood seemed to drain from his face as a shadow of knowledge washed over his expression.

"My very soul would wither away to dust if I lost what I have found with you," he whispered in bleak agony. "My soul did wither away, Chantel. And now, I would know what black magic Galen practiced against me to cause me to forget it."

He released her, moving away from her before turning back to face her, his eyelids lowered until only a sliver of the black color could be glimpsed beneath his black lashes.

"What have you remembered? I will have no more of your deceit, wife. I do not need your protection. I do not need your sacrifice." He looked so outraged, so furious that she would have, in some way, attempted to protect him. She would have found such male pride amusing if her heart wasn't breaking.

"I haven't remembered anything, Devlin." She pushed her fingers wearily through her hair. "Whispered words, a glimpse here and there of things that make no sense, but nothing concrete."

"It's the same for me." He blew out roughly. "Joshua should be out of stasis soon. I suspect he remembers well everything that happened during that time. I'll find out why he allowed me to drift in this manner, unknowing…"

"I don't think he did," Chantel broke in, seeing the dark retribution in his gaze. "Joshua tried, Devlin. No matter his faults, I truly believe he tried, and whatever enchantment holds this castle, and the rest of you in the dark, kept him from telling you."

A silent snarl lifted his lips as his gaze went over her once again.

"This will continue no longer," he bit out. "There are many things that will continue no longer within this castle, such deception being only one of them. The second is the state of your clothing. Remove that rag from your body before I tear it off. Wear one of my shirts, or borrow some decent clothing from Kanna until the designer arrives tomorrow. I'll have that trash Michael allowed you to wear burned."

The abrupt shift of topic had her head whirling. Chantel looked down at her dress, and saw nothing wrong with it. Admittedly, it wasn't silk, but it was fairly new.

"What the hell is wrong with my clothes?" She propped her fists on her hips, more than upset at the insult.

"The seams are crooked and the material inferior. As Lady of this castle, you will not dress like a peasant." He crossed his arms over his chest, his expression disapproving.

Tendrils of psychic awareness filled the room, his power wrapping around her, pulling at her. Chantel shook her head, the feeling that Devlin rarely lost his control long enough to let that power free in such a way, filling her. His anger was a primitive, dark force, all the more dangerous for the very fact that it was escaping in waves of psychic energy.

"My clothes are fine." She faced him, her own anger rising. "There's nothing wrong with them."

They were inexpensive, not cast-offs, she assured herself. She pushed aside the fact that she had admitted long ago that she couldn't afford better, and that her father would never willingly provide any more than what he had to.

"The villagers wear better clothing," he snarled. At the same time, the top button of her dress tore free and fell to the floor.

Chantel's eyes widened as she followed the small disc as it twirled on the stone floor, then lay still.

"Remove the dress." His voice throbbed with the power he was fighting to contain.

She looked up at him slowly, the blood racing hot and thick through her veins as lust overwhelmed her. The feeling wasn't desire. It wasn't passion. It was a hunger, a compulsion, rising deep and hard from the very pit of her womb. Her vagina clenched with a spasmodic reaction to the answering hunger in his expression.

"Make me," she dared him.

His eyes narrowed, and though the intensity in his look never changed, the edges softened with a brief humor. She gasped seconds later as the buttons tore free of the dress, clattering over the floor, leaving the edges gaping along her body.

"There are so many things I could do to you, and never touch you," he growled, his voice dark, rough with lust as his hands unbuttoned his shirt and he shrugged it from his shoulders.

A second later, Chantel fought for breath as phantom fingers eased the material of her dress from her shoulders. She watched him as he stood several feet from her, his eyes glinting with brilliant pinpoints of power.

The dress fell to the floor amid the buttons that had been torn from it, leaving her clad only in a matching thong and bra.

"I want to see you in silk and satins," he whispered, his finger flicking in an abrupt sideways motion.

Amazement surged through her as the front clasp of her bra cracked and shattered, leaving the fragile cups with only a tenuous hold on her swollen breasts.

She watched, barely able to breathe as he sat down in the chair near him and pulled his boots from his feet. His gaze never left her. The heat and hunger seared her body from the inside out. She could feel the juices easing along her pussy, slickening her, preparing her for him. Her vagina felt swollen, needy, a physical ache that echoed in her nipples and throbbed through her entire body.

Psychic energy wrapped around her like whispering fingers of heated hunger. Chantel fought to control her breathing, the rapid pace of her heart, the anticipation that crowded through her with a hard, sensual shudder.

"I've never worn silk," she gasped as the straps of her bra began to ease from her arms.

She trembled, feeling the warmth of his hands, yet knowing he wasn't touching her. Fear and pleasure washed over her, a heady aphrodisiac she couldn't combat.

"You will." He stood from the chair, his hands going to the waistband of his pants and releasing it slowly.

Chantel licked her lips, watching as he undressed. His cock, thick and long, stood out from his body like a sexual spear. The thick veins stood out in stark relief, the hard throb of the plum-shaped head mesmerizing her.

She jerked then as a heated touch caressed her spine. Moaning, her back arched as a lazy, caressing lick washed over her skin.

"Devlin..." She moaned his name, her body trembling, fear clashing with desire as she fought to assimilate the touch that she knew wasn't there.

"Easy." The phantom caress on her buttock did nothing to ease her nerves.

Her eyes locked with his, seeing the flames of sexual hunger that mingled with the glowing points of power surging there. She felt the waistband of her panties lifting, moving as the sound of ripping material echoed around her. Her gaze lowered in time to see the shredded material drift to the floor.

"Devlin." She heard the fear in her voice, as well as the intense excitement.

He came to her then, slowly, almost stalking, like a panther moving in for the kill. She shivered at the thought.

"Mine," he growled as he stopped before her.

His hands twined with hers then, holding them firmly, watching her closely as the essence of his power threaded through her hair, then clenched at the imprisoned strands. Fire exploded in her belly, spreading to her cunt and spilling out to encompass her clit. She was aching, swollen, desperate for his touch now.

His cock was cushioned on her lower stomach, a hard, hot stalk of erotic flesh that had her mouth watering to taste it once again even as her head tipped back in pleasure. The ghostly fingers in her hair tightened, keeping the taut pressure at a level just below pain. Keeping her in a thrall of anticipation that had her blood rocketing through her veins.

As her eyes closed at the exquisite sensations, his lips lowered, taking hers in a kiss that had her nearly climaxing on the spot. The tongue-thrusting, devouring caress had her rising on her tiptoes, desperate to get closer. His tongue twined with hers, curling around it, tempting her into an erotic duel that had her moaning her need to orgasm.

Heat pooled in her cunt, blistering, causing the tender tissue to throb and spasm as the syrupy juices spilled from it, coating the sensitive lips and aching clit with sensual need. And still his lips ate at hers. His tongue licked her, drawing her deeper into the lustful morass of exquisite desires.

"I'm going to make you scream again," he whispered against her lips.

Chantel's eyes opened, her breath catching at the wicked expression on his face.

"Please." She fought for breath as her knees weakened dangerously. Immediately, sensual strands of energy wrapped about her body, holding her in its grip.

"Watch me," he whispered. "Don't close your eyes, Chantel. Watch me, so I can see your pleasure."

"Oh God!" The prayer was torn from her lips as she felt the phantom caress between her thighs.

She tightened her legs instinctively, though it did little to halt the advancing caress of psychic power. Like ghostly fingers, it gathered the thick juices spilling from her cunt before moving with determined purpose to the tightly closed bud of her anus.

"Devlin..." Uncertainty whipped through her body as she felt the pressure at her tender opening.

Like broad, caressing fingers, the touch pressed against her in a gentle thrust.

"Easy." His fingers tightened on hers as she sought to draw away from him.

He stared down at her as she fought to control the hard, rapid breaths that tore through her chest. She tightened her buttocks, fighting to keep the insidious touch from delving further.

"Mine." He fairly snarled the word now as the pressure increased.

Chantel's eyes widened, then closed as a long, husky moan tore from her chest. She felt her muscles part, the biting little pain adding to the pressure against her scalp, a sensual, erotic bite of sensation that had her gasping.

Her anus was slowly stretched, penetrated, a smooth filling pressure that sent flames of greedy need streaking through her womb.

"There are things I can do to you that you can never imagine, Chantel," he promised her, his voice low, husky with promise as he lifted her in his arms and carried her to the couch.

Still, the pressure in her anus delved slowly deeper, thicker. Her body was shuddering, tight and tense from the unfamiliar caress. The slow stretching, then a gentle thrust spearing into her, opening her, preparing her for what, she wasn't certain.

Her hands clenched at his shoulders as he came over her, his lips taking hers in a kiss that had her reaching, begging for more. Her hands tightened in his hair as the tugging force at hers speared fingers of deepening pleasure through her body. She arched, fighting to get closer to him, to tempt him to drive the thick heat of his cock deep inside her desperate pussy. Her strangled scream was followed by the hard arch of her body as the pressure in her ass increased and Devlin slid between her thighs.

One hand held her anchored to the couch as his lips devoured her, his phantom caress in her anus gently fucking her. She pressed back, instinctively needing to drive the ghostly presence deeper, yet it held firm, taunting her, tempting her.

His hands moved then, pulling her thighs higher, pressing them back as he rose before her. The tip of his cock nudged the opening of her cunt, sliding through the hot juice spilling from her. His eyes were black as night, yet filled with a million pinpoints of light as the psychic power flowed through him, from him. Hands tugged at her hair, the presence in her anus slid deeper. Like a cock, first thin and hard, but swelling rapidly, filling her, stretching her, biting at the sensitive tissue as she screamed out at the near orgasmic pleasure of it.

"You will not ever deceive me again, Chantel," he bit out as the head of his cock nudged into the fist-tight entrance of her cunt.

The pressure in her anus throbbed as the thick head pressed into her pussy, opening her vagina for the thrust of his cock.

"I won't," she screamed. "I swear. Please, Devlin, please fuck me now."

The psychic cock tormenting her anus thrust in deep, swelled, throbbed as her cunt clenched, spilling more of the thick moisture over Devlin's cock head. She was aflame from the pleasure rocking through her. She arched to him, gasping, begging as she never believed she would do.

"Never will you want to leave me. Never will you sacrifice any part of yourself for fear of losing this…" His cock, thick and hard, pulsing with heat, split the tight muscles of her pussy as he slid in to the hilt.

Chantel couldn't halt the explosion that tore through her. Her anus was on fire, spasming on the phantom cock as her pussy exploded around Devlin's erection. Her upper body drew up as her womb trembled and fired with a clutching sensation that left her breathless. The pleasure tore through her like a firestorm as her hands fell to his shoulders, her nails piercing his skin, as she shook in the grip of a feeling so rapturous she wondered if she would survive it.

"Oh yes." Devlin's voice was strained, echoing around her as his cock flexed inside her quaking pussy. "Come for me, baby. Show me how much you like it."

He pressed in deeper, stroking his cock against the farthest reaches of her body as she jerked, caught in a mindless series of orgasmic pleasures.

"Devlin." She could barely breathe his name. Her gaze locked with his, begging him, terrified now as her body, her lusts, took control of her.

He was on his knees before her, holding her hips tight as he stroked his cock inside her. His eyes narrowed, watching her as she fought against the madness enveloping her.

"I'm here, baby." His fingers tightened on her skin, his thighs flexing as his cock stroked within her. "Feel me, baby, all of me."

He throbbed in her pussy, flexed in her ass as her thighs tightened on his and she fell back to the cushions, writhing against the penetration of his cock, his energy inside her anus flexing heatedly.

"Devlin, please. Please. Now." The rack of heated, ecstatic torture he had her stretched upon was destroying her. Despite her release, she needed more. The hard, driving thrusts she knew he could give her, the desperate pleasure-pain that she knew would only drive her higher.

"This is forever, Chantel." He flexed within her again, making her scream with strangled need. "Should you leave me, in any way, baby, you leave this…"

She couldn't scream. She couldn't breathe. He came over her, his elbows bracing at her shoulders as his hips began to thrust his engorged erection hard and strong inside her.

Alternate, forceful thrusts of heated energy in her anus provided a bite of sensation that had her twisting against him, fighting for breath. The slap of wet flesh, heated groans and his whispered words of wicked pleasure had the fires raging in her body flaming higher. Always higher.

Her legs lifted to clasp his hips, her body arching as the driving strokes of his hot cock in her pussy, his phantom cock up her ass, became too much, too many sensations. She couldn't stop the wail of intense pleasure as her body shattered once again.

She felt his cock pulse, throb, swell, then the hot blasts of his cum shooting deep and hard inside her as he cried out her name. His hips jerked against her, driving his erection harder inside her as the hot eruptions of his seed blasted inside her trembling pussy. Then amazingly, the same sensation built and exploded in her anus. The feel of his release, hot and wet, inside the ultrasensitive channel had her screaming as she peaked once again.

Sweat dampened their skin, melding them together as Devlin collapsed over her, his breathing hard and rough, his hands gentle as he slowly reined in the power wrapping around her. She felt it ease away, soothing her, bringing her down from the body-shuddering high of the orgasm that still trembled through her.

"Do not leave me again, Chantel," he whispered bleakly, his voice low, throbbing with emotion. "My soul could not survive. There is no magic on earth that could save me a second time."

His face was buried at her neck, his lips caressing her as he spoke. Was this the vow she had forced on her father? To take his memory of her, to take the memory of their love?

Her breath hitched as his arms wrapped around her, pulling her against him as he stretched out in the couch and jerked the small blanket that lay over the back cushions over them. The cool air from the air conditioner vents wafted over steamy flesh, causing her to shiver as he tucked her against his length. His legs encased hers, his arms holding her close.

"I forced a vow on someone," she whispered. "I called him father. I don't know what it was, or why I did it, but the words wrap around me, prodding me to remember."

Devlin was silent for long, tense moments. Finally he sighed deeply, his hand smoothing over her back. "We'll figure out the why and how of it, Chantel. But I am not pleased by this deception of yours or Galen's or whoever had their hand in it. I will tell you now, it will not happen again. Forewarned is forearmed, do not force me to arm myself against you."

Trust was such a fragile thing, she thought. He had little reason to trust her now.

"Aren't you already armed against me?" she asked him, regret and pain tightening her chest.

He grunted, a sound of such male disgust that she nearly smiled.

"Beloved, I'm as weak as a newborn kitten at this moment. I could not arm myself against a wet noodle right now, let alone against one who holds such power over my very soul."

Despite the exhaustion that drew at her, she leaned back, gazing up at him. Her throat tightened at the gentleness, the love that heated his expression. Tears welled in her eyes and her chest ached with the surging emotion that sped through her system.

"You should hate me." She lifted her hand to touch his lips, still full, slightly swollen from their kisses.

"I should paddle your bottom," he snorted. "I do not yet know what you did, Chantel, but trust me, when my memory returns, I may yet turn you over my knee if I find you deserving."

She frowned, her eyes narrowing. "I don't think I would try that if I were you."

He arched his brows in mocking surprise. "We shall see, won't we? Pray your hand in whatever secrets surround us was not as deep as I grow to suspect. If I find you knew of your death, Chantel, and courted it, I will not be pleased. Nor will I so much as let you out of our bed without a shackle after that. There is only so much one man can suffer in one lifetime."

She tucked her head against his chest, though more to keep her own suspicions from being detected by him than out of weariness.

"I loved you then as well," she sighed. "I know I did. More than my own life."

"And this I know." A world of weariness was contained within those words. "Because my love for you goes deeper than any emotion I have ever known. But in the matter of your own safety, I must say, I no longer trust your judgment."

"Hey, that's not fair," she mumbled sleepily, smiling against his chest, comforted by the tenderness in his tone. "I got out of that prison of Jonar's all by myself, didn't I?"

He tensed. "Chantel, go to sleep," he warned her softly. "You do not wish to remind me of the bruises that covered your skin."

"I killed him, Devlin," she said sadly. "I didn't mean to. But I did."

It bothered her, stung at her soul that she had taken a life, even a life as depraved as the guard's.

"He is better off dead by your hand than mine," he promised her. "He would have suffered, Chantel, had I reached him. I promise you this. So rest easy, knowing you showed him mercy, where I would not have."

She shivered, hearing a thread of mercilessness in his voice that she had never heard before.

"Sleep," he told her once again. "You have worn me out. Tomorrow, you may argue the matter."

She closed her eyes, content. Dominant, hard-headed male that he was, she had no doubt they would indeed clash, if not tomorrow, then soon…

Chapter Fifteen

ဆ

Devlin entered the caverns beneath the castle, stepping slowly into the chamber that held the stasis life units. The glow from Joshua's unit was a dim light, the ruby mists almost dissipated.

He was tired of the confusion. The lack of answers that seemed to mount up as each day passed. He had just left a meeting with Alyx, the Prime Warrior assigned to earth. The Prime Warriors were there to verify the deaths of the Seekers, those Guardians who turned to the darkness of their own souls. Guardians such as Jonar. He had hoped Alyx would have more information on the past, for it was well known he had harbored a softness for one of the warrioresses who had fought with Shanar's wife in those days. And yet, Alyx had claimed to know nothing.

With an abrupt mental command from him, the lights along the ceiling flipped on, revealing the technological marvel that the chambers contained. The computers were more advanced than anything earth would see for another century or two. The life stasis units, though individually assigned, could heal any human body laid within them.

Devlin walked over to the unit, staring down at the warrior who had been a part of his group since they were all children. His eyes narrowed at the signs of strain on Joshua's expression. The warrior never rested, never truly slept. Even now, held unconscious under a power that even Devlin's psychic force could not manipulate, he was still aware. A miracle. A testament to Joshua's power.

He was growing in strength by the year and, Devlin admitted, he feared for his friend, because his anger seemed to grow yearly as well. Sighing wearily, he keyed in the appropriate sequence on the keypad to bring the other warrior out of his sleep.

Instantly the unit hummed, hissed, a mist filling it as it began revitalizing the body held in an artificial coma. As the cloud receded, the lid lock released and opened slowly.

As the lid cleared Joshua's body, his eyes opened and locked on Devlin, an expression of dawning surprise on his face. His amber eyes glowed with eerie awareness as he stared up at Devlin. His harsh features were more defined, sharper than before he had gone into the unit.

"The magic is gone." His voice was husky, an edge of disuse roughening it.

Devlin tucked his hands into his jeans pockets and watched the other warrior as he sat up, reacquainting himself with his body.

"What happened, Mystic?" he asked coolly.

Joshua shook his head. "Hell," he sighed. "You should know. I no longer feel the magic that kept you from hearing her name, from listening to sense where Antea was concerned. You should remember now."

"Explain the magic." Devlin kept his voice calm, controlled, when he felt anything but calm or controlled. "Explain to me how I lost all memories of my wife."

Joshua rolled from the stasis unit, his body still a bit uncoordinated. A shudder seemed to wash over his body as his feet touched the stone floor. Everything was more sensitive, heightened after healing, as Devlin knew.

"I'm hungry," Joshua grunted. "I have explained it already. Neither you nor the others heard her name when it was said, nor responded to questions or statements concerning her. Simple. Cut and dried."

He moved stiffly to leave the cavern then, only to stop, unable to pull his feet from the floor. He turned his head slowly, his eyelids lowered as he cast Devlin a half-angry look.

"I gave you an order," Devlin reminded him as though stopping him just with the force of his mind were an everyday occurrence.

Devlin watched as Joshua fought the mental force that kept him glued into position. He was strong, just as Devlin suspected. Stronger than he had let any of them know, but not strong enough to break the bonds of Command. Devlin held ultimate power, he couldn't change that. At least, not yet.

Joshua sighed roughly, pushing his hands through the long, thick strands of midnight black hair. Exhaustion and hunger, both psychic and physical, trembled through his body.

"Ask Galen," he bit out. "All I know is that we went looking for Antea. When we returned, it was to learn that Galen already had her, and she wore Chantel's earth stone. You were set to kill her, and then yourself. When you walked from the great hall, you, Derek and Shane had all lost your memories of those weeks, and you never heard me if I mentioned them. That's all I know."

"How did she die?" It tormented him, not knowing, uncertain of the past or how it could affect this new future.

"Devlin, I'm tired. Answering these questions will only lead to more."

Fury filled Devlin. The chamber shook, groaned, as his anger vibrated through the room. Joshua grimaced.

"You haven't used those powers since her death," Joshua accused him, his amber gaze flaring with his own anger. "Even against Jonar, you refused. Why now?"

"Tell me how she died." Devlin heard the guttural sound of his voice and fought to contain his fury.

"Shit," Joshua cursed in disgust. "Aaron and Antea. Aaron arranged the kidnapping and frightened Antea into betraying Chantel. She gave her a sleeping potion after they were kidnapped and taken to Jonar's fortress. She stole the crystal, told Jonar she was Chantel and procured her release. Jonar and Oberon killed Chantel with the death wand."

So brief and succinctly said. The words sent agony washing over Devlin's body with such force his hands trembled with it. There had been more. He knew it, felt the dread that consumed him.

"He raped her." Distant, misty images swam before his mind.

He had found her, the death disc rotting her insides as the blood of the rape stained her thighs.

"Oberon and Jonar," Joshua admitted.

Devlin's stomach churned as his throat tightened in agony. He could feel the fury resounding through his soul, the horrifying knowledge that the wife who had known only his touch, only his love, had died with the horror of being forced to accept another.

His fist clenched at his side as he fought the emotions raging within him, fought the pain threatening to destroy him.

"Chantel knew it was coming." It wasn't a question. Devlin knew she had, felt it in his very bones.

"I don't think she knew how she would die," Joshua sighed bitterly. "But she knew she would die."

Devlin watched him, feeling his chest tighten, his body rage with the pain of betrayal. "You aided her," he whispered, his tone feral as the knowledge seeped into his mind. "God damn you, Joshua, you aided her."

Dust whispered from the ceiling as the room quaked. The units trembled, the computers shook along their metal tables, and Devlin was only distantly aware of Kanna, Shanar and Derek rushing into the room, only to slide to a shocked stop at the sight of Joshua held still in the center of the room as Devlin faced him, his fury building in the air around him.

"I aided her." The words were like a death knell to his soul.

Devlin stumbled back, uncertain, furious at the betrayal. He shook his head, certain he couldn't have heard correctly, but he knew he had.

"Why?" Devlin wanted to howl out in pain. In all the centuries they had fought together, never, at any time, had he questioned Joshua's loyalty. Now, he questioned everything and everyone around him.

Joshua's eyes met his directly. There was remorse, but no guilt. He stared back resolutely, without fear.

"I did not know she would die," he finally said tiredly. "I saw only the kidnapping, saw only her manipulations to assure a greater good for you, for her sisters. I did not know until too late that she was tempting her own death."

And it was the truth. Devlin pushed ruthlessly past the barrier of Joshua's mind, well aware of the other man's fury as he did so. He went only so far as to gain the truth of his words then backed away. He refused to violate the memories, thoughts or demons of the men he fought with. But he admitted freely that his rage was so intense that it was a close thing, observing that privacy. At this moment, he was a danger to his own men.

He stared at the others then, seeing their confusion, their questions.

"The next man who aids anyone—I care not who— anyone in a deception against me, of any kind, will no longer fight beside me. Remember this well."

He stalked from the caverns, releasing Joshua with a flick of his wrist and a casual display of the strength of his abilities. Fury enveloped him, tightened his body, and made him long for the violence of battle. Slamming the door to the caverns closed behind him, he stalked through the short hall and into the great hall. Chantel came to a quick stop as she rushed through the room, her expression concerned. Behind her, Michael stood, his expression impassive.

"You were supposed to be gone," he told the other man, fighting to keep from crushing him slowly.

Twisted memories whirled about his mind. Aaron/Michael. The warrior, the man who had sworn his loyalty, his friendship. He had betrayed him in both lives. Had betrayed Chantel.

"The plane had a problem," Michael said slowly. "We're supposed to leave later."

"Devlin." Chantel ignored her father, approaching Devlin slowly, warily. "Is everything okay?"

His gaze sliced to her. His heart warred with his anger. His need to shelter her, to rage at her. His jaw clenched, his fingers curling into fists. He would not berate her, not now, not in front of the man who had despised her since childhood. And yet, he knew he was denied the option of dragging her back to their room. Already his body heated in need, his cock throbbing at the memory of her uninhibited response to him. Damn her, would she again sacrifice herself, and all they had? And for what? What had been so important to her that it was worth his touch, his very life?

Centuries of cold, bleak loneliness washed over him. He had suffered to the depths of his soul, and yet, had not known why he suffered, nor why his life was such a barren wasteland.

"I'm fine." He was more than aware that he growled the word. Like an animal in pain. It was a fitting description of him at this moment. "I will be out of the castle for a while." He heard the door close in the hall behind him and knew when the others entered the room. "Kanna?" he called back to the other woman.

"Yes, Devlin?" Her voice was wary as well now.

"Do not let her out of your sight for a moment. Do you understand me?" He ignored Chantel's frown of mingled confusion and anger.

"I understand, Devlin," Kanna answered softly.

His gaze went back to Chantel. "It is your castle. Make certain the help stays where they are assigned, and out of the private rooms. I'll return later."

He ignored her sharp frown, the words trembling on her lips, and headed for the large front doors. His mind whirled with memories still too shadowed to make sense of, and a grief that threatened to shatter his soul. He had to escape before he destroyed every stone of the castle, and in doing so, every memory it ever possessed.

Chapter Sixteen

ဢ

Devlin's anger was a tangible force within the castle. Like a choking tension, it wrapped around them all. The new servants were wary of every movement, often jumping in startled fear at the slightest sound. And there was nothing Chantel could do to ease any of them. Each time she moved to confront Devlin and his anger, the crystal issued a strident command, the heat at her chest nearly blistering, that she stay away.

Give him time, Daughter. The past is a terrible burden, with no memories, no explanations to ease the pain. He will come to you. The words had wrapped around her as she stood in the silence of the gardens after a silent, nerve-racking meal. Give him time. She sighed. He had been given centuries, and still he suffered, raged alone, with no understanding why. What had she done to him in that earlier life, and why had she done it?

Her stepfather wasn't helping matters. For some reason, the journey back to the States had been delayed yet another day, and he took every opportunity to tell Devlin of each transgression she had made as a child. His words were, though carefully chosen to avoid Devlin's fury, like a whip to her soul. A reminder of the whippings and each small cruelty she had faced as a child.

Thankfully, he had left as soon as he had eaten, rather than lingering for drinks as the others had done. His presence had never failed to make her more than aware of each shortcoming he believed she possessed.

As she breathed in the night and sought the comfort of the garden's cool solitude, she became aware of the crystal's increased warning. Pulsing heat and somehow strident, she felt the uncontrolled urge to flee the garden and seek the safety of the castle doors. Shadows, dark and twisting, were lurking behind and within the fragrant depths of the gardens like demons ready to pounce. Shock hit her like a sudden fist to her stomach. The garden. The danger was within the garden. Where she had felt comfort moments before within the darkness, now she only felt exposed and in danger.

Chantel felt her heart speed up with fear as she began to make her way as quickly as possible to the kitchen doorway. The crystal was insistent, its warning like another heartbeat against her skin.

She was so close to safety. The doors were no more than ten feet from her, when the form emerged from the shadows.

"Father!" Her shocked gasp nearly strangled her as Michael stepped from the shadows.

She stepped back, the imperative heat of the crystal warning her of the danger he now represented.

"I told you, I'm not your father," he bit out, advancing on her, blocking her way back into the castle. One arm held carefully behind his back. "I've never been so thankful as I am now that my blood does not run in your veins, you traitorous bitch."

Chantel flinched at the twisted fury in his voice. She could feel her fears nearly strangling her, the strength of the crystal's warning felt like fire against her skin.

"I haven't done anything wrong…"

"He hates you now, can't you see that?" he spat out at her, spittle glistening in the moonlight as a crazed anger roughened his voice. "He knows what you are. He knows who you are, Antea…"

Images flowed through her mind then. She shook her head, fighting to escape them, knowing their distraction could become fatal. Her father didn't appear sane.

She saw him then, not as he was now, but as he was then. A warrior, watching her with bright, lust-filled eyes even as he moved close to another. Antea. Her face was suddenly there, similar to her own, a steady anger burning in her green eyes, jealousy darkening her heart. Jealousy and fear.

"No." She lifted her hand to her head, watching her father, and yet seeing a time and a place that pierced at her heart. "Please, let me into the castle. I'm tired..."

"Why? So you can deceive him more?" Michael snarled, his lined face so twisted with rage that he appeared demonic. "Can't you see you sicken him, you stupid bitch? You would sicken any honorable man."

"No." Danger wrapped around her. She could see the intensity, the black fury that filled her stepfather. Grief washed over her. He had hated her all her life, for no reason. It was like an insane urge, a need to hurt her as compulsive as breathing.

"Your mother knew what you were," he growled hatefully. "That's why she refused to abort you as I suggested. Because she knew, and whore that she was, she gloried in it. She was just like you. So sweet and innocent in appearance, but the minute she thought I was gone, she was in bed with another man. In bed with him and carrying his bastard."

Chantel shook her head. She felt the tears on her cheeks, the need to run, to hide, but she was held powerless by the hatred spewing from his mouth.

"Oh yes." He breathed in deeply, as though fighting for control. "She convinced herself I was dead. That my mission out of the States had failed. That I wouldn't return. Well I did. I did, and I raised her bastard even knowing what a stupid bitch she was. I still protected her, and you. I protected you, even knowing what you were, who you were."

"Father, please." She could barely speak for the tears, the pain clogging her chest. Her mother had been so kind, so enduring in the face of Michael's cold disapproval, hearing him speak of her with such contempt broke her heart. She had sacrificed herself for him and for her children, all the while grieving for the love denied her.

"I am not your father, I am your executioner, Antea." His hand came from behind his back, revealing the long, lethally sharp knife he carried there. "Devlin won't even grieve for you, you've so disgusted him. And he'll continue in his fight, his greatness, without you to foul his life."

Shock held her immobile. The blade gleamed in the moonlight, holding her transfixed as he advanced on her. Eerie chills raced over her skin, even as the crystal burned at her breast.

"Devlin will kill you," she whispered painfully, the words barely coherent through her tears. "You know he will."

"Devlin will never know," he sneered bitterly. "He'll think one of Jonar's men killed you, as they should have done in that damned prison they held you in. How in the hell you managed to escape eludes me."

She backed away as he came closer, the knife held ready, an ageless weapon of deceit and treachery, yet coldly effective.

"I'm not Antea," she finally sobbed, so filled with anger and pain she wondered if the wounds of this final betrayal by him would ever heal. "And I could have loved you. I could have, if you had shown me any kindness at all."

He paused for a moment. Only a moment. Regret shimmered briefly in his eyes before he tamed it ruthlessly and slid insidiously closer, the knife held ready.

"I wanted your love no more than I did that whore mother's of yours."

He was mad. Chantel could only shake her head. He didn't want to be, but he was. Certifiable. Chantel's heart was thundering in her chest, the crystal burning a hole in her skin as she watched the moonlight glint off the blade in his hand.

There was no choice—she was going to have to run. He was getting closer by the second, more confident of his ability to kill her with each step he took.

She screamed out Devlin's name then, her voice rending the air as she turned to run, praying to put some distance between her and the man set on her death.

"Oh no, you don't," he cried out, his hand tangling in her hair, bringing her to an abrupt stop as he jerked her back.

Chantel kicked back, managing to strike against his knee, causing his hold to loosen. She didn't get far before he managed to grab hold of the loose T-shirt she was wearing and spin her around as she lost her footing on the damp soil beneath her.

She fell on her back, her hands rising quickly and clamping on his wrist as the dagger began its descent.

Distantly, she thanked God that he wasn't a young man. He wasn't nearly as strong as he used to be and this added to her advantage as she fought him for the dagger.

She twisted desperately, her body bucking against the larger one that had her pinned to the ground, fighting to keep the dagger from finding its mark. All the while she screamed, crying out Devlin's name as she used every trick she could think of to get him off her.

He was old, but he knew how to fight. Each move she presented, he blocked, and with each block, the blade came closer. She couldn't keep up her strength long enough, she knew. She was already tiring quickly and the body now straddling hers was weakening very little.

The fear rose inside her until it was like a shimmering aura before her eyes and the scream that tore from her throat was nearly inhuman in its intensity. She felt her grip on the wrist slacken, felt its slow downward glide and knew that she had lost.

Devlin stood silently before the newly lit fire in the great hall, staring into the flames, regret and shattered memories shimmering in the brilliance of the fire as he ignored the others in the room. He felt lost without Chantel's presence, without her quiet grace at his side. Through the day, it had come to him that whatever her reasons had been in that earlier life for sacrificing herself, they had to have been reasons she believed in. He knew her. Despite the short length of the time she had been with him once again, he knew her honor. The strength of her conviction was sound. Just as it had been then.

He breathed in deeply, his head raising, as he looked around the room, intent on finding her. She would be hurt, her pride wounded at his surliness, but he knew several ways he could make it up to her. He was moving from the fireplace when the scream filtered through the opened door of the kitchen and shattered the silence of the great hall.

For the space of a heartbeat, he froze, shock rippling over him as the others jumped to their feet. It was Chantel screaming, which could mean only one thing. Jonar had somehow managed to find a way in.

"No!" Devlin's cry ripped from his chest as his feet began to move.

He was only barely aware of the others racing behind him, his only intent, his only thought to get to Chantel.

None of them knew what to expect as they entered the gardens. Chantel lying dead, Jonar standing over her, would have been their first guess. They never expected to see Chantel standing within the eerie green aura of the crystal as her stepfather lay at her feet, his body bound with misty chains of magic. His hand still gripped the dagger as he tried repeatedly to thrust it past the aura at her feet, though the threads of emerald energy did not allow it to go far.

"Not again." Her voice was forceful, angry, as she stared down at the pitiful form of her stepfather. "You will not betray me again, Aaron."

"You will die," he continued to cry. "Die, bitch. Die." He thrust the dagger at the shielding glow over and over, whispering the words each time he did so.

"My God! Chantel!" Devlin could only stare at her and the aura that surrounded her, in shock.

There were no tears, no condemnation because he hadn't been there to protect her. Instead, she stood before him proudly, the glow from the crystal enveloping her as she stared down at the man who still yet tried to thrust the dagger through the green mist.

The blade went no farther than the glow. Michael's frustrated, frightened cries echoed around them.

"You will die!" he cried out hoarsely. "I am the last chance. The last chance to right the past. I will right the past."

"The past is no longer your concern," she told him softly, her voice immeasurably tender. "It never was."

She knelt before him, watching him with regret, with deepening sadness as she touched the tears that ran down his face. "These were never for anyone other than yourself, and because of this, you failed. Even centuries past, you knew no true loyalty. You knew only your own lusts and the broken dregs of the honor you wished you possessed."

Devlin bent beside the broken man, slipping the dagger from his fingers.

"You will kill me now," Michael cried, tears streaking down his face as he raised his head to meet Devlin's amazed look. "I wanted only to protect you. To defend the vow I made to you. To always protect your back. You are the future..."

Devlin could only shake his head.

"Shane." He called the warrior to his side. "Take Michael and lock him in one of the spare rooms until I can decide what to do with him."

"I failed," he cried out as Shane hauled him to his feet, holding him with careless strength as he struggled weakly.

Michael practically dangled from Shane's grip, twisting in an effort to gain his freedom, his hands reaching out for the dagger that lay at Chantel's feet, a cold reminder of his insanity.

Devlin turned his eyes back to Chantel.

"My warrior." Her smile was soft, loving, he thought. How could she have such love for him? How could he have ever thought her to be Antea, ever believed that deceit could be a part of her?

"Chantel." He reached out for her, only to have her step away.

"The memories are so close," she whispered. "I can feel them but a heartbeat away, Devlin."

He shook his head. His own memories were closer than ever before, taunting him with questions and yet no answers.

"Don't you feel them?" she asked him, her eyes soft and so brilliant it nearly hurt to gaze into them. "Don't you feel the memories?"

Devlin felt his heart breaking. His needs, his desires swirling around them both as he fought to think, to bring forth the scattered remnants of thought.

"I feel them, Chantel." He could only stare at the vision before him. "I don't know what the hell they are, but I feel them."

Devlin came closer to her. He wondered if he could touch her, be certain she was real within that aura. As he neared, he could feel a change within himself.

Energy crackled around him, wrapping over his flesh like the softest caress. Warmth filled him, pushing past the anger and bitterness of the past centuries. He felt wrapped in a part of her. He was stronger. It was one of the more distant impressions. He could feel both his mental and physical strength increasing.

When he touched her, he felt her love. Love so strong and tender, it brought tears to his eyes. He felt humbled and yet strengthened by the emotion pouring from her, empowering him.

His hand touched her face gently.

"Devlin," she whispered. "I'm so tired."

It was then that he saw how dangerously white her face was becoming. Her eyes were dimming, dark circles forming beneath them even as he watched. Exhaustion began to line her face, drag at her body, as though the aura was slowly draining even her life force.

"Turn it off, Chantel." Fear washed over him as he backed away from her quickly, terrified that he was somehow the one draining her strength.

Had he, in some way, caused this to happen?

It didn't help. Her body was now leaning weakly against the gnarled trunk of the tree beside her.

"Turn it off," he ordered her again, moving back to her and wrapping his arms around her body. "Let it go, Chantel."

"It's so hard," she cried out, her hand clutching at him weakly. "Just a little longer and I'll remember. Just a little longer."

"No more." He shook her slightly as he stared down at her fiercely. "It can wait. Stop it now! You're safe. The crystal is only draining you now."

"I have to remember." She sagged against him weakly, but the aura still glowed around her.

"Not yet," he told her gently. "It's no longer important, Chantel. Let it go for now. It will come back when it's time."

Chantel shook her head in denial, but he saw the glow of the crystal slowly fade from around her. He well understood her regret in letting it go. The intensity of feeling while wrapped within it was phenomenal.

When the glow was gone, she collapsed. He picked her up in his arms, cradling her small body against his chest, looking down as her eyes closed weakly. Her head rested against him as he rushed her to their bedroom.

Chapter Seventeen

ॐ

He tucked Chantel into bed, his chest clenching at the weariness that showed in the pallor of her skin. She was limp, nearly unconscious in her sleep, and it scared the hell out of him.

He stripped her of her clothes as Kanna retrieved her gown from the closet. As his hand touched the plain cotton fabric, he snarled and threw it to the floor.

"One of my shirts," he bit out. "The white silk. Something cool and light on her skin."

He heard Kanna's muttered curse, but said nothing as she rushed to do as he said. He dressed her in the silk, the material not nearly as soft as her skin, then tucked her gently beneath the blankets. She whispered his name, and he grimaced. The emotions surging within him were almost painful after so many centuries without them. Tenderness, love. They welled within him like a fever, weakening his body, making him long for things he had forgotten existed.

Leaning forward, he kissed her forehead, thankful to see that the stark white of her skin was slowly easing. The soft flush of sleep was filling her instead. His fingers clenched lightly in her hair as he fought to come to grips with his own fears, his own needs.

"Stay with her," he ordered Kanna, though his forehead still rested against Chantel's. His eyes closed as he immersed himself in her warmth. "Do not leave her, Kanna. Not for any reason."

"I won't, Devlin. I promise. I'll watch her carefully."

Devlin clenched his teeth, knowing he had to leave her, had to take care of the man who should have cared for her as a father, yet instead had reviled her, hated her enough to attempt to murder her. What madness could be strong enough to follow such a man through two lifetimes? A man who began with a sense of honor and dignity, but had slowly eroded into a monster.

"I'll be back soon," he promised her softly.

He straightened up, though his hand lingered in her hair a moment longer. He was loath to leave her, but he had to deal with Michael now.

The past was haunting him in more ways than one, Devlin thought later, as he retreated to his office. Somehow, Michael had come into the possession of his former journal, written as the warrior, Aaron. A journal that had described extensively Antea's crimes and deceptions against the Shadow Warriors. Michael had found the journal years before, during one of the extended trips to the castle that he used to make. It had been hidden behind a loosened stone in the small room built for the commander of arms centuries before. The room Aaron had used while Antea inhabited the fortress. Somehow, some vestige of memory, some knowledge of that former life had slipped into this incarnation. The duel memories had driven him mad.

Aaron had been part of the Viper cult. A small group that worshipped a snake goddess and dreamed of finding their way into her graces. As Devlin remembered the warrior, he remembered one who had regretted his deceptions, but only after they had been committed. One who aligned himself with Antea, but only after Chantel's death. A warrior who had fought to give the persona of honor, yet one whose soul wept with black hatreds. Even then, centuries before, he hadn't been quite sane.

As Michael had described the journal, Chantel had never been spoken of, only Antea. Her crimes, her lusts, her betrayals of the Shadow Warriors, recorded in cruel detail. He had been determined that should she return, she would not wreak havoc against the warriors again. His madness had taken the form of an insane honor, one that only a crazy man could validate.

Devlin's first memory of Antea was that of seeing her pale, tearful and sobbing as she stood beside Galen. Shaking, terrified, she watched the broken bodies of the cult fanatics swing from the crudely made nooses in the courtyard of the castle centuries before. Bleak pain had filled him at the sight, and yet a vindictive satisfaction had accompanied it. Had they somehow been related to Chantel's death?

Devlin knew Galen had been the one to wipe the warriors' memories clear of Chantel. Knew that she was the fourth daughter, when he had believed there were only three. But the details of her death were still absent. Those memories had not yet returned. But he remembered Aaron. Remembered him and saw him in Michael.

Michael was insane, he admitted to himself. After nearly an hour of trying to make sense of his ramblings, Devlin had given up. He retreated to his office and made arrangements to have him transferred to an asylum in Switzerland that he knew would care for him.

After hanging up the phone, he slumped tiredly in his chair and closed his eyes. It wasn't the first time he had been betrayed by someone he trusted, but damned if it didn't hurt more than most.

He had known Michael since the other man's days as a young operative in the CIA. He had been fierce then, burning with a sense of justice and honor. Devlin reflected that perhaps that was the reason he had not recognized him for the man he had been centuries before.

The man he had witnessed earlier had held no resemblance to the younger man of honor though. He was ragged and unkempt, with a dazed expression in what had once been kind eyes. He had spewed his hatred of Chantel, and berated Devlin for his lust toward her.

How had he not seen the changes in him, Devlin wondered. How had he missed such madness over the years?

"Wasn't your fault, Devlin." Joshua entered the room quietly, watching him warily as he took a seat opposite Devlin's desk. "I believe such things were written long ago. We're merely puppets, dangling on the strings that Fate and Destiny hold."

Devlin closed his eyes, restraining his urge to roll them in exasperation. The Philosopher Mystic, he thought wearily. Just what he needed right now. There were times Joshua's powers and his attitude combined in a way that appeared less than attractive.

"Let's not overdramatize this, Joshua," he sighed, looking up at the other warrior.

Joshua watched him with somber cynicism. A knowledge Devlin didn't want to delve too deeply into. It was easier, perhaps, to believe they had a choice, rather than believing Fate and Destiny could control anything so important as their lives.

"Shane is preparing to leave for Switzerland," the other man announced. "Any last minute orders?"

Devlin shook his head. What more was there to say?

"I've contacted Barak's group. They're in the States at this moment, to search Michael's home for the journal, but it is most likely destroyed as he claims," Devlin sighed. "So many centuries. You would think in all that time, such a soul would have had a chance to ponder its mistakes, rather than making them again in such a fashion."

"Perhaps the soul rests." Joshua shrugged. "But other problems are arising as well."

Devlin sighed wearily. "What now?"

"Lissa." The name caused Devlin to wince. The double agent placed within Jonar's organization had been trying for years to insinuate herself in Devlin's life, but more importantly, in his bed.

His eyes narrowed at something twisting on the edges of his memory then slipping away as it left a sense of distaste lingering within him.

"And who is she?" he growled. "I have no doubt we have known that one before as well."

Joshua's lips tilted mockingly. "The powers to answer such questions are yours, not mine," he reminded him. "And as you have left them to lie neglected, then I say we have little hope of learning the answers."

And he had. Devlin had cursed the power the Guardians had given him for as long as he could remember. For centuries he had cursed every mention of the aliens, every thought and association to them. He shook his head, regretting now the stagnation of the power he may need to protect his woman.

"Why is she arriving here?" he finally asked. "She's rarely done so before." And on those few occasions, she had caused havoc within the village and the solitude of the castle.

"She has information," Joshua said softly. "Information she wants to use as a bargaining chip. She refuses to speak to anyone but you. And only then face-to-face."

Devlin's eyes narrowed. "What were you able to sense from her?"

"Deception, as always," Joshua sighed. "But something more. The information is valuable, but the price I fear, will be too high to pay."

Devlin waited patiently when the warrior paused. Joshua's amber eyes lit with an edge of humor.

"She intends to bargain for your soul," he said with amused sarcasm. "She knows Chantel is here, and demands one night within your bed in exchange for the information."

Crystal shattered along the high bookshelves that lined the walls. Vases centuries old, exquisite and priceless, fell to the oriental carpet with an almost silent fury.

"She's insane," he bit out coldly.

Joshua smiled mirthlessly. "She is Lissa. You should have known it was coming." He chuckled then, though the sound was bleak and oddly cold. "Ah, the hands of Fate and Destiny apply their pressure as per their whims, moving their tender captives in perfect alignment, watching with gleaming eyes and calculated interest as each scene unfolds."

A crystal bowl shattered nearby. Joshua winced and cleared his throat, shrugging as though in apology. "I could kill her. It would take little effort to manipulate the plane, even at such a distance." He was silent for long moments. "I believe she is not more than an hour or two out of New York at this time."

Devlin stared at the warrior balefully for long moments. Joshua sighed and slumped in his chair, a clear indication that he recognized Devlin's objections to such an action.

"One day," the Mystic mused, "I will find a place where such powers as I possess are welcome." His tone was one of sullen acceptance. "Earth is a pitiful challenge at times, wouldn't you agree?"

Devlin could only shake his head. He rose to his feet, weariness weighing on his shoulders, discontent surging through his system. Lissa was the last thing he needed at the moment. Her blatant overtures had always left him cold, and feeling slightly less than clean. He had a feeling Chantel would take much stronger exception to them.

"I'm going to bed. I'll deal with Lissa tomorrow, or later," he amended as he glanced out the French door, seeing dawn beginning to streak the sky. "Much later."

He left the study quickly, heading back to Chantel. He needed to hold her, to know she was well, that she was still with him. His fears of losing her were growing daily. His need to touch her, to be with her, strengthening with each breath he took.

When he entered the room, Kanna stood up from the chair beside Chantel's bed, watching him inquisitively. The lights had been lowered and only the small bedside lamp glowed brightly within the room.

"Michael?" she asked him softly, sadly.

Such tangled lives, Devlin thought. He knew Kanna had looked fondly on Michael during his Aaron incarnation, and knew well they had been lovers years before, during one of Michael's odd visits.

"I've sent him to Switzerland," he said softly. "Perhaps they can help him there, Kanna."

She smiled bitterly. "Can anything heal such madness?" Her voice was rough with tears. "Are we forever cursed to see those we care for come and go as though they have no bearing on our lives, Devlin? Would we have accepted this life if we had known?"

He hated to see the tears that shimmered briefly in her eyes. The warriors, he knew, were to be blessed with their wives once again, but what of Kanna? She had had no great love that he knew of, no purpose other than to aid them, in the Guardians' overall plans. His fists clenched at the thought. Such gentleness as she possessed deserved greater.

"I don't know, Kanna," he whispered. "I can only pray that with the destruction of Jonar, our lives will resume as they should have." He shook his head. He had no answers for himself, or for her.

Her head rose as she drew in a hard breath, the mantle of pride and strength she always wore pulling around her like an aura of dignity.

"We all pray," she said shortly. "Chantel has rested well. I will seek my own bed now, and hopefully a few hours' rest before the day begins in full. Good night."

Devlin caught her arm as she made to pass by him. She stopped, staring up at him in surprise.

"I will discuss this soon with the Guardians, Kanna. I will not allow your sacrifices to have been made in vain."

She shook her head, the weary tilt of her lips saddening him.

"I have been blessed to raise fine men, and to see them to happiness, Devlin. I could ask no more. There is no way to replace what never existed to begin with," she said cryptically as she pulled from his grip. "I will leave you now. Rest. I have a feeling you will need all your strength in the coming days."

She left the room, closing the door silently behind her as Devlin watched her somberly. Of them all, Kanna's life had held the most sacrifice. No husband or lover she could hold for more than a few hours, no children of her own. Surely there was a future of happiness awaiting her, he thought. There had to be, for all of them.

Chapter Eighteen

જી

"Daughter, the magic pours forth, builds and strengthens. The power of the Shadow, the earth and its gifts. Destiny speaks and Fate moves the pawns. Prepare well, for your greatest test begins."

The Mother stood before her, her gentle light and soothing voice whispering in shades of life and of love. Chantel wanted to reach out to her, to touch the warmth that she knew emanated from that misty vision, but her limbs felt weighted down, weariness pulling at her as she stared up at the gentle face hovering beside the bed.

What test? she asked the vision silently, suddenly frightened of failing, of losing all that mattered to her in this life, and the one before it.

They all await. You are the first, Chantel. Listen for the second. Triumph in the valley of death. Heed your heart. Heed your fears and the strengths you know flow through your veins. You are my daughter. Protected by the earth itself. The very land whispers to you, child, heed its call.

The winds howled, lightning flared and she could hear the steady pelting of the rain at the windows. Whispering to her, crying out to her. Her body vibrated with the summons, her heart speeding up with a sensation of added life, added strength within it.

Shadows twisted, formed and cleared, and there they stood. There were three others facing her, expressions wavering in the misty fog that separated them. The women stood apart, lost and alone. Around their necks hung the crystals, but only one glowed. The violet aura of the first was dim, weak and struggling.

Outside, Chantel heard the keening winds, and in the violet eyes of the woman she saw sadness, loss and pain. Long auburn hair fell across her face as she lowered her head, her shoulders slumping in defeat. Then the mists rose again, shrouding, then obscuring all she would have seen.

No. What was meant to be a scream, a violent protest was a whimper of regret. The woman, her sister, the one who had fought as a warrior and died in battle, was dying once again. *How do I help her?*

Heed the crystal. It will bring life, bring sight, it will whisper and moan, and on the winds of time it will bring the answers you seek. Listen well and listen true. Savage is her Legacy, death was her payment. A test of strength. A trial of love. A whispered cry. A journey made, and yet no travel taken. Listen well and listen deep or forever and always, the wind shall sleep.

With a final fond look, the vision drifted away. The Mother was gone as though she had never been, leaving Chantel to stare into the gray morning light of the bedroom as she realized it had not been a dream. She had not been asleep.

A whimper came from her throat as she heard the winds howl, crying outside the bedroom windows. Her head jerked around, and she stared at the storm that beat against the clear glass. The rain drove in sheets at the castle, lightning flaring, though no thunder sounded, and the winds screamed. They cried out in agony, in pain. At her breast, the crystal throbbed a warning, though it wasn't a warning. The contradictory sensations that assailed her had her trembling in near panic. Sharp, flaring, like the lightning. There one moment and gone the next, the impulses of emotion and memory struck at her.

Chantel clasped the pendant, her heart racing in her chest as she fought to make sense of the riddle and the summons from the stone. She closed her eyes, trying to block out the storm, but the winds raged.

"Are you frightened?" Devlin stirred sleepily at her side, his arm pulling her closer to the heat of his body as she shivered in fear.

Instantly, the raging emotions began to still as his heat and strength wrapped around her.

"The storm is bad," she whispered, snuggling against him, humming in immediate desire as she felt the heated length of his cock against her thigh.

His hand smoothed down her back.

"Hm. Not too bad," he murmured softly as his lips caressed her forehead.

Chantel moved against him, needing the heat and the passion that fairly vibrated from his body. He was strong and hard, and he wanted her. Needed her as she needed him.

Her lips opened, her head moving until she could touch the flat male nipple beneath her cheek.

His body jerked, the little disc hardening as her tongue licked over it. One hand slid into her hair, the other gripped her hip as she closed her mouth on it, her teeth gripping the hard point ever so lightly as her tongue rasped over it slowly.

She heard a strangled male groan escape his chest and smiled with a sense of power. He was stronger, harder than her, but he craved her touch with the same hunger she craved his.

She licked his hard nipple one last time, then her head tilted back to gaze up at his handsome face. His eyelids were lowered, the long, thick lashes casting erotic shadows over his high cheekbones. His black eyes glittered with rising lust and mingled emotion, making her heart beat faster as he continued to stare at her.

"I want to touch you," she whispered, greedy now for the taste of his body. "I need you."

He grimaced with an expression of painful pleasure. "My body is yours," he said hoarsely. "However you want me, Chantel."

She trembled at the power of his words, the trust they implied.

"You've forgiven me?" Her hand smoothed along his chest, down the clenching muscles to his abdomen, to the steely strength of his thighs.

"For what?" His hips pressed against her as she avoided the straining length of his cock.

"The reason you were angry." She wasn't certain if it had been a good thing to remind him. His eyes narrowed further.

"Chantel, we don't want to discuss this right now," he told her softly, though the corners of his mouth kicked up with slight humor. "I believe you were discussing something much more interesting before."

"I was?" She frowned with humorous confusion. "Want to remind me of it?"

Her nails raked lightly over his inner thigh as a hard groan tore from his throat.

"I don't believe you need reminding." He breathed in roughly as his hips moved, pressing his cock imperatively against her thigh.

"Maybe not." She leaned forward, irresistibly drawn to the sensual curves of his lips.

Her gaze was locked with his as she allowed her tongue to trace the velvet roughness of his lips. They parted as he began to breathe harder, his eyes glittering with a surging hunger as he watched her. Her hand rose from his thigh until she could spear her fingers through his hair, the thick black strands tangling around them as she pulled him to her.

It was one of the most intensely erotic things she had ever experienced. Watching him, their gazes locked as her tongue, then her lips caressed his. The kiss was slow, but so hot it singed her nerve endings. It lasted forever, and yet not long enough. Her eyes closed as her tongue slipped between his lips, tangling with his, tasting him, becoming intoxicated on the strength and depth of his passion for her.

They strained to touch each other. His arms tightened around her, pulling her closer to his body as he groaned with a low, desperate male sound. Yet he didn't take control of their passions, he let her set the tempo of the caress, let her explore and taste and tease, as she needed to do.

Their bodies twisted together as the kiss heated, flaring out of control. Chantel fought the hold he had around her until his grip loosened, but her lips never left his. He followed as she moved, until he was stretched out in the center of the bed, his hands lightly clasping her hips as their mouths ate at each other. Hunger, greed, and lustful abandon sizzled in the air between them.

Chantel couldn't keep her hands still. She wanted to touch him, all of him. She wanted to feel the sculpted muscle beneath tough flesh, hear his labored breaths, the way his muscles tautened at her touch.

His hands clenched on her hips as she tore her lips from his, staring down at the heated hunger in his eyes. They were both fighting for breath, fighting for control. Chantel trembled, her cunt tightening as his heavy-lidded gaze drifted to her breasts as she sat up on her knees beside him. His hand moved from her waist, caressing up her side, until he could cup a rounded globe with exquisite gentleness.

Her back arched as a whimpered moan slid past her lips. Her nipple hardened further, ached, set afire by the hot rasp of his thumb over its turgid tip. Chantel watched him, dazed, fascinated by the erotic sensuality in his expression. Black hair fell carelessly over his forehead, lending his hard, honed features a softer, sexy look. Heat radiated from his eyes, lust and love combining in an erotic marriage of sensuality.

Her eyes drifted closed as his head raised, his tongue licking over his lips before they covered the hard peak of her breast. She jerked as pleasure flayed her body. Sharp spears of sensation shot through her abdomen to her womb, causing it to clench in painful need. She shuddered as a near orgasmic explosion pulsed through her body.

She gripped his head, her fingers spearing through his hair then as his tongue curled around the tip, his hot mouth suckling hungrily at it. Chantel felt her heart clench at the sheer gentleness he used when he touched her. Emotion filled her, shifting and growing in her soul until she wondered if there was a cell of her body that didn't pulse and yearn for Devlin's touch.

His hands framed her hips as he rose to her, leaning on an elbow as he shifted to move his mouth to her other breast. His lips covered the nipple, a hum of appreciation vibrating against her skin as her thighs clenched, her cunt wept. She could feel her juices coating the bare folds of her pussy and the sensation only heightened her arousal.

"So pretty," he whispered as he leaned back to look up at her. "So pretty and sweet, Chantel. I could touch you like this forever." His tongue curled around her nipple again as she shook in his grip.

"Come here." His voice was deep, rough with passion as he lay back on the bed.

Chantel felt her breath catch in her throat as he guided her over him until her knees were braced on each side of his head.

"Devlin." The unfamiliar position sent a flare of nervousness through her system.

She looked down at his long body, his flat, muscular abdomen, the thick stalk of his cock as it pulsed against his dark skin, extending nearly to his navel. She swallowed tightly, wondering what to do, how to react.

A cry tore from her lips as she felt a hard puff of air blow across the plump lips of her pussy. Her face flushed, her vagina clenching as she fought to hold back the juices she knew would slowly drip to his waiting lips.

"Shh." His hands held her firm when she would have moved away from him. "Let me, Chantel. Let me have you this way."

She felt him move. The silk of his hair caressing her thighs as his head raised, then the long, hot lick of his tongue from her hard swollen clit to her vaginal opening.

"Oh God, Devlin." Violent shudders wracked her body, tightening her, preparing her for the orgasm that she knew was only minutes away.

"Mm. So good," he hummed against her throbbing clitoris then licked around it with a slow, teasing movement that had her pressing closer to him, desperate for the release she knew was but one firm stroke away.

Her eyes locked on his cock, seeing the small bead of pearly liquid that eased from the tip as the large head throbbed in silent demand. Another shudder attacked her body as he licked her again, probing at the small entrance to her pussy, licking the syrup that eased from her in welcome. Teasing, seductive strokes that had her sitting closer to his mouth, desperate for more. And still he taunted her with the light flicks of his tongue. Never thrusting inside her, nor giving the violently sensitive nubbin above the release it needed.

Desperate to even the sexual battle raging between them now, she bent over him, her cunt still pressed against his mouth, her head lowering to the hard cock awaiting her below.

Chantel gripped the base of his cock, her tongue flicking out to lick the bead of pre-cum from the tip. He groaned, a hard growl of desire echoing around them as his hips jerked, driving his cock closer to her lips. She wasn't about to deny him. The feel of his thick flesh between her lips was too erotic to deny herself.

She licked the bulbous head slowly, teasing him as he had teased her. Blinding sensation ripped through her body as his tongue speared deep into her cunt in retaliation. She enveloped the head of his erection, her mouth stretching over him, suckling firmly in reward.

As though some erotic line had been crossed, control shattered. Devlin's mouth devoured her pussy, his tongue stroking in and out in hard, moist thrusts, the slurping sounds of his mouth against her soaked flesh driving her over the edge of sanity.

When her release came, she couldn't hold back. She shuddered roughly, her clit exploding from the caress of his chin on the sensitive flesh. A second later, her vagina flexed, spasmed, and she screamed around his suddenly erupting cock as she felt the juices rush from her pussy to his waiting mouth.

She fought, even through the violence of her orgasm to catch the spurting streams of his seed that jetted from the tip of his cock. His taste, salty and male, was an aphrodisiac to her senses.

Devlin barely gave her time to lick at the lingering drops of semen before he lifted her and rose quickly to his knees. Before she could protest, before she could do more than gasp in surprise he had her bent over, his cock plunging hard and forcefully into the convulsive depths of her vagina.

The muscles clasped him, tightening around his thickness as she cried out at the renewed pleasure. She was sensitive, so sensitive, poised on such a pinnacle of intense pleasure that it was nearly pain.

Behind her, Devlin moved with strong, powerful thrusts, slamming his cock into the fist-tight depths of her pussy as his groans matched her cries of pleasure. The sound of wet, sucking flesh, and heated pleasure wrapped around them, stoking the flames of lust to melting proportions.

"Mine," he bit out as he came over her. He blanketed her body, one strong arm holding his weight steady as the other moved. His hand tucked between her thighs, his fingers delicately caressing her straining clit as she cried out in rising excitement.

His erection powered into her. Pushing past the slick, tight muscles, massaging and caressing tissue so sensitive, so responsive to his every touch that she was quickly thrown into a vortex of nearly agonizing sensation. She pushed back, fighting to hold him inside her. She needed both the thrusting power of his cock tunneling into her weeping pussy, and the overfilled, stretched sensation that kept her hovering so close to orgasm.

Then he moved. Pulled back, pulled away as she screamed out in an agony of desire. He flipped her to her back then, pushing between her thighs and thrusting hard and fast inside her again.

Her legs circled his hips, her body undulating beneath him as she fought for greater pressure. The thick shaft burrowed hard and deep, forcing gasps of agonized pleasure from between her lips. Her clit swelled, throbbing with a tight tattoo of anticipated release. Her legs tightened around his hips, her head thrashing on the bed as she felt the pressure building between her thighs.

When her second orgasm came, she swore she died. She heard her own keening cries, felt tears drench her cheeks and was rocketed into a level of emotion and physical intensity that left her dazed and gasping for breath as she fought to find her sanity once again.

Chapter Nineteen

ഔ

Chantel stood within the gardens once again the next afternoon, drawn to it, unable to still the rising need inside her to enter the cool confines that the different wings of the castle created.

Inside, servants moved about efficiently, preparing for visitors, working to get bedrooms cleaned and aired sufficiently after centuries of neglect. The village shopkeepers were supplying the castle now with the best cuts of meat, the freshest vegetables, and an array of other needed supplies. And though the castle interior was coming together, something inside Chantel still felt shattered, splintered.

She moved to the center of the gardens, beneath the trees where Devlin had sent her screaming into orgasm two nights before. Why had she been drawn here? She stared around, seeing the twisted branches and thick trunks of the low growing trees. Looking above, she tilted her head, seeing how the branches intertwined and held each other close. Almost affectionately.

The four trees were set close together, their main branches rising like graceful arms, extending out from the trunks as they rose to meet the branches of the sister trees. Over her head, the separate branches entwined there, clasping each other close, twisting and twining with gentle reaches of the sturdy limbs.

Chantel turned in a slow circle, staring at the branches, feeling the soft breeze that blew through the shading leaves. She tilted her head, her eyes narrowing against the small shafts of sunlight that speared through the thick branches. Like sisters embracing. She stumbled as a sense of vertigo swept over her. The crystal pulsed at her breast as the wind rose.

Breathing heavily, she clasped the trunk of the nearest tree, fighting the dizzying feeling threatening to overtake her. The wind moaned. It wasn't a hard, driving wind. It was a gentle force that blew over her, around her, spreading the warmth of the summer day with the cool promise of rain, yet it moaned out in some protest. Like a strangled scream, it echoed through the gardens, vibrating with... Fear.

"Devlin." She whispered his name, suddenly frightened, not of what the garden held, or of any danger that could be coming her way.

The sound of the wind. There was fear there. Pain. As though a message was being born on currents too delicate to glimpse, it wrapped around her, driving at her with an almost physical emotion of deepening pain and fear.

The crystal heated at her breast, urging her, vibrating against her as a dull throb began to build within her head. Lifting her hand she pressed her fingers against her temple, shaking her head, fighting off the sense of unreality threatening to overtake her.

"Chantel." She jerked as Devlin's voice called out to her, worry shading the deep, vibrant tones.

Chantel. The scream seemed to pierce her mind, howling through the wind as she opened her mouth to speak. But it wasn't Devlin's voice. It was female, calling out, in pain. The crystal vibrated imperatively, urging her, yet toward what she wasn't certain.

She sagged against the tree, weak, fighting a compulsion she didn't understand, couldn't seem to fight. The feeling was similar to freefalling, a loss of control, a loss of herself.

"Chantel." Hard arms caught her as she began to fall.

Strength seemed to pour into her, through her, just as it had the night Michael had attacked her. She grasped it desperately, fighting the building vertigo wanting to swamp her.

"Devlin." She whispered his name, hysteria threatening to swamp her now as she bit off a brittle laugh. "I don't know what's wrong."

Don't leave me... She heard the cry within the wind, desperate, clawing for escape. Devlin jerked her into his arms, holding her to him as he pulled her from the small grove of trees.

Sunlight struck her eyes like searing knives as they left the shadow of the intertwined trees. She staggered, slowly regaining her balance, though the fight to do so seemed to drag at her energy, nearly exhausting her.

"Easy, baby, you've had a hell of a week," he soothed her as he picked her up in his arms and carried her back to the castle. "You're still tired. I told you to rest today."

And he had. After they showered she had lain on the bed, watching as he dressed, his gaze going over her with heated warmth. She hadn't been tired, hadn't wanted to spend the day cooped up in their room. There was too much to do now that she knew there would be visitors coming to the castle.

As an agent, Chantel was well aware of the importance of a double agent. Their means weren't always agreeable, but the information was often life-saving. Whatever was so important that only a face-to-face meeting with the warriors could assure its arrival was important enough to make the agent welcome. Even if she was another woman. Even if she did feel as though that woman would accompany even more trouble than the castle had seen thus far.

"I was okay earlier." She took a deep breath as her equilibrium slowly balanced itself once again. "I don't know what happened out there."

"You're tired..."

"Is she okay?" His voice deep, rich and filled with concern. Galen stood from his seat before the fireplace as they entered the great hall.

Devlin paused as Chantel raised her head from his chest and stared back at the older man. He watched her with sharp brown eyes, his expression somber, reflective.

"Let me down," she mumbled to Devlin. "I'm okay now." Besides, she felt at a distinct disadvantage as humor slowly crept into the sorcerer's eyes.

Devlin sighed but did as she bid, lowering her until her feet touched the floor, but staying close, protective, as she faced the other man.

"Where have you been?" She narrowed her eyes on him, images and emotions suddenly flooding her. "You just disappear as though you aren't needed around here at all."

Chantel wasn't certain who was more amazed at her declaration—herself, or the two men. She shook her head, wanting to stomp her feet in fury. Impressions flew at her, one after the other, nearly swamping her with the misty images that battered at her mind.

Father, promise me… The words whispered through her head.

"I agree, you took long enough to show the hell up." She was distracted by the anger in Devlin's voice. "You have a few explanations to make."

Galen drew himself stiffly erect. His powerful shoulders and muscular body stood ready as he frowned at the warrior.

"I don't have to explain anything to you, pup," he bit out. "Especially considering the tone of your voice."

Chantel's eyes narrowed. The words were confrontational, but she detected a seed of humor in his tone. Evidently, Devlin didn't though. He tensed beside her, the hand clasped at her hip tightening briefly.

"Your magic is weakening," Devlin informed him bitterly. "I'm remembering, Galen."

She can aid you, Father, a sister as well… Her own voice, the words whispered in pain, drifted around her.

"Who said my magic isn't merely strengthening?" Galen shrugged. "Do not convince yourself you know my mind, boy. You aren't nearly that powerful yet."

Galen's gaze returned to Chantel then. It softened, filling with fondness.

"Do you remember?"

You are gaining sons, Father...

Father, what have I done? What have I done in the acceptance of this legacy, not just to myself, but to us all?

Father... Father... "Father..." The word was torn from her soul as the memory flooded her, broken, distorted, yet there.

Her father. Not just then, in a time still hazy within her mind, but now as well. Her father. She watched as he swallowed tightly, blinking at the sudden moisture within his eyes.

As she watched him, other memories surfaced. The wreck that had killed her mother, and nearly taken her own life. He had been there. She remembered now. The weeks she had spent unconscious, he had been by her side, whispering to her, urging her to live, to complete the destiny, promising her that as her father, he would always be near.

"Chantel?" Devlin steadied her as she swayed.

"You left me alone with him." Pain seared her heart then as she remembered the years she had struggled with Michael's abuses.

What have I done, Father? She shook her head, hearing the words again.

She clenched her teeth, her eyes closing tightly as a ragged sob tore from her throat. She felt Devlin gather her closer, heard him whisper her name in concern.

"Chantel, you are not to blame." Galen's voice reached out to her as she pushed against Devlin's chest in protest.

"What did I do?" she whispered raggedly, staring into Devlin's tormented expression, rather than her father's.

He returned her gaze, centuries of pain, of loneliness, reflected in the dark depths. His fingers touched her cheek.

"Whatever you did would have been only what you felt must be done," he said gently.

"No." She pushed away from him, anger raging through her now as she put several feet between them. She stared at her lover, at her father. Desperate screams of rage, of pain, echoed inside her.

Do not leave me, Chantel...

She wrapped her arms across her chest, fighting the pain, the fragmented memories, fighting the horrific knowledge that she had sentenced the man she loved above all things to centuries alone. Centuries drifting, fighting, never knowing love. And that she had done so willingly.

Chapter Twenty

ဏ

"He loves you. Always did. More than his own life."
Galen entered the small chamber deep beneath the earth
where Chantel had escaped.

She was amazed Devlin had allowed the escape. He had
watched her with dark, pain-ridden eyes, the half-formed
memories and suspicions twisting in his gaze, and yet it had
been filled with love. Love and acceptance. How did a man
accept such a betrayal from a woman?

"Then he's weak. To love a woman so completely is
foolish," she bit out, still holding back her tears, refusing
herself the weakness they would bring her. Tears cleansed the
soul, they said. Michael had been right—no amount of tears
could ever cleanse the deceptions that her soul held.

Galen sighed. She watched from beneath lowered lids as
she sat with her back to the wall, across from the stone table
that sat in the middle of the chamber. Water dripped farther
along the passage, a soothing accompaniment to the anger
beating in her veins. Self-anger. Self-disgust. What had she
done and why?

"To love a woman with all your strength and compassion
is the height of bravery for any man," Galen said gently as he
sat down beside her. "You do not remember as I do, Chantel.
None of you do, not yet. When you do, perhaps then you can
forgive yourself."

She leaned her head back against the wall, staring up at
the blackened ceiling of stone, holding back the tears, the pain.

"I left him alone," she said, her voice ragged. "Cursing
him to never love again."

Galen chuckled. "Is this what you think you did, Daughter? You did not curse Devlin's heart. You filled it. It was his love for you, his soul's unwillingness to betray that love, that cursed his heart, not you."

Chantel shook her head. She tightened her arms across her breasts, fighting to hold in her fears, her pain.

"How could I have left him?" she asked, feeling lost, locked between hidden memory and an unknown reality.

Galen sighed. "If I told you, it would not help. For even I do not know it all, Daughter. I know those last months were filled with your despair. It beat at me. Even amidst the happiness of finding the man created for you alone, you grieved for what you knew would be lost in such a short time. And I knew your heart. I knew your love, not just for this warrior, but for your sisters as well."

She covered her face with her hands, breathing deeply as she fought for her strength.

"It's hard," she whispered. "Seeing his pain, the loss…"

"But lost no more," he reminded her. "You do not see the changes in the man that I see, child. The rage that once filled him is wiped away. As though it had never been, his pain and his grief have been healed."

"Did I make you swear to take his memory of me?" She asked the question tormenting her now. "Did I make you swear to me you would?"

He patted her arm gently. "You loved him, Chantel. You knew you would return to him in a time when Jonar could be defeated. His life and his triumph were all that mattered to you."

"That isn't an answer."

"It's enough answer for me." Devlin stood in the doorway of the chamber, watching her broodingly. "Are you finished pouting now? If you are, I'm ready for dinner."

Her eyes narrowed at his tone. "I wasn't pouting."

He crossed his arms over his chest, a brow arching mockingly. "And what would you call it? Sitting here in the dark trying to answer questions that you know will not be answered yet?"

She came to her feet, aware of Galen following her. Her hands went on her hips as she breathed in deeply.

"You aren't supposed to be amused," she snapped. "You're supposed to be angry with me."

He grunted. "Wait until I'm actually angry then before you start pouting. We have company arriving. Shane is landing within minutes with the designer I had him bring back to prepare your wardrobe, and dinner is nearly ready. We don't have time for you to practice the pout at this moment."

Amazement held her still, silent. "Wardrobe?" she gasped. "There's nothing wrong with my clothes, and I wasn't pouting." She shook her head. "Dammit, Devlin, you aren't supposed to be so accepting."

He walked to her, ignoring Galen as the older man looked on. Devlin stopped before her, shaking his head as he stared down at her.

"I was very angry when I first suspected what you had done, Chantel. I thought of the years I had spent alone. I thought of the pain, and the emptiness of my life." She winced as he spoke so carelessly of so many centuries. "And then I thought of my life now, since your return. The warmth that fills it, even in this short time, and I wondered what I would do if I lost it." He touched her cheek gently. "Even now, barely past a week of knowing your touch, I would not survive. And I do not believe magic could save me a second time."

She shook her ahead, such acceptance, such love, made no sense to her. Through her life each transgression she had made had been punished with exacting force. And yet Devlin stood here, a testament to a crime she had committed centuries ago. A betrayal that had left him alone, unable to love, unable to enjoy another woman, and still he loved her.

"Why?" she whispered, fighting to understand.

"Because love forgives, Chantel. Just because my heart knows whatever you did to leave me, it was because you loved me. There is no other answer. Otherwise, I would have to spank you, darling. Of course, that might not be such a bad idea. It would at least give you warning not to make the same mistake twice."

She had a feeling he didn't have in mind the leather strap beatings her father had delivered during her childhood. Her eyes narrowed. The thought of his hand warming the cheeks of her ass teased at her imagination, rather than frightened her.

"You can try, of course," she drawled slowly. "It's your funeral."

His eyes narrowed, glittering now with lust, rather than humor.

"This is perhaps my cue to leave," Galen chuckled from behind her. "There are times when a father is not needed."

"Father." She stopped him as he moved to pass her.

When he looked back at her curiously, she felt something inside her soul ease.

"We need to talk," she whispered. "Soon."

He nodded slowly. "Yes, Daughter. And we will. Soon."

He moved from the chamber, clapping Devlin on the shoulder as he passed and headed for the doorway. The door closed behind him with a muffled thud, the sound reverberating around her as the sexual tension in the room thickened

Devlin watched her with black, hungry eyes, his expression savage in its sensuality. The look speared straight to her pussy, causing her juices to dampen the soft cotton of her panties.

"Are you going to stare at me all day, or are we going to dinner?" She arched her brow in question, though she had a feeling she was going to be eating dinner late.

Yes. Definitely late. Her heart kicked in her chest before speeding up in excitement as his hands moved to his shirt, the fingers casually flicking the buttons from their holes. If that weren't sexy enough when combined with the brooding, dark sexuality in his face, Chantel felt the snap of her jeans loosening.

She should be used to the amazing powers he held, she thought in amazement. She shouldn't be surprised at the ability he had to merely "think" his desires into existence. Such as his desire to remove her clothing. He desired it, therefore the buttons of her shirt slowly loosened, just as her jeans did.

"There, this is much better," he crooned, the dark intensity in his voice sending vibrations of pleasure rushing through her body as the shirt smoothed back from her, sliding over her shoulders in a caress that had her breath catching in her throat.

His shirt dropped from his arms, pooling on the stone floor carelessly as the front closure of her bra worked loose, the cups separating and rasping her nipples as it began to slide from her body.

She fought to breathe against the sensuality of each movement, staring back at him, feeling the hunger for him, for his touch, rising inside her like a wildfire hopelessly out of control.

"Take your shoes off, baby," he commanded her, the shadowed baritone spearing into her womb, clenching it with spasms of pleasure as she felt the material of her jeans working past her hips.

Chantel toed her shoes off, watching in dazed fascination as he removed the black slacks he wore, allowing them to fall carelessly beside his shirt, leaving him naked, the flickering candlelight bathing his hard body with a gentle glow, as it emphasized the straining erection between his thighs.

Chantel stepped from her jeans as they fell to her ankles, wondering if a woman could actually lose her senses from pleasure and yet never feel the first touch. The sheer eroticism of the moment was enough to steal a woman's breath. The sight of his heavy, engorged cock standing out from his body, the thick head damp, glistening in the candlelight, was definitely stealing her breath.

"Good girl," he whispered as he stepped nearer, his smile strained as his black eyes roved over her with a wicked look. "Are you ready for your spanking now?"

She would have answered, if he had given her a chance to. Before she could speak one broad palm smoothed over her ass as his other arm pulled her to him, his lips lowering, taking hers, dragging a ragged, tortured moan from her lips as she met his kiss with voracious hunger.

As though his kiss were the stimulus needed to re-animate her stunned senses, a surge of energy, of hunger filled her. Suddenly, she needed more. She needed the hard slam of emotion, of pleasure, the deep thrusts, the building violence of a release she knew she'd die without.

She needed, ached. Her pussy burned as nerve endings inside and out glowed to vicious, painful life. She couldn't get enough of his kiss, his touch.

"Don't wait," she cried out as his lips parted from hers long enough to grab her hips and jerk her forward, pressing the hard length of his cock against her lower stomach.

She twisted against him, moaning as blazing need whipped through her body, her head falling back to allow his lips to claim the tender flesh of her neck.

"Feel me, Chantel," he growled as he nipped at the arch of her throat. "Feel my love for you. Feel the need that has haunted me for untold years. All for you. Then feel your punishment should you ever tempt such an action again."

She gasped in surprise as he turned her suddenly, bending her over the raised stone table as his hand landed on the upturned flesh of her ass.

Chantel's eyes widened as flames consumed her. She should be fighting him. She should be screaming in mortification and fury. Instead, a strangled scream of pleasure ripped from her throat as she pressed back to him, the pleasure-pain of the erotic swat streaking straight to her clit.

"Never again, beloved." His hand met the rounded flesh again, a firm upswing that caught the lower portion of one cheek and heated the curve with subtle fire.

"Never," she gasped, desperate now, the cheeks of her ass clenching as she felt the juices flowing from her pussy to dampen the insides of her thighs. Her cunt spasmed, violent tremors raced over her body, shuddering through her as his hand landed again. Again. Each firm strike building the heat beneath her flesh higher, her lust hotter.

"Such a pretty ass." His voice was tight, a hungry growl that had her moaning in reply. "It blushes so pretty, Chantel."

The next slap had her lifting to her toes, her hands clenching on the sides of the smooth stone, the breath rushing from her lips as she cried out at the pleasure.

It was wicked. Naughty. It was the most fucking pleasure she had ever known.

"Now," she screamed out as his hand landed again, low, the sensations spearing through her pussy as she twisted against his grip. "Fuck me now, damn you. Stop teasing me."

"You call this teasing?" For all the playfulness in his tone, the dark undercurrents of sexual intensity overshadowed it. "This is punishment, beloved." He struck again. "Should there be pleasure in it?"

"Oh God, yes…" Her back arched as his fingers slid between her thighs, two long digits pushing forcibly into the saturated depths of her cunt.

She rode his fingers, bucking against the shallow thrusts, driving them deeper inside her, feeling the fire raging in her womb, the tension building. She was close, so fucking close.

"Not yet. Punishment, remember, Chantel? This is a lesson to be learned, sweetheart." His hand landed on her ass again as her pussy wept with sultry heat.

"I swear, I won't do it again," she cried, desperate to feel him inside her once again, to feel his cock stretching her, burning her, fucking her with hard driving strokes that triggered a pleasure she knew could never be found outside his arms. "I swear, Devlin."

"You sound very convincing." His voice was darker, deeper. His hand smoothed over her ass, his fingers dipping between her thighs to tease the swollen lips of her cunt. "Spread your legs, Chantel."

Yes. Oh God yes. She spread her legs quickly, lifting for him, eager for the hard thrust she knew was coming. What she didn't expect was that sharp, burning heat of his palm connecting with the wet flesh of her pussy.

The blow rocked her soul as her clit exploded. The silky heat of her juices gushed from her cunt as the next slap sent her higher, the third triggering a second explosion that stole her breath, dazed her sight.

Then he was there, the thick width of his cock pressing into her, the flared head stretching her, burning her as he pushed forcibly inside the spasming muscles until his cock was fully embedded inside the quaking flesh.

"God, you bring me life." He bent over her, his lips at her ear as she fought for her sanity. "You bring me pleasure and fill my soul, Chantel. Leave me again and there will be naught but a shell of a broken warrior, uncaring, unable to fight."

The agony of the past centuries filled his voice.

"Never." Tears flowed as freely as the slick cream between her thighs as he twined his fingers with hers, holding her firmly beneath him as he began to move. Slow, gentle, rocking thrusts as he kissed the tears from the side of her face.

"I live for your love," he whispered as he pulled back until only the crest of his cock remained inside her. "I live for your touch." A hard, slamming thrust had her screaming in mindless pleasure. "I love, Chantel, for you..." There was no breath left for words, for screams.

One hard hand gripped her hip as he began to move, slamming hard and deep, his cock raking sensitized tissue, over stimulated nerve endings. Her clit swelled, throbbed as the over-filled channel began to tremble, ripple around each thick intrusion into her pussy.

The sounds of slapping flesh, suckling pussy and ragged moans echoed around them as the tension increased. Chantel bucked beneath him, feeling her cunt tighten as release beckoned. So close... She screamed out her need as he moved, lifting from her back to grip both hips in hard hands as his thrusts increased.

Furious, driving strokes slammed into her as she felt the ripple of electricity burning from her womb, sizzling up her spine as her climax exploded inside her. The detonation ripped through her, clenching her muscles as she heard Devlin's harsh, strangled cry behind her.

Chantel jerked back, her torso lifting as she arched to her toes, tightening around him further, her pussy spasming violently as harsh tremors washed through her, over her, shaking her in his grip as she felt the wash of his semen jetting inside her. Hard, pulsing jets of heat that threw her further, tossed her higher, then stole her last remaining strength.

She collapsed back to the table, her breathing harsh, gasping as Devlin blanketed her back.

"I love you, my Lady," he whispered at her ear then. "I have loved you forever, and will love you 'til time ends. Always..."

Chapter Twenty-One

ઇન

"I want you to fire that old hag." Several hours later, Devlin stepped into the small room Chantel had taken as an office and spat his order out through clenched teeth.

Her body was still languid from his earlier loving, her senses mellowed and relaxed, but it seemed her lover was back to normal. He stood before her, his jaw working, grinding his molars as he glared at her through wicked black eyes.

She noticed he was clenching his teeth a lot lately. Chantel wondered if those amazing healing powers of his extended to worn-down teeth? Hers better, because she knew she had lost precious enamel while enduring the fittings and alterations to the clothes he had ordered from Paris. Too many clothes. Shoes. Purses. The extravagance still grated on her.

"The Widow stays, Devlin. She's an excellent cook." Her eyes stayed on the list of supplies she had been given earlier by the Widow. She adjusted the thin frames of her glasses over her ears as she tucked her hair back. Watching him was only making her hot again. She had to finish these lists. No time for sex, she reminded herself. Though she doubted she would be ready for sex like that again for months. Or at least a few hours.

"She's an interfering old busybody." He placed his hand flat on her desk as she looked back up at him patiently. "And what's that?" He stared down at the list. "That's enough supplies to feed a whole damn army."

She lifted her brow slowly in question.

"Devlin, why are you poking your nose into the running of this household? Are you bored? Besides," she continued, "according to the number of groupies arriving with that agent that Joshua gave me, we will be feeding an army."

"Rock stars have groupies. Lissa has leeches," he informed her coolly.

"Groupies, leeches, whatever. We'll still have to feed them for an unspecified amount of time." Her fingers clenched around her pen.

She couldn't get past the feeling that danger arrived with the agent and her entourage. To say she didn't have a good feeling about this was putting it mildly.

"That's still too much food," he bit out.

She narrowed her eyes. "Are you the one doing the cooking, Devlin? You will be if you don't leave the Widow and my supply list alone."

Devlin rose to his full height, crossing his arms over his chest as he stared down at her.

"I want that woman gone," he informed her softly, "before I have to kill her."

Chantel laid her pen down on the gleaming top of the rosewood desk and folded her hands.

"Okay, Devlin, what did she do?"

"It doesn't matter what she did. She doesn't know her place."

Chantel blinked, then her eyes widened as she fought to hold in her incredulous laughter.

"What exactly is her place?" She cleared her throat, hoping he couldn't see the smile she was fighting to hide.

"Don't laugh at me, Chantel," he warned her darkly. "This is not a laughing matter."

"Of course it isn't," she agreed, adopting a serious attitude. "Being out of place is very serious. Is she still in the kitchen?"

"You're laughing at me," he bit out.

Chantel was amazed at how well they had settled into the relationship developing between them in the past week. He was still overprotective, and worried excessively about her safety, but the emotion that bonded them together seemed to grow stronger each day.

"Oh, come on, Devlin, what could she have done in the kitchen that's so bad? Smacked your hands for tasting something?" She paused when his cheeks flushed ever so slightly. "No way!" A giggle escaped her at the look on his face. "You didn't stick a finger into one of her pots, Devlin?"

She was outwardly laughing now. She didn't mean to, but the thought of it was too much for her.

He sat down in one of the leather chairs across from her silently while she laughed at him. She could see the muscles bunching in his jaw, the way his eyes narrowed on her. He leaned back and she could see the promise of retribution in his gaze.

"Glad to see you find it so damn amusing," he growled at her.

"I'm sorry." She sat back in her chair. "What's she fixing in there anyway? It smells delicious."

"Onion soup, for sure," he grumped. "Damn her."

Chantel laughed again. The day before, the Widow had stated her kitchen rules. Snacks were laid out in the refrigerator. Trays filled with sandwiches and fresh vegetables were also laid out in case the men became hungry between meals. But no one was allowed to touch, taste or hover over any pot on the stove or in the oven. Those were off limits.

Despite her stand, the men insisted on trying to steal tastes of whatever was cooking. It usually resulted in the smack of a wooden spoon to their wrists, and in Derek's case, his rear. It seemed Derek was particularly stubborn about heeding the warnings.

"Lunch should be ready soon," she consoled him.

When he said nothing more, Chantel went back to the list in front of her.

The food and wine lists the Widow prepared looked excellent. The menu she had prepared was in depth and included all the supplies available in what quantities, and the added amounts she would need.

Chantel and Kanna decided on preparing for a week's stay for Lissa and her people. Kanna had assured her that Lissa would stay as long as Devlin would allow it, and that she would be particularly stubborn about giving Devlin the information that he wanted. If she was coming here, then it meant she wanted something Devlin wasn't willing to pay, the other woman had stated. Unfortunately, she often stated her price as Devlin's bed. Thankfully, he hadn't paid it. She would have hated to have to kill him.

A week sounded like seven days too many to Chantel, but she had kept her opinion to herself and began the preparations anyway.

Extra maids were hired from town and the castle had been busy for the last two days getting the extra rooms ready. At least the woman had had the courtesy to let Joshua know how many groupies she was bringing with her.

"You're taking all of this visit from Lissa awfully well." She heard the question in Devlin's voice. "I expected at least one screaming fit."

Chantel stilled the screams on her tongue. He had no idea just how angry she was over the whole mess. If it hadn't been for Joshua letting the information out that the double agent was indeed more than interested in Devlin's body, then she would have still been in the dark.

"What's the point?" she asked him, making a note to call the butcher that afternoon. "I can't change the fact that she's arriving or that she she'll be staying until you find another means to pay her for the information. I don't like it, but there's no way to get the information otherwise, is there?"

"Not an acceptable solution," he agreed.

Chantel was well aware of Joshua's offers to help. The last suggestion being to destroy the plane en route. The man had a bloodthirsty streak.

"Then, we have no choice but to do what we have to." She had been an agent long enough to know just how true that was.

"Chantel?" Devlin's voice was softly regretful. "I wish there was another way."

"We would be better off to discuss something else, Devlin," Chantel told him, fighting the anger building inside her over the need to prepare her castle for a woman intent on sleeping with the man Chantel considered her own.

"Fine. We can discuss the Widow's last day here then." He shrugged.

"I'm not firing the Widow," she told him sternly. "So, if you have nothing else to discuss, then I will return to what I was doing. Which is getting ready to order supplies for your guests."

He heaved a laborious sigh as he rose from the chair.

"Next time she smacks me with that damn spoon, I'm going to smack her back," he grumbled, walking around the desk to her. "Then we'll see who the master of the castle really is."

Without waiting for an answer, he kissed her on the cheek and then turned and left the makeshift office. Chantel watched him go and wondered how much longer they would have before Lissa and her hoard descended on them.

She turned back to her lists and checked over the notes she already had. She was nearly finished when another knock sounded at her door.

"Yes?" she called out, when it became apparent that the person on the other side had no intentions of just barging right in.

The door opened slowly, and the Widow walked in. Her thin, frail shoulders were thrown back militantly, her lean face flushed and her lips pinched. Her dark eyes were narrowed in suspicion as she spied Chantel behind the desk.

"Well, do I still have my job?" She crossed her arms over her meager breasts as she faced Chantel proudly.

Chantel frowned. "Why wouldn't you?" she asked her, in some confusion.

"Because I rapped his Lordship's knuckles." She raised her chin as she admitted her crime. "Poking his fingers in my soup, he was. Grown boy should know better."

"You're absolutely right, he should." Chantel nodded, smiling. How she would have loved to have seen that sight. "And yes, you still have your job. Unless you don't want it?"

Chantel hadn't thought of that. The men had given her a hard time the last few days. She may have had her fill of it.

"Of course I want my job," the old woman grumped, her shoulders relaxing. "He told me I was fired. I refused to leave until you said so."

"Very good." Chantel nodded. "Don't leave unless I say so. Do you think we need to hire a few more girls to help you in the kitchen when these people arrive? It will be quite a handful for you and Benia alone."

"Several girls, if you don't mind," the Widow answered her. "I have some suggestions, if that would be okay?"

Once again, the old woman's head rose proudly. She wanted the girls she had picked, Chantel thought. Obviously she had given it some thought already.

"Give me their names and I'll send out the messages." Chantel smiled. She wasn't about to quibble with this woman over who she wanted to help her.

Finally, silence descended in the office once again and Chantel was able to complete her lists and call the various merchants who would supply them.

She was closing the books up, when the flash of pain hit her. Blinding in its force, her temples were seared with it. Her chest became hot and tight, making breathing difficult.

She heard screams, and wondered if they were hers. How could she scream, she thought distantly, when she couldn't even breathe?

Chantel's fingers gripped her head as she fought to stagger to her feet and to the door. She made it only a few steps when the pain intensified.

She cried out harshly, feeling herself fall to the floor, as the pain wrapped around her head like a cruel, burning vise.

She pulled at her hair, writhed on the floor, fighting it as she attempted to crawl to the door. Devlin's name became a chant within her head as she fought to get to help. The pain intensified, spreading from her head and chest until it seemed to engulf her whole body.

She was distantly aware of the door finally opening and the Widow screaming out to Kanna. She felt the old woman kneel beside her, but couldn't seem to grasp the hands being held out to her.

She tried to open her eyes further, but the pain that seared the sockets was too agonizing. Besides, the Widow was growing so hazy, her face so distant.

Chantel closed her eyes, feeling the warmth of the crystal wrapping around her. The pain bore down on her like cruel fists and she eagerly awaited the drifting sensation she knew the crystal would bring.

A cloud of warmth engulfed her and the pain lessened, though it was still present in burning waves. She felt herself floating, rising away from the castle, much as she felt the day she went to the children.

When she opened her eyes, she wanted to scream in terror. She was once again within the dark stone room where she had died before. Jonar wasn't standing before her now, though. He stood before another.

Chantel could hear gasping pleas from the woman on the other side of the room. She knew it was a woman by the fragile wrists she glimpsed shackled to the wall.

As Jonar started to move, the moment she would have glimpsed the woman's face, Chantel was suddenly jerked away.

The terrible pain of moments before was gone. Weak and lethargic, she collapsed limply within the arms that had been holding her up. Distantly, she heard voices. She wondered if that was truly the Widow she heard sobbing.

Chantel felt herself being lifted in gentle arms and had the feeling of being rushed from the room. She could hear someone calling her name. Desperately, insistently, the voice pulled at her.

"I said wake up now, damn you!" The voice was suddenly much closer than it had been before.

Desperate and enraged, Devlin's voice filtered past the lethargy fighting to control her.

She tried to push him away, but he was holding her much too tightly. The hands slapping at her face were beginning to irritate her. She swatted at them, making a mental note to slap him back when she had the energy.

"Wake up! Open your eyes, Chantel! Now!" She could hear fear in his voice.

"Let me go back," she screamed desperately, despite the effort it took to form the words. "I have to see who she is."

"Chantel, wake up." He shook her again.

Chantel opened her eyes groggily. She could barely make out his pale features. The burning black of his eyes drew her.

"I have to see, Devlin," she whispered. "Let me go back."

"The hell, I will." He lifted a steaming cup to her lips.

"Drink it," he ordered her as he forced the cup to her lips. "Drink it, or I'll pour it down you."

She drank. Slowly, sip by burning sip, she drank the liquid until the lethargy in her limbs slowly began to fade and she could feel the crystal returning to its calm, sedate state at her breast.

"I want to know what the hell is going on," Devlin demanded when she was finally sitting up on her own.

She shook her head.

"Chantel, I can't take much more of this," he warned her, turning her head so he could gaze into her eyes. "The next time, I might not get to you before you stop breathing entirely."

"I wasn't in any danger." She shook her head slowly.

She knew that now. The pain wasn't her pain. She was needed, just as she had been needed with the children.

"Wasn't in any danger?" His voice was incredulous. "You were barely breathing. White as a damn sheet and cold as ice. Don't tell me you weren't in any danger."

She turned her face away from him. As she did, she saw the Widow standing on the other side of the kitchen. Her hands were clasped tightly at her waist as she stared across the room. Big tears ran freely down her sun-darkened face.

"Why is the Widow crying?" she frowned.

Devlin glanced over. "Damn, I forgot about her. She found you. It was her screams that alerted us."

Chantel shook her head. She pried herself off Devlin's lap and did a quick mental check of herself to be certain she really was okay.

Other than a few smudges on the rose-colored sweater she wore and the chill she still felt, everything seemed to be in working order.

"I'm fine." She smacked Devlin's hands away as he attempted to draw her back down on his lap. "Stop holding me, I need to think."

"You need to rest." The Widow came forward suddenly, her thin shoulders shaking, her voice hoarse with tears as her claw-like fingers grasped Chantel's arm. "You go with him. You rest. I'll bring you soup." She pushed Chantel toward Devlin. "You go before I get my spoon, young lady."

Chantel could only stare at the weeping woman, amazed.

"You go." The Widow cried harder. "Go, get out of my kitchen now."

Dazed, Chantel allowed Devlin to propel her out of the kitchen toward his bedroom.

"What's gotten into her?" She tried to glance behind her, but Devlin's broad shoulders filled her view.

"Come on to bed before she smacks both of us with that damn spoon."

She was still weak, but managed to walk the distance to Devlin's room. When she got there, Kanna rushed in behind them with Chantel's gown and robe.

"Undress." Even Kanna's normally gentle tone was harsh with tension as she faced Chantel. "Get into this now."

"What the hell?" Chantel pushed at the woman's hands. "I'm not undressing in this room full of lunatics." She looked around at the concerned faces of the men watching her. Somehow, all four of them had managed to follow her into Devlin's bedroom. "Get them the hell out of here first."

"Leave." Devlin's command, soft-voiced and dangerous, had the other three scurrying out the door. "They're gone, now get into your gown."

Chantel heaved a sigh and let Kanna help her into the gown.

"Some of the village girls will be here in a few hours," she told Kanna as she stepped out of her jeans. "Send them to the Widow, she'll know what to do with them. Also, some supplies will be arriving…"

"I took care of this castle long before you showed up, Chantel." Kanna jerked the gown over her head and Chantel noticed the other woman's trembling hands. "I think I can handle whatever comes up now."

"There are notes in my office that you need to look at," Chantel continued.

"Will you please get into the bed?" Kanna raised her head and stared at Chantel pleadingly.

The tears trembling on the woman's eyes convinced her. Chantel crawled into the bed and propped herself against the pillows as Kanna pulled the blankets to her waist.

"You need to rest," she told Chantel softly. "I'll send a tonic with the Widow, it will help you sleep. You still look half-dead."

Kanna turned away quickly after speaking and rushed from the bedroom.

Chantel could only stare at the closed door, then at Devlin.

"I'm fine," she told him. "It doesn't take long for the effects of whatever that was to wear off."

"Really?" A black brow arched in an exact imitation of her when she was at her most mocking. "Must be why you're still so damn white and shaking."

Chantel looked down at her hands. Even lying still against her lap, they were trembling uncontrollably. She tucked them beneath the blankets.

"You could barely walk from the kitchen, and while you were standing there spouting orders, you were weaving worse than Derek on one of his worst drunken binges. Don't tell me you're all right."

There was anger in his tone. She could see the bunched muscles of his arms, the clenched fists, which indicated the fragile control he was holding over his temper.

"I'm sorry. You're right." She leaned back farther into the pillows and took a deep breath. "I should be resting."

"Don't placate me, Chantel." He shook his head, running his fingers through his hair in irritation. "Tell me what the hell is going on."

Chantel took a deep breath. Quickly, she described what had happened the day she had gone to the children. Then, she explained the similarities of what had happened in her office.

"I need to know who she is. Somehow, I can help her," she explained to him. "I know it was a woman, and I know I was called there to help her. I think it's another of the crystal mistresses."

"Hell." Devlin shook his head as he walked to the chair that sat on the other side of the bed table.

He pulled the chair closer to the bed and sat down, and watched her for long moments.

"I don't know if you're strong enough to do it, Chantel." He shook his head. "You don't know what those episodes are doing to you. You were barely breathing when I found you."

"The pain is no worse than it was the first time," she told him softly.

He started to comment, but turned instead when the door opened.

The Widow stalked into the room carrying a wooden bed table. Behind her came Derek, bearing a tray loaded with several different dishes.

The warrior had a scowl on his face, and if Devlin didn't know better, he would swear there was a blush there as well.

"Good. She's in bed." The Widow's voice was filled with satisfaction.

She proceeded to place the bed table across Chantel's lap, and then had Derek place the tray upon it.

"I've brought you onion soup, baked pears and a bit of wine," she announced, crossing her arms over her breasts as she stared down at Chantel. "You eat, then you will sleep."

"I promise to eat if you promise to stop worrying about me so," Chantel bargained with her. "I promise you, I'll be okay."

The Widow twisted her hand in her apron. "I tried to hold you," she whispered regretfully. "But my hands would not go past the green light around you. You weren't breathing, Mistress."

"I was breathing," Chantel promised her, though Devlin could see she wasn't so certain of that. "And I'm fine now. I'll eat and rest, I promise."

"That's good." The old woman nodded her head. "I will check on you later to see if you would like a snack. And you…" She turned on Devlin with a frown. "You stay out of her food. Kanna will bring you a tray directly. I expect you will stay and watch over her?"

Chantel was starting to think the old woman could give orders better than Devlin could.

"I'll be here, you old bat," he grumped.

"Good." She took no offense to his words, which only seemed to irk him further. "She will have until tomorrow afternoon to rest. Joshua sent a message that the Barracuda will be arriving sometime after noon.

Unaware of the bombshell she had just dropped, the Widow turned and left the room.

Chapter Twenty-Two

ເ໐

Chantel had only seen Lissa a few times, and only then from a distance. Each time Chantel remembered clearly for the simple fact that her nightmares always became worse in the nights after. Barracuda was known for more than just her exceptional abilities to fool Jonar though. She was known for her seductive dark beauty, and erotic sexual acts. The agents with the Terrorist Control Agency sang her praises with a mix of pornographic descriptions and adoring sighs. But Chantel didn't expect the shock she received when the other woman arrived.

The moment Lissa and her traveling companion stepped from the car that had driven them from the small landing strip, Chantel knew exactly what and who she was. And why Lissa had never dared to properly meet her. The crystal flared at her breast, and through the change in appearance, the demeanor of sophistication and money, Chantel saw the girl she had once called sister. But this was no reincarnation. The soul was the same, not reborn, nor refreshed. The agelessness in her eyes attested to this, as did the knowledge within them.

Antea. Deceptive, beautiful, mercenary, and yet she still held that fragile spark of humanity within her that Chantel had witnessed and tried to nurture so long ago. That hunger and need that had nothing to do with riches or immortality. And it explained why Devlin had never recognized her. He would have recognized an incarnation immediately, but somehow, Antea had found another's body to inhabit. One whose soul no longer lived.

Chantel tensed as the double agent sent Devlin a seductive look from beneath lowered black lashes. She was gorgeous, with deep blue eyes, long thick black hair, and skin the shade of caramel cream. She wore a short, figure-hugging navy silk dress and high heels that complemented her curvaceous figure. Seductive and alluring, she was sex personified, and it was more than obvious that she still coveted Devlin.

Chantel barely restrained her gasp as the knowledge flickered through her mind. Antea had always wanted Devlin. She remembered the sly, calculating looks, lust eagerly reflected on the other woman's face.

Chantel stood beside Devlin just outside the double doors that led into the great hall. Her hand was tucked in the crook of his arm, and it was all she could do not to grip his arm in desperation. She could feel the dazed, almost otherworldly sensation that gripped her when the memories began to surface. She wanted to shake her head, fight the overwhelming emotions and sensations that came from the fragments of the past.

The other woman traveling with her was a petite redhead, her hair just as long as Lissa's, but with long corkscrew curls that fell to her hips and framed a heart-shaped face. Dressed in emerald silk, with hazel eyes that looked sleepy and seductive, she approached Devlin and Chantel as Lissa moved behind her.

Chantel watched as Lissa's eyes flickered over Devlin, then to her. There was a question there, a sly curiosity that made Chantel narrow her eyes in warning.

"Lissa, it's good to see you again," Devlin greeted her as they stepped to the landing.

He took her hands in his, raised them to his lips and pressed a small kiss to the back of her graceful fingers. Lissa appeared to shiver in pleasure at the touch.

"It's good to visit again, Devlin," she said, her voice flavored with a South American accent. She gazed up at him in amusement. "We missed you in Caracas last week. Jonar was after yet another artifact at the Embassy. I think perhaps he attained this one."

Blue eyes glanced at the crystal at Chantel's breast. Cold hatred flared in the eyes, mingled with a shadow of fear.

"Jonar is always searching for artifacts, Lissa," Devlin sighed as he turned to Chantel, wrapping his arm around her waist and pulling her near. "I'd like you to meet my fiancée, Chantel Ducaine. Chantel, Elissa Stanhope and her companion, Deanna Sorven.

Deanna was an enigma. A perfect illusion. Chantel delved into the power of the stone at her breast, seeking the answers to this woman. No hopes, no dreams, no fears emerged. Whoever or whatever Deanna was, she wasn't of the earth.

"It's good to meet you, Miss Ducaine. You are the scourge of Blackthorne, I hear. The only agent to ever be taken and escape. You are to be commended." Deanna's admiring voice was light and reminiscent of a New England accent.

"It's nice to meet you, Ms. Sorven." Chantel nodded then turned to Lissa. "It's good to meet you, finally."

A smile flirted with the dimples at the side of Lissa's lips. Her blue eyes were filled with mockery, with knowledge.

"I've seen you several times at the Agency." She nodded in greeting. "Your father was most protective of you though. His favorite occupation was keeping us nasty double agents away from you."

Chantel stared back at her knowingly. "I think we all know that isn't true," she said gently, remembering well her father's attitude of merciless scorn at the offices. "Please, come into the castle. We have refreshments prepared and you can rest before dinner if you like."

Surprise flashed across Lissa's face as she glanced at Devlin.

"She's domesticating you, darling," she said with spiteful laughter. "You never offered me refreshments before."

"I didn't offer them this time," Devlin snorted as he turned and escorted Chantel back into the castle. "Enjoy it while it lasts."

Chantel glanced up at him, gauging the cool expression on his face, the lack of emotion in his eyes and in his voice. Lissa made him uncomfortable. Her blatant sexuality and unvoiced invitations were less than welcome with him. A surge of confidence filled her. He was truly hers. His heart, all that he was. There was no desire there, no interest. Yet when he looked at Chantel, his gaze softened.

As they entered the great hall, Chantel and Devlin stood aside as the two women entered to be greeted by Kanna and the other three warriors awaiting them. Chantel watched the men carefully. After a slight hesitation, Derek moved to intercept the redhead, while Joshua smiled mockingly at Lissa and lifted his drink glass in salute.

The greetings were sarcastic, filled with a friendly enmity and thick with tension. Shane stood silent, watching it all, much as Chantel was. Every now and again he would cock his head, listen closely and close his eyes as though in pain. He had been doing it for the better part of the day, and Chantel understood why.

The winds moaning around the castle were eerie and often shrieking, as though filled with fury. At times, she swore she heard her name in the twisting currents of air that fought to enter the castle, and wondered if Shane thought he was hearing the same.

She took a slow, deep breath. She could feel knowledge fighting to pour into her. Memories and answers and a power unimagined. At times, it terrified. Now was one of those times, while she stood before her enemy, the woman who had betrayed her and caused her death so many centuries ago.

Forgive me, sister. Words whispered in regret. Hers or Antea's?

Chantel accepted the glass of wine Devlin poured for her, standing with him, his hand at the small of her back, his warmth heating her. As long as he was near, she could draw on his strength, keep the fears and the maelstrom of shadows at bay.

"I hear Michael resigned from the Agency," Lissa commented as Chantel sipped from her wine. "Something about an illness, I believe."

Chantel stared into the other woman's eyes, catching sight of a long ruby nail caressing the lip of the wineglass Lissa held.

"I hadn't heard that," Chantel answered her softly. "I'm certain if he did, then he did only what he thought was best for the Agency."

Lissa nodded. "James has been called back from his post in Saudi as well. There's talk he'll take the reins."

Chantel doubted that, but she kept her opinion to herself. Her brother loved his freedom, and his work. He would hate a desk job.

"I don't know what James' plans are," she answered her, still worried at the fact that she hadn't heard from her brother since Michael's breakdown. "I'm sure he'll let me know when he decides."

Lissa propped a slender arm along the back of the couch as she turned fully to them. Her legs crossed at the knee, the dress sliding almost indecently high on her legs. Long red nails now caressed the material of the couch as Lissa's gaze flickered to Devlin.

"We were all concerned at Michael's illness. It was said he was here when it developed." Sly innuendo colored her voice.

"He was here. We're not entirely certain what happened, Lissa. But I am certain the medical attention he is receiving is the best," Devlin answered the other woman coolly.

Chantel narrowed her eyes in warning as she watched Lissa. Her lips quirked in amusement, but she must have decided that today was her day to live dangerously.

"Oh, I'm certain you got him the best treatment available," Lissa sighed desolately. "Poor guy. We all knew he was a shade loopy, but he was brilliant in fouling Jonar at nearly every opportunity. I'm amazed he's still alive. It's a wonder Jonar didn't place a price on his head as well, years ago."

"Lissa, is there someplace you're going with this?" Devlin finally asked her, his patience obviously wearing thin.

She slanted him a mocking look, her blue eyes glittering with barely suppressed amusement.

"Of course there is, lover," she drawled. "Would I bother otherwise?"

"Then perhaps you should get to the point, and have done with it," Chantel said softly, fed up with Lissa's baiting attitude herself. The knowledge of who Lissa was, was eating her alive. The mocking, sarcastic attitude was an insult to the memory of patience and careful fondness Chantel had once felt for her.

Slowly, with dream-like wispiness, the memories were returning. As Chantel watched, Lissa eyed Devlin with seductive, calculated interest. She was more forward now than she had been while under Galen's protection. She no longer needed protection from Jonar, no longer cared about offending those within the castle.

"Just that we all were well aware of Michael's, shall we say, shortcomings." She grimaced. "Really, Chantel. Everyone knew how he treated you and his opinion of you. I'm amazed he didn't get you killed years ago, sending you against Jonar as often as he did."

"What does this have to do with anything, Lissa?" Devlin bit out. "I won't have you taunting Chantel, here in her own home."

Lissa rolled her eyes. "Is the truth forbidden here, Devlin?"

"Not the truth, Lissa. Your snide comments," he growled. "Behave with civility or you can leave now."

Her eyes narrowed. The dark blue glittered with feral intensity behind her thick black lashes.

"I leave, and we will never figure out what or whom Jonar has taken," she told him softly.

"I won't be blackmailed, Lissa," Devlin warned her coldly. "Neither will I allow Chantel to be insulted this way. Behave or I won't care how much or how little you can help. You'll leave."

Chantel laid her hand on Devlin's arm in a silent message that she could handle Lissa's comments. She didn't need a champion, not here, not now.

She felt his gaze on her, watched the calculated interest in Lissa's and wondered what the hell was going on in the other woman's eyes. For a moment, a brief moment, the undisguised lust was gone and something else flashed in her eyes. Satisfaction? For what reason?

Finally, Lissa sighed with ill-disguised mockery. "I do apologize," she said as she rose to her feet. "Perhaps it's my weariness coming out. Deanna and I had quite a long journey. Didn't we, dear?" She cast an amused glance at her companion.

"We did at that, Lissa." Deanna smiled serenely as she rose to her feet again. "I think I'm ready to rest before dinner as our hostess suggested earlier. If someone would show me my room?" She glanced around the room with an innocence that fell far short of her experience.

"I'll take her up, Devlin." Derek came to his feet, his own, darker blue eyes less than serene.

They didn't wait for acceptance, but moved on from the room as Joshua rose and moved to Lissa.

"Come on, wildcat, I'll show you your room and see if I can't help you with some of that excess energy that seems to be getting you in trouble."

Chantel blinked at the sensual interest in his voice. She tensed then, anger stealing through her.

"Joshua." He stopped, turning to her slowly as he arched a black brow questioningly.

Lightning flared outside. Strong, bright, crashing in fury outside the castle walls. She watched him flinch, his eyes narrowing in anger.

He lifted his lip in a sneer before he turned back to Lissa, his hand settling on her back as he led her through the great hall.

"Arriane will kill him and Lissa," Chantel whispered, unaware for a moment the memory that slipped in. "If he fucks her, he's a dead man."

"If he fucks her, it will be no more than he's done to thousands of other women who so closely resemble Arriane." Devlin shrugged. "Should she kill him, she will only give him the peace he's prayed so desperately for all these centuries."

* * * * *

Dinner was strained. Lissa's seductive laughter and cutting comments grated easily on her nerves, and when added to the warning throb of the crystal, made the event more than strained for Chantel.

As she closed the door to her office, she leaned wearily against it and closed her eyes tightly. Too much, she thought. It was all happening too fast. What she was feeling, the knowledge she was absorbing, was too much.

She went to the small settee at the side of the room, sitting down and covering her face with her hands. It couldn't be true.

"Will you tell Devlin who she is?" Her head jerked up as Galen's rough voice echoed within the room.

He stood before her, scowling down at her. There was anger in his eyes, and a tension in his body that spoke of his worry.

"Don't stand there looking down at me like some avenging force," she bit out, leaning back against the small couch. "At least sit down while you're getting ready to lecture me."

Surprise lit his face, but he did as she bid and sat down after rearranging one of the high-backed chairs in front of her desk.

"I have no lecture for you," he told her. "I merely wanted to ask if you will tell him what you know."

"I don't know." She shook her head, confused, and once again wondered if she should be questioning her own sanity. "Would he believe me? She's not an incarnation. How did this happen?"

"It is possible for their souls to inhabit a body of one whose soul has passed on," he informed her. "It only happens when they are half-human. Guardians "die" differently than we do, Chantel, but they can still die. Their souls return to their own world. But in the case of human-Guardian birth, the soul is bound to earth, yet destined to wander instead of rest."

"You swore to contain her within the crystal." That knowledge was only one of the bits that had come to her. "What happened?"

He sighed bitterly. "She escaped me. My energies were focused elsewhere for a time and she had managed to find a way free."

Chantel was silent. Another question answered.

"The car wreck when I was a child. When Mother was killed," she stated softly. "It was you who sat by my bed. The nurses thought it was Father."

"Your 'father' was too busy grieving." Anger charged his statement. "You were dying, with no one to hold onto. You needed hope, I gave it."

"And while you were with me, she escaped," Chantel stated tiredly. "What do we do with her now?"

"There is nothing I can do." He shook his head. "My powers extend only so far. The crystal can protect you, though. You must trust it."

"I want you to tell me everything, Galen." Anger filled her at the missing pieces of information. "I must know everything to fight her."

"I can't do that, child." He shook his head regretfully. "For every destiny, there are rules. I can only help you in some things, in others, you must help yourself."

Chantel sighed roughly. She had known that, she had also known she had to try.

"I'm frightened, Galen," she whispered, looking into his eyes. "I don't know enough to know how to proceed. I feel like I'm stumbling around in the dark here."

"The crystal will guide you through it," he promised her, leaning forward intently. "Listen to me, Chantel. Stop fighting the crystal. When it takes you away, there's a reason. You shouldn't fear it. It will always allow you to return once you've seen what it's bringing you."

"The pain…" She shook her head, remembering the agonizing waves that washed over her.

"Because you're fighting it," he told her desperately. "Don't fight it. Remember what I taught you the first time, with the children. Relax, let it take you where it will, and returning will be at your command. But you must first see what it's bringing you."

"It's not like that." She remembered how the pain became worse. The terror that filled her when she entered that stone room. "There's pain there, Galen. Pain I can feel. It's not part of the crystal."

Galen watched her, his blue eyes saddened. "The crystal must show you whatever it is. Until you face it, the pain will only become worse."

"And on top of it, I have to deal with *her* again." Chantel grimaced. "Does she know who she is?"

"Most definitely." He leaned forward, resting his forearms on his knees as he clasped his hands before him. "Be careful, Chantel. Antea was a very cruel, malicious woman. She could be even more so with all the centuries she has had to nurse her hatred. She may be more of a danger than we anticipate."

He rose from his seat, staring down at her somberly, his expression concerned.

"I'll be careful," she promised him.

"Be certain of it." He nodded in satisfaction. "And be careful in telling Devlin who she is. His reaction may not be…rational."

She shook her head, closing her eyes at the understatement. When she opened them again, he was gone.

She stared around the room, feeling incredibly tired. So much still left to do and she had no idea the task set for her. A crystal searching for a link… She paused. A link.

Then it came to her in a flash of insight so blinding it took her breath. The crystals, all four of them, were linked to each other.

"My God," she whispered, feeling the chill that washed over her. "It *is* one of the other Crystal Mistresses."

Chapter Twenty-Three

෨

The lightning raged outside and the winds howled in horror. Rain pounded at the windows, and Chantel could feel the very elements twisting inside her, echoing their rage. The crystal thrummed against her flesh, almost vibrating as it sought the link to the other women within the elements. What kept the crystals from connecting? Why couldn't she find the path to the other women?

"The lightning always comes when Joshua takes a woman to bed. Rain when Derek dares to. Each must be tempting the forces of nature tonight."

Devlin moved behind Chantel, wrapping his arms around her as he stared out the window with her, absorbing the storm. She was trembling. She couldn't help it. So much anger and rage, so terrible the betrayal. Or was it? Centuries alone. Lost. Men who had lost everything in one terrible battle. Was it such a crime that they would find solace where they could?

"And you?" she asked. "Why didn't you seek another's bed?"

She laid her head on his chest, watching the lightning as it flared outside. Bright, violent forks of jagged rage.

He sighed deeply. "I think because I knew nothing else could compare to the love we had. Even though I do not remember the events, I remember the emotion, Chantel. For Derek and Joshua, I think it was much different. Perhaps the love wasn't as deep, or even there to begin with."

"And Shane?" she asked curiously as the winds moaned.

"Shane has never touched another," he said sadly. "In his room is a portrait of Ariel, painted by an artist that Galen found after her death. It is an exact likeness. He remembers his bride, and that memory sustains him, I believe."

"Why then would it be different for Joshua and Derek?" she asked him, flinching as lightning seemed to crack against the stones of the castle.

He smoothed her hair back from her neck, kissing her nape gently.

"I don't know, Chantel." His eyes met hers in the glass. "Their relationships were different..."

"They deceived, where they should have loved." She shuddered as the knowledge came to her. "I hate this." She pulled away from him, her fingers threading through her hair as she fought the bits and pieces of knowledge, trying desperately to capture the full memories. "Why can't I remember? Why does just the knowledge come, but not the memories?"

The winds moaned and she wanted to scream out at them to stop. It was pain, not betrayal or fury. She felt pain in the sound, a horror unlike anything she had known before.

"Chantel." Devlin followed her, catching her in his arms, drawing her close to his chest as she fought her memories and the elements raging outside. "You can't do it all. Not at once. It will come to you when it's time."

"Listen to the wind, Devlin," she whispered painfully. "It's not anger. It's fear and fury and pain. And I can feel it. Feel it drowning me."

And she could have sworn she heard her name in the keening cries. Her scalp prickled with awareness, and chills chased over her flesh as she held tighter to Devlin.

He was her strength. His arms tightened around her, pulling her against hard muscle and loving heat. Against her abdomen, the hard ridge of his engorged cock pressed against her through the silk of his slacks, reminding her of his years alone. His years in a cold, often violent world.

"I want to take it all away," she whispered as her arms rose to curl around his neck, her cheek lying against the fierce throb of his heart. "I want to make you forget, Devlin, all the years we were apart. All the years I left you drifting in such pain. Tell me what to do. How to ease it all."

"Baby." His fingers threaded through her hair as he pulled her head back until he could gaze into her eyes. "You make it up with just a smile. Every night in my arms, every sigh from your lips, every breath you take. You wipe it all away, and ease any pain I may have had. Just never leave me again, baby. That's all I ask."

Her arms tightened around his neck as she lifted herself closer, her lips going to his neck, her tongue licking, her teeth nipping, lips kissing as she tried to satiate the need for his taste.

She moaned as his fingers tightened in her hair, exerting just enough pressure to make her scalp tingle, to make the slight, edgy pinch blend in with the arousal suddenly raging through her body. She arched in his arms, needing the dominating force of his passion, the aggressive lust that seemed to only fire hers in flames so hot and bright they seared her from the inside out.

She could feel her breasts swelling as he stared down at her, his eyes heavy-lidded and filled with sexual intent. Her nipples hardened, ached, as her pussy wept in shameless anticipation. The storm still raged outside, but in Devlin's arms another, fiercer storm began to rage within her body.

One hand smoothed down her back, caressing her spine, then filling his hand with the rounded mound of one buttock as the other hand pulled at her hair, tipping her head back. His lips went to her neck, his tongue a greedy flame as he licked at her flesh.

She arched into his body with a low moan of need, letting the tidal wave force of arousal and sensation overtake her. The pain echoing in the winds receded. The fury in the lightning no longer had her flinching at its ragged emotion. Only her own cries and the hard male growls of need from the man holding her could affect her now.

Chantel was distantly aware of the dress falling from her body minutes later after Devlin released it, and pushed it from her shoulders. Clad only in the black half bra and thong now, she shivered in anticipation as he stared down at her.

"God, you're beautiful." His head lowered, lips opening until he covered the hard, throbbing peak of one breast.

A cry broke from her lips as she went to her tiptoes, the sensation ripping from her nipple to her womb as he began to draw heatedly on the hard tip. His tongue flickered over the aroused point, rasping sensitive flesh as he licked at her greedily.

Her hands speared into his hair as he leaned her over his arm, suckling at her lustfully as one hard thigh inserted itself between hers. Cool silk caressed her inner thighs, then pressed hard against her aching cunt. The hard muscle beneath the material flexed, bunched, as she rubbed the swollen folds against it, her clit swelling, throbbing in reaction.

Her hands shook as she moved them to the clasp of his slacks. She could barely focus her thoughts, or her movements, for the slight erotic pinch of his teeth against her nipple.

It took forever to release him, but when the hard length of his engorged cock sprang free, she felt she had accomplished a miracle. But Devlin was the miracle to her. His erection pulsed in her hand, beating with imperative demand as he reluctantly released her nipple, raising his head to stare down at her with hot, lust-filled eyes.

He didn't bother to remove her panties. He ripped them from her hips as she gasped at the explicit eroticism of the act. Her half bra quickly followed those tattered remains to the floor.

"Lie on the bed," he ordered, his voice edged with a growling demand.

Chantel smiled, moved back from him, then went to her knees instead. Before he could pull her back from him, she had the hard, velvety head of his cock sucked between her hungry lips.

She heard his moan echo around her, but nothing could distract her from the furious heat and steely hardness of the cock she caressed with her lips now. Her tongue investigated the flared head slowly, running beneath the edge, stroking the ultrasoft skin beneath it as his hands clenched in her hair. His hips flexed, pushing the thick head of his cock deeper in her mouth as she moaned around it.

His thighs tightened, his hands pulling at her hair with sensuous tugs as she felt the first warning pulse of his imminent release.

"Not yet," he growled, pulling back from her despite her desperate protest.

She wanted to taste him, to feel the hard, jetting streams of his semen in her mouth, taste his satisfaction on her tongue. He paid little attention to her protest. Lifting her to her feet, he moved her to the bed, pushing her down on it forcefully as he quickly shed his clothes and came over her.

Chantel screamed out his name as she felt his cock push forcefully into the tight, clenching depths of her cunt. Each time he took her it was a renewed journey of pleasure and discovery. The head of his cock burrowed deep, the stalk behind it keeping her stretched, filling her, invading tender sensitive muscles that screamed out in acceptance of the biting pleasure.

"Yes." His growling hiss was filled with his own pleasure. "Take me, Chantel, all of me."

He filled her, overfilled her, the pleasure causing her womb to ripple in hunger as he buried into the farthest depths of her pussy. He thrust in hard and deep. Pulling out of her slowly, then pushing in hard and fast, pounding her cunt with the whiplash pleasure of each stroke.

As he burrowed in again, he picked up her hand where it clenched in the blankets, unfurling her fist as he watched her with his midnight gaze.

"Touch yourself." He laid her fingers at her clit. "Come for me, Chantel. I want to feel you come for me."

He lifted her legs, draping them over his, and he held onto her thighs. Chantel's eyes widened then as he began a rhythmic series of thrusts that began to drive her harder toward orgasm. Her fingers moved on her swollen clit, her body clenching with the racing firestorm of need as lightning sizzled in her veins. The blood rushed hard and fast through her system, ripping through her body, building in intensity as sensation after sensation began to assault her system.

When her orgasm hit, it was like an explosion of light and fire racing through her body. She screamed beneath him, feeling his thrust harder than before, his moans wrapping around her as his seed began to spurt inside her, hot and deep, pushing her higher as her fingers sent her clit racing through its own explosion. Her pussy clenched, gushed its juices along his cock and the pleasure overwhelmed and destroyed her. Only to remake her once again.

Devlin collapsed over her, sweat dampening his skin, his body trembling as hers shuddered beneath him. She was limp, drifting, the echoing sensations bouncing through her body, then slowly easing.

"I love you," he whispered. "More than you will ever know, Chantel. I love you."

Chapter Twenty-Four

ഇ

Chantel awoke suddenly, hours later, her heart beating out of control. The crystal summoned her, heating at her breast with an imperative demand. Her first thought was Devlin, but he lay beside her, sleeping deep and well-satisfied. His hair fell over his forehead almost boyishly, softening the planes of his face and the often savage expression of a warrior ready and prepared for any event.

It wasn't Devlin. The crystal hadn't awakened her to seek him out. She licked her lips, then bit the lower one nervously. Should she awaken him? Her hand was reaching out to do just that when the crystal flared hotter against her flesh.

Her heart was beating so fast she felt nauseous, filled with nerves and a hidden fear. She moved from the bed slowly, snagging the robe that lay on the chair beside the bed table and pushing her feet into the warm house slippers.

She left the bedroom, closing the door quietly behind her as she stared along the hallway.

Well, where do you want me? she demanded of the stone, irritated, put out with the feeling that the stone controlled too much of her life at this moment. For now, the great hall flickered in her mind. She sighed as she walked to the stairwell. Quietly, she moved down the stairs, her eyes probing at the shadows as she moved toward the large room that held the greater part of castle activity. It was a room for entertainment, for everyone to gather in and socialize, just as it had been centuries before.

A low lamp glowed from one of the tables, casting a soft, mellow light through the room. The storm had quieted hours ago, as though the earth finally rested, though Chantel could feel the uneasiness. There was, as yet, no peace.

"I wondered if you would come out of the little love nest tonight." Her head swung around at the sound of Lissa's voice.

The other woman moved from the shadows at the far end of the room. She wore a long silk gown and light robe. As she passed the glow of the lamp, Chantel saw the bruises on her arms that hadn't been there earlier. She flinched, swamped with the images of another woman, similar in looks, her arms bruised, her expression fragmented with an inner pain.

"He hurt you?" she whispered. "Why would he hurt you?"

Surprise flashed on Lissa's face as her gaze went to the arm Chantel was looking at.

"Oh that." She shrugged. "He gets a bit intense. But no true pain." A mocking smile twisted her lips. "Arriane enjoyed it a bit more than you thought she did, I think."

Chantel shook her head, fighting reality and vision as the crystal pulsed, overwhelming her with images.

"You know who I am." Lissa advanced slowly. "I know you do, Chantel. Say my name at least."

Chantel tilted her head, wondering at the somber pain reflected in her eyes, regret and fear, and calculation. What the hell was she up to now?

"I know who you are, Antea." The other woman's eyes closed in bitter acceptance as Chantel spoke.

"Do you know I was sent to kill you?" She opened her eyes again, curiosity now flaring in her eyes as she watched Chantel.

Chantel controlled the smile that wanted to hover at her lips.

"Were you?" she questioned her softly. "Strange, but I don't feel any intent to kill me coming from you."

301

Lissa's brows snapped into a frown. "You never felt so before either," she bit out. "I deceived you, and you never knew."

"Didn't I?" Memories flooded her. As though Lissa had somehow broken the dam needed to pass the first hurdle. "I remember I knew of the deception, Lissa. I allowed it."

Confusion passed over the other woman's face. "Why? Why would you do that? What they did to you..."

"Because the Guardians had no intention of gifting you at that time." Chantel frowned at the knowledge. "I knew this. Jonar would have destroyed not just you, but eventually, everyone I loved." She shook her head, the soft caress of the crystal at odds with the violence of the images washing over her.

There was more going on here. Things she couldn't seem to put her finger on. A threat, an answer? What was it? Her heart stopped as Lissa's arm moved. In her hand she held a lethal metal wand.

"Jonar has the Wind Mistress. He took her last week," Antea said softly. "He would have used this weapon, the last of its kind, on her by now had he not needed to give it to me instead. He believes you should die the second time, as you did the first."

Chantel looked at the wand, remembered her own screams so long ago, the horrendous pain, and Devlin's shattered cries. The crystal pulsed, burned at her breast, filling her with a glowing warmth she had known but one other time.

"Where is Ariel? If you're going to try to kill me, at least give me her location." Chantel stepped back as Lissa approached her.

Chantel felt lost in the events suddenly unraveling around her. There was no fury or hatred in Lissa's eyes. They were somber, sad. Her expression was filled with regret, and yet something more. She shook her head, fighting the crystal's power as she attempted to understand it. But all she could think about was that wand. The pain, the agonizing, wrenching horror of her heart slowly disintegrating in her chest and Devlin's screams wrapping around her.

"She will die soon." Lissa's voice was unemotional now. "She has screamed out in horror for days, the wind carrying her cries, and you've still not heard her. Not found her. Now, it's too late. You'll never find her, Chantel."

"Do you really think I'll stand still and silent and let you touch that weapon to my flesh?" Chantel asked her with soft incredulity. "Put it away, Lissa. I don't know what your plans are, but you didn't come here to kill me."

"And do you think that I must touch you with it to kill you?" Lissa asked her, sarcasm shading her voice. "No, Chantel, I can stand from here and destroy your life, and this is what I will do." She aimed the weapon, her finger caressing the wand as it lit up on the end.

Chantel felt fear clog her throat. Her own screams echoed around her, Devlin's horror, the empty centuries he had lived, the pain and lost destinies of more than just herself. Rage bloomed inside her like blood from a fatal wound. Power surged, beating through her veins, anger and rage beginning to burn like a conflagration that threatened to overwhelm her.

The crystal throbbed as the tip of the rod flared brighter.

"No!" Chantel screamed out the word as she reached inside for the power that built like a volcano inside her soul.

Color shot from the crystal, rich, vibrant, a deep emerald aura that suddenly wrapped out around her, glittering, glowing, infusing her with a power she could have never dreamed. Memories washed through her, power overcame her. Her hand reached out, the rage boiling inside her soul focusing on the metal rod, her fingers tightening into a fist, watching as the aura shot forward to twist and mangle the weapon within Lissa's grip.

Screams rose within the room, as the power of the earth seemed to invade every corner. Like a storm of elemental rage, the aura whipped around her, isolating her, empowering her.

Lissa crumpled to the floor, shrieking out in horror as the trails of lightning and fierce color snapped around her. The warriors rushed into the room, Devlin moving quickly to the fallen form, Shane and Derek flanking Devlin as he stared at her in surprise.

He started forward then halted, shaking his head in confusion. He tried again, only to be stopped once again. He was her protection, even from the crystal. His strength and power wrapped around her any time he was near, pulling her back, intent on protecting her from whatever would harm her. The visions brought pain, the pain of the one seeking her.

"Shane." The winds called out to him as well. She saw the stormy emotions in his eyes and knew he was aware of it.

She reached out to him. "Take me to her, Shane. We must help her. We must go to her before she drifts away from us forever."

Ariel's voice cried out in pain within Chantel's head. The link the crystal had fought to establish was clear now. To find the knowledge, she had needed only to reach inside herself for the power that was hers alone. So much was clearer now, so many answers there for her to take hold of and use.

"Shane, I can't find her without you," she said desperately as the other warrior hesitated.

She reached out demandingly, jerking her hand imperatively as he hesitated. "She will die without us. Is that what you wish?"

He approached the aura, his hand reaching out, his need, his love, his raging fears for the other woman lending her strength. She clasped his fingers, closed her eyes and willed the crystal to take them wherever they must be.

Chantel felt her stomach lurch as her spirit disconnected from her body, thankful that the aura then allowed Devlin to reach out for her. She was only distantly aware of him catching her body, holding her to him as he knelt on the floor, whispering her name with a dark, furious concern.

She was aware only of shifting light, a roller coaster ride on the winds of time as the crystal connected with that of its sister. She was jerked forward, Shane's spirit connected now with hers, following along, adding strength and love to the weakening form that had called out to them.

When they arrived, Chantel opened her eyes and could only gasp in fear and in dread. Had they arrived too late? Had Jonar managed to destroy the second link, and all their lives in the process?

Shane knelt down slowly, his hand reaching out to touch her. Chantel was surprised to see her react to the touch. She appeared comatose, her body bloodied and abused, her face deathly pale.

"Ariel," he whispered, looking down to where the amethyst crystal lay dull against her skin. He raised his eyes to Chantel's. "What do I do, Chantel? How do I save her?"

Chantel shook her head. She couldn't understand any of it. The memories of the powers were returning, but it didn't make it any easier to understand. She stood still and silent, aware that whatever must be done, must be done by Shanar and the crystals now.

"The only thing I can think of is that she doesn't believe," she whispered. "I knew the crystal was power, perhaps she doesn't. Wasn't Ariel the one who believed the least in what they could do?"

Ariel lay on a crude bed of straw, which had been scattered on the floor. The violet linen dress she must have worn when she was taken hung in tatters on her body. Bruises marred her skin from her face to her chest. Her arm was broken, her legs were cut, and her feet were swollen.

She was breathing roughly, her lungs rasping with each inhale and exhale of air. Chantel suspected pneumonia and possibly internal bleeding. Ariel wouldn't last much longer if she didn't receive medical help quickly, or the crystal didn't find the strength to sustain her. The crystal could protect her from the pain and the illness. Just as it had protected Chantel.

"Ariel." Shane lay down beside her, his hand touching her face softly, as he tried to warm her. He whispered her name again, as his hand moved, clasping the crystal at her breast.

Ariel's body jerked, a moan tearing from her chest as he wrapped his fingers around the crystal. Chantel felt her own crystal heat, the aura surrounding them intensified.

"Help me." The words were soft, barely a breath of sound. "Please, help me." Her voice echoed with weariness and a loss of hope.

"Ariel, open your eyes," Shane commanded gently, his rough voice softening more than Chantel would have believed possible. "You must look at me, Ariel. Open your eyes and see who lies beside you."

Her eyes fluttered as she fought to open them.

"Open your eyes," he commanded her again. "Look at me, Ariel. Allow me to help you."

Her eyes opened, just enough for Chantel to glimpse the unusual violet color, which nearly matched the stone Ariel wore at her breast.

"Good," Shane whispered approvingly, a fierce, saddened smile twisting his lips. "Do you know who I am, Ariel?"

Ariel blinked weakly, staring into Shane's face. Chantel felt like an interloper to the scene as she watched the tender smile the warrior bestowed on the woman.

"There you are." Adoration colored his voice and his expression as he gazed into the bruised features of the Wind Mistress. "Such pretty eyes. Do you remember me telling you what pretty eyes you had?"

"Dreams…" she whispered.

"Yeah, in your dreams," his voice was thick with regret. "But what did I tell you in those dreams? Didn't I tell you the day would come when I would find you? I've found you, love."

"'Bout time," she sighed, leaning closer into the warmth of his chest. "Take me home."

How Ariel could feel his presence, touch him as though his corporeal body was there, Chantel wasn't certain. Perhaps it was the alignment of both crystals, hers and Ariel's. But the other woman could touch her warrior, feel him, hold him.

"Soon." Chantel watched as the large, hardened warrior battled the tears gathering in his eyes. "Soon, love. But first, you have to do something for me."

"Take me with you," she cried weakly, her arms struggling to lift and hold onto him. "Don't leave me alone again."

Chantel's throat tightened as a tear ran down Shane's hard face. His features tightened with agony, his body spasming with it.

"Ariel," He kissed her hair tenderly. "Look at me, love. Don't cry. You have to help me."

He moved her head back until he was staring into her swollen eyes once again. "Do you remember the first time you dreamed of me?"

"The closet," she whispered.

"Yes, you were in the closet, in the dark. But when you cried for me, the crystal lit your way. Remember? You had light so you wouldn't be so frightened."

"But you left me," she accused him. "You never came back."

"And you stopped believing in the crystal," he told her gently. "It no longer reached out to me. No longer called to me when you needed me."

"I needed more than a dream," she sighed weakly.

307

"The time has come, Ariel, as I promised you," he told her thickly. "You can whisper the words now, and my strength will become your own. But you have to believe I'm coming for you. You have to believe in the power you carry, before it can ever do you any good."

"The words?" She was growing weaker, Chantel could hear it in her voice.

"Whisper the words now, Ariel, before you die. Believe them as though your life depended on them, because it does. Those words will keep the pain at bay, and keep anyone from touching you until I get here. I'm coming, Ariel, but you must hold on until I can get to you."

Her eyes opened once again. Awareness seemed to spark within them. The crystal, held within Shane's hand, brightened.

"You're coming for me?" The pain and hope in her voice ripped at Chantel's heart. She could see it was doing the same to Shane's.

"I'm on my way now, love," he swore to her. "Whisper the words, and believe. Hold on until I get to you. Believe, Ariel…"

Ariel cried, and Chantel felt tears run down her own cheeks as she did so.

"Savage…" The words came slowly. Weakly, the crystal at her breast began to glow. "…into my heart, part of my soul. Life of my life, lover of my heart, make me whole."

Tears ran faster down Shane's cheeks as the words resonated around him. The aura of Chantel's crystal slowly strengthened as the violet rays of the Wind Crystal began to bleed into it.

"Keeper of the wind…" he whispered in turn, bending until his lips glanced hers with each word. "…Mistress of my heart, bride of my soul. Take to your body my strength, to your heart, my warmth, 'til the time when we are no longer apart."

Seconds after Shane whispered the return words, the amethyst crystal began to glow brightly within his hand. He placed it gently at her breast and Chantel was amazed at the results.

Ariel's eyes closed. Her breathing evened and her body was no longer shaking from chills and pain. Shane leaned close, bestowing a kiss upon the single unbruised spot on her forehead.

"Breath of my life. Take my breath..." He kissed her lips gently, exhaling softly into her mouth. "I lend my strength..." He breathed softly into her mouth once again. "My heart lingers and warms your body, until once again, our bodies can warm one another..." He exhaled once more.

Chantel watched as he closed his eyes tightly, his breath hitching roughly as he pushed himself away from her.

Shane stood, looking down at the woman a moment, his face contorted as he fought to hold in his tears. Chantel knew she had never seen such agony as she saw reflected on this man's face.

"She's much stronger now," Chantel whispered. "The crystal will allow no one to touch her, until she loses her faith again."

"And that doesn't take long, either." He looked around the cold, damp cell she had been placed in. "We have to hurry and get to her."

Chantel nodded her agreement sadly.

"Can you leave now?" he asked Chantel softly.

"You will return with me when I do," she said regretfully. "My presence is all that holds you here."

He nodded jerkily. "The words will help. Galen foresaw this, ages ago. She knows what those words mean in her heart. She'll hold on as long as she can."

Chantel nodded. She closed her eyes, willing herself back in Devlin's arms. When she reopened them, the sluggishness of sleep washed over her. Weariness was dragging her down, as she tried to rise from the couch.

"Easy." Devlin's voice was harsh, but his hands were gentle as he lifted her into his arms. "Joshua." She heard him begin barking out commands. "Take care of Antea, find out everything she knows, and then get her the hell out of my castle."

Chantel didn't hear Joshua's response. She snuggled into Devlin's chest and drifted slowly into sleep.

* * * * *

Joshua sat Lissa gently into the large wingbacked chair in the corner of his room, staring down at her broodingly as she lifted her gaze to him. Resignation filled the dark blue depths as her head lolled against the back of the chair, her body held in thrall, a puppet under his command.

"Do your worst." She forced the words past her lips, lips that were pale, tight with pain.

He should feel pleased that he controlled her so easily. That he finally had within his power the woman who had destroyed all their lives so long ago. Antea had been a plague he could not touch, no matter the strength of his powers, centuries before. Protected by Galen's earth magic, she had been a scourge within the castle, a daily reminder of the loss Devlin had suffered, and the loss they would all know, eventually.

Moving carefully, he pulled the matching chair beside her forward, until he could face her as he lowered his body into it. Leaning forward, he regarded her, unsettled by the morass of emotions filling him.

"They control you...The Guardians..." The words were forced past her lips as desperation filled her gaze. "And Jonar...knows..."

He stilled her ability to speak. The moment no sound could be pushed from her lips, panic filled her expression as tears glittered in her eyes.

"I merely wish you to be silent for now." Why he bothered to whisper the comforting words he didn't know.

The violence that swirled so deep inside him pricked at his control. He could feel it rising fast and hot, taking much of his concentration to keep it stilled. It was her looks, he knew that. He stared into her face, saw the rich midnight silk of her hair framing her delicate expression and he saw another.

"I won't hurt you." He moved closer, brushing back her hair as a tear slid free and ran a slow course down her pale flesh. "Though you deserve the pain, Antea. What tragedies you have instigated. What pain you have been behind. I have long awaited this day, prayed that the Command would be released, allowing me a chance to repay you for the dark evil that has infected all our lives."

His chest ached, but not in grief or in emotional pain. The scar that had never healed, the feel of the blade that had pierced his heart centuries ago, still lingered within his mind. The blade his wife had wielded. Antea had not forced Arriane's hand, but she had instigated so much with her betrayal of Chantel. The betrayal was like acid, washing through his mind, tempting the darkness that filled him.

Her lips worked, her gaze filled with beseeching despair.

"Do you know what I intend to do?" His finger smoothed over her lips, but it was another's pouty curves he felt and saw. It was another's fragile body he imagined. "I intend to deliver your reward for choosing a body that you believed would sway my loyalties." He bent closer, allowing his breath to whisper against her lips as he stared into her terrified eyes. "Did you think I had any tender feelings left for the bitch, Antea? Did you delude yourself into believing my lust was aught but a need to punish, to destroy?"

He could feel her fighting against him, feel her mindless fear sinking into him. It should have filled him with satisfaction. Should have given him a measure of peace. Instead, he felt only weariness as he sat back in his chair, his gaze going over her.

Bruises marred the delicate flesh of her arms, drawing a frown to his brow as he remembered the past evening and their confrontation. He had nearly taken her. It would have been so easy, so very easy to allow the self-deception and take her as his body had demanded. To fuck her into submission, to hear her ragged cries as he found a measure of peace inside her well-used body. She was no stranger to the pain, or the pleasure to be found within it.

But, as always, the storms had raged outside. Lightning had struck at the walls, crashing with thundering violence each time he attempted to do so. Inside, Joshua had raged within himself. He ached, ached with such despair there was no release, and yet he had no reason to feel such pain. There was only vengeance, only the need to purge the fury that railed with him.

Yet, when he stared into the eyes so similar to another's, something darker, deeper than his fury clenched in rejection.

"I can do this one of two ways," he finally sighed. "I can bring you great pleasure, Antea. I can fill you with a hunger, a pleasure you could never imagine. Or I can bring you such pain that you will pray for death." If it was possible for her to turn whiter, she did. Her deep blue eyes were like bruises within her face, staring back at him as she struggled to scream in fear. "Settle back within your chair and give me the information I need without a struggle. It is your choice. Don't fight me, and you will leave this castle as you came into it. Fight me, and you will never know peace, Antea. I can ensure you pay. Each day you inhabit that body will be torture. Which will it be?"

And why the fuck was he giving her a choice? He had never, at any time in his life, hesitated to do what he preferred to do. He preferred to make her suffer. And yet, he could not find it within him to do so.

He should have been disappointed as he felt the struggle within her, and then the slow relaxation of her mental guards. She was indeed of Guardian birth, and that part of her was strong. It was also very much under her control.

Regret shimmered for but a moment within him before he struck. He sent himself swiftly into her very being, to the one place where only truth could be found, where the essence of the soul could no longer hide, and had no defenses against one of his strength.

And what he found there sent shock resounding through his mind. He felt his gut clench at the despair he read there, the shame, the need to purge from her soul the mistakes of a past she had been helpless within.

She gave herself totally, completely, and within her he saw the child huddled in the corner, her eyes wide with fear, staring back at him, her fragile limbs shuddering with terror.

Please don't hurt me, Joshau, she whispered tearfully. *I will save Chantel however I must, I swear it. If her hatred is my reward, then at least she will live to know even that dark emotion. It is not over yet. The final battle has not yet come. Do not betray me. Do not betray me, Joshau…*

Give me what we need. He held back both pleasure and pain. The child that watched him was not yet broken, but he sensed the fragile balance within her.

There will be no battle. Do what you may. Jonar will accept Chantel's death, but only if the secret of the burial ground of the Fire is revealed. I seek to give her knowledge, as Jonas seeks to triumph in the race to find the flames.

The child huddled deeper within the shadows as she spoke. *He believes the Wind shall die before the Earth can reach her. He believes the Water shall spill with no place to harbor the moisture. He believes when the Flames awaken, they will be lost and without a foundation. And the Earth could punish him no more, for his hand did not give the killing blow. She lies near death in the fortress Jonar conquered half a century before. In a land of sand, harboring heat and deceit, there the Wind is restrained.*

He saw the Fortress then, rising from the desert, blackened by age and by evil.

Do not betray me, Joshau. I walk the land of the living dead, is my punishment not great enough?

There was no pity in her voice, only irony. As though she felt she deserved no more and perhaps even less than she had gained upon this land.

I existed within dark time, a prisoner of the power I once envied. I felt its warmth, the touch of the Mother's hand, and in that moment of time, I knew love. The child leaned her head against a stone wall...or an altar? Shock filled him as he recognized the same altar Chantel had died beside so many centuries before. The shadows of the room he stood within, the place of safety the inner child had found, was nothing more than a recreation of her sister's place of death.

Go...do not touch this part of me. Do not exact vengeance, either in pleasure always remembered, or in pain never forgotten. Betray me not, Joshau, as those who swore to protect you have betrayed you.

She turned to him then, her eyes glowing within her pale face, compassion, fear and rage reflecting within her eyes. *Where is the child who harbors your innocence, Joshau?*

He fled from the image, from the soul of the woman. He staggered back in shock as reality returned and he was staring once again in the eyes of a woman he had not expected. Aye, Antea lived within this body, a woman stronger, more determined than she had ever been.

Where is the flame? he whispered hoarsely as he allowed her freedom from the hold he had placed on her. *Tell me, Antea. Where is the flame?*

Within your heart, Joshau. Find your heart, and you shall find the flame.

Her eyes drifted closed as her strength waned, the stress of the power he had sent racing through her, taking the last of her strength. He stumbled to the bed, sitting on it heavily as he stared back at her. His hand rose, rubbing at the ache in his chest, the scar that never healed. Outside, the storm had died down, the lightning quieting, for now. But inside his soul raged.

Betray me not, Joshau, as those sworn to protect you have betrayed you...

That thought tormented him now.

Where is the child that harbors your innocence, Joshau?

That question raged inside him.

There was no child inside him.

Chapter Twenty-Five

ஐ

When Chantel awoke several hours later, she awoke to Devlin's arms wrapped around her, his black eyes staring down at her worriedly.

"I have coffee ready," he told her before she could voice the questions beginning to surface. "Are you ready to get up?"

"I think so." She still felt a bit sluggish and dazed. "How long have I slept?"

"Six hours," he told her softly. "I decided to let you sleep until things were ready here to leave."

Chantel looked up at him, seeing the worry in his eyes. "We're heading out soon, then?" she asked him, feeling her energy returning at the thought of rescuing Ariel.

"As soon as some friends arrive." He nodded. "I've had another group join us for backup purposes, just in case the crystal doesn't cover us."

He wasn't expecting the crystal to hide them from detection, Chantel suspected.

"The crystal will disguise us." She was certain of that. "We have to go in at night and avoid a face-to-face confrontation with anyone who could alert Jonar. But other than that, it will hide us."

"Jonar and Oberon left the Fortress, heading to Paris to meet with Antea this morning. She's expected to arrive at the meeting point at dawn. They won't suspect anything until then," he told her as he poured a cup of coffee.

"She wasn't going to betray us." Chantel knew that. "Whatever her plans were, Devlin, she wouldn't have hurt me."

The truth had come as the aura surrounded her. A game. So much of what she had played had been a game, a manipulation, for what, Chantel wasn't certain. But this time, Antea had been determined that Chantel would live rather than die.

"Who knows what she planned." Devlin sighed as he helped her sit up in the bed and then handed her the cup. She had a feeling he may know more than he was saying, but something inside her urged her to leave the matter for now. "Drink that. It's good and strong."

Chantel sipped at the coffee as she watched Devlin pace the room.

"What's wrong?" she asked him as he paused beside the bed once again, staring down at her intently.

He shook his head, then sat down in the chair that had been pulled from the wall and placed at the bedside.

"Nothing." He exhaled slowly, and Chantel knew he was lying. She also had some idea what was on his mind.

Her sleep had been filled with dreams, though they lacked the nightmare quality of the past weeks. Most of it was gentle, memories of a life she had led before and the sister who had betrayed her.

"Have you remembered?" she asked him, staring at him over the rim of the coffee cup.

Surprise lit his features. "Have you?" He was being cautious.

Chantel hid her smile as she watched him. He was like a little boy with a secret he was afraid he wasn't supposed to tell.

"You've gained patience over the centuries." She smiled softly. "I remember a hot-blooded warrior who would have never let a moment alone in our bed go without at least a kiss."

The smile that lit his face was roguish, and fitting with the man of her dreams.

He rose from his chair with a surge of energy, taking the cup carefully from her hand and setting it on the table beside the bed.

Laughter rang through the room as he picked her up in his arms, and then fell back into the bed with her. There, with those bands of steel-hard muscles wrapped around her, Chantel gazed up into the passionate, loving face of her warrior.

"Galen knew I couldn't live without you," he whispered.

"No, love, I knew." She sighed sadly. "I made him swear to take your memories of me and to use Antea, if he could. I saw your grief and I feared for you."

Sorrow filled his eyes. "I died inside, anyway," he whispered. "My dreams were tormented, then forgotten when I awoke. I was dead inside until your return."

"But you lived until my return." She touched his face tenderly, her fingers feathering over the lips that had always brought her so much pleasure. "I was frightened then that you wouldn't."

She had known the battle with Jonar would be a vicious one, even then. She had foreseen the Guardians' final gift of complete immortality to her lover and knew he would have never accepted it willingly if his one wish had been to die himself. To live, his reason to die had to be taken from him. His need to join Chantel, if only in the afterlife he believed in, had to be obscured.

They would have wandered time forever, always lost to each other because he would have given up the fight for the earth.

"We're together now, and we remember." He kissed her lips softly. "But so help me, you ever allow that to happen again and the next time I remember, I'll paddle your backside."

"There will be no next time." Fear skated down her spine. "We must succeed this time, Devlin. If Jonar wins, if he manages to defeat even one of the mistresses and her warrior, then we're all lost. This is our last chance."

That knowledge terrified her. Jonar was weakening the earth with his destruction and the terror he was beginning to spread. Countries were at a loss how to deal with him and the men he could send out, willing to die for his cause.

Blackthorne's forces were growing as humanity lost hope. Something had to be done now.

"We will succeed this time, Chantel," he swore to her, his hand threading through the hair at the back of her head. "We've stopped Antea, and we will stop Jonar."

"Not without the other crystals." Worry still edged her voice.

"We will rescue Ariel tonight," he promised her. "Barak's group will be here soon. We'll have the girl and be headed home before dawn."

Chantel took a deep breath. She trusted Devlin. He had always prepared according to the battle before him, and she knew he would have covered all bases possible.

She also knew that all the forces of the earth were backing them. The crystals weren't together yet, but their mistresses lived. Chantel could draw from the power of those crystals, if needed.

She was the Earth Mistress. Her crystal was the strongest of the four.

"We will succeed." She moved until she was leaning over him, smiling into the soft adoration of his gaze.

This was how it had been then. The bond they had created together, in that first life, had transcended anything she could have ever dreamed of.

"Yes, we will." His hands framed her face, drawing her closer for the kiss he had been dreaming of for hours. "We're together, that's all we need to succeed."

She looked into his eyes and he watched her quizzically as she began to speak.

"Shadows of the past. Shadow of memories darkened by the haze of magic," she whispered. "Shadow of my heart, and all my soul holds. Into your heart and into your soul, I share the light of the earth, the treasure of forces only foretold." The crystal sprang to life, surrounding them in its glow.

Devlin then whispered the words that bound them for eternity with the crystal and to each other.

"Mistress of the Earth, of light and of my heart. Bride of my soul, wife for eternity. Take my strength, my warmth, all that I am. Binding forever and into eternity my soul with yours."

The crystal flared. A deep burst of light, and the veils of the past were lifted. The memories were returned, but with the vows came something more. Their souls were free now and bound together in ways they could have never envisioned.

Clothes were dispensed of quickly. Both by him, using that wicked, unseen power to rip them from her body as her hands tore at his. Finally, blissfully naked, he pushed her back to the bed, moving quickly between her thighs and pressing the engorged length of his cock deep inside her.

The tight, overfilled sensation brought a gasp from her lips, but he gave her no time to catch her breath. He pushed her legs up and back, lifting her closer, tilting her hips as he began to thrust so deeply inside her she swore he touched her soul. Hard, desperate lunges that stroked, burned, filled her with such pleasure she could only hold tight to his neck and let it sweep her away.

Fire bloomed in her belly, rushed through her system, and in one shocking, blinding second, she felt not just the desperate strokes into her body, but she felt him. His pleasure, the heat and incredible tightness of her body gripping him, his heart shuddering with his love for her.

Her eyes opened wide as he ensnared her gaze, sinking into her, souls merging as ecstasy rose, beating at her with whipping forks of sensation even as it tore through him.

Love, pleasure, completion. They all filled her. Filled him. Until with one last, furious stroke she felt release tear through them both. The combined sensations ripped through her mind, flung her into space and kept her spinning for forever. She felt life, death, rebirth, all within his arms. And she knew, in the moment she began to drift slowly back to earth, that it was only beginning. Forever awaited them.

Chapter Twenty-Six

ဆော

The warriors, with Chantel, were waiting at the airfield when Barak's plane landed that evening. They were dressed in formfitting black fatigues and thin cotton shirts that Chantel had only shaken her head over. The least bit tighter, she had sworn, and they would have been indecent.

Chantel had dressed in her customary jeans, T-shirt and leather sneakers, all in black—the color choice was determined by Devlin.

On her head, she wore a black ball cap, the front and sides of her hair pushed back beneath it carefully. Her gun was clipped behind her hip on the black leather belt she wore with her jeans. On her finger she wore the wedding band he had given her centuries before, as Devlin now wore his. Galen had been awaiting their descent to the great hall, the bands held out in his hand as his eyes shimmered with love and pride.

As the plane rolled to a stop, the door was thrown open and several men stood ready to assist with loading the plane. Each man grabbed an individual duffel bag and, with Chantel ahead of them, quickly boarded the plane.

The small Lear jet was identical to the one Devlin and his men had flown into the desert, Chantel noted as she took her seat and strapped in. On one side, a portable stretcher was strapped to the wall, ready to unfold for a wounded warrior to rest on, or unlock to carry one.

"Chantel." Devlin drew her attention from the memories of that fateful day.

She turned her head, gazing into the most amazingly beautiful face she had ever seen. Brown hair fell long and thick around the strong features. Eyes the color of tobacco stared back at her warmly.

His face was beautiful. Not feminine beautiful, but exquisite in the strong-boned graceful features on one side of his face. The other was savagely marred by a ragged scar running across his right cheek.

"Barak, the woman with her mouth hanging open is my wife," Devlin introduced them with amusement. "I neglected to warn her about you."

Chantel shook her head as a flush warmed her skin. "Forgive me." She smiled self-consciously.

"None needed." The rich baritone of Barak's voice would have soothed the most frazzled nerves. "When the Guardians give gifts, they go all out. Too bad they couldn't do anything with this." His finger ran over the ragged scar that marred the male perfection of his looks.

"Trust me, it distracts me from nothing," Chantel laughed, her eyes finally clearing as the effect of the first sight wore off.

"So, I've learned." His wicked grin was amused, and in it she saw the hint of the rogue she suspected he could be.

Then he turned to Devlin, his face losing its smile as he held his hand out.

"It's good to see your destiny coming to pass, my friend." Barak nodded shortly as they clasped each others' wrists in camaraderie. "What do we need to know?"

The plane lifted from the runway as Devlin began to outline the plan he had put together. It was simple, depending more heavily on the crystal than any firepower or advanced tactics.

Barak seemed to have no problem with this as he looked to Chantel.

"Then nature will be our ally?" he asked her softly.

"The sandstorm will begin as we make our way into the desert surrounding the Fortress. Drawing on the power of the Wind Crystal, I can sustain it, as well as provide a shield about us. We'll be protected from it, Jonar's forces won't be. It will cover our entrance, as well as our exit."

"Sounds simple enough." Barak nodded. "What about the girl? How heavily is she guarded?"

"Not heavily at all," Chantel answered him. "She's too weak to attempt escape. They're merely waiting on her to die from her injuries. There are no guards posted within the cell block."

"The entrance to the cells is unsecured as well," Devlin informed him. "Jonar doesn't expect it, and has no reason to believe Antea didn't kill Chantel as they planned. When Lissa revealed her identity to him and procured the weapon that killed Chantel before, Jonar was confident she would succeed. He's unaware she hasn't."

Devlin spoke matter-of-factly about the odd weapon that had killed Chantel in that former life. Chantel knew he wasn't nearly so unemotional about it. The warriors had seen, on more than one occasion, what that wand was capable of.

The miniature explosive it set off released an acid that affected human skin only. Its destructive, deadly force could not be halted. The healings that the immortal warriors endured were too hellish to even describe.

If the acid contained within that ray was measured properly, then the warriors had no chance of healing. It ate away skin, muscle and organs before the body could repair it.

"Excellent." Barak nodded. "What about our landing? Jonar has spies at the airport, won't they report our arrival?"

Devlin glanced to Derek and Joshua. "The ban on Joshua's powers was lifted last night. He had the pleasure of extracting Antea's secrets. Combined with Derek's gifts, we're confident Jonar's spies won't even notice our arrival."

Chantel studied Derek and Joshua now. Both were quiet, their eyes closed, and their heads were resting on the backs of their seats. She had first thought they were merely resting. Now, as she watched them closely, she could feel the power resonating around them.

They were combining their powers. Derek's power of mesmerism and Joshua's advanced powers of telepathy were working in perfect harmony. But Joshua was drawing on more than just his own powers. Even the power of the air itself seemed tapped, drained as Joshua used it to feed his strength, to reach into the land and gain what he needed.

"So, you finally lifted the ban," Barak remarked. "It's a hell of a chance you're taking, Devlin."

Devlin sighed roughly, and Chantel turned to meet his gaze worriedly.

"Yes, it is," Devlin admitted. "But one we had no choice but to take."

The plane advanced on the small desert country, its occupants planning out each detail to the last second.

As they neared their landing, Chantel's confidence grew. Her powers were stronger. Her bond with Devlin and the combination of his power working in accord with hers made the crystal glow with warmth.

The mission wasn't without danger, but they had covered as much as possible. She knew they would rescue Ariel, but the fate of the Wind Mistress wouldn't end there. Her battle was still ahead of her, and Chantel knew that road would be much rougher than the one she and Devlin had taken.

"We're preparing to land," Barak announced several hours later as he reentered the cabin from the cockpit. "We're cleared to land on a back runway, and there are jeeps waiting for us." He strapped in quickly, but not before Chantel glimpsed the excitement radiating in his face.

Night had fallen and the stars were hidden behind clouds that had begun to roll in. Chantel smiled in satisfaction. The night would hide their advance.

"Nice trick," Devlin murmured in her ear as they buckled up. "But won't any unusual weather alert Jonar if he happens to be watching for it?"

"It's not at all unusual," she whispered back to him. "The weather began changing last week, right after Ariel was taken. By now, he will think nothing of it."

"Can you be certain of that?" Devlin asked her.

Chantel sighed. "I can't be certain of anything at this point. I can only hope my instincts are right, because Ariel is weakening fast. If she gives up on Shane's arrival, then our lives will be for nothing."

"Can you let Shane go to her while covering us?" His voice was still soft as he glanced worriedly at Shane.

"Multitask?" An edge of humor cleared her voice. "I'm very adept. I think it would be easy enough to handle."

Devlin smiled slowly into her eyes, and Chantel felt the world tip once again. The lazy sensuality, approval and love she glimpsed there sent spirals of heat radiating throughout her body.

"Control yourself." She lowered her voice until only he could hear her.

"Hmm, for now," he whispered back, placing a kiss on her brow. "As soon as we land, I'll put you between myself and Shane. If you think you can handle it, then we'll give Ariel a little added incentive. We're still hours away from her, and I don't want to take any chances that we don't have to, where she's concerned."

"Sounds like a plan, then." Chantel nodded. "Warn him first, though. I don't want to throw him into something he isn't prepared for, because I won't be making the trip with him."

She grinned at Devlin's surprised look. "So, I don't have to deal with waking you up later?" That relieved his mind. He was worried how that would affect the rest of the trip.

"No." She shook her head. "My job was to get Shane there. I just didn't know that. It's getting easier to sift through what the crystal wants."

Its demands could be felt, heard by a subconscious part of her mind. Chantel knew the pain and sluggishness before and after each episode were due to her inability to decipher those needs.

Now that she knew how to get Shane there, there was no need for her to go as well.

Devlin nodded, his head lifting as the plane began to slow to a stop.

He released his harness, and then Chantel's. "Shane, you're with me and Chantel." He turned to the other warrior with the order.

Shane nodded, his gray eyes bleak as he prepared to disembark.

Behind them, Derek and Joshua began moving. No one spoke to them or issued orders. They were still intent, focused on hiding their movements from Jonar's spies until they were out of the vicinity.

They ran from the plane, careful to keep close to the shadows of the other planes and the hangers as much as possible.

Two jeeps waited outside the airport perimeter, deserted.

Joshua, Derek and two of Barak's men took one jeep. Devlin, Shane and Chantel jumped into a jeep with Barak and his partner.

"Careful, Shane," Chantel whispered to him as she lifted her hand. "Let her know we're close. She's getting weak."

Shane nodded, taking her hand gently and closing his eyes. Chantel took a deep breath, concentrated and then led him softly into the vision that would take him to Ariel.

"Where's the aura?" Devlin asked her quietly as Shane slumped against the side of the jeep.

She shook her head. "The aura isn't needed for this. It was only used before to isolate me because I was fighting it. You gave me strength, so it had to separate me from you until I figured it out."

Devlin grunted. He didn't like the thought of having been deliberately separated from her.

"How long will he be out?" he asked her.

"Not long." She shook her head. "As we get closer, I'll need more of the energy myself, and will have to bring him back."

They were an hour from the Fortress when Chantel brought Shane back from the vision. He was pale, shaking and his eyes and face were haggard.

Chantel knew it wasn't from the effects of the vision, but the drain on his own strength. Ariel had whispered the vows to him, just as Chantel had whispered them to Devlin that morning. In turn, he had created a direct line into his own strength for her. Without it, Chantel knew that the girl would have already died.

"We're entering the mine field." Chantel closed her eyes as she felt the deadly weapons.

She relayed the position of the mines, and had Barak correct the direction of the jeep to avoid them. She didn't need the map, she closed her eyes and let the earth guide her around the unnatural objects that had been planted inside it.

As they entered the minefield, the dust began to fly, gently at first, then gathering speed as the storm built up around the jeep.

Inside the two vehicles, the occupants were protected as dust swirled beyond the pocket of energy the crystal had created.

Chantel relayed directions through the growing fury as she concentrated on the road painted within her mind.

Finally, she drew the vehicles to a stop. Eight men and one woman jumped from the vehicles. Shane, Devlin and Chantel entered the Fortress with Derek and Joshua at their backs, while Barak's group guarded the entrance.

Derek and Joshua took up a position at the only other entrance into the cool, tomblike atmosphere of Jonar's dungeon.

They entered Ariel's cell swiftly, Chantel and Devlin standing watch at the door while Shane rushed in and tenderly picked the young woman up from the floor.

"Take me with you." Ariel's words rasped from her throat, causing Chantel to wince.

"Yes, love, I'm taking you with me." Chantel heard him whisper.

Getting in and getting out was easy. Too easy, Chantel reflected as they once again boarded the plane and headed for home.

The huge swords the men had worn were not needed. Jonar had not appeared, and no one was hurt, except the woman they had rescued.

Chantel watched as Shane hovered over her, tending to her as she lay on the makeshift bed at the side of the plane.

Shane was tired, she noticed. The dark circles under his eyes and the pale tone of his skin were indicative of the amount of energy Ariel was using just to survive.

"Don't leave me." The words were whispered from the woman's swollen, cracked lips. "Don't leave me again."

"Shh." Shane soothed her as he washed her face gently with a cool towel. "It's going to be okay."

"You'll leave me." As the girl spoke to Shane, Chantel glimpsed the amethyst color of her eyes through swollen lids.

"Did we not say the vows, Ariel?" he whispered to her, leaning close. "Do you not use my strength to live for now? That bond can never be broken, I swear to you."

"And so, the Savage will relinquish hold of his heart, allowing his memory to slip into the folds of mist…" Chantel's eyes widened as Ariel spoke the words. "And so the darkness shall come again, striking…" Her voice faded off with a sob. "He'll come again."

"And you don't remember so good." He smoothed her hair back from her forehead. "And so darkness shall come again, specters rising from a past hidden in the veil of an unjust death. Believed you not, when love was within your grasp, Mistress of the Wind. Remember not, the vows spoken when death harkened at the door. Remember not, until the heart accepts, the soul knows full well, and the whispered vows tremble twice upon your lips. Twice, Mistress. Once for the foolish who refused to believe, twice full measure, for the life you must lead."

Chantel breathed deeply, awed at the charged atmosphere of the plane's cabin. The Legend of the Savage, whispered in the ruined voice of the man who must live it, sent tremors of sadness washing over Chantel.

Devlin's arm came over her shoulder, and she leaned tightly against him. They were together, and she would thank God for that each day. Just as she would pray each day that Shane would survive the battle to come.

"You okay?" Devlin whispered against her hair as she fought back her tears.

"Yeah." She raised her head, smiling up at him softly. "Tired, but otherwise, fine."

"Then go to sleep," he told her firmly. "Your job is finished, my love. You can rest now."

She closed her eyes, dropped the protection the crystal afforded them all, and slept.

Chapter Twenty-Seven

ഔ

Hours later, Chantel walked wearily into the welcome atmosphere of the castle. Shane had already moved Ariel to his rooms, with Kanna and a doctor following.

Shane hadn't halted or even hesitated as he rushed his burden to his room. Ariel was still losing strength, and they knew she would have to be transported to a hospital soon.

Barak had placed a call from the plane for medical transport to head for the castle airfield. It wouldn't be much longer before they arrived.

So, Chantel thought, as she gazed around the great hall, seeing it, not as it was but as it had been centuries before.

It still welcomed her, wrapping around her and reminding her she was home. She smiled softly as she walked slowly to the fireplace, running her hands over the old stones reverently.

She closed her eyes, smiling with bittersweet sadness as she remembered her last day there with Galen.

"You always loved that fireplace. Even as a child." Galen's voice whispered over her.

She opened her eyes, turning to find him standing beside her. She looked around, wondering where Devlin had disappeared to.

"He said something about a shower," Galen told her as he smiled down at her. "I think he wanted to let you enjoy your memories in peace."

"It all happened so fast," she whispered, crossing her arms over her breasts as she looked around the room once again. "It's hard to imagine we made it."

Galen nodded. Chantel and Devlin had completed their part. Devlin's immortality would linger until the final battle, and Chantel's began the moment she whispered her vows to Devlin. Both would resume normal aging when Joshua completed his destiny. So much knowledge. She knew things she wished she didn't now.

Chantel took a deep breath. She hoped Joshua hurried, because she had a feeling this immortality stuff could get old.

"Soon, the battles will be completed, and you and Devlin will have the lives you dreamed of so long ago," Galen promised her. "The one I promised you when we created those stones."

Chantel glanced down at the crystal still lying outside her shirt.

"It was a shadowed legacy the Guardians gave us, Father. I think Devlin and I would have preferred a clearer destiny. But we made it, that's all that matters."

"I wanted to tell you the secrets. Shed light on the shadows, so to speak, but I was silenced by my own vows. Magic comes with a price. In taking Devlin's memory, I was forbidden to reveal that same past to you. You had to remember on your own, as well," he told her regretfully.

"It was better that way." She remembered the love, the emotions racing across her soul the moment she had remembered. "I preferred it that way."

"You told me you would." He nodded sharply. "We spoke of it, when you demanded my oath to take his memory. You were right, he would have killed Antea the moment he had a chance, then fallen upon his own sword, I believe. His grief..." Galen shook his head.

"I understand, Father," Chantel said, her voice soft with fondness.

He was her father, by blood and by love. That knowledge healed the wounds Michael had left over the years.

"Yes, you would." He exhaled sharply, his eyes growing moist as he stared at her. "You are as lovely as ever, Chantel. The most beautiful of my daughters. The most caring. It's been lonely without you."

Chantel closed her eyes tightly, and when she opened them again, he stood there, his arms opening for her to enter his embrace.

She stepped into them, a cry escaping her lips as he hugged her tightly.

"I cannot always be here," he whispered. "Soon, when the battles are done, I will seek my final rest. But know this, my pride and my love for you have no limits."

"I love you, Father," she whispered as he finally moved back from her.

"As I love you, daughter." He touched her face with the tips of his fingers, and then, once again, he was gone.

She sighed wearily and blinked back tears of regret. She was home. Her and Devlin's home.

"Mistress?" Sarah entered the room slowly. "Can I get you anything?"

Chantel smiled, thinking of all the things she had wished for when this adventure began.

"No, thank you, Sarah." She added softly, "I'm fine."

"Very well." She turned and left as quietly as she had arrived.

When Chantel entered the bedroom she shared with Devlin, he was standing in front of the closet, a towel wrapped carelessly around his hips as he pulled out soft sweat pants and a cotton T-shirt.

She stood silently, watching him. Relishing the feel of his presence. She hadn't known how desperately she had missed him, until she remembered him. No, that was wrong, she thought. She had known, in the deepest reaches of her soul, she had known.

She watched as he turned to her, naked, aroused, and she felt grungy and mussed from the air travel, and anticipation of a battle that had never arrived. It was a particular letdown.

"I need to shower," she sighed as he started toward her, his cock lengthening, engorging with his desire for her.

The answering ache in her cunt was sharp and demanding. Would she ever get enough of him? She didn't think she ever would.

"Hmm, let me help you undress for it. I'll even wash your back for you." Devlin took her hand, leading her into the bathroom, and stopped at the edge of the tub.

"You've already showered," she laughed as he stripped the shirt over her head.

"I didn't get my back," his lips quirked sensually. "I don't feel clean enough. You can help me this time."

He stripped her jeans to her ankles, pausing as she toed her leather sneakers from her feet. When that obstacle was gone, he helped her step from the jeans and led her to the bathtub.

He adjusted the water, then poured a healthy measure of the foaming bath salts she had purchased in the village during her shopping trip. When the tub was half-filled with steamy water, he stepped in and drew her to him as he sat down.

Chantel moaned as heated, liquid silk seemed to seep into her bones. Devlin's hard chest cushioned her back, and all around her the silken suds and warming water caressed and relaxed her tired muscles.

"It happened too fast. Too easy." She couldn't get it out of her mind. "Jonar should have been there. He should have known."

Devlin sighed as he lifted the sprayer from its resting hook and turned it on. She tipped her head back as he indicated, moaning in pleasure as he wet her hair and began to lather shampoo into it.

"We'll worry about it later," he told her gently. "For now, we have Ariel, and Shane is with her. We triumphed in this small battle, no matter how, we managed it."

She closed her eyes as the spray directed on her hair once again.

"He will lose her again. It's their destiny."

"And he will find her again, and then it will be forever." He lathered a cloth and began to bathe her quickly. Chantel felt a grin edge her mouth as his hands lingered on her breasts. There was definitely more than cleanliness on his mind.

Behind her, his cock throbbed against her back, demanding attention. His lips settled on her shoulder after he rinsed the fragrant bubbles from her skin, his tongue rasping over the flesh his lips caressed.

The spray was shut off and his hands, so warm and gentle, settled at her waist. He lifted her, helping her to turn, arranging her until she straddled his muscular thighs as his lips settled on hers.

Lips and tongues melded together, stoking the fires that already raged between them, moaning at the heated caress, the touch, the taste of the other. Chantel felt the breath catch in her chest as his hands cupped her breasts, his fingers rasping over her nipples, heating them further as they puckered beneath his sensual touch.

His lips slid from hers then, smoothing down her neck, her chest, until he could catch a hardened peak between his lips. She arched, crying out at the heat and pleasure that streaked through her system. She felt the heated juices easing from her cunt, preparing her for him as his lips suckled firmly at her breasts.

Her hands feathered through his hair, smoothed to his shoulders as she arched her back, pressing her nipple deeper into the greedy heat of his mouth. Her thighs tightened on his, her clit rubbing against the hard, thick cock that pressed heatedly against it.

"Come here," he growled, his hand pulling her close as his head lifted. "Take me, Chantel. Here. Now. Feel how desperately I need you. Love you."

The broad head nudged at her vaginal opening, spreading it, invading her with a slow, measured thrust that threatened to have her screaming out her need. She watched him, her gaze locked with his, his eyes as heavy-lidded as her own as he pressed his cock deeper inside her. Slow, stretching her erotically with a small bite of pleasure-pain that had her gasping in need.

The muscles of her pussy spasmed, rippling convulsively around his engorged erection. Then he was lifting her again, easing her up, his cock stroking her as he retreated. When she thought he would release her fully, he plunged inside again, hard, deep, grimacing in his own pleasure as her muscles clamped around him, her juices spurting along the thick flesh as she arched in his arms.

Heat, almost violent in its intensity, possessed them. Mingled lust and desperate love pushed them harder, demanding a pinnacle of pleasure they had never reached before.

Devlin's thighs bunched beneath her as she began to ride him hard and furiously. His hands gripped her buttocks, parted her, a wicked finger sliding through the cleft until he could massage the tender opening of her anus.

There was no lubrication to ease the passage of his finger there, but his finger, like the lubrication, wasn't truly needed. Chantel screamed in pleasure as he felt the muscles there part, his psychic energy warming her, possessing her once again. Like his cock, thickly lubricated and so heatedly real, she could have sworn another was invading her there.

"Easy," he whispered as she stilled against him. "Lie against me. Let me pleasure you, Chantel." One hand pressed her to his chest as his thighs bunched and he began to work his cock in and out of her in tight, hard strokes.

Behind her, power invaded her. Alternating strokes, identical to his cock, thrust into her ass, parting the muscles there, heating her with a painful pleasure that had her gasping. Her hands bit into his biceps as she held on to him, fighting for breath as he took her with a double penetration all the more heated for the fact that he alone was doing it.

He filled her pussy, stroking in fast and hard and retreating. As he pulled back, the force of the psychic thrust up her ass had her crying out at the prickling heat of the more tender muscles stretching, gripping the thick force invading it. Then it pulled back and his cock slammed deep and hard in her cunt once again. Over and over, driving her higher, harder, until she was screaming breathlessly through the orgasm that tore through her.

One last series of thrusts and he stiffened beneath her, groaning her name, his seed surging inside her body as she milked him, her cunt flexing, drawing on him, sucking each drop of his release from his pulsing cock.

"Damn," he groaned as his head fell back against the lip of the tub. "Damn, Chantel. I could drown in this water now. I don't think I have the strength to move."

They were both breathing hard, fast. Pleasure vibrating through them, the aftershocks of their release causing them to shudder with echoed sensations. She lay against him, replete, fulfilled.

"Forever," she whispered, and knew this time, it would be true.

"Forever." His hand cupped her head, a kiss of promise pressed to her forever.

Forever. The shadowed legacy they had lived under — Chantel for years, Devlin for centuries — was at an end. Forever, and the earth agreed.

Epilogue

🔊

"There is a reason why you did something so foolish?" Oberon was screaming in rage as he threw open the door to Jonar's sleeping chambers, only to pull up short as he caught sight of the Seeker and his companion.

The human female was gorgeous, with long black hair and an impossibly lovely back, buttocks and legs. He couldn't see her face, of course, strapped down on the slanted bench as she was. But he could see the thick plug working between her petite buttocks, the alien device mimicking a slow, deep thrust up her ass.

Oberon was brought up short by the sight. It was rare that Jonar became interested in a female of any culture. His favorite sport was normally male, with the exception of his lust for his granddaughter. But this small female appeared more than tempting.

Her back and buttocks were marked with the faint streaks of a strap. How exquisite the pain must be. He shivered at the thought of the pleasure he would have felt himself.

The female was whimpering with each stroke of the alien dildo up her ass. The device lodged in, the shaft then working the anus as the muscles tightened around it. No manual control was needed, merely a mental order to control the depth and speed of the thrusts. From the appearance of it, the thick, even strokes were lazily executed, stretching her flesh slowly.

Jonar was at her head, his thick cock buried in her mouth as she sucked at it noisily, moaning and whimpering at the trusts up her ass. It was a decadent sight. The woman bound and submissive, swallowing Jonar's erection with noisy desperation.

Oberon doubted sincerely there was an ounce of true willingness in her body. The threat of death often did amazing things for one's libido. And Jonar could make anyone, male or female, beg for the fucking rather than the death.

"Go away, Oberon." Jonar grimaced as he buried his cock between the female's lips once again. "I am punishing Antea for her failures."

Oberon's brow lifted. Antea. Perhaps there was willingness there. That or terrible fear.

He heard her screech, glanced at her parted buttocks once again, and saw the pace of the dildo increasing. Her hips were jerking, the muscles of her buttocks quivering with the faster strokes.

"You let Chantel escape with the Wind bitch," he bit out, trying to ignore his own erect cock. Jonar rarely shared his pleasures. "You knew she was coming."

"I knew." The other man was nearly panting now as he thrust heavily into Antea's mouth, giving her more than she could surely take.

Oberon smiled at the sound of her choking as Jonar entered her throat then pulled back. She loved that part, he knew. He had given it to her just so, several times himself.

"No excuses?" Oberon bit out then, his anger flaring in the face of Jonar's obvious disregard.

Jonar ignored him. His thrusts increased within the woman's mouth, his hands in her hair tightening as his body tensed. He groaned her name, or was it another's? Then he shuddered, his semen splashing in the girl's face as the dildo in her ass thrust her into a screaming orgasm of her own. Ah, Jonar knew the way of exploiting any human weakness. And this one had a weakness where a fine ass was concerned.

Breathing hard now, Jonar moved back from the woman as he jerked a robe from a nearby chair.

"I do not owe you excuses," he bit out.

He moved to the girl's rump. With a wave of his hand the thrusts stilled, though the object, Oberon knew, still pulsed inside her. Moving to the bed table, the Seeker chose another thick dildo. Oberon smiled. The thick device would lodge in her pussy, pulse and swell, deflate and swell again, driving her mad with a need for a climax that would not easily be granted.

He watched silently as Jonar knelt behind her straining body. Inserted the bulbous head, and began to work it slowly up her pussy. Oh yeah, she knew well what was coming. She was one of Jonar's favorite sexual playmates. She fought the pleasure better than any other they had come across.

After pressing the nearly nine inch thick device up the narrow channel of the woman's cunt, Jonar slapped her ass, tugged at it to be assured it could not be pushed free, then rose to his feet once again.

"She let the wand be destroyed," he sighed. "It was, unfortunately, my last."

Oberon doubted the loss truly mattered to Jonar.

"The woman," Oberon reminded him. "You had no guards on her. Nothing to stop the warriors and their Earth bitch from taking her. Why?"

Jonar shrugged. "It is not yet time to battle."

Oberon watched as he paced toward him slowly, lust still glowing brightly within his eyes. His cock throbbed in anticipation.

"Jonar…" he began to protest.

"Your impatience gained us nothing centuries before when we killed the Earth Mistress," Jonar reminded him angrily. "I will hear none of your prattle now, when they are finally returning. Those bastard Guardians have Arriane hidden so well from me, that without the Earth Mistress, I shall never find her again. Until then, I will inflict what pain I can, and settle for that small satisfaction until I have my granddaughter once again."

His face was flushed, and as always when Arriane was mentioned, a maniacal light of lust lit his eyes. "Do you wish to object further?"

Oberon knew better than to argue with the other Seeker when he was in such a mood.

"Of course not, Jonar," he bit out. "I will, of course, abide by your wishes."

Jonar grunted. "I wish for you to pleasure me then, as I watch this one scream out for mercy."

He took his seat where he could watch as Antea squirmed now, the dildos tormenting her body as she cried out, whimpering against the fiery pleasure-pain he knew was attacking her body. Jonar parted his robe, his thick, still-engorged cock rising dark and angry-looking from between the material.

Oberon went to his knees, his hands encircling the flesh as Jonar pushed the broad head to his lips. "Yes," he growled. "As I watch her scream for mercy, make me beg as well."

Soon her screams were filling the room, the thickening of each device within her body, as well as their unnatural thrusts spearing into her, making her insane with the burning pleasure. Oberon pleasured his master, hearing his voice chant out another name, beg, plead, and finally spew his silky semen as her name echoed around them. "Arriane…"

Also by Lora Leigh

ಐ

A Wish, A Kiss, A Dream *(Anthology)*
B.O.B.'s Fall *(with Veronica Chadwick)*
Bound Hearts 1: Surrender
Bound Hearts 2: Submission
Bound Hearts 3: Seduction
Bound Hearts 4: Wicked Intent
Bound Hearts 5: Sacrifice
Bound Hearts 6: Embraced
Bound Hearts 7: Shameless
Broken Wings *(Cerridwen Press)*
Cowboy & the Captive
Coyote Breeds 1: Soul Deep
Elemental Desires *(Anthology)*
Feline Breeds 1: Tempting the Beast
Feline Breeds 2: The Man Within
Feline Breeds 3: Kiss of Heat
Law and Disorder : Moving Violations *(with Veronica Chadwick)*
Manaconda *(Anthology)*
Men of August 1: Marly's Choice
Men of August 2: Sarah's Seduction
Men of August 3: Heather's Gift
Men of August 4: August Heat *(12 Quickies of Christmas)*
Wizard Twins 1: Ménage a Magick
Wizard Twins 2: When Wizards Rule
Wolf Breeds 1: Wolfe's Hope
Wolf Breeds 2: Jacob's Faith
Wolf Breeds 3: Aiden's Charity
Wolf Breeds 4: Elizabeth's Wolf

About the Author

૪౨

Lora Leigh is a wife and mother living in Kentucky. She dreams in bright, vivid images of the characters intent on taking over her writing life, and fights a constant battle to put them on the hard drive of her computer before they can disappear as fast as they appeared.

Lora's family, and her writing life co-exist, if not in harmony, in relative peace with each other. An understanding husband is the key to late nights with difficult scenes and stubborn characters. His insights into human nature and the workings of the male psyche provide her hours of laughter, and innumerable romantic ideas that she works tirelessly to put into effect.

Lora welcomes comments from readers. You can find her website and email address on her author bio page at www.ellorascave.com.

Tell Us What You Think

We appreciate hearing reader opinions about our books. You can email us at Comments@EllorasCave.com.

Why an electronic book?

We live in the Information Age—an exciting time in the history of human civilization, in which technology rules supreme and continues to progress in leaps and bounds every minute of every day. For a multitude of reasons, more and more avid literary fans are opting to purchase e-books instead of paper books. The question from those not yet initiated into the world of electronic reading is simply: *Why?*

1. ***Price.*** An electronic title at Ellora's Cave Publishing and Cerridwen Press runs anywhere from 40% to 75% less than the cover price of the exact same title in paperback format. Why? Basic mathematics and cost. It is less expensive to publish an e-book (no paper and printing, no warehousing and shipping) than it is to publish a paperback, so the savings are passed along to the consumer.

2. ***Space.*** Running out of room in your house for your books? That is one worry you will never have with electronic books. For a low one-time cost, you can purchase a handheld device specifically designed for e-reading. Many e-readers have large, convenient screens for viewing. Better yet, hundreds of titles can be stored within your new library—on a single microchip. There are a variety of e-readers from different manufacturers. You can also read e-books on your PC or laptop computer. (Please note that Ellora's Cave does not endorse any specific brands.

You can check our websites at www.ellorascave.com or www.cerridwenpress.com for information we make available to new consumers.)

3. *Mobility.* Because your new e-library consists of only a microchip within a small, easily transportable e-reader, your entire cache of books can be taken with you wherever you go.

4. ***Personal Viewing Preferences.*** Are the words you are currently reading too small? Too large? Too... ANNOYING? Paperback books cannot be modified according to personal preferences, but e-books can.

5. ***Instant Gratification.*** Is it the middle of the night and all the bookstores near you are closed? Are you tired of waiting days, sometimes weeks, for bookstores to ship the novels you bought? Ellora's Cave Publishing sells instantaneous downloads twenty-four hours a day, seven days a week, every day of the year. Our webstore is never closed. Our e-book delivery system is 100% automated, meaning your order is filled as soon as you pay for it.

Those are a few of the top reasons why electronic books are replacing paperbacks for many avid readers.

As always, Ellora's Cave and Cerridwen Press welcome your questions and comments. We invite you to email us at Comments@ellorascave.com or write to us directly at Ellora's Cave Publishing Inc., 1056 Home Avenue, Akron, OH 44310-3502.